Fire Touched

BY PATRICIA BRIGGS

The Mercy Thompson novels
Moon Called
Blood Bound
Iron Kissed
Bone Crossed
Silver Borne
River Marked
Frost Burned
Night Broken
Fire Touched

The Alpha and Omega novels
Cry Wolf
Hunting Ground
Fair Game

Aralorn: Masques and Wolfsbane

COMHAIRLE CHONTAE ÁTHA CLIATH THEAS
SOUTH DUBLIN COUNTY LIBRARIES

PALMERSTON LIBRARY, STEWARTS, DUBLIN 20
TO RENEW ANY ITEM Tel: 651 8129 or online at
www.southdublinlibraries.ie

Items should be returned on or before the last date below. Fines,
as displayed in the Library, will be charged on overdue items.

ORBIT

First published in Great Britain in 2016 by Orbit

1 3 5 7 9 10 8 6 4 2

Copyright © 2016 by Hurog, Inc.

The moral right of the author has been asserted.

Map by Michael Enzweiler

A CIP catalogue record for this book
is available from the British Library.

HB ISBN 978-0-356-50157-4
C format 978-0-356-50704-0

Printed and bound in Great Britain by Clays Ltd, St Ives plc

Papers used by Orbit are from well-managed forests
and other responsible sources.

MIX
Paper from
responsible sources
FSC® C104740

Orbit
An imprint of
Little, Brown Book Group
Carmelite House
50 Victoria Embankment
London EC4Y 0DZ

An Hachette UK Company
www.hachette.co.uk

www.orbitbooks.net

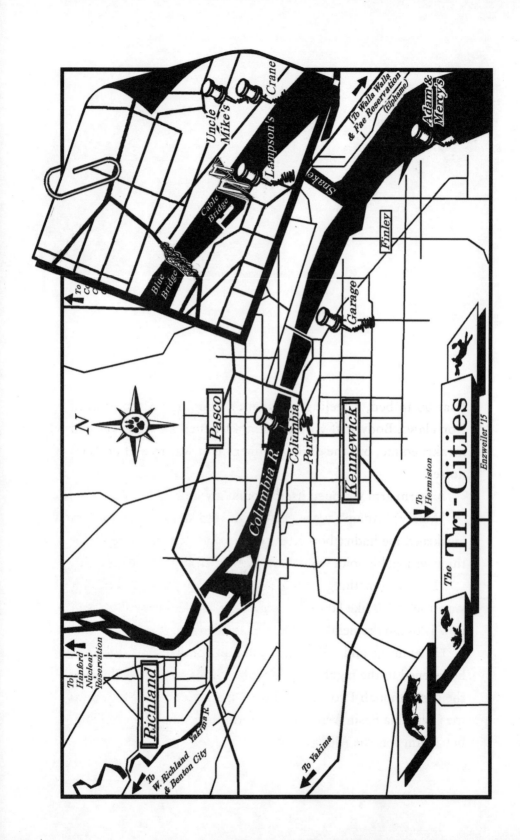

1

I sat up in bed, a feeling of urgency gripping my stomach in iron claws. Body stiff with tension, I listened for whatever had awakened me, but the early-summer night was free of unusual noises.

A warm arm wrapped itself around my hips.

"Mercy?" Adam's voice was rough with sleep. Whatever had awakened me hadn't bothered my husband. If there were something wrong, his voice would have been crisp and his muscles stiff.

"I heard something," I told Adam, though I wasn't certain it was true. It *felt* like I'd heard something, but I'd been asleep, and now I couldn't remember what had startled me.

He let me go and rolled off the bed and onto his feet. Like me, he listened to the night. I felt him stretch his awareness through the pack, though I couldn't follow what he learned. My link to the Columbia Basin werewolves was through simple membership, but Adam was the Alpha.

"No one else in the house is disturbed," he said, turning his head to look at me. "I didn't sense anything. What did you hear?"

I shook my head. "I don't know. Something bad." I closed my fist on the walking stick that lay against me. The action drew Adam's eyes to my hands. He frowned, then crouched beside the bed and gently pulled the walking stick away.

"Did you bring this into bed last night?" he asked.

I flexed my fingers, frowning with annoyance at the walking stick. Until he'd drawn my attention to it, I hadn't even realized that it had, once again, shown up where it shouldn't be. It was a fae artifact—a minor fae artifact, I'd been told.

The stick was pretty but not ornate, simple wood shod in etched silver. The wood was gray with age, varnish, or both. When it had followed me home like a stray puppy the first time, it had seemed harmless. But fae things are rarely what they seem. And even very minor artifacts, given enough time, can gain in power.

It was very old magic and stubborn. It would not stay with the fae when I tried to give it back to them. Then I killed with it—or it had used me to kill something. Someone. That had changed it. I didn't know what to do with it, so I'd given it to Coyote.

My life so far has been a learning experience. One thing I have learned is: don't give magical things to Coyote. He returned it, and it was . . . different.

I opened and closed my hands several times; the fierce knowledge that something was wrong had faded. Experimentally, I reached out and touched the walking stick again, but my fear didn't return.

"Maybe I just had a nightmare," I told him. Maybe it hadn't been the walking stick's fault.

Adam nodded and set the walking stick on the top of my chest of drawers, which had become its usual resting place. Shutting it up in a closet had seemed rude.

He came back to the bed and kissed me, a quick, possessive kiss. He pulled back and looked at me, to make sure I was okay.

"Let me just take a look-see around the place to make sure." He waited for my nod before he left me alone.

I waited for him in the dark. Maybe it had been a nightmare, or maybe something was wrong. I thought about the things that could be triggering my instincts—or things I was worried about.

Maybe something was wrong with Tad and Zee—that would explain the walking stick's presence in my bed. The walking stick could be concerned about them—they were fae. At least, Zee was fae.

When one of the Gray Lords who ruled the fae had declared independence from the human government, the fae had retreated to their reservations. Zee, my old friend and mentor in all things mechanical, had been forced to go to the Walla Walla reservation, which was about an hour away.

The fae barricaded themselves inside the walls the government had built for them. For a month or so, they'd let the humans figure out that the walls weren't the only things that protected the reservations. The Walla Walla reservation had all but disappeared, hidden by illusion and magic. The road that used to lead to it no longer did. Rumor had it that when people tried to find it by airplane, the pilots forgot where they were going. Satellite photos were a gray blur for an area far larger than the reservation had occupied.

Then they released some of their monsters upon the human population. Fae that had been held in check by their rulers were let free. People died. The government was trying to keep a lid on it, to avoid panic, but the media were starting to notice.

I closed my hands again on the gray wood of the walking stick lying across my lap, the one that Adam had just set on the top of the chest of drawers. The walking stick moved on its own, though I'd never managed to catch it in the process.

I hadn't worried about Zee a whole lot at first—he can take care of himself. Tad and I had been able to contact him now and then.

Tad was Zee's son. Half-fae, product of a mostly failed experiment by the Gray Lords to see if fae could reproduce with humans and still be fae, Tad hadn't been required (or asked) to retreat to the reservations. The fae had no use for their half-bloods, at least not until Tad had demonstrated that his magic was powerful and rare. Then they'd wanted him.

Seven weeks he'd been gone. Without Tad, I hadn't been able to activate the mirror we'd used to contact Zee. Seven weeks and no word at all.

"Is it Tad?" I asked the walking stick. But it sat inert in my hands. When I heard Adam on the stairs, I got up and put it back on the chest.

Sitting at the kitchen table the next morning, I paged through yet another catalogue of mechanic's supplies and made crabbed notes on the notebook beside me with page numbers and prices.

I hadn't forgotten last night, but I could hardly sit and do nothing, waiting for something dire to happen. I had no way to contact Zee or Tad. I also had no way to tell if the walking stick had caused my panic over something real, or if I'd had a nightmare and that had called the walking stick.

If something dire was going to happen, in my experience, it would happen whatever I was doing—and waiting around was singularly useless. So I worked.

The wind rustled the pages gently. It was early summer yet, cool enough to leave windows open. A few more weeks, and the heat would hit in full force, but for now we only had the occasional windstorm to complain about. I flattened the page and compared the specs of their cheapest lift to the next cheapest.

We'd managed to scavenge some tools out of my shop when a volcano god toasted it, but a lot of things got warped from the heat—and other things got demolished when the rest of the building collapsed. It would be months before the shop was up and running, but some items were going to take a few months to order in, too.

Meanwhile, I sent a lot of my customers to the VW dealership. A few of my oldest customers—and a few of my brokest customers—I had bring their cars out to the big pole building at my old place. It wasn't really tooled up, but I could take care of most simple issues.

Music wafted down from upstairs out of Jesse's headphones. Her door must have been open or I wouldn't have heard it. The headphones were an old compromise that predated me. Jesse had told me once, before her father and I got married, that she suspected that if she were playing Big Band music or Elvis or something, her dad wouldn't have minded her playing it on a stereo. He liked music. Just not the music she liked.

She also told me that if she hadn't told him that her mother let her play whatever she wanted (true—you don't lie to a werewolf; they can tell), he probably wouldn't have been willing to compromise on the headphones. Werewolves can hear music played over headphones, but it's not nearly as annoying as music over speakers.

I like Jesse's music, and I hummed along as I sorted through what I didn't want, what I wanted and didn't need, and what I needed. When I finished, I'd compare the final list with my budget. After that, I expected that I'd be sorting through what I needed and what I absolutely needed.

Above Jesse's music, I could hear male voices discussing the pack budget and plans for the next six months. Today was, apparently, a day for budgets. Our pack had money for investments and to help support the wolves who needed help. *Our* pack because though I wasn't a werewolf, I was still a member of the pack—which was unusual but not altogether unique.

Not all packs had the resources that we did. Money was a good thing to have in a werewolf pack. Werewolves had to work to control their wolves, and too much stress made it worse. Lack of money was stressful.

It was a fine balancing act between helping the people who needed help without encouraging slackers. Adam and his second, Darryl, and Zack, our lone submissive wolf, who was the one most likely to hear if someone in the pack was in trouble (in all senses of that word), were upstairs in the pack meeting room—Adam's office being too small to accommodate two dominant wolves.

I couldn't hear Lucia, the sole human in the room. She was there because she had taken over most of the accounting for the pack from Adam's business's accountant. She was quiet because she wasn't yet comfortable enough with the werewolves to argue with them. Zack was pretty good at catching what she didn't say and relaying it to the others, though, so it worked out.

Lucia's husband, Joel (pronounced Hoe-*el* in the Spanish tradition), sighed heavily and rolled over until all four paws were in the air and his side rested against the bottom of the kitchen cabinets a few feet away from where I sat at the table. Joel was the other nonwerewolf who belonged to our pack.

He was black, but in the strong sunlight, I could see a brindle pattern. His induction into the pack was my fault, though it had saved my life and probably his. Instead of turning into a werewolf—or a coyote like me—he sometimes regained his human form and sometimes took on the form of a tibicena, a giant, very scary beast that smelled like brimstone and had eyes that glowed in the dark. Mostly, though, he looked like a large presa Canario, a dog only slightly less intimidating to most people than a werewolf, especially if the people weren't familiar with werewolves. We were hoping that someday he'd get control of his change and be able to be mostly human instead of mostly dog. We were all grateful that he wasn't stuck in the form of the tibicena.

Curled up next to him, and nearly as big as Joel, Cookie, a German-shepherd mix, gave me a wary look. She was a lot better than she had been the first time I met her, as a victim of severe abuse who'd been rescued by Joel and his wife. Still, she avoided strangers and tended to view any abrupt movement as a cause for concern.

The sound of an unfamiliar car in front of the house pulled my attention away from the merits of a four-post lift over a two-post lift. Joel rolled over and took notice. Upstairs, the men's voices stopped. There was no doubt the car was for us because our house was the last one on a dead-end, very rural street.

It wasn't the mail carrier or the UPS lady—I knew those cars, just as I knew the cars the pack usually drove.

"I'll check it out," I told Joel, knowing Adam would hear me, too. I was halfway to the front door, Cookie at my heels, when someone knocked.

I opened the door to see Izzy, one of Jesse's friends, and her mom, who was carrying a large teal canvas bag. Izzy usually drove herself over; I wondered if there was something wrong with her car—and if I should offer to teach her how to fix it.

"Hey, Ms. H," said Izzy, not meeting my eyes. "Jesse's expecting me."

As soon as she spoke, Adam and his budget brigade (as Darryl called them) went back to work—they knew Izzy, too. Izzy slid around me and—"escaped" was the only word that fit—up the stairs. Cookie bolted after her—Izzy was one of her favorite people.

"Mercy," said Izzy's mom. I couldn't for the life of me remember her name. While I was fighting with my memory, she continued speaking. "I wonder if you have a few minutes. I'd like to talk to you."

It sounded ominous—but Izzy had just run upstairs, so it couldn't be one of those "I'm sorry but I just don't feel safe with my daughter coming over here knowing there are werewolves in the house" talks. Those usually happened over the phone anyway.

"Sure," I said, taking a step back to invite her in.

"We'll need a table," she said.

I led her back to the kitchen, where Joel had stretched out, big and scary-looking, across the floor, until the only way to the kitchen table was over him. I opened my mouth to ask him to move, but Izzy's mom stepped over him as if he'd been a Lab or a golden retriever.

Joel looked at me, a little affronted at her disregard of his scariness. I shrugged, gave him a small apologetic smile, then stepped over him, too. Izzy's mom sat down at the kitchen table, so I sat down beside her.

She pushed my catalogues away to clear a space, then pulled out a slick, teal-colored spiral-bound book the size of a regular notebook with "Intrasity Living" scrawled in gold across the front.

She placed it gently, as if it were a treasure, on the table, and said, in an earnest voice, "Life is short. And we're not getting any younger. What would you give if you could look ten years younger and increase your energy at the same time? That's what our vitamins can do for you."

Holy Avon, Batman, I thought as worry relaxed into annoyance-tinged humor, *I've been attacked by a multilevel marketer.*

Sounds from the upstairs quieted again, for just a moment, then Darryl rumbled something that was nicely calculated to be just barely too quiet for me to pick out. Adam laughed, and they went back to talking about interest rates. They had abandoned me to face my doom alone. The rats.

"I don't take vitamins," I told her.

"You haven't tried *our* vitamins," she continued, blithely unconcerned. "They've been clinically proven to—"

"They make my hair fall out," I lied, but she wasn't listening to me.

As she chirruped on enthusiastically, I could hear Izzy's voice drifting down from Jesse's room. "Mercy is going to hate me forever. Mom's gone through all of her friends, all of her acquaintances, all of the people at her gym, and now she's going after my friends' parents."

"Don't worry about Mercy," said Jesse soothingly. "She can take care of herself." Jesse's door closed. I knew that with the door shut, the kids were too human to hear anything that went on in the kitchen short of screams and gunfire. And I wasn't quite desperate enough yet for either of those sounds to be an issue.

"I know there are other vitamins out there," Izzy's mother continued, "but of the twelve most common brands, only ours is certified by two independent laboratories as toxin- and allergen-free."

If she hadn't been Jesse's best friend's mom, I'd have gently but firmly (or at least firmly) sent her on her way. But Jesse didn't have that many friends—the werewolf thing drove away some people, and the ones it didn't weren't always the kind of people she wanted as friends.

So I sat and listened and made "mmm" sounds occasionally as seemed appropriate. Eventually, we moved from vitamins to makeup. Despite rumors to the contrary, I do wear makeup. Mostly when my husband's ex-wife is going to be around.

"We also have a product that is very useful at covering up scars," she told me, looking pointedly at the white scar that slid across my cheek.

I almost said, "What scar? Who has a scar?" But I restrained myself. She probably wouldn't get the *Young Frankenstein* reference anyway.

"I don't usually wear makeup," I told her instead. I had an almost-irresistible need to add "my husband doesn't want me attracting other men" or "my husband says makeup is the work of the devil" but decided that any woman whose name I couldn't remember probably didn't know me well enough to tell when I was kidding.

"But, honey," she said, "with your coloring, you would be stunning with the right makeup." And, with that backhanded compliment, she was off and running, again.

Izzy's mom used "natural" and "herbal" to mean good. "Toxin" was bad. There was never any particular toxin named, but my house, my food, and, apparently, my makeup were full of toxins.

The world wasn't so clear-cut, I mused as she talked. There were a lot of natural and herbal things that were deadly. Uranium occurred naturally, for instance. White snake root was so toxic that it had killed people who drank the milk from cows who had eaten it. See? My history degree *was* useful, if only as a source of material to entertain myself with while listening to someone deliver a marketing speech.

Izzy's mother was earnest and believed everything she said, so I didn't argue with her. Why should I upset her view of the world and tell her that sodium and chloride were toxic but very useful when combined into salt? I was pretty sure she'd only point out how harmful salt was anyway.

She turned another page while I was occupied with coming up with more toxins that were useful—and I was distracted from my train of thought by the picture on the page. A mint leaf lay on an improbably black and shiny rock in the middle of a clear, running stream with lots of water drops in artistic places. It made me a little thirsty—and thirsty reminded me of drinking. And though I don't drink because of an incident in college, I sure could have used something alcoholic right then.

Come to think of it, alcohol was a toxin—and useful for all sorts of things.

"Oh, this is my favorite part," she said, caressing the dramatic photo, "essential oils." The last two words were said in the same tone a dragon might use to say "Spanish doubloon."

She reached into her bag and pulled out a teal box about the size of a loaf of bread. In metallic embossed letters, "Intrasity" and "Living Essentials" chased each other around the box in lovely calligraphic script.

She opened the box and released the ghosts of a thousand odors. I sneezed, Joel sneezed. Izzy's mother said, "God bless you."

I smiled. "Yes, He does. Thank you."

"I don't know what I would do without my essential oils," she told me. "I used to have terrible migraines. Now I just rub a little of our Gaia's Blessing on my wrists and temples and 'poof,' no more pain." She slid out an elegant, clear bottle that held some amber liquid and opened it, holding it toward my nose.

It wasn't that bad. I admit my eyes watered a little from the peppermint oil. Joel sneezed again and gave Izzy's mother the stink eye. From upstairs came a gagging noise and loud coughing. Ben wasn't here, and I didn't think Zack was the type. I'd have thought Adam and Darryl would both have been more mature. If I had any doubt that they were teasing me, it would have been dispelled by the way they were careful to be just quiet enough that Izzy's mother couldn't hear them.

Joel looked at me and let his tongue loll in an amused expression. He stretched, got up, and trotted up the stairs, doubtless so that he could join in the next round of fun. Deserter. I was left alone to face the enemy.

"Gaia's Blessing contains peppermint oil," Izzy's mother said unnecessarily because that was the one making my eyes water, "lavender, rosemary, and eucalyptus, all natural oils, blended together." She capped it. "We have remedies for a variety of ailments. My husband was an athlete in college, and for twenty years, he's battled with jock itch."

I blinked.

I tried to keep my face expressionless, despite the laughter from upstairs, as Izzy's mother continued, apparently unaware of the meaning of TMI. "We tried everything to control it." She dug around and pulled out a few bottles before coming up with the one she wanted. "Here it is. A little dab of this every night for three days, and his jock itch was gone. It works for ringworm, psoriasis, and acne, too."

I looked at the bottle as if that would keep inappropriate images from lingering. It helped that I had never met Izzy's father, but now I hoped I never did.

The bottle label read: "Healing Touch." I wondered if Izzy's mother's husband knew that his jock itch was something that his wife brought up in her sales pitch with near strangers. Maybe he wouldn't care.

She opened that bottle, too. It wasn't as bad as the first one.

"Vitamin E," she said. "Tea tree oil."

"Lavender," I said, and her smile wattage went up.

I bet she made a mint on her multilevel marketing. She was cute, perky, and very sincere.

She pulled out another bottle. "Most of our essential oils are just one oil—lavender, jasmine, lemon, orange. But I think that the combination oils are more useful. You can combine them on your own, of course, but our blends are carefully measured for the best effect. I use this one first thing every morning. It just makes you feel better; the smell releases endorphins and wipes the blues right away."

"Good Vibrations," I commented neutrally. I hadn't been

pulled back to the sixties or anything; that was what the label on the bottle read.

She nodded. "They don't advertise this, mind you, but my manager says that she thinks it does more than just elevate your mood. She told me she believes it actually makes your life go a little smoother. Helps good things to happen." She smiled again, though I couldn't remember her not smiling. "She was wearing it when she won a thousand dollars on a lottery ticket."

She set the bottle down and leaned forward earnestly. "I've heard—but it hasn't been confirmed—that the woman who started Intrasity"—she pronounced it "In-TRAY-sity"—"Tracy LaBella, is a witch. A white witch, of course, who is using her powers for good. *Our* good." She giggled, which should have been odd in a woman of her age but instead was charming.

Her comment, though, disturbed me and made me pick up the bottle of Good Vibrations. I opened it and took a careful smell: rose, lavender, lemon, and mint. I didn't sense any magic, and mostly if magic is around, I can tell.

LaBella wasn't one of the witch family names, as far as I knew, but if "Tracy the Beautiful" was her real name, I'd have been surprised.

"Now, this little gem"—Izzy's mother pulled out yet another bottle—"this is one of my favorites, guaranteed to improve your love life or your money back. Does your husband ever have trouble keeping up?" She held up a finger, then curled it limply downward as her eyebrows arched up.

The silence from upstairs was suddenly deafening.

"Uhm. No," I said. I tried to resist, I really did. If Darryl hadn't said, "Way to go, man—for a moment I was worried about you,"

I think I could have held out. But he did. And Adam laughed, which clinched it.

I sighed and picked an imaginary string off my pant leg. "Not *that* way. My husband is a werewolf, you know. So *really* not, if you know what I mean."

She blinked avidly. "No. What do you mean?"

"Well," I said, looking away from her as if I were embarrassed, and I half mumbled, "You know what they say about werewolves."

She leaned closer. "No," she whispered. "Tell me."

I had heard the meeting-room door open, so I knew that the werewolves could hear every word we whispered.

I let out a huff of air and turned back to her. "You know, every night is just fine. I'm good with every morning, too. Three, four times a night? Well . . ." I let fall a husky laugh. "You've *seen* my husband, right?" Adam was gorgeous. "But some nights . . . I'm not on the right side of thirty anymore, you know? Sometimes I'm tired. I just get to sleep, and he's nudging me again." I gave her what I hoped would come out as a shy, hopeful smile. "Do you have anything that might help with that?"

I don't know what I expected her to do. But it wasn't what happened.

She nodded decisively and pulled out an oversized vial with "Rest Well" written on the label. "My manager's father, God rest his soul, discovered the 'little blue pill' last year. Her mother just about divorced him after forty years of marriage before she tried this."

"God rest his soul" meant dead, right? I took the vial warily. Like the others, it didn't *feel* magical. I opened it and sniffed. Lavender again, but it was more complex than that. Orange, I thought, and something else. "What's in it?" I asked.

15

"St. John's wort, lavender, orange," she said briskly. "This isn't quite chemical castration, but it will bring your life into balance," she said, and she was off on her sales pitch as if the phrase "chemical castration" was a common concept—*and* something one might consider doing to one's husband.

And she looked like such a nice, normal person.

I sniffed the vial again. St. John's wort I knew mostly from a book I'd once borrowed about the fae. The herb could be used to protect yourself and your home against some kinds of fae when placed around windows, doors, and chimneys. If it protected against the fae, maybe I should see if we could get it somewhere and stockpile. Maybe we could grow it. Lucia had our flower beds looking better than they had in years, and she was talking about putting in an herb garden somewhere. St. John's wort was an herb.

Eventually, Izzy's mother finished her sales presentation and began the hard sell.

I have a strong will. I didn't join up to sell Intrasity products to all my friends. She could say it "wasn't a pyramid scheme" all she wanted, but that's what it was. When she offered a 10 percent discount for names and phone numbers of friends, I thought about giving her Elizaveta's name. But I wasn't all that keen on sending a perfectly nice woman to the scary witch. I also wasn't sure that the witch really counted as a friend.

I would let Elizaveta know that Tracy LaBella was styling herself a witch to sell her products and let the old Russian deal with it herself.

So I paid full price for one normal-sized and one oversized bottle of Rest Well, which was Izzy's mother's entire stock. I mostly bought it because it was funny, but also because I intended to see what kind of an effect the St. John's wort would have on a fae.

With Zee and Tad stuck on the reservation, I might need something to use against the fae.

I also bought a small vial of Good Vibrations. I hadn't intended to, but Izzy's mother gave me 5 percent off because she'd used it as a demo. I could give it to Elizaveta to make sure it wasn't really magical. It wouldn't hurt anything if I tried a little of it myself first.

It was when I bought some orange oil that I acknowledged that Izzy's mother had beaten me. But the orange oil smelled really good. Izzy's mother told me it was supposed to promote calmness— and it worked in cookies. I'd used orange extract in brownies before, but Izzy's mother said the oil worked better.

I saw her out and put my back against the door once I closed it. Adam cleared his throat. I looked up to see him halfway down the stairs. He was leaning against the wall, arms folded as he did his best to appear disgruntled. But there was a crinkle of a smile at the edge of his eyes.

"So," he said, shaking his head. "I'm too much for you. You should have said something. We might be married, Mercy, but no still means no."

I widened my eyes at him. "I just haven't wanted to hurt your feelings."

"When I give you that little nudge, hmm?" His voice took on a considering air. "Come to think of it, I'm feeling a little nudge coming on right now."

"Now?" I whispered in horrified tones. I looked up toward Jesse's room. "Think of the children."

He tilted his head as if to listen, then shook it. "They won't hear anything from there." He started slowly down the stairs.

"Think of Darryl, Zack, Lucia, and Joel," I said earnestly. "They'll be scarred for life."

"You know what they say about werewolves," he told me gravely, stepping down to the ground.

I broke and ran—and he was right on my tail. Figuratively speaking, of course. I don't have a tail unless I'm in my coyote shape.

I dodged around the big dining table, but he put one hand on top and vaulted it, right over the top of Medea, who was taking a nap on top of the forbidden territory. She hissed at him, but he ignored her and kept coming after me. I dove under the table and out the other side, sprinted through the kitchen, and bolted down the stairs, laughing so hard I almost couldn't breathe.

He caught me in the big rec room, tripped me, and pinned me against the floor. He kissed my chin, my neck, my cheek, and the bridge of my nose before he touched my lips. He put our game right out of my mind (along with any ability to form a coherent thought), so when he said, "Nudge," it took me a second or two to figure out what he was talking about.

I dragged my thoughts from my enervated and trembling body and thought about how many people would know what we were doing down here. "No?" I said hesitantly.

"What happened to not hurting my feelings?" he asked. Even though his body was evidently as excited as mine, and his breathing harder than our little chase merited, there was amusement in his eyes.

"Izzy, Jesse, Darryl, Zack, Lucia, and Joel happened," I said. If my voice was husky, well, I think anyone in my situation would have had trouble keeping her voice steady.

He rolled off me but grabbed my hand as he did, so we lay side by side on our backs with our hands clasped. He started laughing first.

"At least," he said finally, "being a werewolf means I never have to worry about jock itch."

"Every cloud has a silver lining," I agreed. "Even being a were-wolf has its upside."

I expected him to laugh again. But instead his hand tightened on mine and he sat up and looked at me. He pulled my hand to his lips, and said, "Yes."

Of course, I had to kiss him again.

We went upstairs after that kiss, so I didn't end up embarrassing myself. Sure, there were sly grins from the peanut gallery, but since nothing happened, I was able to keep from blushing as Darryl and Zack got ready to leave. Adam and the others had apparently concluded their business while I was finishing up with Izzy's mother.

Darryl kissed my hand formally, and said, "You are endlessly entertaining."

I raised my eyebrow and gave him a "who, me?" expression. Of course, that only made him laugh, his teeth flashing whitely in amusement. Darryl was a happy blend of his African father and Chinese mother, taking the best features of two races and combining them. A big man, he could do scary better than anyone in the pack, but with a grin on his face, he could charm kittens out of trees.

Zack gave me a hug good-bye. Our only submissive wolf, he had been really . . . skittish and worn when he first joined the pack a few months ago. But as he'd gotten used to us, he touched us all a lot. Some of the guys had been taken aback when he'd started, though his touch had nothing to do with sex. But no one wanted him sad: a happy submissive wolf balanced the dominants and lowered tempers. So they'd learned to accept Zack's ways.

I returned Zack's hug, and he slipped something into my pocket that felt like one of the vials I'd just bought. He stepped back, looked me earnestly in the eye, and said, "To protect you from the nudge."

Darryl high-fived him as he stepped out onto the porch. It made Adam laugh.

After I shut the door on the miscreants who *didn't* live here, I turned around to see Lucia, Joel at her side, standing in the doorway to the kitchen with her arms crossed and a big grin on her face.

I frowned at her.

"Don't worry," she said earnestly. "I didn't hear the whole thing, but Zack courteously kept me apprised as it was happening, so I wouldn't feel left out. Why didn't you tell her to go away before she got started?"

"Because she's Izzy's mother—and that sort of thing can have repercussions for Jesse," I told her.

"And because you didn't want to hurt her feelings," said Adam. "Which is why multilevel marketing works. And you bought the oil because you want to see if there's real magic involved because you're worried about her," said Adam.

I met his eyes solemnly. "No." I patted my pocket. "I bought the orange oil for brownies, and I bought that other as a shield for the nudge attack."

He raised an eyebrow. "So, do you wear it, or do I?" he asked.

I frowned at him. "I couldn't actually tell from her story, but I'm afraid it might be fatal for you." Her manager's father had gotten a "God rest his soul" after his name when she was talking about him, after all. "I figure the way it works is that I put it on me. Then I'll smell so strongly that you'll stay away until you are really desperate."

He threw his head back and laughed. Adam . . . Adam tried to downplay it with a military haircut and clothes that were subtly the wrong color—I'd just figured that one out—but he was beautiful. Like magazine-model beautiful. I didn't always see it anymore, the inside being more interesting than the outer package, but with his eyes sparkling and his dimple flashing . . .

I cleared my throat. "Nudge?" I said.

Lucia laughed and turned back toward the kitchen. "Get a room," she said over her shoulder.

Adam? He took a predatory step toward me, and his phone rang.

So did mine.

I checked the number on my phone, intending to let the voice mail catch it, but when I saw who was calling, I answered it instead.

"Tony?" I asked, walking away from Adam so my conversation wouldn't get mixed up in his. Adam was talking to Darryl, whose voice sounded urgent.

"I don't know if you and Adam can help us," Tony said rapidly. In the background, sirens were doing their best to drown out his voice. "But we have a situation here. There is something, a freaking-big something, on the Cable Bridge, and it is eating cars."

"You and Adam" was short for "please bring a pack of werewolves out to take care of the car-eating monster." If they were asking for the pack, they must be desperate.

"Mercy," said Adam, who, unlike me, apparently had no trouble keeping track of two conversations at the same time, "tell him we're on our way. Darryl and Zack are almost on-site."

I repeated Adam's words, then said, "We'll be right there."

21

I hung up and started out the door. The Cable Bridge, which had another name no one remembered, was about a ten-minute drive from our house.

"Mercy," said Adam tightly. The last time we'd faced down a monster, I'd almost died. It had taken me six weeks to stand on my own two feet, and it hadn't been the first time I'd been hurt. The werewolves were two-hundred-plus pounds of fang and claw who mostly healed nearly as quickly as they could be hurt. I was as vulnerable as any human. My superpower consisted of changing into a thirty-five-pound coyote.

He still had nightmares.

I looked at him. "You're going to be a werewolf. Darryl is going to be a werewolf, and I'm assuming Joel is going to be a monstrous tibicena, spitting lava and looking scary. I think you need someone on the ground with the ability to shout things like 'Stop shooting, those are the good guys.'" I took a deep breath. "I won't promise not to get hurt. I won't lie to you. But I do promise not to be stupid."

His cheeks whitened as he clenched his jaw. His eyes shadowed, he nodded slowly. That was the deal we had, the thing that allowed me to give up my independence and trust him. He had to let me be who I was—and not some princess wrapped in cotton wool and kept on a shelf.

"Okay," he said. "Okay." Unself-consciously, he stripped out of his clothes because it would be easier to do that here than in the car. "Joel? Are you coming?"

The big black dog, who already looked a little bigger, padded out of the kitchen. I wasn't certain how much control Joel had about what shape he wore except that it wasn't much. We needed to get to the bridge before he started melting things in the car—the tibicena was a creature born in the heart of a volcano.

I opened the door, stopped, and ran up the stairs. I opened Jesse's door without knocking.

"Monster on the Cable Bridge," I said. "Police are requesting assistance. Stay home. Stay safe. We love you."

I didn't give her time to say anything, just bolted back down the stairs to Adam's black SUV, where the others waited.

We were going to fight monsters.

2

Adam had not quite changed all the way when the traffic on the highway to town bogged down. A traffic jam on this road was unusual, but then so was a monster that destroyed cars. I suspected there was a connection. Sometimes, I'm observant like that.

I slowed until the cars ahead stopped moving altogether. Then I put the SUV into four-wheel drive and pulled onto the shoulder of the road, driving on the sidewalk when I had to in order to get around the parking lot the highway had become.

At the old metals-recycling center, I pulled into their abandoned parking lot and stopped. From here it would be faster to go on foot. As soon as I opened the door, I could hear the sirens.

Joel hopped out of the backseat into the driver's seat. He flowed out of the car and it rocked, because he was denser in tibicena form than a real animal could be. He waited until all four feet were on the ground before igniting the fire inside him. His skin cracked and broke, revealing something that glowed fiercely even in the daylight.

Adam, all wolf now, exited after Joel. He shook himself once, then set off for the bridge. Joel and I followed him.

Even on two feet, I was fast, though the coyote would have been quicker. But I needed to have clothes on when talking to the police—for some reason, I suspected the police wouldn't take me as seriously if I were naked. So I stayed human and ran with the silver-and-black wolf who was Adam on one side of me and Joel, who no longer could be mistaken for a dog, on the other.

We garnered attention. Pack magic operates passively to make it difficult for mundane people to notice werewolves. Adam could run down the interstate at high noon and only one or two people would see anything but a stray dog. We'd discovered that wasn't true of Joel, even though he was a member of the pack. It was as if something in his magic fought to be seen.

Joel's eyes were hot coals that glowed like those of a hellish demon out of a comic book. He was bigger than Adam, and he left oily black marks on the ground wherever his feet touched. People noticed. Once they noticed him, they noticed Adam.

Adam was a public figure, and though he didn't often appear in his wolf form on the national news, locally, even in his werewolf shape, he was a celebrity. A smallish-town hero, if only because he was sort of famous.

"Hey, Mercy," came a shout from the double line of cars. "What's up? When you gonna reopen the shop? Sheba has an electrical problem I can't find."

"Shop phone still gets me, Nick," I called, waving vaguely without looking around. I didn't need to see him to recognize him. Nick's Sheba was a VW bug that broke down with a regularity that was almost supernatural. "Gotta go help the police with a car-eating monster on the bridge right now."

"What's on the bridge?" he called, but I just waved again because I was already too far to yell loudly enough for him to hear me.

But a woman stuck her head out of a car as I passed, and yelled, "Is it werewolf trouble, Mercy?"

I didn't know the voice, but I'd been bathing in the reflected glory of Adam long enough that I wasn't anonymous anymore, either.

"Nope," I told her. "Fae monster, I think."

I was sure that Tony wouldn't have approved: I was informing the public without talking to him. But I figured that in this era of cell phone cameras, whatever was on the bridge was already due to be famous on YouTube anyway.

The bridge was visible from a long way off on both sides of the river. Something big enough to be "eating cars" was certain to attract people with cameras and cell phones. There would be no covering this up.

Up ahead, the Lampson Building came into view, as did the blue and red flashing lights of dozens of police cars. Lampson International builds the world's largest cranes, and they'd built their headquarters right at the base of the Cable Bridge. Four stories tall, the glass-and-steel structure was distinctively odd. It looked very much as though some giant had picked up a pyramid, turned it upside down, and squished it back into the ground.

The police had set up two barricades. The first was at the last intersection before the bridge, to keep cars away from it. There were several uniformed policemen directing traffic there. The second barricade was closer to the bridge, just past the entrance to the Vietnam Memorial, which was on the edge and up the hill from the parking lot of the Lampson Building.

We ran past the first barricade without any of the police trying to stop us, though we drew sharp looks. Probably they were too busy with traffic, but it also takes real moxie to try to stop someone who is running with a tibicena and a werewolf. Maybe they recognized Adam.

The land rose gently to meet the beginning of the suspension bridge. I looked away from the police and the stalled traffic to peer at the bridge.

It arced gracefully over the river, more or less a mile across, the most beautiful of the three Tri-Cities bridges over the Columbia, and the only one that was not a highway or interstate. Drapes of thick white cable descended from both sides of the two towers on either side of the center of the bridge.

From the Kennewick shore, I could only see to the top of the arc, halfway across the bridge, about a half mile off. There were a few cars with their noses pointed (mostly) toward us in the Kennewick-bound lane, stopped and apparently empty. The nearest car, a red Buick, rested on its roof, one of the rear tires missing. It looked, to my educated eye, like something had grabbed the tire and ripped it off the car.

The Pasco-bound lane on the right side of the bridge was clear until about halfway to the center. The rest of it looked as though a five-year-old playing with his toy cars had had a temper tantrum. The illusion was enhanced by the distance that made the cars look smaller than they were, tiny and abandoned. It was a false picture of harmlessness: all of those cars had been carrying people. I've seen enough wrecks to know which cars might hold bodies, waiting in endless patience for us to deal with whatever had done this before we took care of the dead.

I ran into Adam, who'd turned broadside to me. In wolf form, he was tall enough that I didn't fall when I hit and big enough that I didn't knock him over. He waited until I recovered, then looked at the police off to our left. They'd seen us, but, except for Tony, who trotted toward us, didn't approach. There were a few of them who looked battered, and I could smell blood from here. Theirs or the victims' I couldn't tell, but it smelled fresh.

"Okay," I told Tony. "You should have two other werewolves here already. Adam's called in the rest of the pack, but it might take a half hour or more to get anyone else here. What do you need?"

"Can you kill this thing? Failing that, we need to keep it on the bridge until the National Guard gets here—about two hours at last check," Tony said grimly.

He leveled an opaque look at Joel. This was Joel's first public appearance as a member of the pack. To Tony's credit, a black dog that looked as though he'd been half formed out of burning charcoal didn't seem to faze him long. He barely even paused before he continued to speak.

"It doesn't seem to be inclined to leave the bridge, thankfully. At least here it's contained, but it has amply demonstrated that it's staying on the bridge because it wants to be there. Nothing we've been able to do does much more than annoy it."

Adam gave me a sharp look.

"I've got this," I agreed. "You and Joel can go find whatever's playing Matchbox cars on the bridge."

Adam started out, then hesitated and turned back, Joel attentive at his side. My mate looked me in the eyes, his own golden and clear.

"I know," I said, feeling his emotions sing to me through our mating bond. He should be able to feel mine, too, but sometimes words matter. "I love you, too."

He turned and ran, the efficient lope of the beginning of a hunt rather than a racing stride. Joel kept pace at his hip.

Tony cupped his hand under my elbow and tugged me over to the gathered police officers, some in uniform, some in business casual, and some in whatever they happened to be wearing when they got the call. I recognized a few faces, recognized more scents, and Detective Willis, who was regarding me with an expression I couldn't read.

"Don't shoot the werewolves and the tibicena," I told him—because that was the main purpose of my coming with Adam. "They're the good guys."

"Tibicena?" Detective Willis tasted the unfamiliar word, but that wasn't enough to hold his attention for long. He turned to look at the bridge, not at Adam and Joel, who had slowed to take advantage of the cover provided by the strewn-about cars. "What can you tell us about the thing on the bridge? Why can't we shoot it? Bullets don't seem to do anything to it."

"I don't know what your monster is," I told him. "I haven't had a chance to see it yet. The tibicena is the scary black doglike creature running beside Adam. Adam is the werewolf, and the tibicena is a friend. Please tell everyone not to shoot them, okay?"

Willis gave a quick look at Adam and Joel, then frowned and narrowed his eyes, as if he'd finally realized that Joel wasn't just a weird werewolf. "That thing is a tibicena? What the hell is a tibicena?"

"My friend," I said coolly. "Who is risking *his* life to help out."

Willis grimaced at me. "Don't take offense where none is meant, Mercy Hauptman." He put a hand to his face and pressed a button I couldn't see because he said, "Do not, I repeat, do not shoot the scary black dog . . . doglike creature. Don't shoot the werewolves, either. They are on our side, people."

Tony, who'd followed me over to Willis, said, presumably to
me, "We have a couple of SWAT snipers up on top of the Lampson
Building and a couple more on top of the Crow's Nest on Clover
Island—for all the good that's doing us."

Clover Island was a boating and tourist mecca just west of the
bridge, lots of boats, lots of docks, and, on the tiny island itself, a
hotel, the Coast Guard office, and a few restaurants. The Crow's
Nest was the restaurant on the top floor of the hotel. "They can't
get a shot, the wind is too high." His voice was cool and controlled.
"Pasco's got a couple of marksmen up on their side of the river, too.
At this rate, we're more likely to shoot each other than whatever
that thing is. And given how effective our bullets have been, it
wouldn't matter anyway."

"It's over the hump, and I haven't been able to see it," I said.
"What's it look like?"

"King Kong," said one of the officers I didn't know. "If King
Kong were green and covered in moss with a nose set higher than
his eyes. And it is well and truly a him because that part isn't green."

"Like Christmastime," agreed a woman I'd seen before but
hadn't been introduced to. "Red and green."

"That's more than I saw," said a guy in sweats with a long
streak of dried blood on the sleeve. "I was too busy getting out of
there with my battered civilians."

"What's it doing?" I asked. "I mean, why is it still on the bridge
and not somewhere else? Have the werewolves been keeping it on
the bridge?"

"If it wanted off the bridge," said an officer grimly, "it would
be off the bridge."

"Adam's people are doing a fine job of keeping it occupied,"
said Tony. "According to the Pasco police, they've been distracting

it whenever it seems to be thinking about heading off. But it really doesn't seem to want off."

The guy in the bloody sweatshirt spoke up. "One of the victims I escorted out said it just stopped and ran back to the middle of the bridge. It's been back on our side a couple of times, Pasco, too—but mostly seems to be hanging out in the center section." He looked at me. "That thing was coming right for me, and this big black guy ran past and hit it with a baseball bat. I figure I've played baseball most of my life, and I never saw a human swing a bat like that. Broke the bat, which I have seen, but not like that. He saved my life and the lives of the four people I was helping off the bridge, too. Is he one of your guys?"

Darryl. Darryl carried a baseball bat in his car, a baseball bat and a baseball. In Washington, it was illegal to carry *only* a baseball bat in your car. Darryl wasn't out as a werewolf at his work. I suppose that cat would be out of the bag after today.

"Probably," I said.

"Then why wasn't he sprouting fangs and hair?" growled someone else.

I opened my mouth to snap something back, but then I located the voice. She had a compression bandage on her arm, which was in a sling, and a rosy flush that would be black-and-blue tomorrow covered half her face.

"No time," I told her. "Most werewolves take a while to change—ten minutes or even fifteen or twenty. My friends—the two werewolves who beat us here—were driving by when they realized what was going on. They called us, then dove in to help."

"Thank goodness for that," one of the patrolmen said. I didn't think I was supposed to hear him because he said it under his breath.

"The other one was changing," one of the guys who looked familiar said. "It was pretty freaky."

"It's hard for a werewolf not to change when something's trying to kill him," I told them. "A werewolf in midchange isn't helpless, just not as good in a fight because he's distracted." And not as likely to be able to control himself. But they didn't need to know that.

"We were hoping you might ID it for us," Willis said. "So we know what to do about it."

I'd helped the police with fae affairs before. But I wasn't an expert by any means—and my fae connections weren't available. Samuel and his fae wife, Ariana, were in Europe, and would be for another month or more. Zee and Tad were, as far as I knew, prisoners on the reservation in Walla Walla. But I *had* been studying up, and I'd had access to information that most humans wouldn't have had.

"It would help if I could see it," I told him. Green, I thought. King Kong, though, so we were dealing with something that looked like a large, green gorilla that was big enough to toss cars around. And it stayed on the bridge.

I closed my eyes and envisioned the book I'd borrowed once, a book that detailed a lot of the fae, what they were, what they could do, and how to protect yourself from them. It had been written by a fae—Samuel's Ariana, in fact—so the information was pretty accurate.

"Troll," I said, opening my eyes. "It could be a troll. Green— how tall?" Some of them were green.

"Like a semitruck," Willis said. "That tall, not that big, though it's big enough."

Someone let out a shout, and I looked at the bridge. Right at the top of the arc, I could see movement—something green and about the shape of a gorilla. It leaped and grabbed one of the cables—which were bigger around than both of my hands could reach together—and used the cable to climb upward.

"So look at it," said Tony, and he handed me a pair of binoculars.

It had skin the color of a green bell pepper. Sparse, lacy moss green . . . *stuff* grew out of its shoulders and feathered down from its head. It wasn't hair, but it would give that appearance to anyone not holding a pair of binoculars. Smallish eyes were set a little below a wide-nostriled nose. On either side of the nostrils were slits that looked as though someone had cut its face open with a sharp knife. The inner edge of the slits was bright red—gill slits for breathing underwater, maybe. Trolls lived near water by preference and, when they could, around bridges. There is magic in places that are between: crossroads, thresholds, bridges. Which might explain why he stayed on the Cable Bridge rather than running over the top of the police and into Pasco or Kennewick.

It was certainly a he, and he really was enjoying his climb. I was a shapeshifter, and I'd grown up in a werewolf pack—body shy I was not. But bright red was still really, really shocking next to all that green.

"Yup," I said, trying to sound nonchalant because it wouldn't do to run around screaming in front of a group of police people I was trying to impress for the good of the pack. Ever since the werewolves had admitted to their existence, they'd had to fight for the goodwill of the communities they lived in. Goodwill made it safer for everyone. "It's a troll."

Somehow, a troll hadn't seemed as scary when I was reading about it in Ariana's book. The drawing had been about four inches high by two inches wide. The real creature was terrifying, even half a mile away—elephant-sized or a hair bigger, judging by a rough comparison to the cars nearest him.

I couldn't see any of the wolves—not even Adam or Joel. The bridge was slightly angled from where I stood, and the center barricade between the opposite lanes blocked what line of sight was left with the battered cars littering the roadway, but from the agitation of the troll, I expected that they were there.

Having evidently gotten as far up as it intended, the troll swung for a moment from both arms, which were overly long for his body, longer than his legs. That accounted for the instant association with gorillas—though his features and coloring were nothing like one. His mouth was horribly humanesque despite the eye placement, until he smiled and displayed teeth, sharp and wedge-shaped, in double rows like a shark's.

He opened his four-fingered, thumbless hands and dropped from maybe thirty feet up—it was tough to judge from that distance, binoculars or no. I couldn't see him land. The inconveniently placed center cement barricade hid my view. But I could feel the impact on the ground under my feet from half a mile away. I heard it, too, and saw the bridge shudder. I handed back the binoculars. It hadn't landed on any of the wolves, I told myself. The pack sense would have told me if someone had died.

"What's a troll?" Tony asked as he took the binoculars, then made an impatient sound. "I know what it is in the stories—'Three Billy Goats Gruff' and all of that. But how do you stop it? Our guns didn't seem to do much more than tick it off while we were trying to get the civilians to safety."

"They're tough," I told Tony. "Usually more brawn than brains, though they can talk, or most of them can. A troll's skin is supposed to be very thick; the book I read about it compared it to a suit of armor, for whatever that's worth. It must be tougher than most medieval armor if your guns didn't hurt him."

I tried to remember everything I could. "He'll be equally comfortable on land or the river—you should warn your guys in the boats." There were a number of boats gathering on either side of the bridge, more now than there had been five minutes ago. I judged that most of them were gawkers, but I thought I saw a couple of official boats, too.

"Any idea how we can kill it?"

"Back in the day, people used to hunt them with lances," I told him apologetically.

Tony gave me an unamused laugh. "Mercy, we're all that stands between the citizens and that thing when it comes down off the bridge. I don't have any mounted knights down here."

"J.C. has a horse," the guy with the bloody sleeve said.

"Yeah," said another guy absently. Like Tony and a few others, he had a pair of binoculars. He was staring through them as he spoke. "But his lance is too small."

"You'd know about small lances," said still another guy. This one apparently was J.C. because he continued, "But my horse is afraid of sheep and small children. I don't think I could get him within a mile of a troll—and no one's lance is that big."

"How many people do you have injured?" I asked Tony quietly as the other police officers worked off stress and fear by exchanging rude and inappropriate comments.

Tony shrugged. "We got the civilians off on our side. Pasco got them off on theirs. Some idiot tried to protect his car and got thrown into the river. Sheriff's patrol on the river says he hit wrong and broke his neck. We lost one of our guys who was distracting the troll from a car while Pasco officers cleared the passengers out."

"Ate him," said Willis grimly, though he kept his voice down so he was talking just to Tony and me. "I've known that man for ten years. Lousy cop. He was lazy and good at making sure that someone else took the call. He stepped up today, though. No kids, no wife." He shuddered. "No body."

"Willis?" said a muffled voice. I turned my head to see Willis put his hand to his ear and hold the earpiece tighter.

"Yes?"

"You see that gray van? West side of the bridge, Kennewick-bound lane, stopped just over the arc toward you? The one with the caved-in side?"

"I see it."

"There's someone in that van. The left side's smashed, but the right side door slid open a minute ago. Looks like one of the were-wolves, one of the first two, might have opened the door. The one who has been turning into a wolf." That would be Zack, I thought.

There was a pause. "I can see him again. There's still someone else in the van, a woman. They aren't coming out. Shit," he said. "Oh damn. There's a car seat. They're trying to get a baby out of the car seat. But they're having trouble. There's something wrong with the woman, and the wolf isn't equipped to deal with a car seat."

Willis stiffened. "We'll get someone over there."

In my mind's eye, I thought about what would happen to a police officer—a dozen police officers who tried running in front of the troll to get to the car. The troll had eaten one of them already. Adam and the wolves would do their best, but humans were too slow.

I wasn't slow.

I'd promised Adam I wouldn't be stupid. But there was a car seat and a baby. I considered what might be the problem that Zack hadn't been able to get them out of the van. Baby seats attached to the car with seat belts. Babies produced a lot of sticky substances that could make buckles tough to open, and the belts were strong. Werewolf jaws do fine with rending and ripping, but they might have trouble with seat belts attached to fragile babies.

I felt my pockets to make sure, but the only thing I had in my pocket was the essential oil bottle Zack had stuffed there. My concealed-carry gun was in its holster in the small of my back, but that wouldn't be much use if I had to cut a seat belt.

"Hey, Tony," I said casually. "Do you have a knife I can borrow?"

Tony was talking to one of the officers about something else. He didn't even ask me what I needed it for. Just handed me a sleek black pocketknife. I took it and slipped it into my pocket, where pocketknives go, right?

I had watched the troll. He had moved fast, but not as fast as the werewolves could because he had tried to drop on them and failed. If the werewolves could outrun him, so could I.

I was pretty sure I could outrun him.

Willis briefed everyone on the new problem because they were human and couldn't overhear the bluetooth earphone. As he talked to his people, I considered my actions carefully because I'd made a promise to Adam.

I could outrun that troll if I had to—better than that baby trapped in the van could outrun it. Better than any of the officers who already had casualties.

I had to be able to look at myself in the mirror. If I stayed safe when I might have saved someone else, especially a baby . . . that would poison what was between Adam and me.

"I'll do it," I said. "I'm faster than you guys are."

Tony's hand clamped on my arm. "Civilian," he snapped.

I looked at him. "You know what I am," I said dryly, because he did. I'd kept what I was a secret for most of my life. But being Adam's wife, belonging to the pack—that looked like it meant that a lot of my secrets were going to come out. Being Adam's wife meant that being a coyote shifter wasn't going to make me any more of a target than I already was.

The other officers were paying attention while trying to pretend they weren't. We'd been clear with the news media that I wasn't a werewolf.

I gave Tony a smile. "You've seen me run." And so the police would know we hadn't lied to them outright: "I'm not a werewolf, but I'm faster than any mundane person."

He didn't smile back. "Maybe so. Are you faster than that thing?"

A howl echoed from the bridge, and I saw the gathered police officers come to alert, their hands sliding to weapons and their muscles tensing. I understood the instinct; the distinctive howl was as much a weapon of the tibicena as the volcanic heat under his skin. He hadn't loosed the full power of his cry. But despite that, despite the distance between us, the howl sent an atavistic icy finger of fear up my spine, only partially alleviated by my understanding that it was just magic.

"It looks like we're going to find out. Besides, our tibicena"— who had been lion-sized, half-formed, and growing the last time I'd seen him—"won't forget I'm an ally. I'm not sure he'd make the same association with a stranger." I didn't know how much of Joel had stayed in charge when he took full tibicena form. Joel said it was hit-and-miss. So far, the tibicena had been friendly, more or less, to anyone in the pack.

"No," Tony said.

"No," snapped Willis.

"Not your call to make," I told them. Then I twisted using my shoulder and opposite hand to break Tony's grip and slipped by his attempt to regain a hold. As soon as I was free, I bolted for the bridge.

My ears told me no one had taken more than a couple of steps to stop me, but at the end of the bridge, I glanced over my shoulder to make sure. Then I dropped to a walk.

Running would attract the troll's attention if it looked this way. The bridge had four lanes with a central divider. On the outer edge of the outside lane was a guardrail, a sidewalk, and a waist-high banister-style galvanized fence designed to keep people from leaping off into the river. There was a sign, too, that announced there was a $250 fine for jumping from the bridge. The outer coat of galvanization on the metal railings had begun to peel under the effects of the sun and wind, but it didn't look trashy yet.

I gripped the top of the rail and walked steadily up the bridge. I looked at the ground, the sky, the water below, dark blue because the wind was blowing in a storm. I even looked at the men crouching on top of the island hotel. I didn't look for the troll. Some things can feel you watching them. If I made it to the van without attracting attention, it would be a very good thing.

Ahead of me, I could hear the sound of metal crunching and glass breaking. I could hear Adam growling and the sound of Darryl's voice, though I couldn't tell what he was saying. Whatever they were doing, they were doing it on the far side of the bridge.

I made it safely to the first car, the upside-down red Buick. There was blood on the broken glass of the driver's-side door. It wasn't enough to have been life-threatening—but people die from things other than blood loss when their car has rolled. Tony and Willis had only described two deaths, so the occupants of this car were probably going to be okay. I clutched that reassurance to myself and kept walking.

As I passed the Buick, I got a whiff of the troll for the first time. It smelled like water-fae magic and a bit like pepper—something sharp that made my eyes want to water but didn't smell unpleasant, at least not to me.

I took two steps beyond the upended Buick and stopped as the pack hunting song abruptly and unexpectedly flooded through me, connecting me to those of the pack who were on the bridge.

When I'd become one of the pack, I'd learned pretty quickly that there were some downsides. I'd had to learn to shield parts of my mind to keep the pack from influencing my actions. But there were some upsides, too. My favorite was the hunting song. When the hunt was on, we connected. Like a Broadway dance company who had performed together for years, we knew what each member of the hunt would do almost before they moved. It didn't happen every hunt, just on the ones where the outcome of the hunt was important.

It wasn't a matter of Adam's controlling us all. That would have been creepy and absolutely unacceptable. It was a linkage of purpose that allowed us to meld our movements—and it felt like *belonging*. When the song of the hunt sang through the pack bonds, it was the only time I ever felt as though I really was a part of something bigger than myself, that my presence in the pack wasn't an unhappy fluke.

Admittedly, the pack had been a lot better lately. It was me who was holding grudges now, I thought. I knew it wasn't useful, but it didn't matter. The pack was finally willing to welcome me—well, mostly they were. I just wasn't sure I wanted to accept.

But the hunting song only cared that I was part of the pack out risking life and limb together. Between one step and the next, I knew that Adam didn't like the taste of troll blood, that his hip was bleeding but it wasn't serious. I knew that Darryl's shoulder was bruised, restricting the use of his left hand, and that he was sweating with the effort of not changing.

Zack was frantic. He had no way to get the baby out of the car, and the woman's fear was making it hard to control his wolf. Submissive or not, a werewolf was a predator, and his wolf liked the scent of her blood and terror. Even the baby wouldn't be safe if he lost control. He didn't know if he could live with a child's blood on his hands.

Adam wasn't troubled by Zack's fears. I could feel his confidence that Zack would figure out how to rescue the human woman and her child without harming them. And so could Zack. The submissive wolf drew on Adam's belief and used it to control his wolf.

I knew that the troll had lost track of the wolves because they had let him become distracted. He'd found a shiny blue car and was smacking it into the guardrail over and over as if he enjoyed the noise it made.

Adam slunk unheeded along the bridge on the other side of the battered cement barrier from the troll. The barrier hadn't looked like that last time I'd driven over the bridge, so the troll must have played smash the car with that barricade, too. But it was sufficient to keep Adam out of sight as he worked to get in position to push the troll in Joel's direction.

The hunting song told me that while the werewolves hadn't been able to harm the troll much, Joel had been a little more successful, and the troll had quit letting the tibicena close with him. So they'd decided to force the troll into a confrontation with Joel, more to see exactly where the troll's weaknesses were than because they expected Joel to be able to finish him off quickly.

Darryl, crouched low, threaded through the battered cars, heading to a position where he would complement Adam's attack. They'd be two sides of the funnel, with Joel at the narrow end. Darryl had acquired a tire iron and carried it in his good hand. Joel was a foggy presence in the hunting party. His actions were clear, but everything else was murky and hot-rage coated. The rage was unfocused, but I could feel the fury of it building. He let out a roaring cough that sounded more like a lion's hunting cry than anything canine, but he refrained from making the spine-chilling cry that might drive the troll away from him. I took that as a sign that he was cooperating with Adam's planning.

All of this information I received between one breath and the next. At that point, they all realized I was there, too.

From Adam came a flash of betrayal—I had promised to keep safe. That faded as he understood that I was there because of the baby, that I could help Zack. A pause. Acceptance. He knew about protecting the weak.

I knew that he, Darryl, and Joel would do their best to keep the attention of the troll away from the van with the fragile humans trapped inside. Zack and I were to get the people to safety.

Zack was very relieved. More relieved, I thought, than was really justified. I hoped I could help. I hoped not to be just another civilian to protect.

I was nearly to the van, noting almost absently that it had been manufactured in the same era as most of the VW bugs I kept running. It had been lovingly restored to a high polish not very long ago. The front end was crunched, though whatever it had hit was gone—maybe it had been the troll himself.

Antifreeze from the van's radiator ran down the bridge in narrowing rivulets. I could feel Zack's presence on the left side of the van, but it was the right side that had working doors, so I decided to leave it to him to keep an eye out for the troll while I took a look inside the van.

I started around the van but stopped. I trusted Zack—but I snuck around the front of the van and looked for the troll anyway.

I found him in the Pasco-bound lane, the far side of the bridge, smashing the shiny blue Nissan into the metal rails. I caught a glimpse of a white sheet of paper on the rear window with a date written in black Sharpie. The Nissan had been someone's new purchase. I hoped their insurance would cover trolls.

"Smashing" was maybe the wrong word to use for what the troll was doing, I decided, though metal, glass, and fiberglass were getting crumpled. "Smashing" implied that the troll was beating the car into the rails. The troll's actions were more . . . playful than that.

He pushed the car forward, then let go as it rolled with some force into the rails. Bits of car broke off in the impact, then it rolled back into his hands. It was either in neutral, or he'd destroyed the transmission in some interesting fashion I'd never encountered before.

After a particularly hard impact, the front window shattered. The troll bounced around in excitement—the bridge moved under my feet—and then he propelled the Nissan with even more force than before. The car sped into the rail. The rail bent, and the little blue car got stuck.

Mood abruptly altered, the troll tossed back his head and let out an ear-piercing scream of rage. He grabbed the car in both hands, shoved it *through* the guardrail *and* the railing on the far side, and over the edge of the bridge. Hooting in triumph, the troll jumped up and grabbed one of the bridge cables and climbed up it so he could watch the car in the river.

I tried not to reflect on the strength it would take to force a car through both sets of rails designed to prevent just that as I took a chance while it was distracted and moved back to the front of the van with slow caution, so no sudden movement of mine would attract the troll's attention. Then I sprinted to the passenger side of the van.

The sliding door was open and bent, so it would never slide open or shut again. From the marks, I was pretty sure that Darryl had opened it, or maybe Zack before he was wholly wolf.

Zack stood beside the open door, looked at me, then rounded the back of the van again to resume his observation of the troll. I felt him settle into a guard position on the driver's side of the van. If the troll made a move toward us, he'd warn me and do his best to keep us safe.

The car seat was nearest the door. On the other side of it, a woman held a bottle to the baby's mouth, keeping the baby happy and quiet. Smart woman.

"Hey," I whispered.

She was not much older than Jesse. One of her arms was obviously broken just above the elbow, and she held it against her side.

"I'm here to help," I told her. I was being quiet. The troll was making more noise than World War III, but that didn't mean he couldn't hear us.

"I can't get my baby out," she said. She took her cue from me and kept her voice down, but it vibrated with desperation. "The seat belt jammed, and the bottle is almost empty. When it's gone, she's going to start crying."

The baby was not very old, swaddled in a pink blanket and set backward in the seat. She was still in that plastic stage where her mouth and nose looked like every other baby's mouth and nose instead of the person she would someday become. Her eyes were wide and blue and focused on her mom as she sucked.

I took a good look at the car seat. It wasn't one of the ones that the bucket holding the baby just popped out. I didn't know a lot about baby seats, but it looked to me as if it were an older model, and something had jammed the latch, something with a big fang. The button was pressed in, but the catch hadn't released.

I pulled out Tony's knife and started working on the tough webbing of the seat belt. The knife looked good, but the blade was as dull as a bad-skin-cleanser commercial.

"When we get out of this," I said, very quietly, "remind me to give Tony a whetstone and a book on how to use one."

"Who is Tony?" she asked.

"The police officer whose knife I borrowed," I told her. The stubborn belt parted at last, and I pulled the seat free. I took a step back—and that's when I saw that the arm wasn't the only injury the woman had. Her knee was swollen to twice its normal size.

"Can you walk on that leg?" I asked.

She bit her lip and shook her head. "But you can get Nicole out," she said. "Get her out, and I'll be okay. I told the werewolf that."

The baby made a noise.

It was only a little noise, more of a squeak than a cry.

But there were a lot of creatures on the bridge with very good hearing.

The wolves had been letting the troll entertain himself—but the blue car, by now surely sunk under the river, wasn't interesting anymore. The pack hunting song told me that the little noise of something helpless . . . of a helpless human baby . . . had attracted the troll's attention. There was a thump, and the van rocked a little when the troll landed back onto the bridge from his perch among the cables.

I could feel the troll's regard, but he couldn't see me. I rocked the baby seat a little, and the baby settled. We all were very still—until the troll started banging on another car.

I had to get them both out, and I couldn't carry the mother. But we had wheels. The radiator fluid I'd seen told me that it was unlikely we could get the engine going, but we were on a downhill slope, and both Zack and I could push. All I had to do was get the van moving.

I put the baby, car seat and all, back next to her mother, who put the mostly empty bottle back in the baby's mouth. She, the baby, smiled, kicked both feet, and resumed sucking. That made a noise, too, a small, whistly-sucky noise that made the troll grunt in satisfaction. I don't know if it was my instincts, the pack hunting sense, or the sudden lack of smashing sounds, but, with the hairs on the back of my neck, I felt the troll start toward us at a slow hunter's pace.

The fae are attracted to children. Someone, I think it was Bran, told me that children held power because they were in the process of becoming something. In that promise there was magic—and it was like catnip to the fae.

In the past, some of the fae craved children as pets, leaving something in their place because magic required balance—and that I'd learned from Ariana's book. Some of the fae simply ate them. A baby . . . a baby was on the cusp of becoming.

The troll's near-silent approach was filled with an intensity, a lust I could scent. And then the pack hunting song exploded with information.

Adam leaped over the barrier, and Joel bolted from around the car he'd been hiding behind, but Darryl, who'd been a few steps closer, reached the troll first. He struck at the side of the troll's knee with the narrow pry-bar end of the tire iron. The troll slapped the iron away—and knocked Darryl over in the process. Either the touch of iron or the force Darryl had swung it with hurt the troll, who stopped to shake his hand. That gave Darryl a second chance for attack. He took a running leap onto the troll and, without slowing down, climbed up its side, making it all the way to the troll's shoulders. Zack stayed where he was, between the van and the troll, the last barrier. I could feel his determination to slow the creature down so that I could get the human and her child to safety.

Recalled to my task, I scrambled to the front seat, taking a quick glance out the window while I did.

The troll was still on the opposite side of the barrier, so I couldn't see Adam or Joel, but I had a good clear view of the troll reaching behind himself. His shoulder joint was built differently from any ape or monkey I'd seen because he had no trouble reaching behind his neck and grabbing Darryl in both hands and throwing him off, over the railing.

When Darryl disappeared from the pack hunting song, I told myself fiercely that it was only that he was too far away. Werewolves don't swim, but there were a lot of boats down there. A lot of boats. And some of them knew that the werewolves were trying to help.

His abrupt absence hurt, and I couldn't see past the hurt to tell if he was just gone from the hunting song or if he'd disappeared from the pack as well. Zack broke away from the van, running to help the other two keep the troll away.

Darryl doesn't have to be dead, I told myself fiercely as my butt hit the front seat of the van. His sudden disappearance from my awareness was traumatic, and I couldn't reach the subtler pack sense. Couldn't tell if the wave of loss I felt was only from the hunt, or if it was his death echoing through me. I put my foot on the clutch.

"It won't start," the woman behind me said. "My sister, she tried and tried. I told her to get out, that I was right behind her, and she ran. She figured it out, but by then the police had her."

"Shh. It's okay."

I tried to put it into neutral, but the linkage was stuck. It would still roll with the clutch in—but I'd have to push the van and hold the clutch at the same time. I tried to open the door—and it wouldn't open. I remembered the huge crease that something had put down the driver's side of the van.

All the werewolves were fighting for their lives—but the hunting song touched them all, I couldn't block it. They knew I was in trouble, and one of them came to help. Two wolves against the troll weren't enough. But Adam was the heart of the song, its director if not its dictator, and he directed Joel to come help me. He picked Joel because Joel could best protect me if he and Zack failed to hold the troll back.

Out loud because he was ignoring me otherwise, I said, "No, Adam. I'll figure out something."

Joel came anyway. I could see him in the rearview mirror. Joel looked a little different every time he took on the tibicena form. It was the subject of much discussion in the pack. Zack said he thought it might be because the tibicena is a creature of the volcano, and lava doesn't have a hardened shape. That was my favorite explanation.

This time, fully formed and mostly solid, he looked a little like a foo lion, his muzzle broad and almost catlike, with a mane of dreadlocks that crackled and hissed as they moved, breaking the outer black shell and displaying liquid-orange-glowing lava that cooled rapidly to black again as some other part broke open. The effect was a shimmering, flashing, black-and-orange fringe about six inches long.

His body had thickened and his legs lengthened, front more than the rear, so his back had a German-shepherd slant. His tail lashed back and forth, more like a cat's than a dog's, and the end of his tail was covered with the same lava-light-enhanced dreads that his neck wore.

He put his shoulder against the van, and the battered metal smoked and . . . we both felt it when Adam staggered under a blow that shattered his shoulder. Zack was there with Adam, but we all knew, the hunt sense knew, that he was not the partner that Joel was. We felt his frantic efforts to distract the troll from Adam, who had fallen.

Joel heaved, and the van started rolling—and Joel ran back to the battle. The van moved sluggishly around the SUV, but when I got the wheel straight, it traveled better.

By the time we reached the bottom of the bridge, we had achieved a pace that made weaving through the dead vehicles interesting because I had to keep the nose of the van pointed downhill. I passed the last car, the red Buick, and I lost the song of the hunt. The loss was unbearable, leaving me raw—and frantic, because the loss fried some circuit in my brain. I could feel the pack bond, feel the mating bond between Adam and me—but it told me nothing other than that Adam and the pack were there.

I stayed the course until the van coasted past the police barricade—which they had moved so I could get the van through. As soon as I stopped the van, police and EMTs swarmed around it.

The woman and her baby as safe as I could get them, I abandoned them to run back up the bridge. What I expected to do to something the werewolves weren't able to stop, I didn't know. I only knew that Adam was hurt, and I wasn't there to make him safe.

3

As I ran, this time unworried about attracting the troll's attention, my view was blocked by cars and the cement divider, so the fae monster was the only one I could see. I pulled my Sig out of its concealed-carry holster in the small of my back. The Sig Sauer had been a birthday present from my mother. It was a .40, larger caliber than the 9mm I used to carry. I still practiced with the 9mm and the .44 revolver, but the .40 was a subcompact, and it was easier to conceal. It was still small enough caliber that I could fire it and not fatigue until I'd emptied four or five magazines. With the .45, I got five shots before my aim got wobbly. I wished I'd been carrying the .45, though from what the police had said, the gun was unlikely to be useful. But I didn't have a rocket launcher handy.

The troll picked up a Miata in both hands. The shiny green of the car was the same tint as the troll but much darker. Miatas are small, but they still weigh more than two thousand pounds. That troll brought it up over his head and held it there for a second or two.

Then he brought it down and smashed it on the ground I couldn't see, my vision blocked by the cars and the center barricade, though the crash of metal and glass told me when it hit. The troll staggered suddenly. I growled under my breath in frustration because I couldn't tell what had happened. Whatever had caused the troll to stagger hadn't made him lose his grip on the little car, now much more compact. He cried out and smashed the Miata down again, faster than before—like a housewife smashing a spider with her shoe.

Joel howled, and this time it was the real thing, full-throated and powerful, with the magic of the volcano that had birthed the tibicena. I stumbled, falling down on one hand and knees; my other hand still held the gun. My heart pounded in my ears as the resultant wave of fear crashed through me. Even though I knew it was only magic, it was hard for me to stand up and move toward him when fear slid through me and told me to run. But Adam was hurt—I couldn't run away when Adam was ahead of me.

The troll, who was not familiar with the effect of the tibicena's cry, had a much stronger reaction. He dropped the car and bolted, batting a truck that stood in his way so hard that it tipped over. For the first two strides, he was in a blind panic—and then his eyes met mine.

I stopped moving, hoping that he'd stay on his side of the road, that the panic caused by the tibicena would keep him going. I hoped very hard because my biggest magic superpower was changing into a coyote who would have even less of a chance against a troll than I did in human form. I'd come to help because I couldn't stay on the sidelines with Adam wounded, but I was under no illusions that I was a match for the troll.

Though I was past the place where the pack hunting song had kicked in on my first trip, it had not returned. Maybe there were too few of the pack members still whole enough for a hunt. I didn't know, couldn't tell because the pack bonds told me nothing. I felt very alone, standing in the middle of the road with the troll's intent gaze locked onto me.

He bounded over the cement barrier like a dinosaur-sized track star, leaving dents in the pavement where he landed. But Adam jumped the barrier just behind him. He was battered and bloody, running on three legs, and even a werewolf looked small next to the troll. But the front leg Adam had tucked up didn't seem to slow him in the slightest, and Adam brought with him an indomitable determination that made the apparent inequality between the troll and the wounded werewolf meaningless. If I died today or a hundred years from now, I would keep the image of him hunting down that troll in my heart.

They both, troll and wolf, covered the quarter of a mile in a time that would have won an Olympic sprint, but for some reason it seemed to take hours as I stood waiting.

I suppose I could have turned and tried to outrun the troll; I might even have managed it. But I was horribly aware of the humans behind me who had no defense against a fae like the troll. Maybe it would continue to follow me as I ran past them—assuming I did manage to outrun it.

But what if it stopped and attacked the humans instead? I knew some of those police officers. If they saw it chasing me, they would shoot at it. If they hurt it, it would go after them. And then there were all those people stuck in traffic. Easy targets.

I was not going to lead it off the bridge, where I might gain my life at someone else's expense. I didn't know why I'd decided it was my job to keep them safe, but, like Zack standing between the van and the troll, I'd accepted it and would do my best.

The troll moved into my best target range. I took a step toward them, aimed, and shot the magazine of my gun empty as fast as I could pull the trigger. I didn't hit Adam.

I was sure that most if not all of the shots had hit the troll. I've always been a good shot, and this past year, I'd gotten serious about practicing. But the only shot that was important was the one that hit his left eye. I'd been aiming at his eye with all of my shots, but it was small, and he'd been moving.

It brought him to a staggering halt. He brought one hand up to his face—and hit Adam with the other, knocking him out of the air and into the cement barricade. I'd hit the troll and hurt him, but not enough to matter.

I holstered the gun, and my foot landed awkwardly on the walking stick that should have been on my chest of drawers at home instead of the pavement in front of me.

The walking stick had been made by Lugh the Longarm, the warrior fae who'd been a combination of Superman and Hercules in the old songs and stories of the Celtic people. There were no stories I'd ever read about Lugh—and I'd been reading as much about him as I could find since the walking stick had come back into my keeping—that had him fighting a troll. Lugh was a Celtic deity, and trolls were more populous in continental Europe. Maybe the walking stick had come here to fight *for* the troll. It, at least, was fae, and I was not, though it had defended me against the fae before.

I snatched it off the ground because it was better than nothing.

It was probably a coincidence that I remembered the essential oil that Zack had shoved into my pocket as soon as I touched the walking stick. I pulled it out of my pocket and saw at a glance that Zack had gotten it right, grabbed the Rest Well and not any of the other oils that I'd bought. The Rest Well had been mostly St. John's wort.

While I was doing that, Adam rose to his feet, but he was clearly dazed. The troll growled at him, but when the troll went on the attack, he came after me.

I wrenched the cap open. I was clueless how to use it; all that I knew about it was that placing the real plant around the windows and doors of a home was supposed to keep the fae out—like garlic is supposed to work for vampires. It didn't help that I remembered that garlic doesn't work on vampires despite the stories.

For lack of any better idea, or any more time to fuss, I swept my hand out from left to right, scattering the liquid in front of me in a rough semicircle. Adam was running again and gaining on the troll. But the troll would reach me before Adam caught him.

I dropped the bottle and prepared to be hurt. I held the walking stick as I'd have held a spear in class with my sensei, though the metal-shod end had not changed, as it sometimes did, from decorative embellishment into a blade. A bad sign, I thought.

But Adam's presence meant that I wasn't alone. For some suicidal reason, that left me in the Zen state that I only managed at the end of a very hard workout with Adam or Sensei Johanson.

I narrowed my eyes at the troll and thought, *Bring it*. The troll, so close I could feel his breath, stepped on the pavement where I'd dropped the essential oils and staggered back as if he'd hit a wall.

Adam didn't wait for an engraved invitation. He leaped up the troll, in almost the same way that Darryl had, except that when he reached the troll's shoulders, Adam extended his claws and brought his front feet, good shoulder and bad, together in a great swinging motion and dug deep into either side of the troll's head. The troll cried out and reached back, and just as he had with Darryl, he grabbed Adam and pulled.

A sudden burst of pain ran down my shoulder from my mate bond, dropping me to the ground with the unexpected fury of it, as real or worse than if it had been my own pain, the mating bond abruptly opening up clear and full. I screamed with the pain and utter terror because the pain I felt was Adam's and not my own. The terror drove me back to my feet, and I went after the troll with a fury that lit my bones with determination to stand between my mate and anything that hurt him.

I whacked the troll behind the knee with the stick, but it didn't even flinch. So I hit him again, harder, with the narrow end as though the walking stick were a foil and I wanted to stab him. The spearpoint did not form on the end of the stick, as it sometimes did, but apparently the silver-shod end was enough to hurt. The troll whined and turned his shoulders toward me, but Adam pulled the creature's head back where it had been.

From the feel of the pain he shared with me, I knew Adam's shoulder had begun healing from the earlier damage the troll had done, but it was tearing again. Even so, a werewolf's claws are like those of a grizzly: the troll couldn't dislodge Adam. As the troll pulled, Adam's refusal to release his own grip meant that the troll was wrenching Adam apart.

This wasn't the time to be squeamish. I hit the troll in one testicle with the butt end of the staff in the fencing stance I'd used before. As I did, there was a wet, popping noise.

I thought I'd done some damage, but there was no blood where I'd hit him. For a breathless second, I wondered if the troll had broken Adam. But it was the troll who screamed as he pulled Adam loose—and ripped off a cap of moss hair, thick skin, and gray-green bone along with Adam. Then there was a lot of blood.

The troll tossed Adam in a gore-dripping, bloody mess over my head. I heard him hit the pavement, but I couldn't afford to look away. The troll was hurt but not dead. Adam was unconscious, and I was the only thing standing between him and the troll.

Though there was a gaping hole in his skull, the troll didn't seem to be appreciably disabled. I tightened my hold on the walking stick, my only weapon, and prepared to be annihilated.

Something flew through the air, buzzing as it passed me, and buried itself in the newly opened section of the troll's skull. The troll's roar was so loud it hurt my ears.

The projectile fell out of the troll's head and onto the pavement with a clang, revealing itself to be a five-foot chunk of steel pipe, modified with a point on one end and crude fins on the other.

The troll, eyes wild, bashed one fist into the cement barrier between the lanes in a berserker rage. He screamed as cement fell away from his fist in chunks, revealing the barrier's framework of rebar. He grabbed the rebar cage and jerked an entire section of cement free.

I turned and sprinted, visions of a flying Miata in my head. Adam couldn't move out of the way. Adam lay unconscious on his side, blood darkening his fur and flattening it.

I made it to him in four strides. Dropping the walking stick, I grabbed a handful of the fur over his hips and skin behind his neck. I'm strong for a woman, but no stronger than any human woman who worked out four times a week with a werewolf and a sadistic sensei. Adam-as-a-werewolf weighs nearly double what I do. But I lifted him over my shoulders, staggered a step, then ran.

I expected to see the police barricade, though the SWAT team in their body armor was new. Funny how I wouldn't risk aiming the troll at the police to save myself, but for Adam I'd have thrown the whole lot of them to the troll, despite the genuine friendship I felt for some of them.

But it wasn't just the police I saw.

Running toward us was a very wet Darryl, who otherwise looked unharmed by his immersion in the river. He had one hand back in a classic javelin thrower's pose, another pipe weapon pulled back to throw. Keeping pace beside him with visible effort was a too-thin, grim-faced Tad. He held another pipe in his hand, and I watched as he molded it with magic into a weapon that matched the one Darryl held. Darryl took a couple more racing strides and let the pipe javelin go.

I couldn't tell what it did once it flew past me, but something hit the bridge and bounced the pavement under my feet so I stumbled. Cement and broken rebar flew over Adam and me and bounced ahead of me—evidently the troll had thrown his chunk of cement barrier. I managed a couple of trying-to-get-my-balance steps before I lost that battle entirely. I landed hard on my knees, wobbled, then fell full length, chin first, when Adam's weight overbalanced me.

Darryl grabbed the javelin Tad handed him and bolted past Adam and me. I let Adam go and rolled so I could see. The troll was down; the second pipe javelin had struck truer than the first, and the top third of the troll had turned an unhealthy gray color. Darryl, javelin held high, skidded to a stop when Joel, his whole body a bright flaming orange, leaped from the top of a car, over the cement divider, and landed on top of the troll. Darryl backed up until he was level with Tad, who had stopped next to me, as

Joel attacked in a ferocious rage and a heat that I could feel from twenty feet away.

The troll didn't move when Joel tore into it, gulping down the green-and-red flesh. The troll was unconscious or dead, I couldn't tell which, and it didn't matter for long. Its flesh melted where the tibicena touched it, turning first black, then crumbling to gray ashes. The huge body was consumed by Joel's heat in what could only have been a few minutes. The tibicena continued to eat, even when there was no meat left.

We didn't move, none of us, but still, Joel looked up suddenly, his mouth full of ash. He glared at us, his eyes a hot, iridescent red.

I stood up, using the walking stick, which was under my hand though I'd left it a dozen yards away, for balance. I didn't like being on the ground with a predator so near.

I cleared my throat. "Joel," I said. My voice sounded oddly wobbly to me, and I hoped no one else heard it.

Joel's lips curled back, displaying black teeth and a red, red tongue. The fringe of stone mane around his neck rippled as he shook his broad head in open threat, and it made a clattering noise, almost like wind chimes. He growled.

"*Joel*," I said, reaching for Adam's power. "*Stop.*"

I'd done this before, called upon my mate's power of domination to make someone do something—or not do something. But this time, there was no surge of Alpha magic in my words. There were a lot of possible reasons for the failure: the fact that I'd never tried it with Adam unconscious came right to mind. Maybe he was too wounded to fuel my voice. But the reason didn't matter, only the result. The tibicena took a step forward.

Some motion at the corner of my eye attracted my attention. I took a quick glance to my right and saw a kid, a boy maybe ten years old give or take a couple of years, climb over the cement barrier, just a few yards from Joel. I blinked, and it was still true. This stupid kid was dropping on the ground, his face calm, approaching Joel as if he were a friendly dog instead of a slathering tibicena with smoke and heat rising from his body in waves.

"Stay back," I shouted, starting forward—but a hand closed around my arm and pulled me back against a man's body. He only controlled that arm, so I twisted toward his hold, desperate to get free so I could stop the poor dumb kid who was about to die. When I turned, I saw it was Tad who held me back, his face thin, grim, and bruised. I only just stopped the instinctive hit that would have broken his ribs and set me loose.

"Let me go," I snapped at him. But I kept my voice low—I didn't want to set the tibicena off. I jerked to get free, but Tad held me as if I hadn't been practicing how to break this exact hold just last week—if I'd been willing to hurt him, I could have broken away, but I couldn't make myself do it.

"Wait," he said.

"Tad, Joel isn't running this show," I hissed. "He's going to kill that boy."

Joel had quit looking at me at all. His attention was focused on the kid, who was dressed in sweats that were too large for him. They looked suspiciously like the sweats we kept tucked around in the cars of pack and friends of pack members.

Joel wouldn't survive if he killed a child. The thought decided me, and when I started struggling again, I went for blood.

Tad grabbed my hand before I could hit him in the jaw, then pinned me in a lock I couldn't break, my back to his front. "It's okay," he said. "This one isn't just a kid. Watch."

Joel snarled at the boy, who ignored him and touched the tibicena's shoulder. Joel, who was not Joel but the volcano demon who
lived inside him, looked smug, probably waiting for fiery death to
consume the boy the way it had the troll. Horrified, I waited for the
same thing.

We were both wrong.

The skin of the boy's hand flushed red, and the color traveled
through him, and he rocked back a little, then leaned his weight
on his hand.

Whatever he looked like, that was not a human boy. His hand
hadn't burst into flame or blackened with third-degree burns. No
human could have touched Joel when he was running that hot
without getting hurt. Tad released my arm with a pat. I took two
steps so that I stood next to Adam's prone body, in case the tibicena
decided to do something rather than just stand under the boy's touch,
because fire was only one of Joel's weapons.

The hot air on my face faded, replaced by river-cooled wind.
Joel staggered and collapsed. The curious blackened-stone exterior
of the tibicena lost the redness of heat and became entirely black.

"I told you it would be okay," Tad said.

"He's not hurting Joel?" I asked anxiously.

"Joel?" he asked. "Is that the name of the fire-breathing foo dog?
I thought you killed it. How did you manage to take the volcano
god's servant? I assume he's yours from the way he was fighting."

"Not a foo dog," I said tightly. "He's a tibicena. They are very
hard to kill, and when you do, they go out and invade the body
of friends. Like Joel. But we . . . I made him pack."

The black stone surrounding the tibicena cracked and fell away,
leaving Joel in his human body, pale, naked, and unconscious,
facedown on the roadway. The boy stepped back. When he met

my eyes with his own, for a moment I could see that fire lived inside him. Then they were just ordinary hazel eyes.

"Did you hear that, Aiden?" Tad said. "The fire dog is a friend."

"Yes," said the boy, "I hear you. I heard, when the big man who killed the troll told us both the same thing before we set foot on the bridge. I'm not an idiot. I need them. The man who bears the fire dog will come to no harm from this. I didn't kill anything, just banked the fire for a while."

The boy's accent wasn't so much a matter of pronunciation but of cadence. English wasn't his first tongue.

I took a good long breath and took stock.

Darryl, the big-man-who-had-killed-the-troll, was a couple of yards away—in position to step in if the boy hadn't defanged the tibicena. His hair still dripped water, but his various cuts and bruises from the fight had begun to fade.

"How did you get out of the river?" I asked. I didn't move because, beside me, Adam had awakened and was considering rolling to his feet. Where I was standing, my legs touching him, he could use me as an unobtrusive crutch.

His pack was loyal. Two years ago, Darryl might have put Adam down had he come upon him when he was injured like this. Adam's decision to court me had weakened the pack, and Darryl would have viewed himself as the better leader. Part of me didn't like seeing him so close to Adam when Adam couldn't defend himself—even though matters had changed. Darryl respected Adam and had not so much as breathed a desire to move to the top of the food chain.

I don't need protection from Darryl. Adam's voice was clear in my head, though he made no effort to move. *I think you've gotten caught up in the battle that is over now, sweetheart. But there are others watching. I'd just as soon wait until I'm sure I can walk before I try to get up.*

We'd discovered that he had more control of the link between us than I did. The werewolf mating bond seemed a little confused by me. I'd grown to believe that the weird way the mating link seemed to function stronger some times than others was due to my partial immunity to magic. But this time I caught his words just fine.

He was right about Darryl, and about the wound-up feeling in my stomach that tried to tell me that the battle wasn't over yet. I breathed in and tried to relax.

"One of the patrol boats fished me out," Darryl was saying, answering my earlier question. "I got to shore and ran into Tad, Zee, and that one." He nodded toward the boy, who smiled, a wide, sweet smile that sent the warning hairs on the back of my neck straight up.

"The troll," said Zee's voice heavily, "was sent after us, but someone forgot about trolls and bridges and the effect of running water on some forms of magic. Old Jarnvid might not have won in the lottery when they were passing brains out to trolls, but running water was his element, and trolls are difficult to control when they are in the same room with you."

I stayed where I was, one foot touching Adam, but turned to see my old friend. It was unlike him to have sent Tad into battle while he waited on the sidelines.

Zee wasn't looking at me but at the ashes of the troll, which were blowing away in the river's breeze, as he continued talking. "Or maybe they thought they were safe because trolls can't connect to most bridges now. Too many of the bridges today use too much steel. Maybe they—whoever they are—mistakenly assumed the troll would remain under their influence despite the distance and the running water. Or maybe they intended to 'accidentally' lose control and let loose one of the more violent trolls in history on the human population."

Beyond him, I saw a handful of pack members running up the arc of the bridge toward where we were standing. Down by the police barricade, Warren was talking to the police officers. I knew from his body language, and because I knew Warren, that he was keeping them back until we had our vulnerable protected and our dangerous people contained.

"Hey, Ben?"

Our English wolf looked at me, his clear blue eyes missing their usual ironic cast, and sprinted the rest of the way to us.

"Could you go check on Zack? I think the troll threw a car on him just over the crest of the bridge." He wasn't dead. I'd know if he were dead, but I was betting Zack was a long way from healthy.

"Car?" Ben said, and glanced around. "Fucking troll throwing fucking cars. What's the world coming to?" He pointed a finger at Scott and Sherwood, who'd followed his sprint. "You and you, come with me. We're to rescue our Zackie boy, who might have gotten smashed by a fucking car."

Ben's swearing was usually a bit more creative. I had the feeling that he was a little overwhelmed. It didn't stop him from herding his chosen minions over the bridge. Ben had been climbing the pack hierarchy—not by battling his way up but by not backing down. It was a subtler way to do it, more difficult in its way. But it was better for the pack, and for Ben.

Satisfied that Zack would be attended to, I turned my attention back to Zee. "You escaped from the reservation, and they sent a troll after you?"

Zee was wearing his usual appearance, a wiry old man with a small potbelly and a balding spot in the thin white hair on his head. Unlike Tad, he didn't look thinner or grimmer or anything. But Zee wasn't half-human, and his glamour could look any way he chose. He held himself stiffly, as if he hurt—which explained why it had been Tad transforming pipe for javelins and not Zee. But the look in Zee's eyes told me not to mention it.

"Tad told me you destroyed my shop," he said sourly.

I shrugged. "Wasn't me. It was pretty tough to keep up with things with just Tad and me anyway."

He frowned at me suspiciously. "You still owe me the money on it even if it doesn't exist anymore." The fae are very particular about their bargains.

"Insurance and Adam are rebuilding it," I told him. "And I've been making payments into your account the tenth of every month, which you would know if you only looked. I've never been more than a week late since I bought it from you."

"See that you aren't," he grunted. "I love you" can be said in odd ways when you deal with very old fae. I was satisfied, and I think he was, too, because he quit paying attention to me. He frowned at Tad. It was the same expression he had on his face when someone brought a car into the shop before we figured out just what was wrong with it. He was, I thought, checking for damage.

Finished, the old fae glanced at Adam, who was still lying, apparently unconscious, next to me.

"Old man," said the boy Tad had called Aiden. He'd been waiting with apparent patience while Zee and I talked, without moving away from Joel. It wasn't *quite* a threat, but there was something deliberate about it. If it doesn't walk or talk like a ten-year-old, despite appearances, I wasn't going to treat him like a ten-year-old if I could help it. He was dangerous.

No one had gone to Joel's aid, and I realized they were waiting for me to signal them. Was this boy—and I wasn't the only one who knew he wasn't wholly human—an enemy? Joel breathed easily, but his body was lax.

"Old man," said the boy, "I'll have you do as you promised."

"This is Aiden the Fire Touched, Mercy," Zee said neutrally. "I told him that your pack could likely make the Gray Lords back down for a day or two if you chose to."

"You should live up to your word," said the boy, his voice low and threatening.

Zee's eyelids lowered. "You don't know as much as you think you do," he said. *"Boy."*

Nope, I thought. If this boy was as young as he looked, I'd eat my hat—but he didn't smell like fae. I was close enough, and the wind was right; if he were fae, I should be able to scent it.

The boy held up his hand, still ruddy with heat. "One," he said, displaying a finger. "You will introduce me to the Alpha of the pack." He held up a second finger. "Two. You will ask them, as a person friendly to the pack, if they will protect me—even if it is only temporary." He held up a third finger. "Three—you will do your best to see that they agree."

"Snotty," I observed to Zee.

He pursed his lips. Which wasn't actually an agreement. He didn't like many people, my old friend, but he was soft on this boy, and I couldn't see much reason for it. Most people wouldn't be able to tell that Zee liked him, but I'd known the grumpy old man for a long time.

"What did he promise in return?" I asked him curiously.

"He got Dad and me out of Fairyland," Tad said, and when his dad grunted, he added, "Out of the Walla Walla reservation, then. And when he could have left us behind and escaped free without going back on his word, he stayed to help."

The boy had been following the conversation; now he narrowed his eyes at me. "*Who* are you?"

"She's our Alpha's mate," said Darryl in a very unfriendly voice. "That means that right this moment, she's in charge of the Columbia Basin Pack." Then he raised his voice without looking away from Aiden the Fire Touched. *"One of you bring some sweats for Joel."* Apparently, we were going to step down the threat level so we could take care of our own.

"Got it," called Warren. I'd thought he was still down talking to the police. But there was no mistaking the sound of his voice or the rhythm of his footsteps as he ran back down to the base of the bridge.

I could leave Joel's care to Warren and Darryl. That left me to deal with Aiden.

"You aren't a werewolf," he said, but I could tell he wasn't sure.

"No," I agreed. "But I am in charge right this minute."

Aiden made an angry noise.

"If Zee promised to do his best to see that we protected you," I told him, "he's fulfilled his word to you." I smiled grimly. "If he'd come singing your praises, we'd have killed you where you stood. The only way Zee would sing anyone's praises is if someone had managed to hit him with some kind of nasty magic when he had his back turned."

Joel moaned and rose to hands and knees just about the time Warren came up with a pair of sweats in his hand bearing the letters KPD. He must have gotten them from Tony. Warren walked through the invisible no-man's-land between me and Aiden without apparent effect on his usual loose-limbed, big-strided walk. Ignoring Aiden altogether, Warren knelt and began helping Joel. If it weren't for Adam resting against my leg, I'd have run over to help—leaving Aiden until I was sure that our people were okay. I was worried that Ben wasn't back with Zack, yet.

Darryl stayed where he was—to guard me from Aiden, I realized, guarding *Adam* and me. He didn't look down at Adam, but I could feel his awareness and worry.

Warren helped Joel, now modestly covered in Kennewick Police Department sweats, to his feet. Without ever quite looking at the boy, Warren kept himself between Aiden and Joel. That told me that Warren still viewed the boy as a threat.

Joel shivered as if he were cold. Warren started to put an arm around him, then stopped.

Warren was the only gay werewolf in our pack, in any pack that I knew of. The older werewolves were largely male and largely intolerant of homosexual leanings. Gay werewolves didn't last very long unless they were extraordinarily tough or lucky. Warren was tough. He was also careful not to push any of the pack members unless he *intended* to bother them. It wasn't fear, it was courtesy. He glanced at Darryl.

Darryl looked at me, then Aiden, deciding how much of a threat he still was. Then he walked over and wrapped a big arm over the much smaller Joel. "You have this, Mercy?" he asked me. "I'll get him home."

I nodded. "Joel? Are you okay?"

"It doesn't burn inside," he said, his voice husky and a little helpless. "It's gone."

"It'll be back," the boy said dispassionately. "I robbed the spirit of its heat, but it is still there."

"Are you okay, Joel?" I asked again.

This time he nodded. "I think so." He took a deep breath. "I would have killed you."

I shook my head. "We're pack, Joel, even the tibicena knows it. He was just ticked because he got a chance to get out and strut his stuff, and we were cutting short his playtime."

Joel huffed a shaky laugh. "Maybe. But it didn't feel like that from the inside."

Ben and his minions rounded a semi. Zack, still in wolf form, limped heavily on his own four feet. He looked pretty battered, but he'd be all right. Just like Adam, who was fully awake and hiding it from the pack. I didn't do anything to give him away.

None of the wolves looked at Adam. It would be disrespectful to observe their Alpha in a weak position or to express concern that might be interpreted to mean that they thought Adam was too weak to heal. But that left me on my own to deal with the harmless-looking, if hostile, boy who had single-handedly taken down a servant of a volcano god.

"Who are you? What are you? Why do the fae want you?" I asked, because information was always good and because it would give me time to think.

He narrowed his eyes at me. "None of your business."

"You've made it her business," said Darryl.

The boy didn't think much of me, but his expression told me that Darryl had made an impression.

"Darryl," I said, "please arrange for Zack and Joel to make it back home with a couple of guards and someone who can patch them up." I didn't say "and then get back here," but I knew he heard it.

Darryl bowed his head in a move that made him look like he was a thousand years old—though I knew that Darryl was only ten years or so older than he looked. He picked Joel up in his arms and without another word managed to harness Ben, Zack, and a couple of other wolves in his gaze as he strode away toward the police lines at the end of the bridge.

I returned my attention to Aiden.

"I'm a human," he told me sullenly. "I was lost in Underhill until she opened her doors again. The fae want to keep me until they understand how Underhill changed me so that I can do this." He waved a hand at Joel. "I'm tired of being a prisoner, and I need somewhere to stay for a day to put my options together."

"Lost in Underhill," I said slowly, "for how long?"

The boy shrugged. "I don't know."

There was a lot he wasn't telling me.

"It's not a difficult decision," he said. "Tell me to rabbit, and I will. Tell me you'll have my back, and I'll stay." He smiled, and it wasn't a pretty smile. "Don't you wolves always worry about status?" For someone who'd been trapped in Underhill, he knew an awful lot about werewolves. "Wouldn't defying the fae give you the upper hand?"

"Unless we're all dead," murmured Warren helpfully. "Then we don't care about what the fae think of us." He paused. "Come to think on it, we really don't care what the fae think of us anyway." He gave the boy a cold look that seemed strange on my Warren, reminding me that though he was my friend, he'd also survived against the odds more than once, and it wasn't because he was too nice to kill someone.

The boy, unaware of his danger, sneered.

I looked at Zee because it didn't appear as though the boy was going to tell me anything. I knew I should just let him run. I could tell after five minutes that he was going to cause trouble.

But if Zee thought it was a horrible idea for the pack to protect him, he'd have pushed the boy at me as if he were a helpless mite that Zee was determined to help—and I'd have known to steer clear.

Aiden had saved Joel. Despite what I'd told Joel, I'd seen my death in the tibicena's eyes. If Joel had killed me, he wouldn't have survived that figuratively or literally. Joel would have been devastated, and Adam would have killed him. Not just in revenge, but because Joel would have proved himself a danger to the pack. Werewolves had learned to be ruthless to survive.

There was this also: Tad and Zee saw something in the boy to admire.

I wouldn't mind thumbing my nose at the fae, Adam admitted, his voice strong and humorous in my head.

I looked at Zee, who I trusted to tell me what I needed to know. "So what exactly is he?"

"He's human," growled Zee. "Or mostly, anyway. He started out that way a long, long time ago. He's been lost in Underhill since she closed her borders to the fae, and it changed him. He's not the only abandoned one who turned up when Underhill reopened herself to us. He's just the only one who was coherent. Underhill changed him, changed them all, gave some of them elemental powers. Powers of earth, air, water, or fire. Most of those children . . . have been returned to the Mother." "Returned to the Mother," I thought, meant killed, but this wasn't the time to ask. "They were broken by their time alone."

The boy smiled fiercely. "They don't want to kill me," he said. "They want to figure out why I can work fire. They want to know why Underhill likes me better than she likes them. Why she played games with me while leaving them out in the cold for all these centuries. They want to know everything I know about Underhill because they've forgotten what they used to know."

From the expression on his face, I was pretty sure that "played games with me" might have the same meaning to Underhill that it would to Coyote.

"That which does not kill us makes us stronger," I quoted.

"Nietzsche?" murmured Zee. "Appropriate. Also, perhaps this one: *Wer mit Ungeheuern kämpft, mag zusehn, daß er nicht dabei zum Ungeheuer wird.*"

I dragged out my college German and came up with a few words. *Ungeheuern* was "monsters." *Kämpft* was "battles." "Let he who battles with monsters take care lest he become one?" I translated out loud.

Aiden gave the old fae a smile with teeth. "We are all monsters here," he said. "It's too late for any of us to be anything else."

His words sent a flinch through far too many of the pack, including Adam. "That depends," I said.

He looked at me with mild inquiry.

"On your definition of 'monster,'" said Tad. "Who do you allow to tell you what you are? Monster or angel, it's in the eye of the beholder, surely."

"Why . . ." I started to ask, then stopped. Aiden had told me why the fae wanted him. He knew things they had forgotten, secrets about Underhill. And they were jealous because she kept him and gave him power. Any of which, I thought, would be reason enough for the fae to want him.

He'd helped Tad and Zee escape. I owed him—and I wouldn't have left anyone I could help at the mercy of the fae. As a last precaution, I tried to get permission from Adam, but either he didn't hear me (most likely) or he wanted me to make the decision, because he didn't answer.

"Twenty-four hours," I said abruptly. "If you do not harm one who is pack or who belongs to the pack. If you obey the pack leaders as the pack itself does. Those leaders are Adam who is our Alpha, myself, Darryl"—I gave a general wave to Darryl, who had returned sometime during the Nietzsche discussion—"Warren"—Warren nodded as I looked toward him—"and Honey, who is not here. For twenty-four hours, we'll grant you sanctuary in the pack stronghold—with the option to renew this agreement."

I almost missed it, the faint widening of his eyes and the almost imperceptible loosening of his shoulders. Relief. Far more obvious was the rise of outrage from the wolves—that I would risk their lives for a stranger, that I had overstepped my authority. I couldn't tell which wolves were spearheading it, my pack sense was not that clear at the moment. Maybe all of them were unhappy.

For the benefit of those unhappy wolves, I said aloud, "Bran Cornick taught me that the pack only rules the territory it can keep safe from other predators. He taught me that where a debt is owed, it must be repaid."

"What did this boy do for us?" asked Mary Jo, who'd come up with the others of the pack. At her back, as usual, stood Paul and Alec. Mary Jo wore a baseball cap and sunglasses to keep from being recognized. She was a firefighter in Pasco and had chosen to keep what else she was secret from them. But her secrecy felt like a "for now" thing, not a "forever."

We'd been friends, or at least friendly acquaintances, until Adam had courted and married me. She thought he deserved a human woman, someone better than a werewolf like she was. That he'd chosen me, a coyote shifter, had devastated her—but she needed to get over it.

"He saved Joel," I said mildly. She'd been on the bridge long enough that I was pretty sure she knew that.

"Oh. Joel. Your pet, right? The one you invited into the pack." She gave voice to the unhappiness I felt through the pack, the bond we all shared feeling like sandpaper.

I stared at her, and she met my eyes for a whole two seconds before she dropped them. The roar of the pack rebellion died down to a murmur that no longer pounded at me through the pack bonds. Mary Jo's wolf was convinced I outranked her, whatever her human half thought; that left her no room to challenge me, and she knew it.

"Bran also taught me guesting laws," I continued. "A person who asks for shelter will get twenty-four hours if he makes no move to harm. He will get food, drink, and a bed. Protection from his enemies. Safety. It is what we offer any who come to us." Those guesting laws were old. Bran adhered to them, but not all the wolf packs did. From the unease in the pack, I thought that they would be happier if I hadn't mentioned the guesting laws. But the walking stick warmed gently in my hand.

"Can you keep your half of that bargain?" the boy asked me, looking around at the rest of the pack. He couldn't read pack bonds, but he apparently was pretty good at reading unhappy expressions.

"Aiden," I said. "I bid you welcome to my territory and my home." It wasn't enough, but, with the walking stick heating beneath my fingers, I could feel the words that needed to be said. "By my name, Mercedes Athena Thompson Hauptman, by my authority as the mate of the Alpha of the Columbia Basin Pack, I give you as much safety as my pack can provide for twenty-four hours as long as you act as a guest in my house and my territory." I don't know what kept my tongue going, or why I raised the walking stick. "By my word as Coyote's daughter and bearer of Lugh's walking stick, I so swear."

The staff lit up like a lantern. Red fire circled the silver ring at the bottom of the staff and raced up the bark in Celtic knots that spiraled from the bottom to the silver top that had once again lengthened to a spear and glowed as if heated in a blast furnace. It felt as though all of the pack held their breath, waiting.

I kept the staff up in the air, and said, "Let the Gray Lords in their halls know that the Columbia Basin Pack holds these lands and grants sanctuary to whomever we choose."

Yes, said Adam in my head.

Yes, agreed the pack.

In movies, they stop rolling the film after the climactic speech, or they change scenes.

I had things to do.

I knelt beside Adam, but before I could do more, he rolled upright. He rose to his feet with only a little stiffness, then shook himself as if he'd been wet. I could feel the shivers of pain the motion set wracking and howling through his healing wounds, but no one else would.

The others all turned to go, leaving the cleanup for the poor humans whose city I had just claimed—and I already saw a dozen ways that was going to backfire on us. There was a chance that every supernaturally endowed creature in a hundred-mile radius hadn't witnessed my declaration, but I was pretty sure that's what the walking stick had been doing with its light show. It didn't think, not like that, but I was getting better at reading its intentions anyway. Zee started to turn, hesitated, then turned back. "So that was what they were trying. Stupid *verdammt* troll," he said.

I paused. "What who was trying when?"

"What the Gray Lords were trying to do when they sent that troll after me." He didn't say anything for a moment, and when he did, he sounded sad. "There aren't a lot of trolls left, Mercy, not so many that they should have sent this one to die, sad excuse for a troll that he was. And do not mistake me, they meant for him to die—that's what I missed."

"They meant for him to die?" I asked.

"They would know," Zee said. "The Gray Lords are not as forgetful as some of the younger ones. They would know that a troll would not kill me." He sighed and turned back down the bridge and started walking. "You do not send a puppy to kill an old wolf."

I followed him, Adam at my side. Warren and Darryl flanked us. Tad walked next to his father, near enough to help if he faltered. Aiden trailed behind us. It bothered me to have him behind us, but I had his promise.

Tad said, after a moment, "You didn't kill him, Dad."

Zee considered it—or maybe he was just trying to appear thoughtful and disguise how slow he was moving. After a bit he nodded. "This is true. *Interessant.*"

"How so?" I asked at Adam's silent prompting.

"I am not at my best," Zee said. "Things were done." He dismissed them with a shrug. "It would have taken me a long time to kill him and, without your wolves to keep him on the bridge, the battle might very well have engulfed some of the town." He glanced around at the police officers, who were all giving us a little space.

"And even had I managed to limit him to the bridge, I would not have been able to keep the humans away as effectively as you managed. Many humans would have died. You have changed this event, and not to their advantage."

"What do you mean?" I asked.

"Whoever made the decision to send the troll after me, they wanted a train wreck," he said. "They wanted death and destruction followed by a battle guaranteed to terrify anyone who watched it happen. A battle generated entirely by the fae. Something to remind humankind that they spent most of their existence being frightened of the Good Neighbors for a very good reason." He looked back at me, then at Adam, who was walking beside me slowly—as slowly as Zee was moving, in fact. "You have changed the game on them. The fae did not come out of this looking wonderful, but the werewolves defeated the troll, and you defied the Gray Lords themselves. You've set the pack up as the defenders of humankind—and proven that you are capable of taking down the monsters of the fae."

I thought about that awhile. "Is that a good thing or a bad thing?" I was asking Adam, but it was Zee who answered.

"*Wer weiß?*" he said. "Only the future will tell us that. But no good ever came from battling the Gray Lords at their own game. You have changed the rules."

"I would take it as a favor," I said thoughtfully, "if you and Tad would come to stay with us while Aiden is our guest."

Zee looked at me. I didn't want him and Tad alone in his house if the Gray Lords were sending trolls after him. He glanced at the boy, who was trailing behind.

"Yes," Zee said. "I think that would be wise."

4

Tad and Zee followed me to Adam's SUV, with Aiden tagging along behind like a stray puppy uncertain of his welcome. We walked very slowly because Adam was hurt, and so was Zee—and I wasn't certain about Tad. Traffic was still stopped, and people watched us as we walked.

"Hey, Mercy," someone called, "do you know what's up?"

I looked over, but I recognized neither the voice nor the face of the woman who was standing outside her car, a toddler on her hip.

"Troll on the Cable Bridge," I told her. "We dealt with it. They're working on getting traffic moving, but I think the bridge is going to need major repairs before anyone can use it."

"Troll?" A teenager in a minivan filled with other teenagers stuck his head out the window. "You mean like a real troll? Lives under bridges, tries to eat goats? That kind of troll?"

I nodded and smiled but kept walking.

He let out a happy sound. "Trolls versus werewolves. Our werewolves for the win!"

Adam opened his mouth and let his tongue loll out. Someone in the teen's van let out a wolf whistle, and it wasn't because of Adam's big pink tongue.

"Grandma, what big teeth you have," I murmured.

The corners of his lips turned up, but he closed his mouth.

About halfway back to the car, traffic started moving again, though it wasn't going to be breaking any speed records. After that, we got honked at—which made Zee say something rude in German. Tad grinned and waved at everyone.

"Quit frowning, Dad," he said. "If you smile, they'll forget all about us in a day. If you go around looking like that, they'll wonder how many other trolls are going to be wandering into the Tri-Cities."

Zee smiled.

Tad rolled his eyes. "Not like that, old man—that will give them nightmares."

"Be careful what you ask for," I said.

Tad rubbed the top of my head. "I'll keep that in mind, short stuff."

"I told you to feed him more coffee," I told Zee. "Look what happened when he outgrew me."

"Children whine too much," the old fae said. "Just how far away did you park—and why didn't we get a ride there?"

"Sorry," I said, meaning it, because I needed to get Adam home so he could change and his shoulder could be checked to make sure it had healed right. Werewolves heal fast, which was good up to a point—but if a bone wasn't set correctly, it would heal just as it was. Then it would need to be rebroken. "But there is no back way here, and no one could have driven us until the traffic cleared anyway." And the traffic still wasn't cleared.

It hadn't felt like a long way when we were running for the bridge, but with two—possibly three—people who were hurt, it was too long. I'd have offered to run ahead and grab the SUV, but I knew that neither Adam nor Zee would have allowed it unless they were on their deathbeds.

Tad said somberly, "Hey, Mercy? I'm sorry it took us so long to come help with the troll. We didn't know about it until we saw the traffic backed up. We'd taken refuge in one of the old warehouses in the Lampson scrap yard. I was headed out to find someone with a cell phone I could borrow to call you when I saw the troll."

"No one died," I told him, then corrected myself: "None of our pack died. If you hadn't made it when you did, Adam and I would have been toast. You timed it pretty close, though."

"It's all in the timing," he agreed—then grinned at me. "But close is still good."

We walked slowly to the SUV, with its soft upholstery for sore bodies. And I felt Aiden's eyes on me all the way.

Not quite hostile. Not quite. But, my coyote self was certain, not altogether friendly, either.

Our house wasn't really a single-family dwelling. An Alpha's house was the center of the pack, designed to be part meetinghouse, part hotel, part hospital. Sometimes it was just Adam, Jesse, and me who lived there, but Joel and his wife currently were living in the suite on the main floor. There were two extra bedrooms on the second floor, and I'd sent Zee to one and Tad to the other. Aiden had been, not ungently, settled in the safe room in the basement and told to make himself at home. The safe room had camera surveillance, and the doors were alarmed and lockable. When the doors were locked, the room would hold an out-of-control were-wolf. Aiden had merely smiled at the doors.

"These locks won't hold me," he'd told me.

"You're a guest, not a prisoner," I said, more worried about Adam, who was in our mini-clinic getting checked out, than whether or not our guest liked his accommodations. "This is the last private room in the house. If you'd rather, you can sleep in the rec room, which is set up as a bunk room, too. But I'll warn you that there are a number of pack who view those rooms as public property."

"No," he said after a moment, as if he was trying to figure out how to react. "This is fine. I was just warning you."

"You gave your word," I said. "And we gave ours."

"Yes," he agreed. Then he relaxed, as if we'd stepped back into something he knew. "So we did. Twenty-four hours." He gave me an enigmatic smile that did not belong on the face of a child.

The safe room was next door to the clinic. We both heard the crack of breaking bones. I froze, my stomach clenched. Adam's control was back in place because I had felt nothing through our link.

Aiden jumped like a startled cat and showed the whites of his eyes.

"Our Alpha's shoulder healed wrong," I told him, feeling sick. "They had to rebreak it."

We both listened to the silence. "Tough man," he said, finally.

"Oh, yes," I agreed. "If you'll excuse me?"

"Of course."

But Warren stopped me as I headed to the clinic. Before I could say "supercalifragilisticexpialidocious," I found myself chopping vegetables while Warren and his very-human partner, Kyle, barbe-cued hamburgers outside. We were setting up a barbecue dinner because, evidently, in between sadistic-but-necessary medical pro-cedures, Adam had called for a meeting of the pack.

In the front of the meeting room, the only spot of the room clear of chairs, Adam settled one hip on the library table that usually held whatever notes he'd brought with him. Tonight there weren't any notes. If we were going to talk about Aiden and my offer of sanctuary to anyone who came to us for help, I guess he wouldn't need notes, would he? My stomach was clenched. I was causing trouble for him again.

Medea hopped on the table and stropped her stub-tailed body against Adam, claiming him in front of the room of werewolves. He rubbed her under her chin absently, his attention elsewhere.

The meeting room was upstairs, adjacent to the family bedrooms. I'd asked Adam why he hadn't put it downstairs with the rest of the public rooms.

"A pack needs to be family," he'd said simply. "If I don't welcome them into my life, into my home, there will always be a distance between us. They need to trust me, to trust that I will take care of them—how can they do that if I treat them like business associates?"

The meeting room was packed with chairs, the kind you see in a high school band room or at a hotel banquet. More or less comfortable to sit in and strong enough to hold a heavy person, but stackable so we could get them out of the way if we needed to.

Adam glanced at his watch, so I knew he was waiting for a few latecomers. He looked almost normal except for the grim tint to his mouth that I blamed on his shoulder. He moved both arms freely, but I knew it must still hurt. As Alpha, he could draw upon the whole pack for power, so he healed faster than any of the rest of the werewolves. But he'd been hurt pretty badly.

I hadn't had a chance to talk to him, though. If I were a paranoid person, I'd have said he had been avoiding me. I worried that he resented me for making him have this meeting.

Next time I felt the urge to make pronouncements, I'd set down the stupid walking stick before I opened my mouth. I wasn't sure, even now, that it had been the walking stick's fault. I wasn't certain I'd been wrong—but I did know I'd been overly theatric.

Beside me, Warren patted my leg. Warren, bless him, had saved a spot for me right by the door—so I could escape first, he'd told me. But also, I thought, beside him, to show his support for me when I came under fire.

"Didn't the pack used to have meetings a lot more often than we do now?" I asked him. "We have pack breakfast Sundays, but other than that, or some emergency, the whole pack only meets before the full-moon hunt. But I seem to remember a lot more meetings when I used to only live on the other side of the back fence."

Warren laughed soundlessly; I could feel his body shake next to me.

"Oh, meetings," he said after a moment. "Yes, there were meetings. You can always tell if Adam is ticked off with the pack by the number of meetings we have. Some days, when someone was really stupid, we had meetings twice on the same day. I think it's his military background. There are a lot of us who are grateful to you for keeping him happy—saves on our gas bill, and some of us even have time for date nights once in a while. Or hobbies."

I saw Adam's lips quirk before he blanked his face again. Eti-

quette among werewolves was that you tried to ignore private conversations. But like everyone else in the room, he could hear us just
fine.

Ben entered with Zack and Joel, both of whom still looked a
little shaky, but Zack was by far the most battered. The hit with
the Miata had fractured his pelvis and four ribs. Werewolves are
tough, but Zack was as far from an Alpha as he could get; he'd
be in pain for days yet. Ben kept a hand under Zack's arm. The
cool expression on Ben's face meant that he was still working as
their . . . babysitter? Escort? Something. On his own, he might
still have decided to make sure they were safe, but he'd have had
his happy mask on and come in making rude comments designed
to get a rise out of someone. Under orders, he tended to be much
more businesslike, especially lately.

Ben had watched over Joel at the barbecue, too, making sure
he got plenty to eat. Zack had been in our mini-clinic with Adam,
getting patched up.

As soon as Ben entered, Adam nodded to Darryl, who shut the
meeting-room door and went back to his seat in the front of the
room. I felt the pack magic surround us, sliding over walls and
doors and windows, encasing us in secrecy so that no one outside
this room could hear us. It would block our ability to hear anything going on outside, too.

I'd have been more worried about that last, given that we had
a stranger in the house, but Tad had promised, out of Jesse's hearing, to keep Adam's human-fragile daughter busy and safe "while
the werewolves discussed what to do with their fae . . . guests."

Adam crossed his arms, and said, "Do we have anyone who
would like to start?"

Mary Jo shot to her feet, body tense, though her eyes were lowered.

"Not you, I think," said Adam thoughtfully. I'd never seen him refuse to allow a wolf their say in a meeting. "Someone else."

Mary Jo's mouth squinched down until it was hard to be sure it was there. But she sat down without saying anything because there had been something in that thoughtful voice, an edge that was not calm, not quiet, no matter how relaxed Adam's posture was.

A wave of . . . unease swept through the room as Adam's werewolf gold eyes passed over them. Adam was well and truly angry. I wondered if there was some way I could fix it. I'd set the pack up against the whole of the fae. I had no trouble fighting with Adam when I knew I was right. Over this? I found myself wishing I hadn't eaten the half of the burger I'd consumed at the barbecue to appease Kyle, who had, he said in his usual sardonic fashion, cooked it just for me. Warren must have told him what I'd done because the two of them had mother-henned me just as Ben had Joel.

Now that food sat, an indigestible lump, in my stomach.

Ben stood up, his body language casual, confident that he, at least, wasn't the subject of Adam's ire. This time.

Adam raised an eyebrow.

Ben took that as permission. "Tad told me that his father will be fine, and it was probably better just to leave him alone unless he asks for help. He also assured me that his father is more than capable of dealing with . . ." Ben stumbled.

"Aiden," said Zack. "Probably not his real name, 'cause it means 'little fire.'"

"Welsh?" Warren asked.

"Irish, I think," said Zack. "Which doesn't mean it couldn't also be 'fire' in Cornish, or Welsh, or a hundred and one related languages." I'd known English wasn't Zack's original language any more than Zack was his real name. When he'd first come to us, he'd hesitated answering to it, as if he had to remind himself that "Zack" meant someone was addressing him. It wasn't unusual for wolves, especially old ones, to adopt new names. I wouldn't have picked him out as Irish. Maybe he'd just spent some time in Ireland, the same way he'd spent some time in the US. Maybe I was over-analyzing, and he just knew that "Aiden" meant "little fire" because he'd read it in a book somewhere.

Zack's speech had been a little blurry. The troll had crushed his jaw, too. But his eyes were happy. Very happy.

I leaned forward in my seat so I could get a better look at his face. He looked like a man who knew something no one else did. He'd been closeted with Adam in medical.

I frowned at him, but he didn't see it.

"So Mercy's fae friend can save us from her other fae friend," said Alec bitterly. There were subpacks in the pack, groups of people who just liked one another and hung out together. Alec was one of Mary Jo's cadre.

He didn't get up because Ben had the floor. But Zack's contributions, made while he was sitting down, had opened the way for audience participation.

Adam stared at him until Alec dropped his eyes. It didn't take very long.

"Indeed," said Adam, very softly. "Zee has shown himself to be a friend."

Alec, his head bowed very low, tried not to squirm. Ben didn't react at all, just waited for the drama to be done.

I tried, but couldn't recall any time Zee did anything to help the pack. Okay, he had helped Adam find me when a fairy queen wouldn't let me go—but that didn't really count because he was helping Adam find me, helping me, not helping the pack.

"Are you finished, Ben?" asked Adam.

Ben glanced at Joel, who didn't do anything I could see, but Ben nodded and sat down. Joel stood up.

Adam said, "How are you?"

Joel smiled. "Better than I've been in a long time," he said, sounding it. "The boy told me he hadn't killed the tibicena, and he's right. I can feel it. But so far, I've been able to stay *me* for the past four hours."

"The boy—Aiden—helped you," said Adam.

Joel glanced at me. "I haven't been able to stay human for longer than an hour or two since Guayota gave me to the tibicena," he said. "Since Aiden drew out the fire, I'm in charge. I don't know how long it will last, but absolutely he helped me." He waited to see if Adam had more questions. When Adam didn't say anything else, Joel sat down.

George stood up. George was pretty far up in the pack hierarchy. A good man and steady. I liked him.

Adam invited him to speak with a tilt of his head.

"We are werewolves," George said heavily. "Mercy is not, so maybe she doesn't understand how this works. We are pack, and we look out for ourselves. We cannot afford to take on the world and lose focus, forget what's important. We take care of pack."

"And that's why you became a police officer, is it, George?" I couldn't help myself, though I knew I should hold my peace. "Not to protect and serve all the citizens of Pasco, but to take care of the pack."

He flushed angrily. "That's got nothing to do with it."

I met his gaze and held it. "Okay," I said mildly.

"I do my job," he said.

"Okay," I agreed. He did.

George worked for the Pasco Police Department. From what I'd overheard during the barbecue, he'd been in among the police on the Pasco side of the bridge today. Pasco had lost two police officers and had another three in the hospital in various states of non-life-threatening injuries, one of whom he'd dragged off the bridge—right out from under the nose of the troll. Which was why I thought he was being pretty hypocritical.

"Mercy, quit playing games with the grumpy werewolf," murmured Warren. When I glanced at him, he was staring at George. "You might start a fight. Remember, werewolves look out for pack." He bit off the last word.

George sat down and stared away from me—away from Warren, too.

"He's right," Paul said earnestly, standing up but not waiting for an invitation from Adam to talk. "George, I mean, not Warren. We cannot be responsible for everyone in the Tri-Cities, like Mercy said. Like she tried to make us be." Paul had been on the bridge for my grand declaration. Paul was not one of my staunchest supporters. "Some of you think this meeting is to discuss the boy she brought home. But she did more than that. Mercy offered sanctuary to anyone who came to the pack for help."

"Point of fact." I stood up, though there wasn't supposed to be more than one person standing (other than Adam). I wasn't going to talk to Paul from a position of weakness. "I reserved the right of the pack to offer sanctuary to anyone we chose to help. A small but important distinction." I sat down again.

"You challenged the Gray Lords," Paul said. His short reddish beard tended to hide anything but strong emotions, but there was a tone of entreaty in his voice. "We can't take on the Gray Lords, Mercy."

He had a point. But he was looking at what I had done from the wrong point of view. I stood up again. And then hesitated, waiting for Adam to ask me to sit down until it was my turn to speak. Adam was a stickler for order and proper procedure in the pack meetings. But he simply watched me with an expression I couldn't read. So I decided to go ahead and answer Paul's statement.

"I grew up in the Marrok's pack," I said.

"Good for you," said Mary Jo.

I pulled out as much patience as I could manage and ignored her. Getting in a snark fest with Mary Jo would not be useful. Instead, I looked around the room at everyone else. "Can any of you imagine the fae sending a troll into the Marrok's territory? Into Aspen Creek—or, say, Missoula?" I let them think about it. "Can you imagine what the Marrok would do if they did?"

I saw a few appreciative grins. No. Bran would not allow a rampaging troll in his territory.

"What's your point?" asked Auriele, Darryl's mate. She wasn't one of Mary Jo's crowd, and recently, we'd been cautiously cordial.

"The fae in Walla Walla either do not respect us, or they did not think that we would come to the aid of the human inhabitants in this city," I told her, told them. "Maybe both. As a result, people died, and wolves got hurt. If they know that we will defend our territory against them, maybe they'll think twice before sending in another troll. Or something worse. My point is that right now we cannot afford *not* to take on the Gray Lords."

"But the Marrok isn't here," Paul, still standing, said.

Paul wasn't the smartest person in most rooms, but he was just saying what I saw in other people's faces.

"No," I agreed. "Do you think Bran would go kill the troll himself? He has more critical work to do." Facing the troll himself would give it too much importance, would acknowledge that it was a real threat.

"He'd send Charles," said Paul. "Or Colin Taggart, or the Moor." He grinned suddenly. "I'd like to see a fight between the Moor and a troll."

"Or he'd send Leah," someone muttered. Bran's mate could take care of business—I didn't have to like her to acknowledge that.

"And then he'd go after whoever sent it and make sure they didn't make that mistake again," said Alec.

"Right," I agreed soberly. "The point is that the fae would never send a troll into Bran's territory because they'd go through exactly the same thought process that we just did."

"This is not the Marrok's pack," said Paul. "We don't have Tag or Charles."

"No," I agreed. "We have Adam, Darryl, Warren, and Honey. We have you, Paul. We have Auriele, George, and Mary Jo. And we *did* take down that troll, with only a fraction of our pack: Adam, Darryl, Zack, and Joel. We had no casualties."

"They didn't do it alone," said Mary Jo. "They needed Tad."

I held my hands palm up. "We have friends and allies," I said. "Good. Those are assets, too. Right now, we are in a position of power. We've killed their troll and drawn a line in the sand. It's up to them to cross that line—and maybe they won't."

"Maybe they will," said George. "And before this, we weren't an enemy of the fae."

"Weren't we?" I asked. "Weren't we? Then why did they feel free to send that troll into our town?"

"It's not *our* town," said Alec. "We're werewolves. We're a pack. We don't own the town."

I looked around at the stubborn faces. I'd been waiting for

Adam—or Warren or Darryl or *someone*—to throw in with me. Without support from someone the pack respected, they'd never listen to me.

I threw up my hands, both figuratively and literally.

"Fine," I said, and sat down. I couldn't help but send an apologetic look Adam's way because I was pretty sure I'd made everything worse. But he wasn't looking at me. He had folded both of his arms and closed his eyes. There was a white mark growing on his cheekbone that told me he was gritting his teeth.

If he was mad at me, I thought, then we'd have it out in private. But, sitting next to Warren, I'd had some time to review my actions today. Other than feeling a little squirmy about the drama level, I was okay with everything I'd done on that bridge. I prepared arguments to defend myself. If I felt hurt that Adam hadn't understood, I tucked that hurt down and away. I didn't want anyone here knowing that I was hurt.

Warren's long-fingered hand closed over my knee. He squeezed, then patted it, his face serene. Warren, at least, understood what I'd been saying.

Honey stood up and looked around. "I am ashamed," she said.

She let that statement hang in the air for a moment. Then she continued, "I am so ashamed of all of you. I look around, and all I see are stupid people."

"It's not stupid to be afraid of the fae," said Mary Jo hotly.

"No?" Honey disagreed. "But that's not what makes you stupid, Mary Jo. You aren't arguing with Mercy because she's wrong, you're arguing with her because you don't know who she is. You still think she's some dumb bimbo who seduced our Alpha and stumbled into a stupid magic trick that allowed her to become part of the pack. That she is a mistake. That she is a weakness."

She looked around the room. "Idiots. Every one of you. We drove a *volcano god* out of our territory, and you are afraid of the fae?" She made a noise. "Oh, that's right. It wasn't us—it was Mercy, wasn't it? She put herself between Guayota and us. She nearly *died* to protect us—and you are all still wondering if she should be a member of our pack."

"She is a weakness," said Darryl reluctantly. "Guayota saw it, too. She was the first of us he went after."

"And she defeated him," Honey said. "She drove him out of her garage."

"Tad and Adam defeated him," Mary Jo said.

"That's a theme here, isn't it?" said Honey. "Mercy stands up for what is right—and her friends back her up." She paused. "Why do you think that is?"

Her lip curled when no one said anything. "Because they know she'll have their back in return. Pack is about *not* standing alone. About having people you trust to have your back. There is not another person in this room that I would rather have at my back than Mercy."

"What about Adam?" asked Mary Jo instantly.

"Not excepting Adam," Honey told her stoutly. "Your pardon, Adam, if you find that offensive. But because you are our Alpha, you have other considerations, other responsibilities. Mercy, once she has your back, she has your back."

Adam didn't open his eyes. He just waved her apology away.

"Offering sanctuary to the fae boy was the right thing to do," Honey said. "He'd given aid to our fellow pack member. It is right and proper that he ask for something in return."

"And Joel wouldn't be a member of the pack who needed help if it weren't for Mercy," said Mary Jo fiercely.

Honey opened her mouth, but Adam spoke first.

"Enough," he said, and his voice was silky-soft. "Sit down, Honey."

She sat, but her mouth was screwed up in anger.

Adam opened his eyes and surveyed the room with bright gold irises. "Y'all are mistaken about the reason for this meeting." His Southern accent was unusually thick. It should have made his anger sound softer, but it didn't.

Beside me, Warren's mouth quirked up.

"We are not here to discuss Aiden and the sanctuary he was promised. We are not here to discuss the fae in any way, shape, or form. We are here to discuss Mercy. And your attitude toward my wife. My mate."

He rocked to his feet and began pacing slowly back and forth. "Mercy is a tough, smart woman. She can defend herself—I do not have to protect her. She is not weak or dependent or needy. She doesn't need the pack. She doesn't need me."

I shot to my feet. "That's not true," I said hotly.

He tilted his head a little, his eyes meeting mine. His eyes softened. "I misspoke," he said in a steady voice. "She doesn't need me to make sure she has enough food or a place to live—that is my privilege, but she doesn't need me to do that. She doesn't need me to keep her safe or to make her a whole person. She doesn't need me to do anything except love her. Which I do."

Well now, I thought, abruptly breathless. I nodded at him and plunked down in my seat before my weakened knees gave out.

After I sat down, Adam started that slow pace back and forth again. It was a hunter's gait. When he spoke, it was even more quietly than he had before. "When she agreed to be my mate and when she agreed to be part of the pack, I understood that she would not welcome my standing between her and you. She's defended herself all of her life, and she is capable of defending herself from you when she cares enough to do so." He stopped and looked around, an eyebrow raised in challenge.

Warren coughed the words "blue dye" into his hand.

Adam's smile flickered into being, then disappeared. "She has rightfully earned the reputation, that goes back to her days in the Marrok's pack, of being someone people respected. No one in Bran's pack wanted to get on her bad side because Mercy always comes out on top. And she has acquitted herself very well in my pack, defending herself from whatever you've thrown at her. But today on the bridge, I discovered something."

He let the pause linger.

"I'm done with it." All hint of softness was gone from his voice. "I am done with listening to you attack my mate while she is trying to save you. Again. I called this meeting to give notice. If I hear or hear about any of you saying anything to my mate that is in the least bit disrespectful, I will end you. No warnings, no second chances. I will end you."

And he walked through the aisle left between the chairs and out of the room without looking me in the eyes.

Darryl stood up in the silence and addressed the room. "Adam has authorized both Warren and me to help anyone who wishes to leave this pack in light of this announcement. Do not go to Adam. I assure you that he is quite serious."

I sat where I was, dumbstruck. On the one hand—that was pretty sexy. On the other—holy cow. He couldn't *do* that. I'd just started making real inroads into the general prejudice of the pack. He'd silenced them. My life was going to be hellish, full of people who hated me but couldn't say anything out in the open so we could hash it out. It would just fester.

"For what it's worth," Warren said to me, "if he hadn't done that, I think Honey would have. And that would have been a disaster." He looked at my face. "It'll be okay, kid."

I opened my mouth. "He can't do that."

Ben grinned at me. "Of course he can. This isn't a democracy, Mercy. That was brilliant."

I shook my head. "That was a disaster."

"How so?" asked Mary Jo, who had gotten up and was standing in the queue to get out of the room. "And I mean that respectfully, Mercy."

She didn't sound sarcastic, but it lurked in her eyes.

"He can't dictate how people feel," I said.

"Some people need to shut their mouths in order to use their brains," said George. He sounded . . . thoughtful.

I stared at him.

"And I'm beginning to think that I'm one of them," he said. "I think . . . I think that you're right. The Tri-Cities is our territory. If we don't police our territory, then who could blame the fae for thinking we wouldn't do anything when they sent a troll through downtown? It never occurred to me that the pack wouldn't help. I saw Darryl up there, and thought, 'Good, they've made it.' And if I know that—maybe we should make sure that the rest of the world knows it, too. It might stave off incidents like the one we had today."

He crouched so his head and mine were at an equal height, ignoring the way that meant he blocked the path out of the room.

"Honey was right," he said. "If it had been Darryl up there on the bridge, promising the sun, moon, and stars, we'd all have backed him. And you not only outrank Darryl, you've proven that you deserve that rank to anyone who isn't an outright idiot. We should have backed you. And now we will."

"This isn't a third-world dictatorship," I said.

"Yes," said Mary Jo slowly. "Yes, it is, Mercy." Her voice softened. "It has to be. We are too dangerous. Controlling our wolves is much, much easier when we are a pack, following a leader. This needed to happen a long time ago."

Warren stayed by me as the room cleared of strangely happy werewolves. When Honey made it to us, she slid into the row of chairs in front. She pulled out one chair and stacked it on its neighbor, then took another and turned it around until she faced us. She sat on this one, crossed her legs at the knee, and waited, bland-faced, for the room to clear. Under her gaze, it cleared a little faster than it had been. Darryl gave her an ironic salute as he passed, which she returned.

When we were the only three left, she said, "Okay. Any ideas on how this petitioning for sanctuary is going to work? Word of it is going to spread, and I expect that this Aiden character isn't going to be the last. There are a lot of people in hiding from the powerful groups—the fae, the witches, the vampires—who will look upon this as an invitation. Do we take them all? What if the bad guys demand sanctuary?"

"Like Gary," said Warren in a serious voice.

Gary was my older half brother. My very-much-older half brother who was smitten with Honey and had made no bones about it—he wasn't, strictly speaking, a bad guy. On the other hand, he wasn't a poster child for the heavenly choir, either.

Honey flushed, raised her chin, and said, "Like Gary. Are we mediators? A hotel for the night? And how will we deal with expenses?"

"Do you really think that it's going to get that big?" I said, taken aback. "I was looking upon it more like a line in the sand. A 'this is our territory and we will defend it' rather than a clarion call of blanket protection for anyone who wanted to show up."

She examined me with a small smile. "Who knows?" she said. "I was just trying to distract you from your intention of cornering Adam in a private place and ripping him a new one. I figured it would be easier for me to do it than whatever Warren had planned."

Warren grinned at her, but when he turned to me, his face was sober. "He had to do it, Mercy. I'm surprised he let it go this long, but he was worried that you would run if he stepped in too soon."

That startled me. "Did he tell you that?" I asked.

"Today," Warren said. "Darryl and me both, while he was getting fixed up. And Zack, too, I guess, because Zack also needed repairs. You were a tough hunt for him. He had to all but turn himself inside out not to scare you away." He looked up at the ceiling, then he looked at Honey. "The rest of this conversation is private, I think. You've distracted her from her panic, thank you."

Honey nodded her elegant head and left, the foggy shape of her dead husband's ghost followed her. Peter was fading now, I thought with sad satisfaction. It wasn't safe for the living to cling too hard to the dead; it pulled the living in the wrong direction.

She shut the door behind her.

Warren closed his eyes a moment, and I felt when the pack magic slid back into place, locking us into a private space where no one could overhear.

When he opened his eyes, they were yellow, but that faded. "When you found me alone all those years ago and sent me to Adam, I thought that it would be the usual talk—don't get in our way, don't make a stink, and we might not come for you some night and run you out of our territory."

"That's not Adam," I said.

He nodded. "No. He's not the usual Alpha at all, is he? For which we are all grateful. He's taking a lot of flak, you know. Not from Bran, but from other places. We are the only pack on the planet that has members who are not werewolves or human mates of werewolves, and even that last is right uncommon."

"Yes," I said.

"And you upset the applecart over how our female werewolves are ranked, much to the betterment of their lot everywhere, no matter how much Honey hates it," he said. "And she hates it less every day. You and Adam, you've broken a lot of traditions between the two of you. You are probably lucky you haven't become targets of other packs. It may not have happened since Bran assumed control— but our history is full of packs who were exterminated when they got uppity."

"What does that have to do with anything that happened tonight?" I asked, honestly puzzled.

"Most of the pack members are actually pretty happy about a lot of the changes. That one about the women, that is the best one because it allows the pack power structure to lay as it should instead of how the Alpha thinks it best. Makes our bonds tighter, healthier."

I waited, and he smiled at me. "Well, now, Mercy. Today, you did the right thing—and whatever he said today about not judging that decision, he and I and Darryl talked a lot about it. We all think it was not only the right decision, it was the only decision you could make." His Texas accent got momentarily thicker. "An' when you held up thet flaming walking stick, thet was ahlmighty somethin'." He grinned, and his voice went back to normal, which still had a Texas flavor. "But it's going to cause a real whoop-de-do all over the place, and we cannot afford to have the pack focused on you instead of on business, or some of our people are going to get hurt."

"The vampires?" I asked. "Adam thinks Marsilia is going to be up in arms because I claimed the Tri-Cities for us?"

"No, ma'am," said Warren. "Darryl is worried about that, but Adam says, and I reckon he's right, that Marsilia will be pleased at having that little bit to throw at any other vampires who think to come here and challenge her like that one did a while back. Besides, we can handle the vampires. Stefan won't move against you"—he didn't say why not; Warren was one of the few who knew about the bond between Stefan and me—"and that leaves Marsilia herself, and Wulfe. The rest of them aren't old or powerful enough to give Zack a fair fight."

"So where is the problem?" I asked. "The Gray Lords?"

"Uniting the pack against the fae won't be no trick." Warren reached up to tip his cowboy hat—and rubbed his ear instead when he realized it was sitting on his knee because we were inside. Warren didn't wear hats inside a building because it was rude. He was also perfectly capable of speaking with good grammar, he just didn't always bother. "The fae are pretty good at making themselves unlikeable—excepting Zee and Tad."

"Excepting Tad," I said. "Zee can be as obnoxious as the best of them when he wants to be." But I was still working through what he said—and I figured it out. "Oh holy wow. Oh wow. Oops."

Warren smiled. "See, I knew you'd think of it when you got going. But if it helps, Adam thinks that pot was boiled when Darryl and Zack jumped in to face off with the troll."

"Bran," I said. "Bran is going to be livid."

"Yes, ma'am," he said.

"He just got things smoothed over from when Charles took out that monster in Arizona," I said. Livid wasn't even in the ballpark of what Bran was going to be.

"We figured he'd get the news when it broke on the national front—about twenty minutes ago."

"National news," I said.

He tipped his imaginary hat to me. "Yes, ma'am. One of our local reporters was close enough to get your declaration on camera, complete with fiery sigils lit up and down your walking staff."

I sucked in a breath. This wasn't my fault. At least, it wasn't all my fault. It was the fault of the fae for letting a troll loose in my town.

There was no way we could have left that troll to the police. The troll's appearance was outside my ability to affect—therefore this was not my fault. I felt guilty anyway.

"So what does Bran have to do with Adam's sudden, knuckle-dragging declaration of protection?" I asked.

"Wait a moment," Warren said. "He wrote it down because he was worried I might mess it up." He lifted his hip off the chair and dug around in the back pocket of his jeans. "Here it is." He handed me a three-by-five card that had seen better days. He'd folded it in half to stick it into his pocket—and Adam had bled on it. There was writing on both sides.

In small, neat engineers' block lettering I read:

1. I've wanted to do this for a long time.
2. I cannot afford dissent in the pack over anything if we are to square off against Bran. If they are showing disrespect to my mate, they are not committed to me. They need to be loyal to me, that will matter to Bran.

3. The rest of the packs all over will now have to decide what they are going to do. If they don't follow our example, they are going to appear weak. If they follow our example in this, in making our territories truly our territories, they will follow, will they or not, the other changes that have begun in our pack. For this to happen, we must be united.

4. Even if Bran eases off, the fae will not. I had a little talk with Zee. They want Aiden. They will not be gentle, and Aiden has done nothing to raise their ire, but that won't save him from torture or worse. I'm not ready to turn someone over for torture just because it would be easier for me. So—here, too, we cannot afford for the pack to be divided.

I turned the card over. The writing on this side was different, more angular, larger, and the pen had dug into the surface of the card.

5. Most importantly. I love you. And I am done with standing by while my pack thinks it is acceptable to disrespect you. I am done.

After the last "done," he'd written, "I'm sorry," but it was crossed out. Evidently he wasn't sorry.

Warren tapped the card. "The back side he wrote after we had to break his shoulder blade a second time. Apparently, all we did the first time was open a hairline fracture into a full break in the wrong place. Which is why we'd brought Zee down. He's better with a hammer than any of us."

I flinched. "He should have let me be there," I said.

"He needed an excuse to be strong," said Warren. "He was afraid that he couldn't hold the illusion of strength if you were there."

I tucked the card into a front pocket. "You win," I said. "I won't yell at him about his declaration. I wouldn't have even if you hadn't added that last bit."

Warren wrapped his long-fingered hand around the back of my neck and pulled me over so he could kiss the top of my head. "Go ahead and yell at him," he said. "He's tough, he won't mind. Just don't leave, and he'll be good."

"I wouldn't have left him over this," I said, feeling insulted. Then I rubbed my face. "It's just . . . Warren, I was raised with werewolves. I was raised among the wolves in the Marrok's pack, where no one was allowed to say anything bad about Bran's mate, Leah. Sometimes I still wake up in the middle of the night and use phrases I learned from Ben and aim them at her because now I can."

"Adam told me that your experience with Leah would make you madder about Adam's stance," Warren said. "I've met Leah, and she deserves the worst Ben's potty mouth can offer. Adam knew putting you in Leah's position wasn't going to make you happy."

I opened my mouth to agree, but honesty stopped me. "It's going to rankle," I said. "But I'm all right with it." I looked at the bloody note. "It's the idea that he thought I might leave him over this that he's going to pay for." I gritted my teeth. "Idiot."

Warren grinned and hit his leg with his hat. "I told him he was worried over nothing. If we are okay here, I'm going to go get Kyle and head home. He's got a meeting with a new client tomorrow. Couple who've been married twenty-five years. Their youngest child just graduated from high school. I guess they were waiting for that."

"Sad," I said.

He looked at me with wise eyes. "Take happiness where you can," he said. "It seldom lasts—'course, neither does sorrow, right?"

5

I stalked out of the meeting room and ignored the surreptitious looks aimed my way as I stomped down the stairs. Adam wouldn't be in our bedroom—he tried not to bring conflict there. Given his temperament—and mine—he was only partially successful at this. But he did try.

He wouldn't want to linger among the wolves, either, not after his exit. He'd let them stew and absorb his edict on their own. Speaking of the wolves, as I got over myself enough to look around, the pack was still here. Lately, some of them lingered after meetings, choosing to go downstairs and play computer games, or stay to chat. They were lingering, chatting (pointedly not about me) and, if my ears didn't deceive me, playing computers downstairs. But almost no one had gone home.

I thought about that a moment. Of course no one was going home—I'd made our home a target, and we needed the pack to keep everyone here safe.

"Where's Zack?" I asked Ben, who was leaning against a wall scarfing down a couple of leftover hamburgers held precariously on a saggy paper plate.

He swallowed and ran his tongue over his teeth before opening his mouth. "Asleep. Tad suggested he take half the bed in his room, as it was likely to be quieter than anywhere else he could sleep tonight."

That's not exactly what Ben said, but I'd gotten good at ignoring the swearing ever since I figured out it was a defense mechanism. Occasionally, he got me with something truly creative.

"And our guest?" I asked.

He shrugged. "I think he went to bed, too. But honestly, Mercy, I don't care, right? We promised to grant him sanctuary, but if he doesn't stick around like a fly on a whore's mattress, then I guess we're off the hook."

I wasn't sure of that, but I was pretty sure, from his reaction on the bridge, that Aiden wasn't going to be running off while he was still safe.

"Adam?"

Ben grinned at me. "In his office."

Of course he was. Because he wasn't a coward, he wasn't afraid of fighting with me. The only reason he'd left Warren to talk to me was so that he could face off with Bran.

I knocked on Adam's office door. Adam's office was sound-proofed, mostly. Which meant I had to be leaning against the door to hear anything inside.

"Who?" he asked.

"You know who," I told him.

"Come in."

I slipped in and closed the door behind me, locking it. Despite my expectations, he wasn't on the phone. That was good, because I still had a few things to say to him.

"Afraid someone will interrupt us?" Adam asked, his face politely wary.

"Afraid you'll run," I told him seriously. "Apparently. From what you told Warren. And Darryl. Oh. And Zack."

He flushed a little. "I only said that because—"

"Because you were afraid if you jumped in between the pack and me, I would run," I said.

He folded his arms and looked unhappy.

That was okay. I was unhappy with him, too.

"Because," I said with fierce irony, "you can't count on me not to take off when the chips are down. Because every time we fight, I run away and lick my wounds. Because if you do something I don't agree with—and we'll get back to that—I'll desert you and go looking to find myself like your ex-wife did."

"Because," Adam said carefully, "Bran told me that if I treated you the way I did Christy, you'd leave me, too. Maybe not that day, or the one after that, but eventually you'd burst free of any chains I tried to wrap you in, even if it was for your protection."

I froze. Raised an eyebrow. "Did Bran really compare me to your ex-wife, or are you just saying that so I'll be mad at him instead of you?"

"Would I do that?" he asked.

I narrowed my eyes at him. "In a heartbeat, you would."

He laughed.

"Okay," he said. "I deserved that. But those were his exact words."

I took a deep breath. "There are two of us in this relationship, Adam. I love you. If you need to establish a rule I disagree with, but it is necessary for you—I can compromise." I took a deep breath because I really, really didn't like the gag order he'd issued. "I can live with the law you laid down on the pack tonight—I don't like it. But I can deal—and so will they." Just like Bran's pack dealt with his wife, Leah. I hated her when I lived with Bran's pack. But I'd never disrespected her to her face.

Adam relaxed.

"Of course," I said, "not letting me know how badly the initial treatment of your broken shoulder had gone, that might get you in real trouble. But you would never try to keep something from me, like having to break your shoulder twice because the first time didn't work, would you? Because you know that I would be really, really ticked off about that."

He looked at me.

I held my hand up at hip height. "Here's my irritation level when someone jumps in to protect me when I don't need it." I thought about it and bent down until my hand was at my knee. "Nope. This is where my irritation level is. My irritation level is here"—back at my hip—"when he does it without warning me. My irritation . . . anger level is here"—I held my hand up to my eyes—"when you keep me out of something that is my concern. When I landed in the hospital after your ex-wife's stalker tried to kill me"—he'd been an insane volcano god, the same one who'd destroyed my shop and turned my friend Joel into a tibicena—"*I* wasn't trying to make everyone keep you away because the sight of me all beaten up might make you feel bad."

"You were dying," Adam said. "You had no choice." But his

face was tight. He didn't like to be reminded about how close I'd come to dying.

"Yes," I snapped. "And if you keep me away again, you only *hope* you'll be dead when I find out about it."

I was absolutely serious. The force of my anger took me by surprise. Adam was mine. I'd belonged at his side, not setting up a stupid barbecue. He'd sent me away—and I'd let him because I'd felt guilty for setting the pack up to face off with the fae, the vampires, and a host of other people and not-people who might take offense at my declaration that the Tri-Cities was our territory. It was probably myself I was maddest at, but Adam was a good substitute.

The computer chimed.

I marched around and saw that Skype was up, and hit the ANSWER button.

Bran appeared, his eyes half-lidded in the way they were when he was furious.

"Not now," I told him. "Adam and I are having a fight about stupid wolves who don't tell their mates when some damned iron-kissed fae has to break his shoulder because your son the doctor is running around Europe. We have some competent EMTs, but EMTs are not up to bone work—which they proved by breaking his shoulder wrong. Excuse us. I'll call you back when we are done here."

"Mer—"

I hit the button to hang up, turned to Adam—who was laughing. Laughing. It was going to be the last thing that he ever did.

"That might be the last thing either of us ever do," he answered, and I realized I must have said that last thing out loud. "Bran doesn't really appreciate being hung up on." He sobered. "I plead stupid," he said. "And prideful. In my defense, I was pretty badly hurt, and no one wants to get their shoulder broken. Three times today, actually, if you count the first one."

"Four," I said, hopping up to sit on his desk. "Because Warren said the reason their attempt failed was because you also had a hairline crack they didn't know about. For it to be a hairline crack an hour later, it was a break at first."

"Four," he said. He moved his keyboard and mouse aside, then slid me sideways across the desk until I was sitting directly in front of him, one leg on either side of his. "And I was worried about what I had to do tonight. I couldn't make everything work—my shoulder included—if I didn't think. And if you were in that room, I wasn't going to be thinking very clearly."

"And getting Zee down into medical would let you talk him into letting someone take a look at his wounds, too," I said thoughtfully. "Did you?"

"I can't say," he said. "I promised someone something as long as he wasn't so bad that we couldn't help."

I didn't say anything.

"He's a tough old smith," Adam said. "But they had a real go at him." Bad, I thought, but not bad enough he needed more help than Darryl and Warren could provide. "For what it's worth, they left Tad alone. Zee managed to convince them that Tad was fragile, and they don't know enough about humans to torture without killing him." Adam smiled coldly. "But what they did to Zee—one of their own—puts me squarely behind your offer of sanctuary for Aiden."

"Good to know that you are both on the same side of this disaster," said a voice.

I wiggled and ended up on Adam's lap. He caught me and helped me manage a not-very-dignified pose across his lap that was still better than the floor, where I'd been headed.

"Good evening, Mercy. Adam," said Bran from Adam's computer screen. There was none of the usual Skype screen stuff—just Bran's face. "Courtesy is for the courteous."

"Thanks, Charles," I said. "Always nice to know that your computer skills are still cutting-edge. And good evening, Bran." I wrinkled my nose. "Courtesy is for the courteous? Really? Did you find that in a fortune cookie?" I felt awkward on Adam's lap in front of Bran and Charles, but when I started to slide off, Adam held me where I was.

"You're welcome," said Charles's voice from somewhere on the other side of the computer screen. Impossible to tell from his voice, but I think I'd amused him.

"My mother's phrase, actually. Though not in those words. She didn't speak English," said Bran in a very soft voice. I don't know anything about his mother except that Bran only mentioned her when he was seriously unhappy. "Are you finished, Mercy?"

If Adam wanted me to stay on his lap, he had a reason for it. However, it felt really awkward to deal with an irate Bran while sitting on my husband's lap. Still, I trusted Adam's instincts, so I stayed where I was to mount our defense. And the best defense is a good offense, right?

"You really would have preferred we let a troll loose in a major human-population center?" I asked. If he was going to be mad, he was going to aim his mad where it belonged. At me. "Like you would have let one run around throwing cars all over Missoula without lifting a hand against it?"

Adam kissed my cheek—and I got it. He was worried Bran was

going to be mad at me, and he wanted Bran to remember that we were a team. If he thought a little PDA would help, I was willing to let him run with it.

"You can stop at any time, Mercy," Adam said. "As much as I'm enjoying your stepping in to rescue me, it is not only unnecessary, it's likely to backfire."

He turned his attention to Bran. "We got a call from the Kennewick police that they needed our help with a troll. We had no idea it was anything more than that. I had two wolves already there, so I grabbed the other pack member and Mercy and we headed in."

Bran pinched the bridge of his nose. "Of course you did."

Behind him, someone snorted.

"Go on," Bran said.

"I have some video I e-mailed to you. Did you watch it?"

"It made the national news," said Bran. "I've already watched it five times."

Adam nodded. "Okay, then. You saw Mercy and Zack rescue a woman and her baby at the risk of their own lives. You saw Darryl get thrown off the bridge, get fished out by concerned citizens whom he did not hurt, and go running back up to fight the troll some more. 'Heroic efforts' was the phrase I heard over and over again. 'We could not have stopped that thing without more lives lost,' the police chief said. 'We are grateful to Adam Hauptman and his werewolves, who saved a whole lot of people.'"

"Just wait until they get the bill for the bridge," murmured Charles's voice—earning an irritated look Bran sent over his shoulder.

Charles was trying to calm Bran down, I realized. I shook my head. Hard to be dignified when you're sprawled across someone's lap, but I tried. "They will send the bill to the fae."

"If they can find the fae to give it to them," Charles said.

"Werewolves fighting the fae," said Bran.

Silence fell.

"I've been trying for six months to keep that from happening." Bran's voice had a rare growl in it. "To keep *this* from happening."

"Neutral doesn't work," Charles said. "When you watch your allies commit atrocities and do nothing, who is more reprehensible? Those who rape and plunder or those who could have stopped it but do nothing?"

"You are misquoting your grandfather," said Bran. "And you have caused me enough trouble. At least we could argue that the fae struck the first blow against us when you hunted down that fae lord in Arizona. Here, we are clearly the aggressor."

He took a deep breath, raised his chin, and stared at Adam—who stared right back, though I could feel the pulse of his effort not to drop his gaze.

"Very well, then," Bran said—and he was looking at me, not Adam. "Defend your territory."

"You heard that part," I said, fighting not to squirm. In retrospect, I regretted that my speech would have been at home on the set of *Cleopatra*, *The Ten Commandments*, or one of the other epic films from the middle of the last century before Hollywood decided to tone down the overacting. I could have done something more *Dirty Harry* and been just as effective—and less embarrassing.

"It's been playing in various cuts on the news stations all afternoon," said Charles. "CNN has a special show scheduled for tomorrow to discuss the fae and the werewolf pack that, and I quote, 'protected the people who live in their territory.' Unquote."

Bran tapped the top of his desk. "So you two, you see if you can back up Mercy's words. Your territory to hold when the fae come calling. There is a slim chance I can still keep this from being an all-out war between werewolves and the fae. There is a case to be made that we always have protected our territory from the fae—a fiction that stands only because they have not moved against the humans in five hundred years." He took a breath through his teeth. "If you succeed, I'll have to convince the other Alphas who live near the fae reservations to do the same—there are only two of them." He leaned his head back and closed his eyes, thinking. When he opened his eyes again, the anger was gone, though there was a grimness to his expression that I didn't trust. "Adam, be aware that if you let that boy go after twenty-four hours and something happens to him, all of the good publicity could easily turn against you."

Adam nodded, his body stiff. There was something going on that I wasn't reading, something hard and tense between Adam and Bran. I was getting a bad feeling about this conversation.

"Your pack has made enemies among my Alphas," said Bran. "Change is not easy on the old wolves. Your wholehearted embrace of it has created a lot of conflict, and they know, the old ones, exactly where to aim their ire. You should expect some challenges to your leadership from outside the pack, Adam, from other Alphas."

That was so unusual as to be almost unheard-of. Outside challenges usually came from lone wolves too dominant to be welcomed into a pack on their own. One of the secrets of Bran's successful rule was that he tried to keep track of the lone wolves and found places for them to be useful—even building new packs—to accommodate their needs. It didn't save them all, or even most of them, but it helped.

One Alpha only challenged another when two packs were too

close together—or if an Alpha had a personal vendetta against another. Such battles were supposed to be one-on-one, but, historically speaking, unless an Alpha was utterly useless, his pack would fight for him, too. Quite often both Alphas and most of both packs would die in the fight.

"I am aware," Adam said.

One of the things Bran had done was virtually eliminate fighting between packs. He'd send Charles out at the first hint of real conflict—and none of the werewolves wanted to have Charles land in the middle of their business. If he thought an Alpha was taking liberties without provocation, he was likely to take out that Alpha. He'd done it a couple of times I knew of, and I expected that the werewolves, who had longer memories, would know of other times.

So why was Bran issuing a warning now?

"Make her declaration real," Bran said in a low voice. "Give us grounds to make some places safe. Let us be heroes as well as monsters." He looked at me then. "And do *not* make this into a full-scale war."

"Unless you can't help it," murmured Charles.

"You know what this means," said Bran.

"I do," agreed Adam.

The two of them stared at each other for a moment, then Bran said, "I repudiate you and your pack. You are sundered from me and mine."

Something happened to the pack bonds, a shivery pain slid through them into my head and was gone a moment later. It hit Adam harder; he took a deep breath, and his whole body broke out in a light sweat.

Bran's eyes caught mine. He started to say something, then shook his head.

The monitor went blank for a moment, then the familiar Skype screen reappeared.

"He had to do that," Adam said. "Or else there would have been a war between werewolves and the fae. By cutting us off, by making us a rogue pack, he made sure that this stayed a local matter. We should expect that he will get word to the other packs and to the fae immediately, or else there would be no point."

He waited, then said in a soft voice, "Mercy, he had to do this."

"Of course he did," I said, still frozen on Adam's lap.

He leaned sideways and grabbed his cell phone off his desk. I started to get up, but his arm wrapped around my middle. He hit a button on the phone.

"Yes," said Darryl.

"We're on our own," Adam told him.

"I felt that," Darryl said, "and you warned us. I'll let the pack know."

"Tell them they can leave if they want to," he said.

Darryl laughed. "Like that will happen. After your performance tonight, you couldn't pry anyone out of this pack with a crowbar and a bucketful of dynamite, as Warren would say. No worries, we've got this."

Adam disconnected and set the phone back on the desk.

"I suppose," I said, my voice more wobbly than I liked, "that it's a good thing you yanked the pack's chain. If it's going to be us against the world, we better all be fighting the enemy instead of each other."

My stomach felt like I'd been kicked. Bran wasn't my father, wasn't even my foster father, but he had raised me just the same. "You knew this was going to happen?"

"I thought it might." Adam relaxed back against his seat and pulled me more tightly against him.

"I'm sorry," I whispered.

"Not your fault," he said.

"Uhm." I considered the progress of events again. "Yes, it is."

He shook his head. "Nope. If you hadn't given notice to the fae—what would they do next? I'm not willing to allow them to prey upon our town." He paused. The Tri-Cities are three towns . . . and a bunch of small towns tucked right up against them. "Towns. Our towns." He growled, and I made a sympathetic noise. He said, finally, "Our territory." That sounded right.

Bran might have cut me loose, but Adam would never do that. Adam was mine, and I was his. Sometimes I chafed a little at all the belonging I'd been doing lately: belonging to Adam, to Jesse, to the pack, and having them belong to me in return. Oddly, the responsibilities of taking care of them didn't bother me at all; only being taken care of brought out my claustrophobic reactions. I had spent most of my life being independent, and it took an effort to have to answer to other people, no matter how much I loved them. Loved him.

Right now, belonging felt a lot better than being alone. The last time Bran had abandoned me, I'd been alone.

"Are you done being mad at me?" Adam asked. He was changing the subject for me, I knew. There was nothing more to be said about Bran.

"I wasn't really mad at you," I told him. It wasn't a lie, because it had been myself I'd really been angry with. "You'd have known if I'd really been mad."

"For a good time, call—" he said, and I gave a watery laugh and put my forehead against his shoulder—his good shoulder.

The old VW still sat facing the backyard of this house, looking more and more disreputable every day. Once, Adam threatened to have it towed, and Jesse—not me—told him, seriously, that it was a bad idea.

"As long as Mercy has that way to torment you," she'd told her father, "you'll know where it's coming from. If you get rid of that now, you'll never know what to watch out for."

"She just wants to save it because she likes the bunny she painted on the trunk last week," I'd said.

Adam had laughed, and the wreck stayed where it was, with "For a Good Time Call" followed by Adam's phone number scrawled across it for anyone (in our backyard) to see.

"I am not mad at you," I told him. "But you should be aware that if you try to keep me away from you when you are hurt again, I will take you down when you least expect it."

"Seriously," he said, "I didn't expect it to work."

I lifted my head and looked at him. Maybe I hadn't been the only one I disappointed when I hadn't hunted him down in the infirmary. "I thought you were mad at me," I said. "I mean—look what I did when you couldn't defend the pack. I agreed to protect a boy that the fae had sent a *troll* after, and to cap it off, I told the world that we would protect the whole Tri-Cities from whomever and whatever. I figured that you needed time to cool down. I didn't realize how bad it was—though I knew it was bad enough—until I talked to Warren later. If I'd known, I wouldn't have let your anger, however righteous, keep me away."

"You stayed away because you thought I was mad?" he said, sounding . . . smug. Which was better than hurt.

"I stayed away because you wanted me to stay away," I growled at him. "That's not going to happen again."

He hugged me hard. "Good," he said, his voice muffled in my hair. "Don't let it happen again."

"We'll be okay, right?" I said. If I'd been sitting on anyone else's lap, I'd have been embarrassed by how little my voice was.

"You and I," he said, "will always be okay. I can't promise anything more."

"Me, either," I told him. "So what do we do about Aiden?"

What we could do, evidently, was let him sleep.

Tad was sitting on the floor in the rec room directly in front of the lockup-room door (which was shut, not locked). Cookie was curled up next to him, asleep. His legs were crossed in front of him, and they held a battered laptop. He had earphones in, and his fingers made castanet sounds on the keyboard. His mouth was moving silently. Reading his lips and making some educated guesses, he was saying, "Come on, come on, come on. I've got this, see? And boom, boom, boom. Like that, suckers. Just like that."

"Success?" Adam asked.

Tad looked up. For a moment his face was somber and . . . old. Then his mask came back up. "You betcha. I have really missed"— he raised his voice—"playing with you guys." There was a universal, but friendly, groan that echoed through the room where people, intent on their own laptops, were draped over various seats and couches like cats in a dry sauna, limp and happy.

"And they all died before me greatness, the scabbied old lot of 'em," he said. "Who is the greatest pirate of all?"

"Me," declared Paul. "The king of CAGCTDPBT. The ruler of ISTDPBF." CAGCTDPBT and ISTDPBF were the pack's favorite computer games. Codpieces and Golden Corsets: The Dread

Pirate's Booty Three, and Instant Spoils: The Dread Pirate's Booty Four, respectively. "You talk too much—and now you are dead, you lowly deck scrubber. Nothing but a landlubber with salty aspirations. Yarr harr and yohoho."

"Argh, verily, argh!" chorused the rec-room occupants obediently, though none of them raised their gazes off their monitors. Cookie woke up and barked a couple of times.

Tad looked at his laptop and scowled. "Now, that's not right. No one should die buried in fish eggs."

He looked back at us. "Jesse's in her room—she said something about 'homework waits for no woman,' and barred the door. I decided keeping an eye on Aiden would be useful. But after the barbecue, he wandered around the house, then retreated down here. I think he's asleep now." He frowned at his keyboard, debating with himself. Then he said, "He locked the window bars and came out ten minutes later and locked the door from the inside. He looked pretty spooked, and the locks make him feel safer." Tad glanced at the door to Aiden's room and shivered. "I don't know how long he was in Underhill, but a week would be enough to make me sleep in the closet with the door shut. It's not a place that feels like it could ever be safe."

I'd been there once, by accident. It hadn't lasted long, but it had not felt safe. I crouched, balancing on my heels, so my head was more on a level with Tad's. "What can you tell us about him?"

Tad shook his head. "Not much. Your buddy who broke us out brought him to us." He waited.

"What buddy?" I asked.

Tad raised his eyebrows and waited.

"You know which buddy," said Adam. "Think about it."

There was a certain Gray Lord who'd promised to help Tad and Zee in return for my giving him back the walking stick. But the walking stick hadn't stayed with Beauclaire, so I'd figured that he would count that bargain null and void. "Buddy" wasn't a word I would ever apply to Beauclaire.

"Okay," I said. "I know what buddy you're talking about. Though I'm a little surprised because—" Because I still had the walking stick. I swallowed my words. If Tad didn't think it was a good idea to talk about Beauclaire, then I would go along with his judgment. The whole pack knew that Beauclaire had come to me to get the walking stick, so I couldn't mention the stick or the reason I was surprised Beauclaire had helped them.

Tad waited until I'd finished working it out. Then he nodded. "Your buddy talked to me a couple of times. So I was prepared when he opened the cell where I'd been spending my alone time when they weren't torturing Dad to get me to perform for them." He sucked in a breath, and muttered, "Don't look like that, Mercy. They'll regret that for the rest of their short lives because . . . hey, it's Dad. And they've forgotten what Dad can do."

There was something dark and not-Tad in his voice. I was used to that when dealing with the werewolves. Sometimes in the middle of the conversation, there would be a switch, and instead of talking to my friend Warren or my husband Adam, I was talking to someone a little more direct, someone who could eat little coyotes for breakfast. So I was used to it, but I'd never seen something . . . someone so dark and violent in the man I thought of as a kid brother, a guy who was a little bit of a clown to cover up just how competent he was.

It was only for a moment. His voice was faintly cheerful as he said, "So your buddy opened the door, and he had Dad with him—and this kid. He told us that was as much as he could do, but that the kid could get us out and on our way. The kid, Aiden, had agreed to do this in return for my father's help in gaining him a little time—twenty-four hours of safety under the pack's protection. Hoping—as you probably have figured out—to see if he could finagle that into something really useful, like getting him away from here to somewhere else. Somewhere that he's not so likely to end up back with the fae"—the darkness was back, just for that one word—"who would like to take him apart to see how he works."

"We'll see," said Adam, as if Tad had asked him a question. "We need to know a lot more about him than he's told us. I'm not unhappy to thumb my nose at the fae—but I won't do it over someone who will turn around and stab my friends in the back. Not even if that someone looks like a helpless little kid."

Tad looked down at his computer screen and brushed it with a forefinger. "Sometimes it's hard to remember he's not just a kid, Adam. He was just human, not witchborn or anything. No one knows how he can do fae magic the way he does—not even the fae. They know it's something Underhill did, and they're jealous—as if Underhill stole something they thought belonged to them and gave it to a human."

Like Tad, I thought. Mostly the half fae were just messed up, but Tad had come out with a powerful talent for metal magic—which was rare even in full-blooded fae. Were they jealous of that, too?

Tad rubbed his face. "He's just human. But all I can think of is *Star Trek* and 'Charlie X.'"

"*Star Trek*?" I asked, puzzled.

Adam grunted. He put a hand on my shoulder. "Charlie is a

kid who survived a spaceship crash and was rescued by aliens," he said grimly. "They gave him powers so that he could survive. And, after a very long time, the *Enterprise* and her crew show up and rescue him. So he survived and is rescued . . . but he has all of this power and is turned loose on the universe without the experience of growing up human. He doesn't understand how to interact with people, how to listen when someone tells him 'no.' And because of his power, no one can make him stop. Eventually, the aliens have to come and take him back with them, where he will be alone for the rest of his life—because it's not safe for him to be out with the rest of the universe."

Tad nodded earnestly. "Now, your buddy who was repaying a favor to you, for a fae, he is pretty softhearted. I think he couldn't stand to watch what the fae were prepared to do to figure Aiden out. They killed the last one of these kids they found—last year. That one was water touched. They told Aiden that the water-touched boy was crazy, but from what your buddy told me, he wasn't crazy when he came out of Underhill. That happened later." He took a breath. "I don't think your buddy knows any more about what this kid is like than you or I do. I think he felt sorry for him. I do, too. He sure deserves a chance, don't you think? After surviving Underhill for all those centuries?"

"But 'Charlie X' weighs on your mind," Adam said. "Are you guarding him from harm, or us from him?"

Tad smiled. "Both, if you don't mind."

"You need to sleep," I said.

He nodded around the room at the occupied chairs and sofas. "I'll sleep down here just fine. Let Zack have the bedroom." He took a breath and smiled brightly. "I'd just as soon not be alone for a while anyway."

Paul glanced at him obliquely, met Adam's gaze, and nodded. Our pack had Tad's back. Tad could keep Aiden safe, and us safe—and the pack would keep him safe.

I made Adam strip and let me look at his shoulder.

There were bruises and swelling—a testament to how bad it had been. There had been other hurts, too. Places where I could see the faint remnants of bruises and damage. I touched those to make sure that what I was seeing was true healing and not some inner bleeding finding its way out.

Something that had been tight since I watched him run up the bridge for the first time relaxed. He was okay. He'd fought a troll and come out okay.

"Your turn," he said, while I ran my hands over a bump on his lower ribs.

"My turn?" It was an old bump, gotten before he'd become a werewolf. He'd told me that it used to be much worse: ragged, purple-edged scars over a broken rib where someone had shot him in another life on another continent. Some of his scars had disappeared overnight after he was Changed. But that one was fading gently. Someday it would be gone.

"Your turn." His voice was dark with something other than pain. "That's how we do this, remember. You check me out, I check you out."

I looked up at him to meet his eyes and saw heat that had nothing to do with the room temperature. "I don't think you are looking for bruises," I told him.

He put his hand under my chin, and without any kind of force, lifted me to my feet. "I've been a soldier," he told me, his home state of Alabama thick in his voice. "Been Alpha longer than that. Sometimes I think that I've been on the front lines for most of my life, one way or the other. And no one, but you, wants so badly to keep me safe. You'll have to forgive me if I find that sexy." He kissed me, and when he pulled back, the Southern gentleman was gone. "But I am not blind, so although I want you naked in the worst way," he told me conversationally, "I've also been watching you limp around all evening. So strip down and let me take a look."

I snickered. "You get many girls with that line?"

"Which one? The 'sometimes I think I've been on the front lines'?"

I waved my hand. "Nope. The"—I dropped my voice down in imitation of his—"'strip down and let me take a look' line." In my own voice, I said, "On the other hand, if you pulled out the wounded-soldier line, you'd be batting them off like flies." I paused, frowned at him. "You do know that the time for your using that line is gone, right? No more pickups for you. Alpha or no, I'll torture you to death, one day at a time." I looked at him, and he didn't seem to be taking me seriously. "Drip. Drip. Drip," I said. "If you even think about another woman like that."

He waited, a small smile on his face. "I understand," he said after waiting a courteous moment to make sure I was finished. "And just to keep such matters on the up-and-up, if I catch you flirting seriously with someone, I will rip out his throat."

"Fair enough," I said. "For the record, the 'strip down and let me take a look' line is not very sexy."

He raised an eyebrow. "Mercy"—he deepened his voice—"strip down and let me take a look."

I shook my head. "That's not fair. The voice doesn't count." But as I talked, I stripped down. Because underneath the sexy voice was worry, as if just because he'd hidden how bad his wounds were from me, I would have done the same to him.

My knees were skinned, one shin was bruised, and when Adam touched my chin, it hurt.

"From tripping while I was carrying you," I told him.

He nodded and turned his attention to a scrape on my hip. He was tanned, but my skin was still a shade or two darker than his, so mostly my bruises don't stand out as much as his. "This didn't come from a fall."

"It's just a scrape," I said.

He raised an eyebrow. Okay, it was a scrape and bruises that were still blossoming in glorious profusion.

"I honestly have no idea," I said.

He put his forehead against mine. "I'm sorry."

"About what?" I asked.

"Fussing," he said.

I wrapped my arms around him, trying not to see the troll lift a car over his head. "I fussed first," I said shakily. "I fussed first."

When he kissed me, it was a gesture of comfort. But with the both of us naked, it didn't stay that way for long. We made love on the soft carpet, and afterward, he fell asleep on top of me. Exhausted, I thought, from the fight and from the healing that followed. I held him and wondered what I'd done to us. Wondered what changes the boy would bring.

Coyote had told me once that changes were neither good nor bad—but brought with them some of both.

I closed my eyes and prayed for more good than bad, for Adam's safety, for Jesse and the pack. Then I thanked God for helping to return Tad and Zee out of the hands of our enemies. I fell asleep before I was finished.

The phone rang at four in the morning. My face was buried in my pillow—though I didn't remember moving from the floor to my bed. Adam moved, and the phone quit making that annoying noise—I almost fell back asleep.

"They told me, *Wulfe* told me, I should call you. That you're taking care of such matters now," said a high-pitched but sexless voice.

Wulfe's name had me sitting upright on the mattress.

"I see," said Adam.

The voice said, "We are paid to watch the hotels and motels around town and to call the Mistress's people when one of their kind shows up."

"I see," said Adam again.

There was a pause. "Are we going to get paid?"

"I am sure you will," Adam said. "I will call the Mistress and discuss the matter with her further. Is this a good number to reach you at?"

"Yassir," the voice said.

Adam ended the call.

"Do you know who that was?" I asked.

"Probably a goblin," Adam replied. "But I'm going to call and check."

Wulfe answered the phone himself. "Adam," he purred. "How lovely to hear from you."

"Goblins?" Adam asked.

"I see they contacted you," Wulfe said. "They are a little unreliable, so I wasn't sure they would."

"How much are you paying them?"

"Three hundred for every stray vampire they find," Wulfe told him. "And a thousand a month to keep them looking."

"I'll pay the three hundred," Adam said. "But I won't pay the thousand."

"Good luck finding the vampires who show up around here, then, darling," said Wulfe.

"Oh, I'll find them all right," Adam told him. "From what I understand, most of them are after Marsilia. I'll just keep an eye on the seethe, and when they find her, I'll find them."

There was a little silence. "Smart boy," said Wulfe, "aren't you just a smart boy. Fine. We'll pay the thousand. But they'll report to you, and you will pay for the actual sighting."

"Yes," Adam agreed.

The first change, I thought.

Adam disconnected and called the goblin back—explaining the new order to . . . him or her, I couldn't be sure from the voice alone.

Goblins, according to Ariana's book, were neither fish nor fowl. They qualified for status as fae—they could disguise what they were with illusion spells. But the fae didn't want them. For human purposes, the goblins counted themselves fae, without argument from the Gray Lords, but the goblins didn't want to be fae, either. Part of the problem seemed to be that goblins could reproduce as fast, if not faster, than humans, and the other part was that many of the fae considered goblin flesh a delicacy.

When Adam got off the phone, I said, "So the vampires are punishing you because I got uppity?"

He shook his head. "They're seeing if we're serious. Do you want to come with me to the hotel?"

I considered it. "Bran sends minions; he only goes himself if he needs to rain death and destruction down upon the world."

"Yes," Adam said. "But I'm awake, I might as well go check it out myself. I thought you might like to go along for the ride."

I couldn't help smiling—and it was stupid. There was a strange vampire in town, and my own hasty words meant that we had to go confront him or her. But Adam wanted me with him on an adventure.

"I'm coming," I said. I glanced at the clock. Six hours of sleep was plenty.

6

Adam put on one of the suits he had for work, power suits designed to let people know who was in charge. That they looked spectacular on him was a bonus for me and a matter of indifference, if not embarrassment, for him. I'd chosen this one, so the colors were right—steel gray with faint chocolate stripes that brought out his eyes. The tie he wore with it was the same chocolate brown. He might not care about looking pretty, but he did care about the impression of power he made.

People who were impressed by him were not so likely to try to screw him over, in business or with fang and claw. He enjoyed fighting, though I didn't think he'd ever admit it to anyone else. What he didn't like was the way fights could spill over onto the people he was responsible for: the people, human and other, who worked for his security company as well as the pack. He preferred to stop trouble before it happened when he could—thus, the suits.

After some serious consideration, I put on a blue silk blouse, a pair of black slacks, and shoes I could run in. Next to Adam, I didn't look underdressed, precisely—I looked like his assistant. But that was okay. Adam and I worked best together when he took point and I faded into the background. It suited our personalities. Adam was a "what you see is what you get" kind of guy, but I was happy to be sneaky.

We pulled into the Marriott parking lot, and I looked up at the balconies and sliding glass doors outside each room. The sky was still dark, but it wouldn't be in an hour.

"Unusual hotel for a vampire," I murmured as I got out of the car. The Marriott was covered with huge windows. Not that there was much choice; the Tri-Cities had mostly grown up during and after the Second World War, when the old hotels of small-windowed rooms, chandeliers, and ballrooms had given in to the practicality of the motel, efficient and graceless—with lots and lots of windows. Still, it seemed to me that the Marriott was awfully light and airy for a vampire to feel comfortable with.

I tucked my arm through Adam's, and we started for the hotel. We hadn't gotten three steps from the car before the sound of hard wheels on blacktop had us both turning to see a skinny teenager approaching us rapidly. Casually, I dropped Adam's arm and stepped back. The kid hopped off the skateboard with a kick that threw the board up so he could catch it without bending down. He stowed it under one arm as he walked.

"Hey, man," he said, his voice familiar from the early-morning call, but it was far more laid-back—less meth-head and more stoner. "I looked you up on the Internet to see why suddenly I'm dealing with the werewolves and not the vampires. Nice work on that troll."

"Was it?" asked Adam. "There aren't many trolls left, I am given to understand."

The boy spat on the ground. "They can all rot for all I care. Nasty pieces of work, trolls—killing 'em ain't no cause for tragedy. Now, I'd like to get paid and get out of here before someone wonders why I'm riding around on this toy at five in the morning."

"What did the vampire look like?" I asked.

He shrugged, but there was something sly in his eyes when he said, "Weren't me what saw him." He held out his hand.

Adam handed him an envelope. The goblin in human guise dropped the skateboard back on the ground and hopped on the battered and scarred surface. He didn't stop it when it started to drift backward. He gave Adam a salute with the hand that held the white envelope, dropped a toe, and spun his board around to speed off into the night.

Three cars down from where Adam had parked there was a white Subaru Forester with California plates. I remember cars, a hazard of my job. I tugged Adam to a stop and examined it more carefully.

Subaru Foresters weren't uncommon—there were three others in the parking lot. But I'd followed this one for miles last winter. I sniffed at the driver's-side door and smelled a familiar vampire.

"Thomas Hao," I said. I'd fought beside Thomas a couple of months ago, and we'd helped Marsilia destroy a nasty vampire. I wondered if Marsilia had known who he was when she turned him over to us this morning. I considered the goblin's half lie about not being the one who saw the vampire and decided she did.

"This should be interesting," said Adam after a moment, but he'd relaxed a little, and so had I.

Thomas Hao was the Master of San Francisco. That's all I'd known about him the last time we met. But it turned out that he was something of an enigma, even by vampire standards. Like

Blackwood, the vampire I'd helped kill in Spokane, Hao ruled without other vampires in his city. Unlike Blackwood, Hao was the opposite of crazy. He'd never had a large seethe, but a couple of years ago he'd shooed the few vampires he controlled out to other seethes and remained in San Francisco alone. No one knew why, though there were lots of stories about Thomas Hao, about what happened when someone made a move against him. I'd seen him hold off two very powerful, very old monsters all by himself.

There was no question that Thomas was a very dangerous vampire. But he was also a man of principle and logic, not driven by ambition. It wasn't just me who thought so. As vampires went, Hao was almost a good man. I liked him.

It didn't take long to find his room. We got on the elevator that smelled of him and hit every button on the way up. His room was on the top floor. We followed Thomas's scent down the hall.

"There is a fae here, too," I whispered. I'd first scented her downstairs, and her track followed Hao's too closely for coincidence.

Adam nodded and knocked softly at the door where Thomas's scent had led us. No need to bother the neighbors, and a vampire would hear us.

"A moment," said Thomas's voice. It would not have carried to human ears, so he wasn't expecting room service.

The vampire opened the door and regarded us for a moment. He was dressed in a brown silk button-down shirt and black jeans. His feet were bare, and his hair was damp. I never had been able to read his face, but I could read his body language. Whoever he'd been expecting, it had not been us.

He was not a big man, but in vampires, that didn't mean much. His hair was cut short and expensively. He smelled of the fae woman whose scent trail had paralleled his, as if he might have been touching her just before he answered the door.

He stepped back and gestured us in, closing the door behind us when we accepted his wordless invitation. His room was a suite with a pair of chairs and a couch in the living area and a view that, in the daylight, would be of the Columbia River. There was a door toward the back of the room, and it was shut.

"Please," he said to us, "take a seat. May I get you some refreshments? If you do not enjoy alcohol, there is soda, I believe, as well as water."

Polite vampire. It was a good thing that Adam and I had come, that we hadn't sent a pair of werewolves who could have misread Thomas and tried to issue threats—assuming Thomas would have been polite to other werewolves.

"Water," Adam said. "Thank you."

Thomas looked at me. "Water is good for me, too," I said. "Thank you." We all had good manners here, yes, we did.

He served us the water and took a glass and filled it from an already opened bottle of red wine. He took a sip of wine and smiled politely. "To what do I owe this visit?"

"I'm afraid that is our question," Adam replied.

"You were expecting Marsilia or Wulfe, right?" I asked.

"I called them when we got in," he said. "And Wulfe assured me that someone would be over before long. I did not expect to see the Alpha of the Columbia Basin Pack and his wife running errands."

Marsilia had known who was here all right.

"Errands," said Adam thoughtfully.

None of us had taken a seat, I realized.

"Marsilia can't send us on errands," I told Thomas. "We inherited this job." I thought about that. "'Inherited' is the wrong word. Co-opted. Not quite the right word, either. Had it dumped on us unexpectedly."

Thomas frowned thoughtfully. "I saw a news program earlier," he said. "You killed a troll and proclaimed the Tri-Cities your territory."

He was looking at me. I cleared my throat. "I didn't kill the troll. That was Adam and some of the pack. And, technically speaking, the whole of the Tri-Cities has always been our territory."

I caught something in Thomas's gaze, and I realized that he was highly amused—though it didn't show on his face except for a quirk of his eyebrow. But I was positive I was right.

"As you saw"—I was going to have to find the news clip myself so I would know exactly what people knew about it—"I made a true but unpolitic declaration on the bridge yesterday. The fallout of that is still settling." I pinched the bridge of my nose hard to distract myself from that thought. No need to panic in front of a vampire. Adam's hand touched the small of my back.

"So when one of the vampire's snitches called us to tell us there was a vampire visiting," I continued. Adam was letting me do a lot of the talking, and I wondered why. "We contacted the seethe. Wulfe indicated that Marsilia was ceding the job of policing stray vampires to us. He didn't say *you* had called them, just that his minions had found a strange vampire who'd checked into this hotel."

"We'll have to discuss that with him," murmured Adam.

Hao laughed then, showing his fangs in a manner that might have been accidental if he'd been a new vampire or someone less subtle. I'd noticed before that the vampire only laughed or smiled for effect rather than because he was actually amused or happy. I was pretty sure that happy and he were seldom in the same room at the same time. He stopped abruptly.

"What do you need to feel that you have successfully defended your territory?" he asked.

"The usual," drawled Adam. "What are you doing here and how long are you staying? Restrict your feeding to nonfatal and non-publicity-gathering ways. Be a good guest."

Thomas nodded. "Fair enough. It's no more than I told Marsilia. I am here as escort for a friend traveling to Walla Walla. I will stand at her back while she tells the Gray Lords where they can stick their decrees."

Apparently, we weren't going to pretend that he didn't have a fae in his bedroom.

"Marsilia," Thomas Hao continued, "owes me on several fronts, which made the Tri-Cities seem safer to rest in than Walla Walla." He paused.

"I have no quarrel with you," said Adam.

Thomas inclined his head. "We'll stay here all day and one more day, then return home the following evening. I have no need to hunt at this time. If that changes, I will kill no one under your protection who has not harmed me or mine."

"Thomas." The door to the bedroom opened, and a woman came out. She walked steadily with the help of a pair of crutches, the kind that wrap around the forearm instead of the ones that fit under the armpit. "You sound like a fae driving a bargain." She didn't sound as if she were complimenting him, even though she was fae herself.

The social temperature in the room dropped to well below zero. Thomas Hao lost his humanity, a very dangerous predator, with a half-empty glass of wine in his hand.

They weren't lovers, I didn't think. The body language and scent were wrong for that. The scents of lovers tend to blend rather than lie on top of each other. His fierce protectiveness told me that whatever their relationship was—he would kill to protect her, and he was ready to do so right now.

Like Hao, she was dressed in silk, an opaque shift that covered her from shoulders to midcalf. The gown was simple and might have been plain if it weren't for the color, which was white for the first few inches, then a yellow that deepened all the way down the garment to a rich, bitter orange at the hem.

Also like Hao, she was barefoot. Her eyes, as they met mine, were crystal-clear gray. Her hair was very close to the fiery color of the hem of her gown. With that hair and the milk-white skin, she should have had freckles, but I saw no sign of them—of course, she was fae. If she had freckles and didn't like them, she could have hidden them. But I suspected she just didn't have them, because she'd made no effort to disguise more egregious barriers to the out-and-out beauty that I suspected was hers by nature.

She was so thin that I could see both bones in her forearms. Huge red scars wrapped around her wrists and ankles as if she'd been bound and all but ripped off her extremities trying to get free.

"Introduce me, please," she said. Adam glanced from the vampire to the fae. He took a step back. He reached out and grabbed my hand so that when he sat down on the overstuffed couch, he pulled me down as well. He settled back, letting the couch half swallow him. I sank down next to him, and he wrapped one arm around my shoulder. Even so, Thomas stared at Adam for a count of three until the fae woman made it to his side.

"Manners," she said without reproof, though she repeated, "You should introduce us, Thomas."

"Margaret Flanagan," said Thomas, pulling his gaze from Adam's with an effort, "may I make you known to Adam Hauptman, Alpha of the Columbia Basin Pack, and his mate, Mercedes Thompson Hauptman. Adam and Mercy, may I make known to you my friend, Margaret Flanagan." His voice was thick as he fought for control.

The fae woman inclined her head in a motion that reminded me forcefully of Thomas's gestures. "I have heard Thomas speak of you, Ms. Hauptman. He said you fought well—high praise from him."

She sounded cool and gracious, not to mention very Irish. Thomas smiled at Adam and me in clear warning. He was marking his territory.

"I should have stayed in the other room," she told us, but she was watching Thomas with . . . some odd combination of affection and worry. "Doubtless, Thomas will scold when you have left. He chooses to forget that though my body is still weak, my power is not. I appreciate that you gave him the courtesy of removing yourself as a threat, Mr. Hauptman. I am in your debt."

The vampire whirled on her. "No. You should know better than that, Sunshine," he growled. "The last time you owed someone, it turned out badly."

"Did it?" she asked. He stared at her. "I don't think it did, Thomas."

"No debt necessary," said Adam. "Just common courtesy—and I know what it is to try to protect someone who insists on putting themselves at risk." He didn't look at me, but he didn't need to.

"Nonetheless," she insisted, "Thomas is important to me, and he would regret your deaths."

"Why didn't you go to the reservations when all of the rest of the fae had to?" I asked, to change the topic before Adam could respond to that.

"I am *the Flanagan*, Mercy," she said without arrogance. "As was my father, the Dragon Under the Hill. They have not the authority to tell me where to go or what to do. The courts of the fae are long gone, but my father was king, and that means power of the like many have forgotten. He saved the world, and they let him die while they sat congratulating themselves on how well the fae were blending in with the humans in this new land. They let him die because they were afraid of him. He died very, very slowly, and there are some on the reservation here to whom I would extend that same courtesy if I am given the opportunity."

Adam and Thomas had fallen silent while she talked, her voice as pleasant as if she'd been discussing the weather. If someone had asked me at that moment who was the most dangerous person in the room—the werewolf alpha, the powerful vampire, or the skinny and broken fae—I wouldn't have hesitated to name her. I didn't know what her mojo was—her talk of courts, kings, and dragons went largely over my head—but *she* was certain that she could take out the Gray Lords. I was willing to give her the benefit of the doubt.

"Good to know," I said.

She smoothed her skirt. "I am the Flanagan, and that means they *asked* me to come. I have decided that it would be better to make some things clear in person." Her gray eyes were chilly.

"He's in love with her," said Adam. "Poor fool."

The sun was sneaking out to greet the day as we drove home. I twisted around until I could see his face.

"A blind man could see that," I said. "Why 'poor fool'?"

"Because he hasn't made a move on her," he said. "I recognize that half-crazed desire to say, 'Mine, mine, mine,' tempered by love that would never do that without a permission that will never come."

"Yours came," I told him.

He snorted.

"Hey," I said, holding up the chain on my neck where my wedding ring held court next to one of his dog tags and my lamb charm.

"Nudge?" he said.

I looked at the cars traveling beside us as we trekked down the interstate. "Here? Seriously?"

"Permission that will never come," he said.

"That's not funny," I said.

He took my hand and gently tugged it away from my necklace and kissed it. "Yes, it is." He winked at me. "But yes, it only seemed like forever before you gave in. It left me with sympathy for other guys in that situation."

I thought about how the fae woman had put herself in our debt, something not lightly done by any fae, because Adam had backed down and allowed Thomas space.

"She's not uninterested," I said, settling back in my seat. "Did you parse what she said about her place in the power structure of the fae? It didn't sound like the Elphame court of the fairy queen." I'd met a fairy queen: a fae with the rare ability to make anyone with less power than she had into a follower—a form of magical slavery.

Adam shook his head. "No. It's a real court system. I've only heard a little of the fae courts. They were gone before the fae traveled to this continent. Nothing to impress the Gray Lords—except that it is a measure of the power her father and, evidently, she holds. They wouldn't be asking her to join them; they'd be issuing orders if they weren't convinced of her power."

"Like Ariana," I said.

"For different reasons," Adam agreed. "Ariana made herself unwelcome because of what she held. No Gray Lord is going to want to be around something that can siphon his magic away—or any fae who could have created it. Thomas's fae is powerful. Did you smell what I did?"

"Fire," I agreed. "Like Aiden—only more so. We're sure knee-deep in fiery things right now."

"You think it's more than coincidence?" asked Adam. It is a mark of how much he loved me that his voice was merely bland, not cutting. Adam believed in God all right, and they were not best buddies.

"Mmmm," I said. "Karma or coincidence, or something, maybe. Doesn't really matter."

We pulled into the driveway, and I examined the silver Accord parked in Adam's usual spot and managed not to growl. What was Adam's ex-wife doing here this early? In two more weeks, she was supposedly moving back to Oregon, where she had a new condo and her old job waiting for her. I would celebrate when she actually left and not a moment before then.

I hopped out of the SUV and noticed that a lot of the cars and trucks that had been parked here when Adam and I left were gone. It took me a moment to remember that this morning was a Monday.

Adam would work from home, as he often did, but most of our pack had more mundane employment that involved schedules. Before my shop was trashed, I'd had a place to be and a reason to remember what day of the week it was, too.

Adam paused by Christy's car. He looked tired.

"Why don't you get started arranging guards for Hao," I said. "I'll go see why Christy came over today."

We'd discovered that if he wasn't standing there, Christy and I could come to a meeting of minds. There would be snark and snarling, but in the end we could deal with each other. Mostly, I suspected, because without Adam's presence to remind her that I'd won the prize she'd tossed away, she remembered to be afraid of what I might do if she made my life too unpleasant. It was a pretty good return for a box of blue dye, if I did say so myself.

"She's not your problem," he said.

She couldn't hurt me, but she could hurt Adam. She'd had years of practice to develop her aim. "It's no trouble," I said.

He smiled. "That's a lie."

"It is my privilege," I said carefully, trying not to tweak his pride, "to do those things that are easier for me than for you. You do the same for me. Let me deal with her."

That was the truth.

Adam hesitated. It was in his nature to protect the people around him. I'd been working on him to let me do the same for him.

"If she's here for you, there's nothing I can do," I told him. "But if she's just here for Jesse, keeping you out of the picture might keep the nastiness quotient down a fair bit—and that will make things easier for Jesse."

He leaned forward and kissed me. "You know the magic words," he said.

I bounced on my heels and grinned.

Adam headed for his office as soon as we came in, and I headed for the kitchen, where I could smell breakfast. I'd gotten a few steps farther when I realized that it wasn't just bacon I could smell cooking. Then I noticed that there was a funny sort of silence in the air.

There were four people in my kitchen. Jesse was plastered

against the counter with the same "someone's gonna die today" look I'd seen on her father's face a time or two. Adam's ex-wife Christy stood in front of Jesse with a damp dishcloth in her hand. Aiden was pressed tightly against the refrigerator with his feet about a foot off the floor because one of Darryl's very large hands was wrapped around his throat. Darryl's hand was smoking, and his eyes were glowing bright yellow.

All righty.

"Drop the munchkin, Darryl," I said in as relaxed a voice as I could find. There were too many fragile humans in here to allow this to break out into a real fight. "We promised not to let him get killed for twenty-four hours, right?"

Darryl took a step back, but his hand was still wrapped around Aiden's throat. Then Darryl shook his hand, and Aiden dropped to his feet, lost his balance, and fell on his rump, a feral snarl on his face as he scrambled out of the vulnerable position.

"If you do what you're thinking about doing, Aiden," I said, "I'll let Darryl loose."

"Then he'll die," said Aiden, who'd managed to find his feet and stood in an angry crouch.

"Mmmhmmm," I said. I wasn't sure Aiden wasn't right, but it's never good to show fear in front of your enemies. I really, really wished I had some idea of just how powerful Aiden was.

There was a cardboard box of doughnuts on the counter: ah, Spudnuts. Probably Christy had brought them, but I took one out to eat anyway, as it was unlikely she'd poisoned them: she wouldn't have known which one I'd eat.

I like most doughnuts, especially Spudnut doughnuts—but the glazed one I ended up with, covered with pink sprinkles, was not one of my favorites. But the point of eating was to give everyone time and reason to cool off.

"You kill Darryl, and I don't think you're going to walk out of here alive," I said, conversationally, around a bite of glazed-with-sprinkles doughnut. I ignored Darryl's indignant grunt when I agreed that Aiden might actually accomplish his death.

"I've faced creatures that would kill every living thing in this house without an effort, and I'm still alive," he said grimly. "Try me."

"Good doughnuts, Christy," I said. Jesse put her finger to her lips when her mother would have said something. I licked my fingers—a waste of time until I finished the doughnut. "Look, Aiden, you are counting on our being enough that the Gray Lords back off, right? If the Gray Lords are afraid of us, don't you think you should at least consider being afraid enough to back down from outright aggression into a position where negotiation can take place? If you aren't worried about *us*, I might point out that the Dark Smith of Drontheim is upstairs."

The tile under Aiden's feet cracked with a loud pop, but he stood up from his defensive crouch. The tiles surrounding the cracked tile were discolored by the heat he was generating. It was ceramic tile. I wasn't sure how much heat was required to crack ceramic tile, though I rather suspected that it was less heat than was needed to burn a house to the ground. We all stared at it a moment—even Aiden.

"My floor," gasped Christy.

Yes. She had picked out the tiles in the kitchen, hadn't she? I regarded Aiden with a little more favor than I'd felt before.

"Information first," I said. "Does anyone want to tell me what happened?"

"I was watching the bacon," Jesse said coolly. "And the next thing I know, the little creep was grabbing my butt."

I trust I caught my instinctive clench of teeth before anyone saw it. No one touches my daughter without her permission—since Darryl had already made that clear, there was no need for me to come unhinged. Adam, whom I could sense listening from his office—he must have left his door open—apparently felt the same way, because Aiden was still breathing and Adam wasn't in the kitchen. Yet. I started a countdown in my head.

"They were treating me like a child," Aiden said.

"What does that have to do with anything?" I asked.

He looked at me as if I were an idiot. "Children are victims— I am neither child nor victim, despite what I look like. It was necessary that I do something to remind everyone that I might be in a child's form, yet I own more years than anyone here."

I blinked at him, so totally nonplussed that I was robbed of anger. That was an excuse I'd never heard before.

"So," Jesse said in the same cool voice, evidently not as distract-ible as I was, "not regarding him as a child, I smacked his face with the spatula."

That was my Jesse. She'd hit him hard, too, because, now that the flush of color he'd acquired while Darryl was strangling him had faded, I could see the rectangular red mark on his face.

"Mom had just come in with doughnuts, and we were talking, or I'd have seen him sneaking up on me." She paused her story to answer the question on my face. "I don't know why she's here, Mercy, she hasn't had a chance to say. She yelled at him—and that brought Darryl."

Succinct, I thought, a little out of order, but with all the essential information.

"Grab my daughter's butt again, and you draw back a stump," growled Adam as he strode into the room two seconds after I expected him. He thanked Darryl with a nod but never took his eyes off the fae. "And I don't care what you were trying to prove."

"She's your daughter?" The anger drained away from Aiden, leaving him looking like we'd just pulled the rug out from under him. "She was making *food*," he said. "And I saw her carrying food and drink yesterday. I thought her but a servant." He looked around, and indignation replaced his look of helpless confusion. "She called that woman 'Mother,' and I knew you were mated to this woman." He gestured toward me. "How was I to know that you had two wives?"

Whiny, yes, I thought, wrong on many fronts, but also truthful. He was upset, not because he'd grabbed Jesse's rump without permission but because it had been Adam's daughter's rump. Not a stellar individual, I thought, finishing off the doughnut, but look how he was raised. Feral didn't begin to describe the likely result of being human and raised by . . . Underhill? The fairies? But he might still be salvageable.

I took the damp cloth from Christy's hand and wiped my fingers with it. Salvageable by someone else. He was only going to be with us for another six hours or so.

Darryl flexed his hand, and bits of burnt flesh dropped to the floor, leaving his skin raw-looking but no longer charred. "Little man," he growled, "you don't touch unless you are invited. Not in this house—and if you are a gentleman, not ever. Servant, slave, or lady of the house."

"I've broken my word," Aiden said, gathering his dignity around himself. "I'll leave."

I almost let him go. But Zee had asked me—in the only way Zee would ask such a thing. I owed Zee.

"I knew I missed something," I said. "I should have put in a clause about protecting yourself, right? Grandstanding is a very bad way to make bargains—it's too easy to leave things out. But I can do that now. Let's see." I cleared my throat. "I declare that you can use the minimum force necessary to protect yourself until misunderstandings are cleared up—as long as you apologize right now and don't do it again."

Darryl gave me a look. Adam did, too. It was probably a very good thing that Aiden looked like a ten-year-old.

"Are you hurt, Darryl?" I asked.

He rubbed his hands together. "Not anymore," he said.

"Darryl's job is to make sure people are safe," I said. "Did you disobey him?"

Aiden screwed up his face. "You are very strange," he said. "I insulted your . . . stepdaughter, yes? Then I hurt the man who stood up for her honor."

Jesse made a growling noise. "I stood up for myself, you little perv."

Aiden looked at her.

She glared back.

"Okay, then," I said. "Aiden, it is good manners to apologize when you offend someone. In your case, it means that you can continue to enjoy the protection of the pack for a few more hours."

He turned to Adam, and said, sincerely, "Please accept my apologies for importuning your daughter."

He turned to Jesse's mother. "I am also sorry that I distressed you in any manner." He bowed to Darryl. "I sincerely apologize for burning you. You weren't hurting me, just scaring me. There was no cause."

Jesse cleared her throat. He looked at her, and they eyed each other with mutual loathing. His lip curled. "I'm very sorry you don't appreciate the honor I did you," he said. "I won't make that mistake again."

He was lucky she didn't hit him a second time, I thought.

"I'm very sorry," Jesse said sincerely, "that I didn't have a kitchen knife in my hand instead of a spatula. Next time, maybe I'll be more careful."

"Jesse," I said, "your eggs are burning."

I looked at Adam. "You take Aiden, and I'll take Christy?" I mouthed.

"I'd like to speak to Adam," Christy said, her tone making it clear she'd seen me. No help for it once she asked.

I shrugged. "Aiden, step outside with me."

Darryl smiled. "I'll go check the perimeter. It'll let me keep an eye on you."

"You could stay with Jesse," I said because I didn't trust that smile: it was a little too eager. "Help her with breakfast or something."

"I can cook eggs," said Jesse, scraping the blackened remnants into the garbage disposal, "assuming I don't have to teach some ancient punk kid how to keep his hands to himself. Yuck." She left it to her audience to decide where that last word was directed.

Aiden turned back and narrowed his eyes at her.

"Aiden," I said.

He stiffened but followed me out to the backyard, where he stood, his arms wrapped around himself in hostile rejection . . . or possibly fear. Darryl trailed after us, then broke into a jog and headed for the river side of the property.

"What happened in there was all about power," I said thoughtfully after Darryl was a sufficient distance away.

151

Aiden didn't say anything.

I thought about power, about how Adam had sat in the soft hotel sofa to make Thomas Hao feel more at ease. So I sat down on the grass. The seat of my pants was immediately wet and cold— evidently the lawn had just been watered. At least my slacks wouldn't show the water stain the way my usual jeans would have. Aiden looked at me, frowned, then took a seat on the nearest lawn chair.

"You felt it was dangerous for us to consider you a child," I said, "because in your world, children are vulnerable, and the fae like to prey upon them." I pushed my fingers into the soil. "Werewolves are not fae. For the pack, children are fragile, and the wolves, most of them anyway, see them as a charge, someone to be protected from all harm."

"I would be safer, here, pretending to be the age that my body appears?" he asked warily.

I sighed and shook my head. For all that we both spoke English, we were alien, weren't we?

"No," I said. "Pretending is a lie—and wolves can tell if you lie. But you didn't have to make a big deal of your real age in order to be safe. But I was talking about power, not specifically about you." I looked up at the sky and thought about how to explain twenty-first-century manners and morals to someone who had last been human before Europeans had set foot on this continent.

"Touch," I said, "is basic to the human condition. Mothers touch their babies to bond with them. Touch brings comfort or pain. Touch is important. The most powerful person in a room is the one who can touch anyone else—and no one can touch him back without permission." The Romans would have substituted "sex" for "touch," but I thought I didn't have to go that crude. Sometimes, when dealing with very old creatures, my history degree was unexpectedly useful.

"Lady," Aiden said sincerely, "you are strange. You are saying that I am less powerful than the girl." He held out his hand and showed me the fire he held. "I do not think so."

"Think about what happened in there," I said. "Who ended up winning that encounter?"

"She hit me," he said, "but I could have killed her—or hurt her so she never would have tried to hit me again."

"But Darryl stopped you," I told him. "Because he is more powerful, and his job is to take care of Jesse. To make sure no one touches her without permission."

"I could have killed him, too," said Aiden.

I shrugged. "Yes. But he has those who protect him, too. And you are not stronger than Zee—the Dark Smith."

Silence.

I nodded. "So what is power for, Aiden?"

"To be safe," Aiden said without hesitation.

A sociology professor of mine had asked that in my college class. She got answers ranging from wealth to the ability to do whatever you wanted to whomever you wanted. She said that when she'd asked that question in a village in a South American country that was on its fifth dictator in ten years, she'd gotten only one answer: safety.

"Okay," I said, wondering what it said about Underhill that Aiden had that much in common with people who'd lived with uncertainty and terror for generations. "So what did you do when you touched Jesse without permission?"

There was a long pause. "I made her feel unsafe," he said.

I shook my head. "Not really. She had no trouble defending herself—and she knew there was a houseful of people who would make sure she was safe. What you did do was tell her that you had no intention of letting her be safe with you."

He said nothing.

"You are safe with us," I told him. "We will not touch you nor allow anyone else to touch you while you are under our protection."

"The big man with the dark brown skin touched me," he said.

"Darryl." I nodded. "You're right. So unless you threaten one of our own, we will not allow you to be touched without your permission. We have the power to do that, and we extend that power to you—to our pack and to Jesse. Power comes from three places, Aiden. It comes from the power that you have as an individual. Some people have a lot of that—Zee has a lot of power just from being himself. Someone can leverage the power they have to take more power—but power taken by force only lasts as long as you can hold it. Most dictators don't live long lives."

He said, sounding offended, "The third way to gain power is to have others give you their power. I am not a child; nor am I stupid."

I nodded, though I thought the jury was out on the last. "I'm pretty weak as far as creatures of magic are concerned. I have a few tricks. But I was able to grant you sanctuary from the Gray Lords— because I have friends, I have pack, and I have people who love me." I turned my head, met his eyes, and frowned at him. "You are going to need a lot of power to stay safe from the Gray Lords. Right at this moment, that means you need to work at making people want to help you—instead of wanting to strangle you and shove your head through a refrigerator."

He threw up his hands and cried out with honest frustration,

"But how do I do that? I don't understand you people. I don't know your customs. I don't know anything about this place."

"Okay," I told him. "Sometimes you have to start just knowing you don't know anything. But if you assume that you are on the bottom of the pack—that means no touching anyone without invitation—you will be safe because I have promised you that, and I have the power to make that stick. But I cannot protect you from your own bad decisions; if you go around grabbing women's butts, they might hit you with something a little sharper next time."

Aiden stared at me. "You are very strange. I have no intention of coming anywhere near the Alpha's daughter again."

"That's probably safer for you," I agreed.

Jesse opened the back door. "Mercy," she said, "Dad's still in his office with Mom, and we have *a visitor* who wants to see you or Dad." The subtle emphasis meant that Jesse knew who it was but didn't think she should mention it in front of Aiden. That meant fae.

I stood up and dusted off the back of my pants, which were wet. "Okay," I said. "In the interest of keeping our word, Aiden, you should come inside."

"Why?" he sneered. "There are two werewolves watching the backyard. Aren't three enough to give alarm? Or do you acknowledge that the fae can come into your territory and take me?"

Warren and Ben weren't being obvious—I could smell them, but I couldn't see them. Darryl had disappeared while I wasn't watching.

"If we keep the weakest of us—that's me—and the one most likely to be attacked—that's you—in the same place, we keep our defense stronger than if we scatter them between us." And there is a fae here to see us. I realized I hadn't told him that because he looked

7

I sent Aiden to wait in the kitchen, and Jesse headed upstairs to get ready for school. I didn't think that Uncle Mike had come here to take Aiden by force but decided that keeping him discreetly in the heart of the house would be prudent.

Uncle Mike was . . . not a friend. The only fae I trusted enough to consider a friend was Zee. But Uncle Mike was someone I knew and mostly liked. He'd run an eponymous bar in Pasco where, in days before their sudden retreat, the fae had hung out with various members of the local supernatural community.

That Jesse had opened the door to him and left Uncle Mike in the living room was a testament to the neutrality that Uncle Mike had built while running his bar. Jesse trusted him more than I did. I'd have been happier if she'd left him on the front porch rather than letting him in herself, but no apparent harm had come from it.

As I crossed the foyer, I could hear the low murmur of voices coming from Adam's office, but, with the door shut, the soundproofing was too good to hear anything specific. Uncle Mike stood, arms clasped behind his back, looking out the window. He was so intent that I looked out, too, but I could see nothing that should have inspired such interest.

After a moment, he turned, and said, "Mercy."

Uncle Mike looked like a worn and distilled version of himself. The Jolly Innkeeper persona was almost gone, leaving in his place a broad-shouldered, broad-handed man with reddish brown hair and tired hazel eyes.

"Uncle Mike," I greeted him. "It has been a while. I'm surprised to see you here."

His lips curled into a shadow of his usual smile. "Not as surprised and four times as pleased as my compatriots, I vow."

"You've been reading *The Lord of the Rings* again," I said, and he grunted.

"So the people ruling the reservation these days don't know you're here and would be upset to know it," I said. "Why *are* you here?"

"Not to interfere with your rash protection of the Fire Touched," he said in an overly loud voice obviously intended to reach the far ends of the house—and Aiden's ears. Then, in a much softer voice, he said, "One of my flitflits told me that she'd heard that the Dark Smith and his boy were on the bridge with you yesterday. I discounted it until I heard that the Fire Touched escaped and that he was under the protection of the pack. My news sources aren't as reliable as they once were, but it was not hard to connect both stories." He flexed his short fingers and put them down on his knees, leaned forward, and said, "Several weeks ago, I was told that the Dark Smith had been executed for failure to cooperate sufficiently, and also that his son died soon after—half-bloods being so much more fragile than we."

"The fae cannot lie," I told him, wondering what a flitflit was. I puzzled over it too long and missed my cue, though.

He'd relaxed as soon as I'd spoken, and I realized I'd pretty much given away Zee's still-alive status by not freaking out when Uncle Mike said he'd heard that he was dead.

"Yes, we cannot lie," he said. "And after I heard the stories, I thought on what I was told and by whom. I think that the one who told me believed what she said, and the one who told her was cunning with his words—as his reputation leaves him to be."

"Zee's alive," I told him. "And what's a flitflit?"

And even though he had known that from my reaction, he still drew in a deep breath as if he hadn't had many deep breaths in a long time. "And so it is true."

"And if it is?" asked Zee from the stairway, his voice arctic.

Uncle Mike smiled. This time it was the full-force, hugely charismatic smile that made the part of me that detected magic sit up and take notice. "Well, then," he said, satisfaction lacing his voice. "Some people are going to be looking over their shoulders, now, aren't they?"

Zee tipped his head to the side. "That is an interesting notion. I'm not sure I know what you're talking about."

"Don't you, now," said Uncle Mike in evident satisfaction. "Just don't you, old friend."

"What," I asked again, "is a flitflit?"

"Lesser fae," Zee said. "They flitflit around and hear things. Uncle Mike has a number of them who are personally loyal to him."

The other fae nodded. "What do you want me to do about what I know?"

Zee frowned. "You see me standing before you. I trust you aren't in the mood to change my status?"

"Someone wanted us to think you dead," Uncle Mike said. "Do you want me to disabuse them of that notion—or let it play out?"

Zee gave him a sour smile. "What do I care? I don't play those games—I don't play any games."

The smile that spread over Uncle Mike's face was sharklike and sharp. "Someone forgot that, forgot whom they were dealing with. Good." He breathed out deeply, and said, "Very good."

He walked to the door and opened it, pausing on the threshold and turning back. "I am reassured as to your health, old friend. I look forward to being in the audience for your next act." He bowed his head to Zee, then to me, before stepping outside and closing the door, very gently, behind him.

Zee watched him leave, listened to the car as it drove off, and came the rest of the way down the stairs. He did it without limping or making noise or any other thing. But he did it very slowly. He was badly hurt.

When he got to the bottom, I said, "Breakfast in the kitchen, I think. If Jesse didn't leave extra eggs, then there will still be leftover doughnuts."

As if the mention of her name summoned her, Jesse descended the stairs in a tenth of the time it had taken Zee.

"I used up the eggs," she said. "But I can reheat the French toast I put in the fridge if anyone wants some."

"That would be good," Zee said.

Jesse ignored Aiden entirely and began rummaging in the fridge. Zee, who was very good at reading between the lines when he cared to, gave Aiden a speculative and not-altogether-friendly look.

Warren came in from outside, still tucking his shirt into his jeans.

There was something in his face that told me his wolf was lingering close to the surface, but his smile was real when he offered to give Jesse a ride to school.

Jesse brought a plate of French toast over and set it in front of Zee. "A ride?" She heaved a big sigh and rolled her eyes, to demonstrate that she wasn't fooled—Warren would be sticking around the school to make sure she was safe.

Warren frowned at Jesse, hunching his lanky length as if he'd absorbed a blow. "If you'd rather ride with someone else, thet's ahlraht, Jesse. Darryl would take you." The excessive Texas was to let Jesse know that he really wasn't hurt. "Or Ben," he said innocently. Ben had caused quite a stir when he'd gone to her school—subtle, the foul-mouthed Englishman was not. Warren would be a lot less likely to attract notice.

She rolled her eyes again because she knew what he was doing. But she couldn't help but pat his shoulder and laugh, too. "Oh, let's not bother Ben. It's fine. We should go before I'm late."

Warren kissed my cheek, and I gave him a hug. "Thanks," I said.

"No worries," he said. "Boss asked me last night if I'd take her and set up watch. Work's been quiet lately. Kyle's started to complain about the number of polite divorces he's been handling. Says if they're that civil, they probably should stay married." Warren's partner, Kyle, was a divorce lawyer, and Warren was a private eye who did odd jobs for Kyle's firm.

"Quiet is good," I said.

"That's what I told him," Warren said. "I don't think he's convinced." He gave the room a general wave, then, with a hand on her shoulder, escorted Jesse out of the house.

"So," I said, sitting down at the table with Zee and Aiden as soon as Warren and Jesse left. "We should talk about options for Aiden."

Aiden looked away from me to the floor of the kitchen, where the cracked tile bore witness to his first clash with the pack.

"It might be interesting," Zee said, "to determine whether the troll had been sent after me, after Tad, or after Aiden. If it was after Aiden, you might have more trouble with the fae."

He meant that if the troll had been sent after him or Tad, he would handle the fallout. I had all the faith in the world that Zee could protect himself—when he was healthy enough to walk down the stairs with something approaching his normal grace. Not that it mattered. If the fae operated anything like the wolves as far as power games went, it was the pack they'd have to go after first, or they'd lose face. Bran had seemed to think we could negotiate with them—I just hoped he was right.

"I think we might be looking at trouble either way," I said. "But let's talk about Aiden, because he has a time limit. How hard are they going to look for you, Aiden? Would it be enough to relocate you somewhere far from the fae reservations, or are they likely to send people after you wherever you go?"

"I don't know," he said finally. "It seemed to me that they were most interested in how I use fae magic when I shouldn't be able to touch it because humans can't." He put both hands flat on the table. The nails were bitten to the quick. "They used to take Underhill for granted. She was their home, their due, and their servant. Then she shooed them all out the door and locked it up tight against them." He shivered. "There were other things in Underhill," he said, not looking at any of us. "Not just us human-born changelings. There were places where the fae kept their prisoners. I suppose some of

them were normal—as normal as any fae—when they were first
locked up. But when she opened the prison doors—because she was
lonely, she said—there was nothing remotely normal about what
came out. When they killed us by the dozens, she was sad, so she
gave us power to protect ourselves. She gave me the gift of fire. As
far as I can tell, the fae are mostly jealous. They've killed enough of
us that they are convinced they can't take the fire from me and keep
it themselves, though."

Zee pursed his lips and whistled. "Did you tell any of them
that she'd opened up the prisons?"

Aiden shook his head. "But they know, right? She's opened the
doors, so they've seen."

"I think not," Zee said. "I think she's been playing games with
them." He sat back, grunted, and sat straighter. "Mercy, I think it is
safe to assume they will come after him. He is beloved of Underhill."

Aiden snorted, trying to sound nonchalant, I thought, but
mostly he sounded scared.

Zee gave Aiden a sour smile. "Last night, while I slept, she whispered in my dreams. 'Where is my beloved?' she asked. 'What have
you done with him, Smith? Bring him back to me.' If she is talking
to other fae, they will hunt you until you are dead or they can give
you back to her."

Aiden's eyes showed white all around. "Don't take me back
there," he begged Zee. "Please, don't."

"Underhill addressed you?" I asked Zee. Unlike Aiden, I knew
that Zee wouldn't even walk across the street at the bidding of the
fae—not after they put Tad in jeopardy. And what was Underhill
but another form of fae? Aiden was in no danger of Zee's returning him anywhere.

Zee nodded. "I don't like it, either," he said. "I never had much to do with Underhill, though I've attended a court or two there. Underhill, like most of the fae, is sensitive to metal, and iron-kissed is my nature. We don't get on." Zee tapped on the table. "It disturbs me that Underhill knows my name."

"Me, too," said Aiden, thoroughly spooked. "Your name, my name—I wish she'd forget them all." He glanced over at me. "Would you keep me safe for one more day? So I can think on this? I will do what I can to stay out of your way."

"What do you expect to accomplish with another day?" asked Zee.

"I cannot promise anything yet," I answered Aiden. "I have to talk to Adam."

Before he could remind me that I'd given him sanctuary in the first place without talking to Adam, a door opened, and Christy burst into the kitchen. Tears slid down her pretty face, and she furiously wiped them away. She met my eyes, raised her chin, and said, "He is a bastard."

Adam stalked in after her, temper in every muscle of his body. "Where's Darryl?" he asked the room in general.

"Outside," Zee told him. "Perimeter duty." He must have been listening to what had gone on in the kitchen before he came down.

Adam opened the back door, and said, "Darryl, I have a job for you."

Christy crossed her arms under her chest and glared at me. "This is your fault," she said. She uncrossed her arms and wiped her eyes again, with special attention to not smearing her mascara.

I made a neutral sound.

Adam gave a look to Christy, who bit her lip and turned her head away.

"No," he said. "It isn't. Darryl?"

The big man slid into the kitchen. "Yes?"

"I need you to take Christy to her apartment and let her pack. Tomorrow, at six in the morning, she's getting on a plane. You'll be on it with her. She'll change airplanes in Seattle for a flight to the Bahamas. You have the choice of waiting four hours for your return flight, which is paid for, or renting a car at the pack's expense and driving home."

"What's up?" I asked.

"There was a note pinned to her door this morning," Adam said. He reached into his back pocket and withdrew an envelope that he'd folded in half.

It was thick paper, the kind that comes with invitations to weddings or graduations. I took out the card inside. It was inscribed by hand by someone with incredibly good penmanship.

It read:

Dear Christina Hauptman,

Please give the attached message to your husband.

I grimaced at the "your husband" part. Christy had thrown Adam away, and she didn't get him back. I raised the card to my nose. It smelled of Adam, Christy, and very faintly of the ocean and something . . .

"The Fideal," I said. The Fideal had attacked me, once. I'd run to the pack, and they had driven him off. Cantrip would have classified him as a boogie monster—a creature used to frighten children into being good or staying safe in their beds. That was one way to look at it. I looked upon him and his ilk as a fae analog of the human pedophile, but the fae version usually ate its prey.

Adam nodded. "I smelled him, too."

"There's another note?" I asked, putting the first on the table so that everyone could look.

Adam pulled it out of his front pocket and gave it to me. Like the first, it carried the Fideal's scent. I pulled the card out.

The fae hadn't bothered with a polite address here, though the fancy paper and the elegant writing were the same.

Adam Hauptman:

Your coyote said that you intend to protect your territory— we can make that promise cost you dearly even unto your last breath. We can bring war and destruction to your territory until not one stone stands upon another, until there is no soul left to cry over your dead.

But we are willing to bargain. You have something we want. Call this number if you are interested in what we have to say.

Like the other note, this one was unsigned.

I frowned. "They don't say what we have. Do they mean Zee, Aiden, or Tad? Or maybe something entirely different, like the walking stick?"

"Yes," said Zee. "Or maybe no. They may want you to tell them what you have—or they may not be in agreement." He sighed. "Getting all the fae to point in the same direction is like herding cats. And once you accomplish that—they are still more likely to stab the person next to them instead of the enemy they face. This might not even be from someone who can bargain for the fae as a whole. It seems . . . more secretive than the Gray Lords usually manage."

Darryl looked at Adam. "I'll tell work I'm on vacation for the week."

"I want to stay here," Christy said. "I only have two weeks to pack before moving to Oregon. I can't afford to spend a week in the Bahamas."

"Here is dangerous for you," Darryl said, tucking his hand gently under Christy's elbow. "They've already picked you out as a target. You need to be out of town, somewhere you aren't going to be easy to get to. Auriele and I will help you pack when you get back."

"Adam and the pack can keep me safe if I moved back in here," she said. "In the Bahamas, I'll be all by myself."

"Adam is going to be hard put to keep himself alive," I told her, though she was an idiot if she didn't know it. "The whole of the fae host on the reservation is about to drop on our heads. That's what this note is all about. And we are out of room in this house."

She looked at Adam. "Why are they after you?"

What had they been talking about that she didn't know that? I wondered. Then I saw the temper in Adam's face, and realized that she knew good and well it was my fault. She just wanted everyone to hear it again.

"Because," Zee said grimly, before I could admit my guilt to the world, again, "they have friends who are fae, and they are dangerous friends to have. If I were younger, I might apologize."

"In this case," Darryl said, "it is smart for you to go and have a free vacation in an island paradise that Adam is paying for." He tugged her out of the room and talked her out of the house.

"Are you both married to him?" asked Aiden, looking, of all people, at me. "Or are you a paramour? And why did they call you Adam's coyote? Is a coyote not a small wolf who lives in this area?"

"Mmmm," I said. "More like a large fox than a small wolf. I'm a shapechanger, but not a werewolf. My other form is a coyote."

"Christy and Adam were married," said Zee. "But they did not suit. Human law allows for dissolution of marriage vows." He glanced at me. "The fae have a rather more direct method of dealing with unwanted spouses." Returning his attention to Aiden, he said, "Marriage is not as necessary for survival of the species as it used to be, and it has suffered somewhat from the change. After the marriage was dissolved, Adam married Mercy." There was a small pause. "I was at the wedding." That last sounded a little bemused.

"Who told you about coyotes, but didn't tell you what they were, Aiden?" asked Adam.

"What?" Aiden looked up. "Oh, coyotes. Someone, I don't know who because I was too busy dry heaving to see which one, inflicted a translation spell on me. They needed to talk to me, and I refused to understand any of them no matter what language they used."

Zee said, "Language is more than just words, it contains concepts and ideology unique to the people who speak it. The best of those recognize that and attempt to fill in."

"With mixed results, usually." Tad came into the room. He looked tired behind his usual cheery smile that mostly had ceased to be real sometime while he was away at college. He looked at me. "Ask Dad about the one he used when courting my mother."

"Or not," said Zee coolly.

There was a little more real warmth in the grin Tad aimed at his father.

"Aiden asked for sanctuary for one more day," I told Adam.

He looked at the boy, who glanced up, then away from my mate. It isn't just posturing, the werewolf Alpha thing. It might not be safe to meet an Alpha's eyes because they see it as defiance, but it is also *difficult*. Even humans have instincts, evidently even humans who spent most of their very long life trapped in Underhill.

"Why?" Adam asked.

Aiden drew himself up and plastered on a vaguely patronizing smile that made me want to slap him. "Never mind."

"He'd like to be safe for a day more," Tad said. He was getting a coffee cup out of the cupboard, so his back was toward us.

Aiden stiffened.

Tad filled his cup with coffee and turned to face Aiden. "I slept in front of your door," he said softly.

I'd thought the boy-who-wasn't couldn't hold himself any stiffer, but he did. If he were a glass, he would have shattered.

"Safe," said Tad heavily, "isn't something that Underhill is full of anymore, I think. How long were you there?"

Aiden shook his head. "It doesn't matter."

"Underhill was mostly closed down by the ninth century," said Zee conversationally. "There were a few bolt-holes until the fifteenth century."

"What would you do for one more night of safety?" Tad asked softly.

And Aiden broke. Completely. And he did it without moving or saying anything. Tears welled and slid down his face while he breathed as if it hurt.

Children don't cry that way. Silently. Without expression. His face was a stony blank, and only the tears betrayed him.

It was the first time I'd seen him look his age.

Adam moved first. He approached him and put a hand on the top of the boy's head. When no objection followed, he drew him against his chest and let him rest in the shelter of Adam's arms. It had nothing to do with Aiden's childlike appearance; I'd seen Adam do the same for any of his wolves who was in distress. That's the base component of what an Alpha does for his pack: he provides a safe place to be. Touch is better than any word.

The boy's feet drew up and he curled into a fetal ball, still crying soundlessly. Babies make noise when they cry, trusting that an adult will hear them and make things better. As children, we learn that tears have power to move the people who care for us. We make noise when we cry in a bid for attention, for help, for support.

Aiden was silent and tried silently to disappear into the safety of Adam. My husband looked at me with troubled eyes.

I said, "Look what followed me home. Can we keep him?"

Adam's eyes warmed, and he smiled. "I think we have to, don't you? Until we can find a better home."

Tad raised his coffee cup to Adam—and his father grunted sourly.

"Aiden?" I said.

Adam shook his head, "Not now. He isn't even hearing us right now."

He picked Aiden up, as if he were the child he looked to be. He started to sit on the kitchen chair, but Joel had fallen asleep against it last week, leaving a leg half-burned through. Seeing what he was looking at, Tad retrieved a chair from the dining-room table. Adam sat in that and held the boy as if it were something that he was used to doing.

I grabbed a dining-room chair, too, and sat opposite Adam, next to Zee.

"So the fae who wrote the note could want the walking stick, Zee, or Aiden," Adam said. "Or some combination thereof."

"Or Tad," said Zee.

"Right," Tad said, sounding exhausted. "Let's not forget about me." He took the chair that Adam had rejected, spun it around, and sat between Zee and me.

Zee said, "That note is not signed—it is probably not a coordinated effort of the Gray Lords."

"So we don't have to worry?" I asked.

"I didn't say that," said the old fae. "If they say they can destroy this city . . . these cities—then they can. But even if you bargain with them, you still might not be safe."

"'Always look on the bright side of life,'" I quoted, though I didn't try singing it. My British accent is terrible enough without music. "Okay. We do have some options, even if they suck. First, we can call the number—they can't zap us through the ether, right?"

Zee raised an eyebrow, so I continued blithely, "And if they can, they don't need a cell phone connection to do it. Second, we can ignore them. Maybe we could send a message to the Gray Lords in residence—Zee should know who they are, and if not, Uncle Mike will—and request a face-to-face meeting. Get the reaction of the governing body"—Zee snorted—"to our rescue of Aiden, killing of the troll, and protection for Zee and Tad straight from the horse's mouth."

"If you request a meeting," said Tad, "it puts them in the driver's seat."

"They win the dominance fight," Adam agreed. "But it is the only way we know we are dealing with the people in charge."

Zee grunted.

"Wait a minute," I said. "Wait a minute." I looked at Adam. "Thomas Hao is meeting with the Gray Lords tonight in Walla Walla. We might be able to finagle the definition of some guesting laws so that we could attend that meeting. Since we are in the process of defining what our duties for our territory are right now, they're pretty fluid."

Adam laughed, but quietly because Aiden had fallen into an exhausted sleep. I'd seen things like that happen with the wolves sometimes, mostly while I'd lived with the Marrok. He took in the wolves who needed help, whatever the reason. Some of them arrived in really bad shape—mentally and physically. In Bran's touch, they found safety. Sleep would come and just knock them off their feet.

"Fluid duties is right," Adam agreed. "Would the Gray Lords Thomas is meeting with be able to negotiate with us?"

"I don't know," I said, "but I bet Zee will."

"Thomas Hao is a vampire," said Zee.

I nodded. "But that's not who the fae are interested in." I told them all about our early-morning call and whom we'd found when we went visiting Wulfe's stray vampire.

Zee bowed his head when I was finished. "The Dragon Under the Hill is dead," he said heavily. "I had not heard. So many of my old enemies are no more." He gave me a wry look. "Happily, there seem to be adequate replacements ready and waiting."

"Her father was really a dragon?" I asked.

"The Dragon Under the Hill is a title. The Flanagan was not a dragon in that sense," said Zee. "He was a powerful fae lord whose elements were both fire and earth in a way that was similar to the Red Dragon of Cymry, who was—for all I know, still *is*— a true dragon."

"So," said Adam. He moved Aiden around until the boy's legs dangled limply off one side of Adam's lap. "Assuming Thomas and Margaret agree to our joining them, we have several options. We can call the number on the note, then go to Walla Walla with Thomas and his fae to negotiate with the Gray Lords. We can not call the number on the note, and still go to Walla Walla. We can ignore the fae entirely."

"I would not recommend that last," said Zee, "not as long as we have bargaining room."

"Do we?" asked Tad in a raw voice. "What would you bargain?" He looked around the room at us. "Dad bargained his safety for mine—they twisted that and tortured my father to get my cooperation."

Zee smiled. "Which you didn't give them."

"I would have," snarled Tad. "Don't think I wouldn't have, old man—but you told me you had a plan. You didn't tell me it would take two weeks."

Zee patted Tad's shoulder. "If you had not held out, all would have failed. As it is, we are safe, with allies—and I will deal with those responsible in such a way that it will not happen again."

Silence fell.

"We were talking about bargaining room," Zee said, sounding almost kindly. "You probably won't know what you have until you talk to them."

"I won't hand Aiden over to them," Adam said. "Nor stand by while you or Tad are taken."

"There's some room between what we will do and what we won't," I said. "Should I call Thomas?" I didn't have his phone number, but I could call the hotel.

"Your justification for escorting the Flanagan and her vampire is that they are in your territory?" Zee asked. "How big is your territory, Adam?"

"As big as I can defend," Adam said, his eyes hooded. "If there is a war, I will take it right to the door of Underhill, should it be necessary. They will not find us an easy enemy to defeat."

"Cost them so much in the winning that they never do it again," said Zee thoughtfully. "That is a tactic. Not a good one, but a tactic. Usually, the result is a Pyrrhic victory."

Adam nodded. "Let's just hope that someone other than you remembers that, and they don't force us to go to war."

"Or we can just refer to the guesting laws," I said. "Guests can request help in their journey without us claiming Walla Walla as our territory. It's stretching the rules a little, but not changing the letter of the law."

"Guesting laws aside"—Adam took a deep breath and gave a decisive nod—"the first thing we really need is information. And I have one place we can get more without risking anyone." He hitched his hip up off the chair and pulled his cell phone out of his pocket. "So I vote that we see what our note writers want first." He dialed, then set the phone on the table with the speaker on—apparently done with his nod to democracy.

It rang three times and stopped. I could hear breathing on the other side of the connection. They waited for us to speak—but that's not how an Alpha plays the game.

Eventually, a voice that could have been a high-pitched man's or a low-pitched female's said, tentatively, "Who calls?"

Aiden jerked awake at the sound of the voice and dug his hands into Adam's arms, then slid off his lap and backed into a corner of the kitchen. Zee knew the voice on the phone, too. His eyes narrowed, and he pursed his lips, but he nodded at Adam.

"You give this number to a lot of people?" Adam asked.

"Mr. Hauptman," said the voice, the tentative quality disappearing, buried in cold confidence. It was a woman's voice, I decided. "We do not desire a war with you."

"Could have fooled me," he growled. "You set a troll on my city."

There was a pause. "Your city?" she said. "I believe you are the Alpha of the Columbia Basin Pack, not the mayor of Richland, Pasco, or Kent-Kenta-Ken . . ."

Adam smiled in satisfaction. "Kennewick," he said, "is the name you're looking for. And my territory is where I say it is."

"What your woman says it is," she snapped, implying, I thought, that the power in the pack was not Adam, but me.

"Exactly so," agreed Adam to my surprise. I wasn't the only one. Tad looked at me with an odd expression. "She is my mate and speaks with my voice. It doesn't sound as though we can work together. You are wasting my time." He reached out and hit END, cutting off the call.

Aiden said, "It is dangerous to play games with them." His shoulders were hunched, and he did not look at any of us. "Especially dangerous with that one."

Tad murmured, "Listen to Captain Obvious." That earned him a quelling glance from Adam.

I started to ask Aiden—or Zee—just who we were dealing with, but Adam spoke first.

"We are dangerous, too," my husband told Aiden, not unkindly. "They need to remember that." He looked at Zee. "How long do you think she'll wait before calling back?"

Zee pursed his lips. "It depends upon how much she wants—"

The phone buzzed, and Adam glanced at the screen. "Apparently quite a lot," he said. He hit the green button on the screen and set it back down on the table.

"You have something I want," she said.

I frowned at Adam, and he nodded. He'd caught her change from the "we" of the note to "I."

"You've said that before," Adam said. "I probably have several things you want, pick one."

"The boy," she said.

"No dice." Adam hit the red button, and we all waited. Aiden stared at the floor and wrapped his arms around himself.

"Adam offered you indefinite protection," Tad told Aiden. "You probably missed it in the middle of your panic attack. But he won't allow you to be given to the fae against your will. Not ever. Nicely played."

Aiden opened his mouth.

The phone rang again.

Adam touched the green button, and said, "You bore me."

"I need the boy," she said.

"And you offer?"

"The note told you we are willing to allow you your territory."

His body relaxing like a cat's, Adam smiled, his teeth white and even. "So the note said." His voice was very soft. "No one *allows* me anything." He paused and continued in a more normal tone. "That doesn't mean we can't negotiate. What are you, yourself, willing to offer me, and why are you answering this phone instead of whoever wrote those notes?"

The Fideal was male—and I would have recognized his voice. The woman might have been working with him, or some group of fae—but she was trying to work out a deal alone. Adam had just let her know that he understood that.

She responded with silence. Hard to tell if she was panicking or just thinking.

"Fae can lie," Adam told her conversationally. "But I understand that they are punished for it. Removed from all that is and was and could be. A curse of rare power levied against your race by those who went before."

I raised my eyebrows. I didn't know that. Zee focused intently on Adam. I assumed that Zee knew that fae could lie but wanted to know where Adam had gotten his information.

"You will regret—" she spat, but Adam had already disconnected his phone.

"Well, that one wants you, Aiden," Adam said. "But as entertaining as that phone call was, we didn't learn what the fae as a whole want. Who was she, Zee?"

"The Widow Queen," he said. "Neuth. She has other names. The Black Queen."

"A fairy queen?" I asked. I'd met one of them.

But Zee shook his head. "No. She's sidhe fae—a Gray Lord. She likes to play with the humans, though, causing misery—which she can feed upon. She made her way into more than one folktale. I'd heard that she was at the one in Nevada. I did not see her while I was at our local reservation."

Aiden shook his head. "No. She is here. She—" He took a deep breath. "No. She was one of the ones who came here when I escaped Underhill and was recaptured by the fae."

"Tell me about her," said Adam.

Zee frowned.

It was Tad who said, "In the far past, the Widow Queen was known for seducing men, men powerful in the human world, but also good and beloved men. Gradually, she would separate them from everything they loved until they were obsessed with her. She could use magic to accomplish this—but preferred not. It was better when they followed her of their own will. Then she would destroy the man, the people he once loved—physically, mentally, in all ways at her disposal—then move on to the lands he ruled. The stories of Snow White and Cinderella probably were first conceived as a result of incidents involving her. When Underhill closed, she lost a great deal of that kind of magic, and more to the point, she lost her ability to feed off human misery. That wasn't her greatest power—she is a Gray Lord—but she enjoyed it the most."

"So why would she want Aiden?" I asked. Then answered myself, "Beloved of Underhill, right? Possessed of magic she bestowed upon him. And the Widow Queen wants her abilities back."

Tad shrugged. Zee grunted. Good enough supposition, I read from the vague noises.

"At least she doesn't prey upon children," Adam murmured with a sigh. "So now we know that one fae wants Aiden. We need a plan for tonight. Will the Gray Lords meeting with Thomas's fae be of sufficient status to bargain?"

He looked at Zee, who sighed. "Probably. The Flanagan was a Power, and his daughter showed signs of being the same." He tapped on the table. "You should bargain with them that they respect the boundaries of your territory—and be very clear what your territory is. Too big, and they will not believe you can hold it; too small, and you tell them that you are weak."

"What do we have to bargain with?" Adam asked. "I won't turn the boy over to them." He looked at Tad. "Or you or your father. Bran has made it clear that we are on our own."

"There is the walking stick," I said.

"That's a nonstarter," said Adam. "It won't stay with them in the first place. And in the second place . . ."

"Yeah," I agreed. "It's changed, hasn't it? It's not just an artifact anymore. It has a mind of its own—which makes it . . . not something I'm willing to bargain with if I can help it."

8

Thomas had been suspiciously amiable about my request to include us in his fae lady's meeting.

"I am," he'd said when I'd called him, "very happy to have more security for Margaret."

I cleared my throat. "You might not be so happy when I explain exactly why we'd like to come along." He'd listened as I expanded on the tale of the trouble I'd caused with my little speech on the bridge.

"So," he said when I'd finished. "You wish to come in the hopes of taking the Gray Lords by surprise—and are fairly sure that those fae you will corner are people who know the situation and have the power to make bargains."

"Yes," I said.

There was a little pause. "You don't think that the Gray Lords are responsible for the threatening message sent to Hauptman's ex-wife. Worse, you don't think that the person, this Widow Queen, you talked to on the phone was the person responsible for the message, either."

"She may have been one of them," I said, "but there are others—who may or may not have a different agenda than she does. Or they want our refugee, too, but not for the same purpose. You see our problem."

"You don't know who wants what—and where they sit in the halls of power." Margaret Flanagan had taken the phone. "Too many possibilities and not enough information."

"Exactly," I told her. "We don't want war with the fae—and I don't think they want war with us, either. But we won't give them the boy, who has been a victim of the fae for a very long time. We won't give them"—I paused, because in this instance I probably couldn't speak for the pack—"*I* won't give them Zee or his son. Ideally, the Gray Lords will decide we are too much trouble or not important enough to screw with, and they will take over and police their own. Otherwise, we'll try to bargain with them to get them to respect our territorial boundaries."

"Zee?" Margaret asked. "You said his name to Thomas, too, as if he were someone we should know?"

"Siebold Adelbertsmiter," I said. "He's had a lot of names over the years. You might know him better as the Dark Smith of Drontheim."

There was a long pause. "You are a friend of the Dark Smith?"

"Zee is a grumpy old fae," I said. "But he is my friend."

She drew in a breath. "He was my father's much-admired enemy."

"If it helps," I said, "when I told him your father was dead, it hit him pretty hard. I'd say the admiration went both ways."

She laughed.

Thomas said, "Margaret is what is important."

"We will protect her," I said.

"All right," he said. "But you come. You and your mate. I've met you, and I'll have you at my back, but no strangers."

"Deal," I said.

Which is how I came to be riding shotgun instead of someone more useful like Warren or Honey—but we were hoping this wouldn't turn into an actual battle.

Zee came, too.

I hadn't asked him. Adam hadn't asked him. Zee hadn't said anything, he'd just been sitting in the backseat of Adam's car when we were ready to leave. He wouldn't say anything, and he wouldn't get out. None of the other cars parked at the house would start. So, instead of being late, we drove to the hotel with him in the backseat.

Thomas and Margaret came out to meet us. The sky wasn't quite dark, and Thomas wore gloves and a black hoodie with the hood pulled over his head. The hoodie made him look . . . smaller, and less dangerous—more like a gang member and less like a vampire.

Adam started to explain our stowaway to Thomas, but Zee got out of the car and looked at Margaret.

He frowned at the crutches and the scars on her wrists. "Your father was an honorable enemy," he told her. "He deserved better followers. Are you as tough as your father?"

She raised her chin, but it was Thomas who said, "Tougher. They were both trapped underground in mining tunnels for decades. He died, and she survived."

"My father was injured," she said sharply. "I was not."

"I did not know about this imprisonment," Zee said. "Or I would have put a stop to it. I heard only afterward how it happened that you were trapped by those who should have cared for you." He raised his eyes to her. "I would have broken my old enemy out of a prison he did not deserve—if only to ensure that a worthy opponent still walked the earth. For the error of my ignorance, I will do my best to make sure that his daughter walks away unharmed today."

She looked at him. "That's not why you came here," she said.

"It is," he said. "But it isn't the only reason, nor the most important, until I saw your face. The Dragon Under the Hill lives in your face. You have his eyes. Your father was one of the few enemies I had who was capable of giving as good as he got. He fought with cunning, skill, and honor; those three qualities are seldom found together. I disagreed with him, and he annoyed me—but he was a worthy opponent. I have other reasons to speak to the Gray Lords, but your safety will be my primary concern."

They faced off with each other, the delicate woman with her scars and her crutches, and the wiry old man with his bald patch and his potbelly.

"Say no," said Thomas. "Sunshine, he is dangerous."

"So am I," she said, but gently. "So are we all, isn't that the truth? But he is more dangerous to our enemies." She frowned at Zee. "You aren't what I expected from the stories."

He glanced around the parking lot, then back at her. "This is a different time." He shrugged—the movement a little shallower than his usual shrug, but she wouldn't know that.

"I see," said Margaret. "I agree to your unexpected proposal, Smith."

"You aren't riding in the car with him," Thomas said.

She smiled at Thomas. "All right. We'll take both cars." She looked at me. "I'd like some time to talk with you." She glanced at her vampire guardian, then at Adam. "I think we have a lot in common, and I'd like to compare notes. I had hoped we'd all have a chance to talk on the way to Walla Walla."

"Maybe we can get together before you leave?" I asked.

She nodded gravely. "I hope so."

"Walla Walla" was a term the Nez Percé used for a place where a stream flowed into a larger stream—or so I was told, though probably the pronunciation had changed quite a bit from the original. The most common translation was "many waters," probably because it was both shorter and more lyrical than "where a stream flows into a bigger stream."

Walla Walla was a town of a little over thirty thousand people, though it felt smaller than that somehow. I think it was the old-fashioned feel of the downtown district, an atmosphere invoking the days of horse and buggy or Model T cars. It was the kind of town that got voted "most friendly," "most picturesque," or "best place to live" on a regular basis.

Despite its many fine qualities, before the Ronald Wilson Reagan Fae Reservation was plunked down west of the town, Walla Walla was most famous for the nearby site of the Whitman Mission. There, the Protestant missionary Dr. Marcus Whitman, his wife Narcissa, and twelve other white people living at the mission were killed by Cayuse Indians in the middle of the nineteenth century.

Whitman was a doctor and a missionary, and he gained a reputation in the local tribes (Walla Walla, Nez Percé, and Cayuse mostly) as a spiritual leader and a man of powerful medicine. When measles swept through the Cayuse tribe, they turned to him for help he could not provide. The disaster that ensued was not, strictly speaking, the fault of either the Cayuse or the Whitmans, who were all doing what they believed to be right.

The symbolic irony of this meeting between werewolf, vampire, and fae at a hotel named after Marcus Whitman did not go over my head. I hoped our results were better than those Whitman and the Cayuse achieved.

The road to Walla Walla was one of those winding highways that meandered through small towns along the way instead of speeding right past them with nothing more than an exit to mark their place. As I rode shotgun next to Adam, following Thomas Hao's white Subaru down the narrow highway to Walla Walla, we passed the road that used to lead to the fae reservation. "How do you want to play this?" I asked Adam, abruptly tired of the quiet in the car. I felt itchy with readiness, and the quiet, centered calm in both men irritated me.

"Nothing to plan," he said.

When I snorted, he grinned at me. It wasn't a lighthearted grin, but there was amusement in it. "There is no reason to overthink things, Mercy. We don't know who we're going to see or what they are going to say. We can't plan except in the most general of fashions. We'll let Margaret get her say in first—that's courtesy. We'll work our business in as we can. Probably that will be very short and sweet for our part. We'll let them tell us what they are looking for if it gets that far. That part is up to them as well. It may be that we all just snap threats at each other and go home. I won't know how to play it until we at least know who we're playing with."

He was right. I knew he was right. But I needed something to do, something to think about, so I could quit scaring myself with what-ifs, even if that meant talking about what-ifs. Adam was very good at making them less scary than my imagination did.

"There are only a few things we know for certain," he said, as if he could hear my restlessness. "Zee isn't going to let anything happen to Margaret. Thomas can take care of himself." Then his voice dropped into a low, dangerous tone that was nothing like the easy, relaxed attitude he'd been portraying. "And *nothing* is getting past me to you."

I absorbed that—the tone, not the words or intent behind it; those I already knew. Part of the magic of his voice was the Southern softness that blurred his consonants even when his accent wasn't strong. Part of it was the reliable confidence behind every word—I just *knew* there was no guile, give, or hesitation in this man the first time I heard him speak. At the time, it had been frustrating and annoying.

But mostly, when he dropped his voice that way, it caressed something inside me—like he'd stroked the back of my neck without touching me. It made me want to melt into a puddle at his feet and settled my restlessness right down.

He knew it, too. He smiled a little and turned his attention back to driving. I glanced at Zee. "How about you? Are you planning or running by the seat of your pants, too?"

Zee smiled happily. Somehow it was worse than his usual tightly sour smile—even though the happy was real. Maybe it was *because* the happy was real. "I will keep my old enemy's daughter safe. Sometime soon, I will deal with the fae who have offended me in such a way that others avoid annoying me for another century or two. That's a good plan for the next few weeks, I think. *Findest du nicht auch?*"

He didn't really expect an answer. "Don't you find it so?" is usually a rhetorical question, especially with Zee, who seldom cares for other people's opinions at the best of times.

We drove for a while longer, and I got restless again. Maybe if

I started fidgeting, Adam would let me drive. Maybe someone could start a conversation so I would quit worrying about how wrong this night could go.

"Why so quiet?" I asked Adam.

"I'm planning my moves," he said. "I think I'll walk to the left of Thomas and Margaret. Studies show that right-handed people look right before they look left. That will give me a psychological advantage. Then I'll walk at half speed—"

"I *could* smack you," I said. "Just saying."

"I'm driving," he answered meekly. "And you shouldn't hurt the one you love."

"Flirt on your own time, *Lieblings*," advised Zee. "I am too old for it—you could give me a heart attack."

"You'd have to have a heart for that threat to work," I said, and happily settled in for a game of insults with Zee.

We parked next to Thomas's car. It was nearly full dark—close enough to it that the vampire had discarded his hoodie and stood, looking elegant, in his usual bright-colored silk shirt. This one was an iridescent pearly blue, with an embroidered dark blue or black dragon crawling over his shoulder and down his arm.

He opened the door for Margaret and stood watching her struggle to get out. He didn't move a muscle, but I could feel the willpower it took not to help. Adam was right, Thomas was a goner. People who say that vampires don't care about anyone except themselves are mostly right—but sometimes they are very and lethally wrong.

Margaret's pain was too private to watch, so I looked up at the hotel.

In downtown Seattle, the Marcus Whitman Hotel wouldn't stand out, but in Walla Walla, it was about a hundred feet taller than anything else around it. From the bones of the original structure, it had been built in the late nineteen twenties. Several colors of brick and the very modern entrance evidenced more than one renovation over the years.

"All right," Margaret said, her voice a little husky from pain. "There are supposed to be three Gray Lords meeting with me, and I'm allowed to bring my people with me. I had intended it to be just Thomas, but they allowed me six. With your permission, I'm going to give you, Adam and Mercy, a little glamour, nothing fancy—just something that will help them dismiss you as thugs numbers one and two. If you do something to draw attention, the glamour won't hold." She looked at Zee. "You, I expect, can do your own and be thug number three." She turned back to Adam and me. "It won't hold if they really look at you, but it should give us the element of surprise. And any advantage is to your favor—they'll respect you for it."

"Fine," said Adam. I nodded.

Her magic settled over me like a cool mist. Sometimes magic doesn't stick to me, but this time it seemed to.

"Thomas?" I asked.

"He doesn't need it," she said. "He can do it without magic. When he doesn't want people to notice him, they just don't."

I rubbed my pleasantly tingling skin, and said, "You're just going in to tell them 'no,' right? Which you could do with just Thomas. The glamour is to help us?"

She smiled. "It's fun. I don't like them. Don't like the games they are playing. I'm happy to help. Now hush, someone could be listening."

"Probably not," I said. "I would smell anyone close enough to listen."

Thomas looked at me as though I were interesting. "Better than a werewolf?"

"For fae and magic, yes," I told him. "To be fair, there is a lot of ambient noise right now. Someone would have to be very close to overhear us." I didn't tell them that fae glamour might be awesomely powerful, but it seldom worked on scent. Let them think I was special.

We walked into the hotel, following Margaret. She didn't travel fast, but no one evinced even the slightest impatience. Adam took the left-rear position. I don't know if he did it for the reasons he'd told me in the car, or if that was just where he happened to be. Zee took the right rear. Thomas walked in front of Adam, and I took the leftover spot next to Thomas.

Inside, the lobby was overflowing with beige tuxes and unflattering teal gowns. They were most densely clustered near the bride, recognizable as such by her thirties-style off-white lace gown. She was patting the back of a middle-aged woman in a bright green sparkly suit who was sobbing on the bride's shoulder. The whole lobby was trying not to watch—and so no one noticed us at all.

As if she'd been in the hotel a hundred times, Margaret headed for one of the banks of elevators. We waited in silence for the doors to slide open. When they did, we stepped inside—it was a tight squeeze. The elevators weren't built for a fairy princess and her guards. Fortunately, it was a fast elevator, and we got off on the second floor. Margaret headed down the hallway, and we spread out behind her like a wedding train.

She passed a couple of doors on her left before opening the door on her right, discreetly marked WALLA WALLA. She waited while we flowed around her to precede her into the room. There was a conference table and someone, maybe the hotel, had put bright bouquets of carnations in shades of red on either end of the long table. Five people were already seated on the side of the table that faced the entry door, two more stood against the far wall in parade rest. All of the fae were wearing their human glamour.

I knew some of them. Beauclaire, the handsome former lawyer who'd declared fae independence, was seated on the far left. Next to him was a dark-haired woman whose sunglasses concealed her blind eyes—Nemane, the Morrigan, who'd once been the Irish goddess of battle. I didn't know the man next to her. He was pale-skinned, bald, and fine-boned, with bulging eyes and broken blood vessels on the sides of his nose that were so bad it was almost hard to focus on anything else. Next to him was an extraordinarily beautiful woman with childlike features, porcelain skin, and deep red lips. The final seated person was a middle-aged woman who was comfortably plump and clothed in a badly fitting, three-piece business suit in salmon pink. Her hair was gray and brown, and her features were absolutely unremarkable.

The two people who stood before the wall were Uncle Mike and Edythe, who I still thought of as Yo-yo Girl because the first time I'd seen her, she'd been playing with a yo-yo. Edythe looked like a young girl—like Aiden, she appeared to be somewhere between nine and eleven. Unlike Aiden, she chose that guise because she enjoyed looking like a victim. Which she very much wasn't. I'd seen her do some scary stuff and watched other fae skittle out of her path. She met my eyes and gave me an ironic lift of an eyebrow. Apparently, Margaret's magic wasn't working for her. The two Gray Lords who knew me looked past me without the hesitation that they'd have given if they'd really seen me, and so did Uncle Mike. I filed Edythe's immunity in the mental file I kept marked Why Edythe/Yo-yo Girl Is Scary. It was a big file.

Margaret looked at the five people seated on the opposite side of the table, letting her gaze linger meaningfully on the last two. "You told me there would be three of you," Margaret said coolly. "Do the fae negotiate in falsehoods now?"

"It's my fault, Margaret," said the beautiful woman in a husky voice that I'd last heard coming out of Adam's phone a few hours earlier. "I was visiting this reservation and heard that you were expected. My associate"—she touched the middle-aged woman's arm lightly—"and I asked to be included for old times' sake. I once knew your father very well, and I couldn't resist the chance to see his daughter."

Margaret spread her hands, as if to display herself. "As you now do."

"You look bad," said the man who sat in the middle seat. His voice, high and fussy, fit his outwardly meek appearance. "You need to come home with us, and we will see you restored to your proper self. It's been several years since the incident, hasn't it? So it is obvious that you need help to recover from your ordeal."

Margaret directed her attention at him even as she waved a hand over her shoulder at us, and we four spread out on the wall behind her. The door was on the far left-hand side of the wall, so we didn't have to worry about anyone's coming in from outside between us.

She walked with painful slowness—more slowly than I'd seen her move before, in fact. When she reached the table, she pulled out a chair left of the middle, directly in front of Nemane. I couldn't tell if it was deliberate, or if the chair was closer to the door so she didn't have to walk so far.

She took her time seating herself and arranging her crutches so that everyone in the room could see just how crippled she was.

Only when she was comfortably seated in the leather executive chair did she speak.

"Incident," she said. "What a curious word. 'Incident.' So . . . bland and small. I truly appreciate your words, Goreu, but I think not. I am healing at precisely the correct rate for full recovery."

Goreu. I should remember something about that name. I'd been reading a lot of stories about the fae lately. Goreu sounded like it should be French, but I was thinking it came from *The Mabinogion*, which was Welsh.

"You are fae," said the beautiful woman. "You belong to us."

I couldn't see Margaret's expression, since I was directly behind her, but a raised eyebrow was evident in her voice anyway. "Curious choice of words. I do not belong to you."

"You are fae, child," said Nemane. She took a deep breath through her nose, tilted her head in a birdlike gesture—and smiled at me. She couldn't see me. But Nemane didn't need her eyes for much. She chose not to say anything. My dealings with her had been almost friendly, but she wasn't an ally. Instead of asking Margaret why she'd brought the Alpha of the Columbia Basin Pack and his mate to a fae meeting, she said carefully, "Neuth chose her words poorly. You belong with us."

"You think so, do you?" asked Margaret. "I disagree. Which I have explained in several letters, e-mails, and one . . . no, two phone calls, if you count the one where I hung up on the Council representative. I am here, now, to explain it in person. I will not go. I will not put myself in your power. I have been under the power of the fae before, and I will not do it again."

"You *are* fae," Beauclaire began carefully, but Goreu went on the attack before Beauclaire could make his point.

"You think you can resist us?" asked Goreu, though I don't think he meant it as a question—his tone was too confident.

"Do you mean to try to force me?" Margaret countered. She looked at Beauclaire. "You—who set the world on this course in search of justice for your daughter—you would seek to imprison me for the crime of being my father's daughter?"

"There are many," said Nemane, "who would rather be elsewhere. But we are few, child. Too few to survive a war—no matter what some say. We have to make a show of strength. We need you in order to survive."

Margaret raised her head and squared her shoulders. "Do you know what I learned when I was trapped in the earth for more than half a century? With neither food to eat, nor water to drink, nor light to see by, when there is no sound except that you make yourself, some things become very clear. Death is not to be feared. Death is easy. It is living that is brutal. The fae may survive or not. I do not care. I am not one of you except through my parents—and they are both dead."

Goreu reached across the table with the speed of a striking snake and slapped something on Margaret's wrist that closed with a click—a fine silver bar bracelet with a red cabochon stone. Goreu held a similar bracelet and shut it on his wrist. As he clicked it closed, he drew in a breath as if it had hurt.

Margaret sat frozen.

It wasn't one of the set of bone cuffs, Peace and Quiet, that had once been used on me. Tad had destroyed those.

"If you cannot be persuaded any other way," the Widow Queen said, "then you leave us no choice. We owe it to your father to protect you and return you to health."

Margaret looked down at her wrist. Then she looked at Goreu. "You have made a mistake."

I couldn't help but look at Thomas. He was very, very still.

"Perhaps," said Goreu. "I did argue that there were those who might be of more use to us—we have only one artifact that can hold a fae against their will for very long."

"You are so arrogant, all of you," Margaret said. "Goreu, Custennin's son, you may be powerful, I do not contest that. But it has been a long time since you beheaded your uncle—and that you did after he was already defeated. But these bracelets are not about how powerful your magic is. You have made a mistake."

The name Custennin rang a bell. Margaret focused on the bald little fae. She said, "Crawl across the table to me."

Custennin had been a shepherd who had twenty-four children. I remembered that because it was twice twelve, and twelve is a number that occurs quite a lot in fairy tales.

Goreu opened his mouth—then lost his smirk. He braced himself on the edge of the table.

"*Crawl*," Margaret said.

All but one of Custennin's children had been killed by a giant, Custennin's brother. The single son who remained was named Goreu.

Slowly, very slowly, sweating and shaking, the fae boosted himself up onto the table and crawled. The bracelet made a scratchy sound as he dragged it across the gleaming cherry finish of the table. He bit his lip, and blood dripped from it onto the wood.

There must have been some sort of protocol at work because none of the other fae in the room gave him any aid. They stayed in their seats and watched Goreu struggle. The Widow Queen looked mildly amused. The middle-aged woman took out a file and became engrossed in buffing her nails with vicious, jerky movements.

Nemane and Beauclaire looked as though they were competing for who could look the most relaxed. Unseen by the other fae because of her position at the wall behind them, Edythe smiled at Margaret, lifted a finger to her tongue to wet it, then drew an imaginary point in the air.

If Margaret reacted, I couldn't tell. I'm not sure she even saw Edythe's gesture—Margaret was engrossed in the strange battle she was engaged in with Goreu.

According to *The Mabinogion*, the Goreu who was Custennin's son had traveled with King Arthur and his knights, eventually returning to his home and killing the giant, his uncle. He was a hero—unless I'd gotten the story wrong, because the Goreu in this room didn't look at all like a hero.

When the unheroic fae arrived at Margaret's side of the table, she reached out and grasped his wrist. As soon as she touched it, a thin red line began drawing itself across the plain silver of Goreu's bracelet. It began slowly, then, as Goreu breathed in quick pants, moved more and more quickly, drawing glyphs that became part of more complex patterns until the bracelet was nearly solid red.

Margaret sat back in her chair, took the bracelet off her wrist and caught the other as it fell off Goreu. She tossed both of them to Zee.

It broke the effect of the light glamour we'd all been wearing. Goreu scrambled backward off the table, half falling in his effort to get away—not from Margaret, but from Zee. The middle-aged woman dropped her file, and the Widow Queen froze.

Uncle Mike smiled—and so did Beauclaire. Nemane kept her relaxed pose, but then she'd known who was in the room the whole time.

I glanced over at Zee, who had his happy face on again. It was just . . . *wrong* to see a happy face on Zee.

"Hello, Goreu," Zee said. "Interesting to see you once more. I'm sure we'll meet under different circumstances. I'm looking forward to it." He looked at the Widow Queen. "But not as much as I'm looking forward to some other meetings. You look more pale than you did the last time I saw you, Neuth," he said. He looked at the middle-aged woman, who was frozen in her seat, and his smile grew brighter. He said nothing at all to her.

The Widow Queen, I knew, hadn't been one of the fae who'd tortured Zee. I thought that Goreu was in the clear, too—though they were not allies. Goreu was afraid of Zee, but there hadn't been any particular maliciousness in Zee's voice when he addressed him. The middle-aged-looking woman was a dead fae walking.

"We came to provide protection to Margaret and her guard, who were traveling through our territory," said my husband, breaking into Zee's moment with a conversational tone. "We thought we'd use this opportunity to express our sadness at the death of the troll yesterday. Please do not send fae who put the citizens of our home at risk. We do not enjoy killing for the sake of killing."

Adam's sense of timing is superb. The Gray Lords, even the ones who had nothing to fear from Zee, were so caught up in that drama they had trouble shifting gears to Adam. Their distraction let Adam hold the floor.

"We'd also like to inform you that we are unimpressed with threats. Some of your people"—he looked over the fae at the table, except for the Widow Queen—"composed a letter and put it on the door of my ex-wife's home. Please see to it that it doesn't happen again." He took in a breath, and when he continued, it was in a very soft voice. "We do not want a war with you. But we will not stand by and see our friends captured and tortured. We will not allow you to harm those under our protection. You should know that the fire-touched boy is ours. We will go to war if you force us to it. And if we go to war, it will not stay localized, it will not stay between your people and ours, because our human citizens will fight beside us."

Zee tossed the bracelets up in the air and caught them, one in each hand, and closed his fists. Air left my lungs, driven by the magic he called. His hands glowed with a white light that was so bright I had to turn my face away. I fought to breathe, fought to stay on my feet—and it was gone.

Zee dropped two blackened chunks of metal on the table. "Those," he said, "were an abomination."

"How is it," murmured Beauclaire, "that you are not on our Council? That you are not a Gray Lord?"

"No one asked me," said Zee.

"Join us," said Nemane.

Zee smiled at the Gray Lord who sat on the far side of the Widow Queen, the one in the salmon-colored suit. She swallowed noisily.

"Not today," Zee said, his voice a purr of menace. "I have a few scores to settle, and I take too much pleasure in the planning to hurry. I'm swamped."

"'I've got my country's five hundredth anniversary to plan, my wedding to arrange, my wife to murder, and Guilder to frame for it,'" I murmured very quietly. I wasn't sure that Zee was quoting the movie, but he sounded so much like Prince Humperdinck, I couldn't help myself. Either Adam was the only one who heard me, or no one else appreciated *The Princess Bride*.

"So," said Margaret, pushing herself back from the table. "You have my answer." This time she let Thomas help her to her feet and hand her the crutches. "Not that it hasn't been interesting. But you'll understand that if you want to discuss anything with me, you'll have to do it long-distance."

She made good time out of the room, and we followed her. As soon as I shut the conference-room door, Thomas picked Margaret up in his arms. I took the crutches—as the least able fighter, I could most easily be spared to carry things. And the crutches would make pretty good weapons if I needed them.

The bride and her entourage were gone when we got back to the lobby. One of the hotel people saw us get out of the elevator and, upon seeing Margaret in Thomas's arms, hurried over.

"Is there anything I can do?" he asked.

"No," Margaret said with a charming smile. "Thomas was either worried that I've tired myself out, or just wanted to get out to the car sometime in the next hour or so." Her tone told him not to take her seriously, and he smiled appreciatively before he got a good look at Thomas's unamused face.

"Don't mind him," Margaret said. "He worries too much."

"We have a wheelchair," the young man offered.

"Thank you," said Thomas, bowing a little despite his burden, though he kept walking in the direction of the exit. "This is not the first time I've carried her out to the car. She pushes herself too hard, even though I've explained that when she does that, she only slows down the healing process."

The hotel employee looked worried.

"I should recover fully," Margaret told him. "Given time. It's just a lot of boring therapy between now and then. Tonight I really am fine, just a little tired."

He escorted us out to the front entrance, offered to drive the car up, and when his help was refused, held the door open for us to leave.

We'd gotten halfway across the dark parking lot when Adam murmured, "Someone is watching us. I can feel it on the back of my neck."

I bent down to tie my shoe and took the opportunity to scan the parking lot behind us. "The nice guy who escorted us out is still watching us. Is that it?"

"She affects a lot of people that way," said Thomas, as Margaret waved at our observer over his shoulder.

"It's the tragedy," said Margaret cheerfully. "Some people can't stop themselves from wanting to help. It's a compulsion." The man waved hesitantly back and left the doorway for the depths of the hotel, presumably to do his job.

"That's not it," said Adam in a low voice. "Let's get to the cars."

"I don't scent anyone," I said after finishing with my shoe. "But I'm with you. There's someone."

"They're around," agreed Thomas.

Margaret leaned her head against him. "This would be a perfect time for an ambush," she said, sounding delighted. "Maybe there's a troll or ogre around."

"How about a witch?" asked a woman's voice.

As soon as she spoke, I saw her, a young, muscular woman wearing a summer dress with brown army boots, walking beside Margaret and Thomas as if she'd been beside us all along.

9

As soon as she appeared, I could smell her. Her scent held a mix of cinnamon, brimstone, and honey, but no witchcraft. She smelled like a fae, but with overtones of earth and water rather than a clear allegiance to either, which was unusual in my experience.

Thomas jumped ten feet sideways, Margaret in his arms. Adam moved in front of them like a trained bodyguard. I recognized her scent and stopped my instinctive move to draw my carry gun. Instead, like Adam, I put myself in front of Thomas and Margaret. Zee stood where he was but put a hand on his hip, where I knew he kept one of his bladed weapons. He didn't just use magicked swords—he *made* them.

"Dangerous to surprise us like that," he said coolly, because he, of course, knew who it was.

I did, too. It's not that I remember everyone I scent. It's just that some people make a definite impression. Though some of the fae have favorite glamours they wear, visual impressions are not a definitive way to recognize a fae. Scent is much more difficult for them to change.

"What's life without a little danger?" The woman looked at me, and said, "And didn't I tell them to keep an eye on you? No one who carries Coyote so strongly is going to be resting on the sidelines. But they never listen to me."

Thomas set Margaret on her feet.

"You aren't a witch," I said. I'd been as surprised as anyone when I met Baba Yaga the first time. The most famous witch in the world—wasn't.

She shrugged. "You say tomato, and I say tomato." She used the phrase backward, the second "tomato" carrying the long "a." "A million people and a hundred tales can't be wrong. You say fae, I say witch, and I am bigger than you—so I can call myself what I want." She leaned toward me and sniffed and twitched her nose in a very unhumanlike way. "There's a Russian here," she said to me. "I can always tell. And it's not *you*."

She took a wide, awkward sideways step until she was in front of Zee. She frowned at Zee a moment. "I remember you as better-looking."

"I remember you as an old *Topfgucker*, who sticks her long nose where it doesn't belong," said Zee, unimpressed.

She dropped her head and cackled, a real witch's cackle—as if she'd watched too many cartoons. "*There's* my Loan, darling. Oops, I forgot. You are calling yourself Siebold Adelbertsmiter now, aren't you? Adelbert was such an old stick-in-the-mud—he deserved what he got, but he was a wimp, no one *I'd* brag about smiting. Siebold, darling, have you missed me? You never call, you never write. A person would be forgiven for thinking you didn't like them. *You* certainly aren't my Russian."

She looked at Thomas, put a hand on Zee's shoulder so she could lean past him to sniff the air. "Not you," she told Margaret. She looked at Thomas, and said, "*Obviously* not you. Too much Earth Dragon, too little air of the steppe." She took that odd sidestep again; this time it put her directly in front of Adam. She leaned too close to him and inhaled.

"So it is you!" she exclaimed, with the air of a vaudeville cop finding the villain. She waited a moment, relaxed, and said, "You smell of my home. True *russkiy dukh*. I should take you home for supper—I would have just a few centuries ago. Sharpened my brass tooth in your honor . . . silver would be more appropriate, but I broke that one in 1916." The brass tooth threw me for a moment, then I remembered that Baba Yaga was supposed to eat people with metal teeth that she would take out of her mouth and sharpen in front of her victims. In the stories I'd heard, the teeth were supposed to be iron, not brass.

Baba Yaga had not slowed down her patter, though. "More to the point," she said, then giggled. "Point—tooth, do you get it? I am so funny. But as I was saying, I am *civilized* now. *Tamed* for the sake of the others, you know. A fine handsome man as you? Now I take him home for other things." She licked her lips hungrily.

Adam growled at her.

"Stop it," I said to her, because I was afraid that if she kept talking, someone would make a stupid move and get themselves killed. "Everyone's on edge, there's no use pushing them over. What do you want?"

"Who *are* you?" asked Margaret.

The witch, who was a Gray Lord, took the sides of her sundress, one side in each hand, and curtsied. "Baba Yaga, at your . . . well, not at your service. That would be a lie. Say rather I'm not opposed to you—or not *as* opposed to you as I am to some others who were in the hotel tonight." She dropped her skirt and held up a hand, displaying a business card with a cartoon Baba Yaga figure on it and a phone number. "For if they bother you, dearling. Just give us a ring. They being the other Gray Lords, of course." She dropped the silliness for a moment. "Margaret, I owed your father, and he cannot collect. Take the card. Put it in the bottom of a drawer somewhere, but remember it. When you need me, you can call the number or rip the card in half, and I will come to your aid, once."

Margaret put her hand on Thomas to steady herself and walked a few steps forward so she could take it. "My father told me stories about you," she said. "He spoke well of you. Mostly."

Baba Yaga smiled, her teeth white and straight. "How good of him. I speak well of him, too—mostly." She looked at me. "I like what you're doing, Coyote girl—even though you had to kill my favorite troll. That's not your fault, though. I know who sent him. They are claiming they forgot how strong the call of water would be on him—that it was an accident that they lost control. You and I know better." She held out another card, this one poison green.

"You don't get to call upon me for a favor," she said when I took it. She glanced at Adam and licked her lips again. "Not unless you want to share the Russian wolf."

"No," I said, closing my fist on the card so it crumpled into a ball.

She cackled again, and said, "If you rip that one up, it will just be harder to read. You should call me for information—I think you might need advice soon. And I will call upon you from time to time. No obligation on either side, of course. You don't have to tell me anything, nor do I have to tell you anything. But I don't want a war with the humans, and some idiot among us—or more properly, some *idiots* among us—are determined to start one. If I know trouble is coming your way, I'll tell you. Keep that card—you'll need it soon."

"All right," I said slowly. "No promises implied or given."

She smiled. "Just so." And she disappeared. No mortar and pestle this time, she was just gone. Her scent lingered behind her.

"That's all right, then," said Margaret. "We needed a finale."

"Don't trust her," Zee told me. He looked at Margaret. "You're probably all right, if you're cautious."

"I am," she said, tucking the card into the small handbag she'd been carrying. "And if I'm not cautious enough, Thomas is happy to point it out." She looked at me. "Mercy. I really would like a chance to talk to you. Would you mind driving our car?" She gave her hands a rueful look. "I'm getting better, but my hands aren't trustworthy to drive yet. Thomas, would you mind riding with Adam?"

The answer I saw on Thomas's face was that he minded very much, but he said, "I can do that."

"Sure," I said. "We'll have a girl's car and a guy's car. It'll be fun."

Thomas picked Margaret up and put her in her seat, and watched gravely while she belted herself in. He shut her door and handed me the keys.

"Drive carefully," he said.

"I will," I promised.

He gave me a stiff nod and strode over to Adam's SUV.

I didn't have to adjust the seat to be comfortable. Thomas wasn't very big to be that scary. I took a moment to familiarize myself with the car, so I wouldn't have to do it while I was driving.

"Thank you," Margaret said.

I gave her a startled look, because, as a rule, the fae don't thank you—and you'd better not thank them, either. "Thank you" implies debt, and most fae will hold you to that. Margaret laughed.

"I'm not that old, Mercy," she said. "About a hundred years, and most of that was spent in the Heart of the Hill—underground, imprisoned in a forgotten chunk of mine tunnel."

She'd said that she'd had no food, no drink, no light. I tried to imagine what going without food and water for almost a hundred years would have been like. A werewolf would have died, starved to death like a human in that situation, maybe even faster than a human. There were degrees of immortality, some more terrible than others.

Unaware of my thoughts, Margaret had kept talking. "My father thought that it was important that we blend with the normal folk, so I don't have a lot of the taboos the old fae do. 'Thank you' means just what it would to you."

Adam's SUV lit up, and I rolled down the window to wave them ahead. I didn't spend much time in Walla Walla. If I'd been alone, I could have found my way out to the highway, but why bother when Adam could lead the way? He flashed his lights and took point.

"How did you survive?" I asked her.

"Not very well." She held her hand up and moved it. "It's taken me years to get this far—and the first year I spent as a total bed-ridden invalid. But I am better now, getting better almost every day. A month ago, I would not have been able to stay on my feet as long as I did tonight." She paused. "That's sort of what I wanted to talk to you about. You are human."

"Half," I said apologetically. "My father is . . . not human." I wasn't up to explaining my complicated parentage to her, likeable as I found her. Besides, I was pretty sure my bloodlines weren't what she wanted to talk about. "I can change into a coyote, and I have a few other tricks up my sleeve."

"But your husband is still far stronger than you," she said.

I nodded. "He is."

"How did you get him to stop treating you like a fragile thing that might blow away in a harsh wind and take you to bed?" she said.

Holy cow. The girlfriend talk. I tried to remember the last time I'd done the girlfriend talk. Char. It had been with Char, when I'd talked her out of the very handsome but not very bright young man who would make a lovely date for someone else. That was all the way back in college.

I smelled Margaret's sudden embarrassment. "I had a much more tactful way to ask that," she said. Then she let out a frustrated growl. "We've been living together for two and a half years, and the most passion I get is a kiss on the forehead. And I don't have anyone but Thomas to ask about it. And I *can't* ask Thomas."

"Obviously not," I said. The reason I hadn't had the girlfriend talk with anyone in a long time is that I sucked at it. I could barely talk to *Adam* about our relationship, and I *loved* Adam.

"Right?" she said.

I liked Margaret. I wanted to help her if I could, even if only as a sounding board. But. I couldn't forget what Margaret was. Despite the easy way she'd thanked me and how she'd just established that she was not under the power of the Gray Lords, she was still fae. If there was one thing I'd learned about the fae, it was that being in their debt was only a little more dangerous than having a fae in my debt. If she wanted my help—I'd ask for her help, too.

"I have a proposition for you," I said. "I'll try to help you—as much as one clueless person can help another—if you'll give me some intelligence on the people in the room tonight." Like, say, the name of the middle-aged woman in salmon who had tortured Zee. "I could ask Zee—but he tends to hate everyone uniformly."

It hadn't been an accident that Tad had been the one to talk to

Adam and me about the Widow Queen. I could call Ariana, maybe, but she was in Europe, and she hadn't been in that room tonight.

"Deal," she said promptly. "What do you want to know?"

"Don't you think I should go first?" I asked. "I see your problem, but I'm relationship-challenged. Since Thomas sounds like he's relationship-challenged, too, you might be better off talking to Adam, who has experience dealing with stupid people."

She leaned back in her seat and smiled sweetly. Unlike when Zee smiled sweetly, it didn't send the hairs on the back of my neck up with nervousness. "I'm not in the inner circle of the Council, either. All I know is the stuff my father drilled into my head. But he was pretty sharp. I have to tell you, that if all you do is listen to me whine, it would help me a great deal. Let's do politics first. I have a feeling it will be less depressing. What do you want to know?"

"Let's start with the woman in the salmon-colored suit," I said.

"Órlaith," she said. "She is the sister of Brian mac Cennétig."

I frowned because she said the name of Órlaith's brother as if I should have known him. "Who?" I asked.

"He was the high king of Ireland," she said. "He defeated the kings of Ulster."

I only knew one of the high kings of Ireland named Brian. Okay, I only knew the name of one of the high kings of Ireland, and *his* name was Brian.

"Do you mean Brian Boru?" I asked tentatively. "The one who united all of the Irish against the Vikings?"

She let out a huff of air. "And a good thing it is that my father died before he heard you say that. Boru is a nickname given him years after he died by people who didn't know him. And the Vikings weren't driven out, they were assimilated . . . not that it is important to our current conversation."

Not being an expert on Irish history, I didn't feel the need to argue. "Okay. So Brian Boru was fae?"

"No. His father married a fae lady who saw to it that he thought her daughter Órlaith was his. She soon grew bored of him and went on her way, but she left her daughter behind." Margaret huffed. "But that's not what you need to know, is it? Still, despite her chosen appearance, Órlaith is very young for a Gray Lord. Even so, my father said she is too tied to the glories of the past. Her greatest strength is in her ability to persuade people to follow her. My father liked her a great deal."

"I think she tortured Zee," I said. "I don't think I'm going to like her."

She smiled, but it was a sad smile. "My father did not like your Zee. The Dark Smith was not, even by the flexible standards of the fae, a hero."

I knew that. I *knew* that. But I'd worked side by side with him for most of my adult life. I'd seen him do a lot of small kindnesses, and I suspected that there were some I'd missed because he was embarrassed by them. He was not petty, and *I'd* never seen him be cruel.

I decided it would be safer to change the subject. "So the Widow Queen?"

"Neuth?" Margaret focused her gaze on the dark beyond the windows of the Subaru. "She's not a nice person. Dangerous. She takes pleasure in the misery of others. She despises humankind—despises those weaker than her, and most people are weaker than she is."

That dovetailed with what Tad had said about her.

"Goreu," I said.

She looked at me. "My father didn't know him well. Goreu didn't take an active role among the fae until after my father died.

Much of what I know of him comes from the research Thomas did for this trip." She smiled, as if at some memory. "The vampires follow fae politics for entertainment. Thomas gathered a lot more information about current politics than the Gray Lords would be comfortable with if they knew." She tapped a finger on the dash. "So Goreu. King Arthur wasn't a king, really, and the stories of the knights of the round table are only very loosely factual. But Arthur was a hero, and Goreu rode with him. He killed a giant. The troll you killed was but a rabbit to the wolf that a giant would have been." She paused. "But that was a long time ago. Goreu has done nothing important since except for his selection into the Council of the Gray Lords. I wouldn't have thought one of Arthur's men would have stooped to the foulness of those slave bracelets." She hummed a little; it was on key and pretty. "I also wouldn't have thought a Gray Lord would have been so easily defeated."

"Nemane." Her name seemed to hang in the air longer than sound should have. Suddenly it was very dark in the car, the dash lights only a candle in the night.

"The Carrion Crow," Margaret said slowly, and for the first time I smelled fear rising from her skin. "One of the three fae who could be Morrigan, the goddess of battle. She is smart and very old. And very, very clever. My father respected her—and feared her. The only one of the fae he truly feared. She is capable of playing a very long game. She is patient." Margaret swallowed. "And bloodthirsty."

Maybe if we hadn't been in a dark car, driving through the dark, her words wouldn't have been so . . . frightening. Like how a story told by firelight has more power than one told in the light of day. But I hadn't been afraid of her back in the hotel. Neuth, yes, but not Nemane.

I could just be affected by Margaret's fear, but it felt like more than that. Maybe it was just that we spoke of someone who was a Power and had been a Power for longer than I could imagine, and we spoke of her in the loneliness of the night.

"Okay," I said. "Now that you've scared us both . . ." I had the sudden conviction that Adam and I were in way over our heads. We had just met with five of the Gray Lords—but those weren't the only Gray Lords on that reservation.

"When I saw her sitting there . . ." Margaret said. "I was very grateful for Thomas at my back."

There was still one we hadn't spoken of.

"Beauclaire," I said. I knew him best of the Gray Lords and liked what I knew.

She smiled and relaxed. "My father said that Lugh's son likes to be underestimated. It helps him that so many of the fae remember his father, Lugh, and judge the son from that scale. Lugh . . . Lugh was everything they say he was. Sometimes the humans called him a god, and they weren't far wrong." She didn't exactly stiffen, but she eyed me. "He was good, glorious, and kind—and your Dark Smith killed him."

I knew that. Zee had killed him because Lugh had, like many very old creatures, started to become a monster. It was why Zee and Beauclaire did not deal well together—and another reason I'd been surprised when he helped Zee escape.

"Beauclaire and Nemane are allies," she said. I'd picked that up from tonight's meeting. "From what happened when Adam spoke, I think that those two have a use for you and your pack. Zee distracted Órlaith and Neuth. Goreu was still recovering from the slave bracelet. But Nemane and Beauclaire could have responded to Adam when he spoke. By not doing so, they gave legitimacy to Adam's claim—unless they rule against it out loud, all of Faery must respect the borders of your territory. That tells me that Adam's claim played right into whatever those two have planned."

"Okay," I said. Being part of any fae's plans wasn't a good thing. I'd have to warn Adam. And speaking of warning . . . "You should know that Edythe didn't have any trouble seeing through your glamour."

Margaret frowned. "Edythe?"

"There were two guards the Gray Lords brought with them," I said. "She was the one that looked like a girl."

"They weren't guards," she said. "The Gray Lords don't use guards. They were servants, to be sent to fetch food or whatever else was required." She frowned. "She saw through the glamour?"

I nodded.

"There are some who see truth," Margaret said. "But it is a rare gift. It may be that gift was the reason they brought her to the meeting. Interesting that she didn't speak when she saw who accompanied us."

"I'm not a threat," I said. "And I'm the only one she looked at."

"Okay," she said. She dusted her hands on her thighs and took a deep breath. "So tell me how you got an Alpha werewolf to treat you like a partner instead of a princess who needs protecting."

I pursed my lips. "I can tell you that, but I don't think it will be useful in your situation. By the time I'd met Adam, I'd spent my whole life proving myself, Margaret. I knew who I was and what I could do—and I didn't let anyone make me less."

"Damn it," she said. "I hoped that you could give me some useful advice. I don't know many women—have never known many women. And your situation seemed so similar."

It hadn't been, really. Not the beginning of Adam and me—but . . . "A couple of months ago, this volcano god—a great manitou—came after Adam's ex-wife," I told her. "We defeated him, but in the process, I was badly injured. Our pack doctor told Adam I was going to die."

"But you didn't," said Margaret.

I drew in a breath. "I *was* dying, no question. Only by the weirdest circumstances ever did I survive. Not quite dumb luck, but unexpected enough that it was worse really." Coyote counted as weird circumstances—and he was unpredictable.

"It took a while for me to recover completely. Adam, who has been very, very good about not indulging his wolf's need to be overprotective, has had to deal with his perceived failure to protect me. Sometimes he wakes up in the middle of the night to listen to me breathe." I didn't tell her about the nightmares, or the times when he pulled me close to him to listen to my heart, and his skin was damp with the sweat of fear. Or that sometimes, in the darkness of our room, he cried. Those moments weren't for public consumption. "But Thomas didn't fail to keep you safe, so the situation isn't completely analogous."

Margaret said nothing, but I felt like she was going to, so I kept quiet.

"That is," she said, "I think, very much what is between Thomas and me." She paused. "I don't talk about him to other people. He wouldn't like it. But I need advice, and I don't know how I'm going to get it without giving you the whole picture."

I didn't say anything.

"Excuse me," she said. She took out her cell phone and began texting. The phone chimed as her message was returned. She texted back and forth a bit more.

"He says I should talk to you," she said. "He" was obviously Thomas. "He says Adam says that you are a deep well. That secrets are safe in your keeping." She gave me a considering look.

"That's me," I said. "Damp. Also, cold and dank."

She laughed. "All right." She quit laughing and looked out into the darkness. "I met Thomas when I was thirteen in Butte, Montana. Butte was . . . not what it is now—small and forgotten. Gold, then silver, and finally copper, which, in the age where all the cities of the world were stringing copper wire for electricity, meant money, and money is power. The people who flocked to the boomtown were not just human. My father came, hoping to set up a new court, I think. But his people weren't the only fae, and there was conflict."

She hummed a little, reached out, and turned on the radio. Classical music filled the car, replaced by country and then eighties rock before she turned it off.

"My father's enemies used me against him. They stole me away and chained me in the mining tunnels." Her restless fingers played with the fabric of her slacks. "The mining tunnels in Butte were five thousand feet below the earth and more, a mile deep. My father and I, our power comes from the sun."

Silence stretched.

"Which is ironic, given that you love a vampire," I said, trying to help her.

"Not . . . not as ironic as you might think." She played a little more with her slacks.

"So you were trapped there for decades?"

She shook her head, gave me a quick smile, then went back to her narrative. "Not that time. For a couple of days only. But it gave my father's enemies the idea for what they did to me later. It was still dark and frightening. I was hungry and alone, and I heard a sound."

She swallowed. "I don't have any friends," she said. "Except for Thomas. I don't quite know how to go about this."

She didn't know me, and it was hard to tell someone you don't know about private things. "My foster parents both died when I was fourteen," I told her, breaking the awkward silence. Then I realized that was the wrong part of the story to start with. "Let me backtrack. My mother was a buckle bunny when she was sixteen."

"Buckle bunny?"

I nodded. "That means she followed the rodeo and slept with rodeo cowboys. I guess her parents were a real freak show. She left home when she was fifteen or sixteen. She took the truck and horse trailer she'd paid for and her quarter-horse mare and hit the road. Traveled wherever there was a rodeo and barrel raced. She was good enough she made money at it. But she was lonely, so she chased after the cowboys." I paused. "Rodeo cowboys aren't universally horrible, but they are macho, and some of them, usually not the more successful, are brutal with their animals and with women. She had hooked up with this bronc rider in Wyoming, and he got drunk and pretty rough one night. They'd been sleeping in his horse trailer—"

"In a horse trailer?" Margaret asked.

"Some of them have campers in the front," I said. "I guess his did. Anyway, the fight spilled to the outside and attracted attention. My mother is a lot shorter than me. She was sixteen, and he was twenty-eight and big for a bronc rider. He outweighed her by a hundred pounds or more. He was snake mean when he was drunk, and the other rodeo riders were afraid of him."

It had been a long time since I'd told this story to anyone. Even knowing what I knew about my father now, it was still pretty cool.

"But my mom was nobody's punching bag, and she doesn't believe in fighting fair. She kicked his butt in front of his friends. Then she

215

turned around to get her stuff out of his trailer, and he got to his feet and came after her while her back was turned." I could see by the tension in Margaret's shoulders that the story was getting to her.

"There was this Native American, a Blackfeet man from Montana." Which he sort of had been, and sort of hadn't been. "He rode bulls, Mom said, and those bull riders are all a little crazy to do what they do. Anyway, he coldcocked that man before he got close to my mother again."

I smiled as I got to the best part. "And my mom punched him in the stomach. She said, 'I have a gun, you stupid son of a bitch. I could have *shot* him, and no one would have said it was anything but self-defense. Now he's going to get to beat up some other woman, and it will be your fault.'"

Margaret laughed.

"I know, right?" I said. "Mom is scary. Even Adam walks softly around her. She and that bull rider hooked up for a couple of months. Then one day, he just didn't come home. Died in a car wreck." He'd been hunting vampires, and they'd caught up with him. "Mom was pregnant with me. Imagine her surprise when she came in to change my diapers and found a coyote puppy in my crib."

It was my turn to be quiet for a little while. "She eventually ran down a pack of werewolves—do you know who the Marrok is?"

Margaret nodded.

"Right," I said. "That's whose pack she found. He agreed to take me—but she couldn't come with. She decided that it was the best place for me." Mom never said exactly what had made her decide to do that, but I figured it was pretty bad, considering the stories she did tell me. I did know that she'd negotiated for visitation rights over Bran's objections. "So I was raised by a pretty neat couple. She was human, and he was werewolf. She died, and he committed suicide to be with her. I was fourteen, and I didn't want to live with anyone else, so Bran let me live on my own." Bran was from an age when fourteen was an adult. "I was raised a coyote in a werewolf pack. I know exactly what it feels like not to have anyone to talk to. Tell me as much or as little as you'd like. I won't swear not to tell Adam, he's my mate. But if I'm a well, he's a . . . bottomless pit." I glanced at Margaret, then looked back at the road. "When we last left you, you were alone, chained in the dark, and hearing monsters."

"Thomas found me there," Margaret said, but she sounded more comfortable. Good. I'd worried that the "monster" talk would throw her. If so, she didn't stand a chance taking on someone as . . . closed as Thomas. He reminded me of my foster brother Charles, and, for Charles, it had taken an Omega wolf with a backbone of titanium to learn how to make a relationship work. Omega wolves didn't come around very often; maybe a fairy princess would do.

"He was . . . he was a very, very angry man. I asked for his help. He refused. I asked him what he wanted, and he said . . . no, that's not right. *He wanted.* I felt what he wanted as if it were water, and he'd doused me in it, so I could feel his need in my bones. But what he *asked* for was to feed from me."

There was a long moment as she weighed what had happened with how much she wanted to tell me. She smiled. "I was frightened—but not so frightened I didn't see the hurt that caused his anger. I didn't think he'd be happy to know how easy it was for me to see."

She took a breath.

"I gave him what he wanted as well as what he asked for, even though he'd done that last because he knew I'd refuse. That I'd give him an excuse to walk off. If I'd known him then as well as I do now, I'd have known there was no way he'd have left me. I'm not sure *Thomas* knows that." She gave me an incredulous look. "Talking. Who would have thought talking to someone would be so useful. I bet he, too, needs to know that he would not have left me there."

Oh, I knew that battle. "Good luck," I said. "When your man is responsible for the world, heaven forbid they aren't guilty of every little thing."

She giggled. Looked at me and broke down in whoops of amusement. "Isn't that the truth, now," she said when she quieted, wiping her eyes.

She laughed again and shook her head. "Anyway. We struck a bargain that night, but it was more than either of us expected. There is magic in bargaining with one of my kind that has nothing to do with what I had the power to do or not do. There, that's some repayment for you. That's why so many of the fae are willing to strike odd bargains—they can gain power from it. And mine wasn't the only bargain present that night. Thomas's father had bargained with the master vampire who made him. Two bargains in the Heart of the Hill—there is power in the deep places of the earth, Mercy. There was also my fire magic, tempered to a stronger force by my royal birth and his . . ." She hesitated. "Some things are his secrets to give. But there is magic in Thomas's heritage, too. I gave him three gifts. His freedom from the vampire who had bound him—that was Thomas's own power made manifest. From my magic, I—" She sucked in a breath. "You are easy to talk to. I think that is something else that belongs to Thomas."

I nodded. "I can live with that." It was the truth, but I was very curious anyway.

She laughed. "That was almost a lie." She looked at me. "I tell you what. I'll tell Thomas what we talked about, and he can tell you if he chooses."

"I can live with that better," I said. "Or at least, it isn't any worse." But then I got an inkling. A terrible horrible very, very scary inkling.

No normal vampire would have chosen a hotel like the Marriott. There were too many windows—and the ones in their room all faced the east, where the sun would rise.

And Margaret said that her power, like her father's, came from the sun.

Unbidden, I remembered walking at night once with Stefan, a friend who was a vampire. At one point, he stopped, looked up at the moon, and said, totally out of the blue, "I miss the *sun*." And the last word sounded as though it had been dragged up from the depths of his being. If someone asked Stefan what he would wish for, I think that the ability to walk in sunlight would be very high on that list.

Could Thomas walk in the sun?

As soon as I thought that, terror screamed up my backbone. Vampires are evil. Even though I like some of them, I know that they are evil. Symbols of faith can work against them, repel them and cause them pain. Wood works against vampires because it was something that once was living that became dead—sympathetic magic of a sort. But it is sunshine that is the real weapon against vampires.

"Mercy?" Margaret said, her voice concerned.

That was a secret too dangerous for anyone to have. They would hunt him down. Which they? All of "they." Vampires would hunt him down to steal his secret. Everyone else would hunt him down to kill him to get rid of the fear I had coiled in my stomach.

"Don't ask him," I said, my voice hoarse. "This gift from your power, I think I know what it was." Thomas called her Sunshine, I remembered. "That's a secret too big for acquaintances, no matter how friendly. When we're friends, we can pretend you told me then. For now we can say that I have an idea—and I'm going to pretend I'm wrong because that would make Thomas the scariest vampire I've ever heard of."

We drove for a few miles in silence.

Then she said, "Thomas isn't a monster—though he'd disagree with me on that. I don't know how he managed it, with his father, who was the single coldest being I have ever known, but he's a good man."

I nodded, though I wasn't as sure of it as she was. I cleared my throat. "So the third thing you gave him was your blood."

"It sealed the bargain," she said. "That's what my father said. For the next seventeen years, I always knew where he was, whether he was . . . well, not happy. Thomas doesn't do happy very much. But he was content. Or if he was unhappy or cold or whatever . . . He says that he did not feel the same connection—not the same way."

"That's backward to the way a vampire's feeding usually works," I said. I knew that because apparently my . . . Stefan felt that way about me. He knew when I was sad or hurt. He'd known when I had nearly died. I knew that because he'd shown up at the hospital and sat with me all through the night. I'd been pretty high on pain meds, but Adam had told me that Stefan hadn't said a word the whole time.

Margaret nodded. "Backward, yes. That's what my father said. Then he said he thought it was the thing that Thomas gave me back for my gifts. Thomas was raised to be a guardian, to protect his father's interests. When his father betrayed him, he still guarded, but he no longer believed in what he was doing. He gave me himself, everything of what he was, when we sealed the bargain with blood." Voice tight, she said, "My father said that the vampire usually takes ownership of those he feeds from, but Thomas reversed that in an effort to balance our bargain."

"That's . . ." I hesitated, not wanting to be offensive.

"Messed up," she said. "I know. If I think of it as a gift of service, it helps. But I used him—and now . . . we're so lopsided. It's like he thinks of himself as my devoted . . ."

"Slave?" I suggested. "Servant?"

She laughed, wiping tears from her eyes again. "Can you imagine Thomas as a slave? He'd have the person who thought he was his master committing suicide in an hour, all the while helping out with solicitous advice on the proper length of blade. And even as the knife slid in, the master would think it was all his own idea."

"Guard dog," I said.

"Yes," she said. "That one. It's as if he sees me as this fragile thing to be protected." She paused. "That's not quite right. It's not as though he doesn't respect me, respect my power. But he sees me as different from him. Separate." She sighed. "I hoped you could help me."

I thought about it. Sometimes simple is best when dealing with men. It's not that they are simple. Simple and Adam didn't belong in the same room. But dealing with them . . . that was simple.

"So seduce him," I said.

"I'd love to," she all but wailed. "But how?"

Okay. Seducing Adam wasn't exactly . . . difficult. It was fun, actually, just how much I could get him to react with subtle cues. A nudge. He did it back to me, too—with interest. But Thomas was more like Charles. Thomas needed a sledgehammer first.

"Victoria's Secret," I said. "No. That's too feminine. Too much what women think is sexy." I tried to channel Adam.

"Have you looked at me?" she said. "I am covered with scars, and I'm too skinny. I have no muscle. I'm ugly."

I wasn't a guy, so I knew better than to argue with that last statement. What I thought didn't matter—what she thought mattered.

"*Thomas* doesn't think you're ugly," I told her. "No one who watches him watch you—no one who saw his face when he picked you up back there in that hotel would ever, ever be under that impression."

"I've tried lingerie," she said after a moment.

"Big guns are required," I said. "Subtle won't work. Naked."

"But I don't have big guns," she said. Then she dropped her head in her hands. "I can't believe I just said that. I can't believe I said that to someone I've just met."

"Thomas will like your guns just fine," I assured her. "Just ask him."

Her jaw dropped open. Then she closed it and laughed.

We talked awhile more. I offered improbable suggestions, and she responded in kind. Just outside of Pasco, she fell asleep.

It had been a long time since I'd talked with a woman who was just my friend. I'd called Char, my old college roommate, over Christmas. Maybe it was time to call her again.

I parked the Subaru, and before I had the engine off, Thomas had the passenger door open. When he saw Margaret asleep, he extracted her from the seat without waking her up.

Yep, I thought with satisfaction, *he's a goner.*

I got out of the car, locked it with the appropriate button on the key fob, and handed the keys to Thomas.

He took them, looked at me, then glanced over his shoulder at Adam, who was standing beside the black SUV in the parade-rest position that he habitually fell into when waiting for someone. Zee had the hood of the SUV up and was tinkering.

I frowned at Zee. There was nothing wrong with the SUV. I kept all of our cars in excellent running condition.

"You should come visit us in San Francisco," Thomas said, his voice quiet. "I would be delighted to serve as your escort." Then he smiled. A real smile. He didn't have Adam's dimples, but it was a good smile anyway. "In the purely tourist sense of the word."

"We'll do that," I said. "Margaret and I had fun."

Margaret opened her eyes and, in a sleepy voice, said, "Take care, Mercy. And thank you. I hope not to need the big guns."

I laughed. "I think you'll find that your guns are plenty. Safe travels."

Thomas turned and headed for the hotel entrance.

I stalked to the SUV, and said, "There is nothing wrong with the SUV." Zee kept tinkering. I stood on my tiptoes to see what he was doing. "Is there?"

Zee removed himself from under the hood and held up a small device. "Not anymore. Someone's been tracking you."

Adam held his hand out, looked at the device, and snorted. He passed it to me. It bore a neat label with the SUV maker's logo on it. I'd never had to do anything more complicated than an oil change on the SUV. If I'd noticed the little box, I'd have assumed it belonged.

"Feds, I bet," Adam said. "We are persons of interest."

"How did you find it?" I asked Zee.

"Nothing you could do, *Liebling*," he said. "I felt it transmit. It didn't bother me much, but since we had a moment here, I thought I'd take a look."

Adam stuck it under the bumper of the Chevy parked next to the SUV. The Chevy bore all the signs of a rental vehicle, including a license-plate surround that advertised for Enterprise. I patted its trunk. "May someone rent you for a very long drive to Alaska," I told it.

Adam snorted, then asked Zee, "Could you tell how long it has been there?"

Zee nodded. "Six months, maybe a bit more. Someone wants to keep tabs on you, Adam."

This time it was my turn to snort. "If I'd known it was there, we could have done something more interesting—like drive out to the middle of the Hanford Reach every full moon and park for the night." Which we did, mostly. We had other hunting spots, but the Reach was the best. "Sorry I didn't find it, Adam. I'll keep a better eye out next time."

"No worries," said Adam softly. "I'll have a talk with a few people I know about boundaries that shouldn't be crossed. It won't happen again."

We arrived home to find every door and window in the house open, and the smell of burning wool in the air.

"Hey, Boss," said Warren, as we came through the doorway, his expression somewhere between pained and amused. "We had a little mishap. Aiden was sleeping when his blankets burst into flame. Happily, Mary Jo was here. While we were all trying to figure out what to do—besides hold our ears to try to shut out the fire alarm—she grabbed the fire extinguisher from the garage and put the fire out. Mattress is a goner, but the room's okay. We have the situation under control."

About that time, Mary Jo came up the stairs, carrying an armful of sodden, blackened fabric that had at one time been a Pendleton wool blanket. She looked at me, and said, "Life is never boring around here." Then she grinned at me, an expression she hadn't turned on me in a very long while. "Your fire demon says that he needs to leave. We convinced him that it would be rude to leave before you got back, but I'm not sure we could have kept him here much longer."

As she finished speaking, Aiden came up the stairs. His hair was wet, and he was wearing sweats from the pack stores—I made a mental note that we were going to have to get him clothes if he was going to stay here long.

"My apologies," he said as soon as he reached the landing. He didn't look at either of us. "I am not safe to be around. I didn't light fires in my sleep when I was in Underhill—at least, not that I know of. I will find somewhere else to sleep tonight. I appreciate the help you have given me thus far."

"Why are you planning on leaving?" Adam asked.

That made Aiden raise his face briefly. "I have damaged your home."

Adam shrugged. "We house werewolves here, Aiden. I don't think anyone has tried to burn the house down before—"

"No," I agreed, "that was my house."

Adam gave me a rueful grimace. "At least you weren't in it. Werewolves can be very destructive. My contractor sends me Christmas cards and most-valuable-customer presents every year."

"And this time the damage was confined to a mattress and some bedding," I told him. "That's cheap by werewolf standards."

"The mattress might have been all right," Mary Jo said, "if Ben hadn't dumped a five-gallon bucket of water on it. I told him I had it under control with the fire extinguisher. So the mattress isn't really Aiden's fault." She wrinkled her nose. "Excuse me, though, I'm going to get rid of this blanket."

Aiden opened his mouth, then shut it again.

"No worries," Adam said. "We'll just make sure to keep a fire extinguisher around. Until the situation with the fae stabilizes, we'll have to have twenty-four/seven guards at the house anyway. I'll just make sure that they keep watch for fire, too."

10

"It's not quite the biggest crane in the world," said the Lampson guy to the police officer. He'd introduced himself as Marley.

The Pasco police officer, whom I'd seen before but didn't know personally, was Ed Thorson. He was the only police officer left on the scene because I'd asked him to get rid of as many people as he could. No one is proud like a dominant werewolf in front of an audience. If there were too many people here, we might end up with him jumping, even if he didn't intend to do it in the first place.

Above us, nearly forty stories up, on the top of the Transi-Lift LTL-3000, was one of our werewolves. I couldn't see him, I'm not sure I could have seen him even in the daylight without binoculars, but he'd been seen climbing up it at the end of his shift, and everyone was very sure that he hadn't climbed back down—or jumped.

Three days had passed since we'd confronted the fae in the hotel meeting room—and we hadn't heard anything from them. We'd had to step down our security because we just didn't have enough people to stay at high alert for very long.

Though Adam made sure that there were at least two were-wolves at our house at any given time, mostly everyone's lives had returned to normal. Even Aiden's setting something on fire when he slept felt normal—one of Adam's techie guys was working on rewiring some smoke alarms so that instead of shrieking, they just buzzed a little.

Back to normal meant when Adam got called to work after dinner, he left me in charge. So when the police called to tell me that one of our wolves was sitting on the top of the big Lampson crane and they were worried about him jumping, I was the one who got to go fix it. If Darryl, Warren, or George had been our guard wolves, I'd have sent one of them because I'd exchanged about four words with Sherwood Post. "Yes, ma'am" and "no, ma'am" only counted as four words, even if they'd been said every time I'd tried to strike up a conversation with him. But as luck would have it, Ben and Paul were the watch wolves on duty, neither of whom I could trust not to drive a suicidal werewolf right off the edge—both metaphorically and literally speaking. Sher-wood Post had come to us a month ago from the Marrok. He was too quiet, too polite, and missing his left leg. Werewolves heal. They heal broken things, they heal crushed things, and they heal amputated things. But apparently not if witches were involved.

About four or five years ago, there had been a nasty coven of witches in Seattle. Their leader had been killed by the Emerald City Pack. When the pack went to clean out the home of the leader, to make sure that there were no nasty magical surprises left behind, they had found, among other things, an emaciated were-wolf in a cage. He was missing his leg.

He hadn't remembered who he was or where he came from—
and neither did any of the packs. He also didn't remember what
had happened to his leg. As best anyone could figure out, he'd
been brought over from Europe and traded around among various
black witches for years, if not decades.

Bran took him home, eventually coaxing him back into human
shape. When he couldn't do anything that could make Sherwood's
leg regrow—yes, that's as bad as it sounds—he sent Sherwood to
doctors who provided a prosthetic for the human form. The wolf
just ran on three legs.

Sherwood took his name from two books that happened to be
lying on Bran's desk when Bran told him to pick a name. That
Bran would read Sherwood Anderson was not surprising. I wasn't
sure if I was more amused or horrified that Bran had been reading
Emily Post.

According to Bran, Sherwood had approached him in January
and asked for a transfer to somewhere with a shorter, more congenial winter than Montana. Most places have more congenial
winters than Montana, so Bran had a lot of places he could have
sent Sherwood, but he sent him to us.

When the call came in about Sherwood and the crane, I hadn't
been able to get in touch with Adam other than to leave him a voice
message. His office wasn't answering, either, which meant whatever
he was involved in was some security issue with the government
contracts he held. I couldn't feel anything through the pack bonds
that suggested Sherwood was about to kill himself, but Bran hadn't
been able to tell when my foster father had gone out to commit
suicide, either. Sherwood felt just as he always did to me—quiet.

I squinted, trying to see him, but he was too far up, and it was
too dark.

I might not have known Officer Thorson, but I liked him. When I explained that all the extra people who'd been there when I arrived were problematical, he'd listened gravely. Then, without arguing, he'd dispersed everyone until there were just two guys from Lampson, Officer Thorson, and me. Marley continued to talk to the officer about his crane with the enthusiasm of a golf addict describing his new putter. "So not the biggest—that mark keeps moving. But it is the largest twin-crawler crane in the world, and the biggest crane *we've* ever built. So far, anyway."

I hadn't quite worked out if Marley was the night manager who'd summoned the police or if he was security, the CEO of the company, or someone in between. He wore scruffy jeans, a Western-style button-up shirt, and needed a shave. He also smelled like beer, but I think most of that was coming off his boots, so maybe he'd come over from a bar or party. I did wish he'd shut up about how big the stupid crane was because I was pretty sure I was going to have to climb it and see if I could talk Sherwood down.

I'd seen the crane before; you can't help but see it when you drive across the suspension bridge—which we had not been able to do tonight. There were no estimates about when that bridge would go back in use. They had to figure out how badly it had been damaged, first. I didn't know why I felt guilty about that—I didn't turn loose a troll on the city. Still, even without being on the bridge, you could see the crane for a long way.

Lampson's Pasco yard was located in a warehouse district near the railroad. The whole area still showed signs of the army depot it had once been with long wooden warehouses laid out in orderly patterns. It was haunted. If I looked—and I tried not to—I could see a few ghosts flickering around. There was one, dressed in a World War II army uniform, who watched me. I was pretty sure he was one of the rare self-aware ghosts. If I stared at ghosts for very long, even just the repeaters, they tended to start following me around.

This wasn't the first time I'd come out here—there were a couple of junkyards not too far away. But I'd never seen the crane up close and personal before, and it was a lot bigger than it looked from the bridge.

"So Hitachi commissioned it to build nuclear power plants," Marley was saying expansively. "Then along came that tsunami that hit the Fukushima Daiichi plant and, well, no one is building nuclear power plants in Japan now, are they? So here it sits."

The big crane was part of the Pasco skyline, which admittedly was not much of a skyline compared to Seattle or Spokane. In the daylight, the crane part of it was bright orange with sections of white, and the crawler part—this thing moved with two tanklike treads that were taller than I was, each with its own control booth—was bright Lampson blue. Obviously, no one with a hint of estrogen in their veins had designed the color scheme.

In the dark, though, it rose above us, black against the lighter sky. We were standing right next to one of the treads, just beneath the crawler that allowed the humongous structure to move. Above the crawler, the crane rose like the orange, Leaning Eiffel Tower of Pasco. If I squinted and used my imagination, I could, just barely, see that someone was sitting on the end of the boom head—the highest point of the crane.

"We could start it up if you want," said Marley, following my gaze. "But we waited until you came out because if we start moving it around, he could fall. I don't know how you feel about your people, but we like ours to survive their tenure with us." He squinted up. "So this guy's tenure is going to end as soon as we get him down."

The nameless guy standing next to him, the only one of the

four of us standing there to whom I hadn't been introduced, murmured, "Marley, that's Sherwood Post. He speaks Russian and
English without an accent, in either language, I'm told. That means
when he's on shift, everyone can communicate with everyone else.
Let me say it again: everybody knows what they are supposed to
be doing. And his shift mates say he can move a three-hundred-
pound bar of steel all by himself."

Marley made a growly sound. "So maybe we give him a second
chance. But I hate to encourage this behavior. What if he jumps?"

"Then you probably don't have to worry about firing him," I
said.

"What I don't get," said Officer Thorson, looking up to the
top of the crane and saying it once more with feeling, "what I
don't get is how you let him get up there in the first place."

"One of my guys saw him start to climb up," the other Lampson
guy answered. "He went running for help, and by the time they got
back, he—Post, I mean—was most of the way up. He didn't respond
when they yelled, but truthfully, it is windy up there. I don't know
if he could have heard them." He frowned, then shook his head.
"But he sure as hell should have noticed all the police and the fire
trucks with their sirens and lights."

Yep. It had been a real circus when I got here.

"How much can you drop that arm down?" Thorson asked.

"All the way to the ground," Marley said. "We'd have already
done it, but it doesn't happen instantaneously, and if he wanted to
jump off and kill himself, he'd have plenty of time to do it. Seemed
to me that we'd be putting pressure on him to do that very thing."

"How high is that?" Thorson asked.

Marley smiled like a proud father. "She's 560 feet tall and she
can lift six million pounds. Six million." He shook his head. "I don't

know how he managed to climb all the way up there with one leg—that boom isn't exactly equipped with a ladder."

"He's a werewolf," I groused. "They are hardwired to do dumb stuff." Maybe I wasn't being fair to Sherwood, whom I didn't know well, but, since it looked like I was going to have to follow him up there, I was entitled to be judgmental. I bent down to make sure my shoes were tied. I didn't want to have to tie them while 560 feet in the air, though I supposed since the boom wasn't at a ninety-degree angle, more like a sixty-five, it wouldn't really be that high. Probably only like 400 or something. My long-ago unlamented geometry class was too far in the past to be of much help. I straightened up and started for the crane.

"What are you doing?" Marley asked in the tone of someone used to getting answers. "Stop." But I didn't work for him.

"Someone's got to talk him down, and he didn't bring his cell phone," I told him, and hopped the chain that blocked off the metal stairway on the side of the crawler. Once I started moving, I moved fast; I was up and on top of the two-story-tall crawler before they'd considered doing anything but talking. By then it was too late to stop me because they were human, and no one who was just human could catch me unless I wanted them to. I heard Marley swear, but it didn't feel like he was emotionally involved—his voice had a frustrated sound rather than honest anger. He wasn't coming after me.

The boom was built of scaffolding-like bars that crossed and crisscrossed the heavy outer beams that were the corner supports of the boom. Everything was size huge. There was a catwalk along the left edge of boom that ran all the way to the top. It would have been easy to use if the boom had been flat. As it was, I was forced to scale the thing, clinging to the top rail like Batman in the old sixties TV series.

I don't have a problem with heights, generally speaking. But, I decided, clinging to my perch and fighting an attack of vertigo, when cars started to look like they belonged in a Matchbox set, that was too freaking high. No more looking down.

Jaw clenched and sweating, as soon as the dizziness subsided, I climbed and climbed some more. My shoulders and arms ached, but my hands took the worst of it. I wished I'd brought a pair of driving gloves. My palms grew blisters that burst. My fingers were sore from grabbing the rail.

"What do you think you're doing?" said a man's voice. He sounded pretty close, and it startled me.

I froze, then wrapped myself around the bar I was climbing on before I looked up. Just a car length from me, Sherwood sat on the last, highest rung of the boom, his leg and prosthetic both dangling off the side. He wasn't holding on.

Reflexively, I looked down before I remembered how bad an idea it was. I put my forehead against the cool metal and swallowed until I knew I wasn't going to throw up. I looked up at him again.

His words had been pretty aggressive, especially for a wolf addressing his Alpha's mate, but the tone was soft and relaxed. I answered the tone, not the words.

"I'm climbing up after you," I told him.

He turned around—balanced on his rump until he could get all the way around—so he could see me easily. I was going to take a wild guess that the height didn't bother him at all.

Bastard.

"That's dumb," he said. "Where's one of the werewolves? If they fall, they might be able to catch themselves. What's Adam thinking to send you up here?"

I growled at him. "Adam is otherwise occupied. Next time you decide to kill yourself, wait until he's home and can climb up here himself. If I have to do this again, I might just push you off myself." It probably wasn't what I should have said to someone sitting five hundred feet—more or less—in the air, but my hands hurt, and I had made it up here by concentrating on how mad I was at the stupid werewolf who made me do it. Also, I have a problem with suicide, and have ever since my foster father had left me alone at fourteen because he couldn't bear to live without his wife. I couldn't take my anger out at him, so I let Sherwood be the scapegoat.

He laughed.

"And yes, I agree with you," I said. "Climbing up here is very, very dumb. I know why I did it. Why did you?"

He sighed and spun around again, making me cling more tightly to my bar. "I'm a useless freak," he said, gesturing at his leg. "It's hard to kill a werewolf, but I'm pretty sure that drop would do it."

Me, too. But that wasn't a productive thing to say, so I found something else. "Marley was going to fire you for climbing up here until the other Lampson guy told him who you were. Apparently you are too useful to them to fire."

He snorted, and I had a thought. He'd been working here since the third day he'd come to the Tri-Cities.

"Just how many times have you climbed up here without getting caught?" I asked.

"All of them but one," he said.

"You came here to get out from under Bran's eye so you could kill yourself," I said.

He didn't say anything, which was a "yes" in my book.

I thought of the kind of courage it would take to climb all the way up here to kill yourself, decide not to, and climb all the way down nearly every day for the better part of the month. And the question that occurred to me then wasn't "why?" but "why not?"

"What stopped you?" I asked his back.

He raised his head and looked up, gesturing to the night sky with one hand, waving with what I considered to be reckless abandon. "Look at that. Do you see the lights? And the sky? Beautiful. Up here? It feels like the huge tightness in my spine that contains all those things I've forgotten loosens up a little." He tapped his forehead. "I can feel those things, curled up inside me, waiting like the sword of Damocles. And I think, maybe I should wait and see if I can find myself. Then I'll have a better idea of what I have to lose."

I made sure my grip was tight, then I looked—out, not down. And he was right. It was beautiful.

And the wind decided right then to blow hard enough to send a buzz through the rail I was holding on to. I felt the vibrations of it under my fingers and had to reassure myself that this crane had been sitting here for at least a couple of years and hadn't fallen down yet. It was certainly designed to hold up more than the three or four hundred pounds that Sherwood and I represented between us. Surely.

And still, the metal vibrated.

"I see your point," I said tightly. "But I think your hiding place has been found out. You think maybe we could talk with our feet on the ground? Fair warning, if I fall and break every bone in my body, Adam will never forgive you."

He laughed again. "Okay," he said. "Do you need any help getting down?"

About halfway to the ground, I stopped to rest. He was below me. When I'd told him I'd get down the same way I got up, he'd scrambled around me to get underneath where he could catch me if I fell. He hadn't said it, but he hadn't had to.

After a minute, I said, "You know what makes me crabby? I didn't need to go up there, did I? If we'd waited for you, you'd have come down just like you always have."

"Yes," said Sherwood. Then he said, his voice a little dreamy, "Probably. But maybe I'd have come down another way."

He started down again then, moving slower than he had to so that I didn't hurry.

"You missed your chance," I told him. "I think your days of climbing up here unseen are over."

"Yes," he said. "But there's always the suspension bridge."

"If I have to climb up the suspension bridge," I told him. "I really will push you off."

He must not have understood I was serious because he laughed again.

So neither of us got arrested for trespassing, though it was, I understand, a near thing. I got Sherwood into Adam's SUV. The Vanagon's radiator had developed a leak and I hadn't found it yet, so Adam had taken a Hauptman Security SUV and left me his. I had to think a bit to get the lights on and the SUV in gear, but I remembered not to swerve to avoid the ghost of the guard who stepped into the road in front of us. But I couldn't help but mutter, "Sorry, Sorry," under my breath when the bumper went through him.

Sherwood looked at me and raised a brow in query.

"Ghosts," I said. "I see dead people."

"Do you?" he said.

I nodded.

"Sucks to be you," he said.

"Beats climbing 560 feet up a crane trying to talk down an idiot who couldn't avoid being seen."

"True," he said thoughtfully. "But doesn't take away from my earlier observation that it sucks to be you."

I had to drive back to the interstate and over the Blue Bridge to get home. It added fifteen or twenty minutes to the trip. Having the Cable Bridge down was going to get old really fast.

My phone rang through the stereo system, an unfamiliar number. It wasn't my car, and my purse with my phone in it was tucked under my seat. And then Sherwood helpfully hit the ANSWER button on the stereo's touch screen—I think he thought I was having trouble reaching it. Any number not in my contacts list I usually let leave a voice mail. It saved me from the guilt of hanging up on someone trying to sell me auto warranties on cars I didn't own.

"Mercy," I said.

"Stay away—"

"Pastor?" I said. "Pastor White. Is that you?"

He cried out, and the connection was reset.

I turned on my turn signal, hit the gas, and headed to church. Maybe they were at Pastor White's house, but I didn't know where he lived. The best I could do was the church.

"What's up?" asked Sherwood.

"That's my pastor," I told him. Pastor White was new; our last pastor had left to take over his father's church in California. Pastor White wasn't quite as engaging or accepting, but his faith was real. "Somebody wants me to go to church," I said.

I hit a button on the stereo, and said, "Call Adam." Sherwood and I listened to his phone ring. When the voice mail picked up, I said, "Someone attacked slash kidnapped my pastor, and I'm heading to the church right now. It is eleven fifty-four." I disconnected. Whom to call? Ben and Paul were home with Jesse and Aiden.

"Call Honey," I said. And got her answering machine. I didn't leave a message. "Call George." Another answering machine. I pounded a fist on the steering wheel. "What the heck good does it do me to be a pack member when there's never anyone home?"

"I do not understand 'what the heck good,'" said the stereo. "Please say a command. Some commands you might find useful are 'call' or 'search address book.'"

I growled, then said, "Call Mary Jo."

She picked up immediately. "Hey, Mercy," she said, her voice wary.

"I need you to gather anyone you can find who is not guarding the house," I told her, "and bring them to the Good Shepherd on Bonnie." I gave her terse directions because it was hard to find, even with the address.

"Got it," she said.

I hit the END CALL button and settled in to drive.

"I'm not much good in a fight," said Sherwood tightly. "My leg."

"You can pick up a three-hundred-pound bar of steel, you can fight," I told him, not looking away from the road. I was driving too fast, and I didn't want to hit anyone.

There was a pause.

"I guess that is so," he said, like it was a revelation. "Okay."

The church was small. It had been a house that someone converted into a church about twenty years ago. It was tucked unobtrusively into the most mazelike section of Kennewick, a little residential area on the north side of the railroad that ran along the Columbia. There were only two ways in or out, one on the far east side, one on the west. The east-side entrance was the easiest to navigate.

The church grounds backed up to the railway, and between a couple of empty lots and the parking lot, it was half a block from the nearest house. There were two cars in the lot, parked next to the handicap parking. One of them was Pastor White's. The other was a Ford Explorer that had seen better days.

I parked Adam's SUV on the side of the lot farthest from the cars and the church building. I gathered the Sig's two spare magazines from my purse and stuck them in the back of my waistband because my stupid jeans didn't have pockets. Sherwood scrounged around and came up with a tire iron. I shook my head at him, opened the rear hatch, and pushed back the mat to expose the big locked box. My handprint released the lock. I opened the box and revealed Adam's new treasure chest. Inside was a collection of guns and various bladed weapons.

"Any idea what we're facing?" Sherwood asked, examining the contents of the box.

I shook my head. "Probably fae, but it could be one of the anti-supernatural groups or Cantrip or anyone. If they are here, in the church, it probably won't be vampires." Sherwood had spent a few years in the Marrok's pack. He'd know how to fight whatever we'd face as well as I did. "If you figure it out first, let me know."

He picked up an ax and checked it for balance. "This works for the fae," he said. Then he picked up the HK45 compact, checked it. (It was loaded.) "This will do for anything else." He decocked it and put it in the pocket of his jeans. "Compact" was an optimistic label for that gun.

"That's a dangerous place to carry it," I told him.

He grinned at me. "Nah, that's my bum leg. Can't shoot my foot off 'cause someone already did that. What does the interior look like?"

"The church was a house, once upon a time," I told him. Then I described it the best I could.

We paused for a moment by the cars. By now, the scent of fae magic lingered in the air, so I was pretty sure that was whom we were facing. However, the Ford Explorer belonged to a human male who did a lot of smoking.

"Do you recognize him?" asked Sherwood in a voice that wouldn't carry.

I shook my head, but the church wasn't empty during the week. I was grateful that it wasn't a Tuesday when the choir practiced or Thursday when the youth group met to plan their monthly community service. On other days . . . "The pastor has a degree in sociology," I told him, softly. "He makes most of his living as a counselor for recovering addicts."

"Not a lot of money in that," Sherwood observed. He was looking around alertly; the conversation was to keep relaxed and ready. It wasn't how I functioned, but I'd fought side by side with enough people—mostly wolves—to know that it was a technique that worked for some people.

I said, "Not a lot of money being a pastor of a small non-denominational church, either. I expect that if he wanted to be rich, he'd have gone into a different business."

"Does this change our strategy?" Sherwood asked, patting the car soundlessly.

He was acting as if I knew what I was doing.

"I don't think so, right?" I said. "Two hostages, or two victims if the fae have already killed them."

"The humans aren't dead," said Zee, startling a squeak out of me and an annoyed look out of Sherwood. "I was alerted that something was planned—and apparently my information was correct."

"Where did you come from?" I asked him.

He frowned at me. "Where your enemy might be next time."

"Nah," said Sherwood. "He was waiting around the corner of the building, Mercy. Downwind, but I caught a glimpse of him when you parked. I figured he'd been waiting for us. If he'd been the enemy, I'd have said something. I didn't see him approach, though."

"Do you know who they are?" I asked Zee. "What do they want?"

"Nine or ten idiots who follow a greater one," Zee answered. "These are the ones who left a letter on Christy's front door. According to my source—and Adam's telephone conversation—they want Aiden."

I frowned. "I can scent at least three." One of whom I knew.

"Four," said Sherwood. "One of them is flying, but I caught something where it landed on the top of the car."

Zee considered the church. The lights in the upstairs rooms were on, but the windows had all been replaced with stained glass. It was impossible to see inside.

"The humans are upstairs with Uncle Mike," Zee said, confirming my nose. "I heard them set him to watch."

"Is he the one who told you about this?" I asked.

"Probably," Zee said. "I can't imagine that he'd be this stupid unless he's working as a spy for the Council."

"What's stupid about it?" asked Sherwood. "They take hostages Mercy cares about to get an unlikeable ancient in the shape of a boy who is doing his best to burn down Mercy's home. Trade the hostages for the boy—and it's a win-win for all."

The dry dislike in Sherwood's voice told me that he'd had an unpleasant encounter with our Aiden. Aiden was prickly and very good at getting under people's skin when he wanted to. If I hadn't seen him vulnerable, hadn't heard his nightmares, maybe I would be more ambivalent about him, too.

Zee snorted. "Only if you don't know Mercy or Adam. Or anyone else involved. As if either of our idiot-heroes would ever turn someone who looks as helpless as Aiden over to the fae."

"Hey," I protested softly. I'm not an idiot or a hero. But he had the last part right.

By mutual consent, we left the Explorer and headed into the church. The front porch had been modified with a wheelchair ramp next to the stairs, and both led to a double-door entryway that wasn't original to the house. The changes had been made with an eye to economy rather than harmony.

We could wait for reinforcements, but if the fae thought themselves outgunned, they were likely to kill and run. We had a better chance going in now and hoping the cavalry made it in time to help with the cleanup.

"Mercy," said Zee in a nearly soundless voice that was hard for me to hear even with my ears, and I stood two feet away. "You go upstairs with your werewolf. Wolf?" Zee met Sherwood's eyes and didn't look away. "You keep her alive. I *think* that it's only Uncle Mike up there with the human hostages, and I *think* that he'll let you get them free."

"Meanwhile?" asked Sherwood in the same very quiet tone.

Zee smiled wickedly and snapped his hand down—where a narrow, black-bladed sword appeared. "I'll keep the others occupied."

"Zee?" I said. "Are you okay to fight?" He still wasn't moving right.

Zee nodded. "Against these fools? I could fight them off if I were blindfolded and tied hand and foot."

I let it go—though I was still worried. The fae speak the truth—as they know it. Just because Zee was an arrogant old fae didn't make him right.

We walked up to the doors with me in front and the others flanking me. I pulled the right-hand door open, and Sherwood reached around me to pull the left so we could enter as one group.

The entryway was a twenty-by-ten room cut off from the rest of the church by a wall with a walkway on either side. There was a kitchenette to our left with a refrigerator, a sink, and a stove. The interior wall had a counter and a half wall that opened into the main room, with a curtain that could be shut or open. It was shut.

On the right was the stairway that led up to the pastor's office, three rooms that were set up as classrooms, and the bathroom. Zee slipped around the wall and into the sanctuary that encompassed the rest of the first floor. Sherwood and I, in that order, headed up the stairs.

Below us, in the sanctuary, there was a huge crash, a wary cry, followed by the clashing sounds of weaponry engaging.

The top of the stairway led to a hall with five closed doors. The door to the immediate right of the stairs was the pastor's office, to the left was the bathroom. Then there were the three classrooms, one left, one right, and one at the end of the hall.

My sense of smell was of limited use for finding Pastor White—his scent was everywhere. The man who'd driven the Explorer was better. He'd gone into the pastor's office, but I caught his scent farther down the hall—where he'd have had no reason to go.

I tapped my nose and pointed at the classroom door at the end of the hall. Sherwood nodded as a huge crash below us spelled the end of one of the stained-glass windows. My fault. The fae had only come here because of me.

Sherwood took point, the ax in one hand and the big gun in the other. I reached past him to turn the knob, and he elbowed the door in.

The classroom was the largest of the five upstairs rooms. The pastor and a stranger were tied to folding chairs, gagged with duct tape. The floor of the room was covered in a dark brown carpet that showed the triple ring of salt someone had placed around them.

Between them and us stood Uncle Mike, a crossbow in his hand. He'd brought it up—but let the nose point down to the floor as soon as he saw it was me. There were three containers of Morton salt. Two of them were open, but the third still had a seal on the spout.

"Shut that door," he said. "There's a sprite lord out there, and I don't want his sprites seeing what I have done until Zee's through with them. Stupid louts."

"What's this about?" I asked.

"I can't tell you," he said. "All I can tell you is they gave me my orders—to bring these two upstairs and secure them." He grinned fiercely. "My orders didn't say secure them from whom. As long as those idiots"—he paused as the whole building vibrated—"don't burn the place down, your pastor and this gentleman are safe from most of my kind. Who did you bring with you?" he asked. "Is it Zee?"

"Can't you get across the salt?" I asked.

He shook his head. "This isn't just salt, but salt bonded with magic. I've locked out most fae, including myself. Zee might manage it. One or two of the Gray Lords—but the only one of this group, the one who gave me my orders and is powerful enough to break this, isn't here." He stared hard at me. There was something he couldn't tell me. He'd said he couldn't tell me why they were here. I'd thought it was obvious—but if it were obvious, Uncle Mike wouldn't have bothered to talk to me about it.

What did they gain from their actions so far? Two hostages—but they were human hostages, near enough to me that I'd respond. But, as Zee pointed out, if they knew anything about Adam or me, they'd never believe that we'd turn Aiden over to them. So what had they gained? They'd called me, let the pastor talk until they were sure I knew who he was, and hung up. And I'd come right over, hadn't I?

I pulled out my cell and called Mary Jo.

"We're on our—" she answered.

"No. Go to the pack house," I said. "There are some fae coming for Aiden."

Uncle Mike smiled.

I called the house, but no one picked up. I called Jesse, and it went to her voice mail. I called Warren, Darryl, Ben, and George with the same results.

I called Adam.

"Not a good time, Mercy," he said tightly.

"Don't hang up," I told him. "Did you listen to my message?"

"No. I'm discussing bugs with Cantrip. We're—" He would have said more, but I interrupted him.

"The fae are attacking our home," I said. "Don't listen to my message, waste of time." Don't worry about me—worry about Jesse, about Aiden and our wolves. "There's a fae attack at the house," I repeated. "And no one is answering their phones."

"Headed home," he said, and hung up.

Uncle Mike's smile widened and took on a patronizing edge, as if he were a proud father, which he had no right to do.

"Zee says this is a small group," I said. I didn't want to be here; I needed to be home. "They aren't likely to have all of Faery attack us at our home, right?"

"This group wants the Fire Touched," he said, so apparently my question was not what he was forbidden to discuss. "Underhill talks to people in their sleep and whispers at them when they are awake, asking for the Fire Touched. We've been searching for a way to make nice with her for a decade or more. We need her to survive—and she's been fickle and nasty. Some of us figure that if we give her the boy, she'll be grateful. Truthfully, others of us figure if we give her the boy, she will shut up about him and we might be able to sleep for longer than five minutes at a time. It's like Chinese water torture or that noise a car makes when your seat belt isn't fastened."

He frowned at me, but it wasn't a directed frown. "Still, more of us aren't happy that Underhill can *do* that."

"Do what?" I asked.

"Talk to us in our heads."

I nodded. The sounds from below weren't getting louder, but the frequency of the crashes was denser. Zee should be finished soon.

Uncle Mike bent down, picked up the unopened container of Morton salt, and handed it to me.

"Here," he said. "I will keep watch on your humans and secure them for you. I so swear. You two should get downstairs with the salt before Zee gets really upset."

"We need to release them," I said, nodding at the hostages. "Get them out of here, where they will be safe."

Uncle Mike shook his head. "Once the salt circle is broken, I don't have enough magic to renew it. They are safer here. Take out the threat, then release them."

Pastor White made a wild sound and shook his head. The other man stared at me with old eyes, closed them, then opened them again. He was okay with our plan—which made me very curious about him.

I met Pastor White's wild gaze. "Uncle Mike doesn't lie. He'll keep you safe—has kept you safe tonight. I'm going to make sure we stop the bad guys before he lets you out of the safe zone."

As we trotted down the stairs, Sherwood said, "Salt is protection against fae?"

I shook my head. "Some fae. Mostly the lesser fae, because it neutralizes magic. Uncle Mike apparently used it as a component in his spell—which fae aren't supposed to be able to do. Salt *neutralizes* magic. What Uncle Mike did is the equivalent of using water to start a fire."

"So don't count on it," he said, as we reached the ground.

I nodded, stepped around the (broken) wall, and looked out into Armageddon meets Apocalypse.

I'd learned some things from playing computer games with the pack. "When you first enter a room, look around for your enemy" was one of the golden rules of the Dread Pirate games because the scallywags like to hide behind furniture and doorways and get you from behind. So I ignored the splintered furniture and the brightly colored glass shards that littered the room and looked for the bad guys.

Enemy number one was flattened beneath a pew. She was unconscious. She was breathing, but judging by the crushing injury to her back, she wasn't going to be mobile anytime soon.

Enemy number two was dead. His head was a good twenty feet from his body. Not even the fae could survive that, I didn't think—certainly he wasn't going to get up and fight in the next ten minutes.

Enemy number three was a slender man fighting Zee, both of them armed with swords. There was no enemy number four that I could sense via eyes or nose. Zee fought, a wiry old man who moved like a demon. Not a wasted motion, every strike and parry clean and quicker than humanly possible. There was blood on the thin white t-shirt he wore, and some of it was his.

The smaller man he fought moved oddly, though it didn't affect his control of his blade. There was something wrong with his shape—and with his face. As I tried to pin it down, Zee hit him and . . . the part of his body that Zee's sword would have hit just dissolved in front of the blade, releasing little bits of sparkly light about the size and color of a yellow jacket. I finally got a clear look at his face—and he didn't have one, just a suggestion of features that moved constantly, as if all that was under his skin were the little bits that had fled the iron of Zee's weapon.

Some of those little bits sparkled all the way to Sherwood and me.

"Ouch," I said, slapping my forearm.

Sherwood swore, and started fighting with the ax. I've met a few werewolves who had lived when swords and axes were the weapons of choice for humans as well as fae. He moved like a man born with an ax in his hand—and I don't mean to cut down trees. His ax sang a little as it cut through the air. The little hornetlike fae things dropped to the ground like miniature falling stars, some of them in two pieces. Sherwood put himself in front of me, and very few of the little vicious beasties made it through him.

Skilled with an ax was our Sherwood. Very skilled—and very fast. His prosthetic leg hindered him occasionally, but it seemed more a matter of annoyance than a real problem because those sparkly lights kept falling.

Couldn't fight, he'd claimed. Couldn't fight my aching rump.

I closed my fingers on the wings of one of the critters that had made it through his slicing and dicing as it bit my thigh. I had to rock it back and forth to dislodge it so I could bring it up to my face to see what it was.

Up close, and without the beauty of the fluttering wings, it was utilitarian in design. Or she was. She looked vaguely like a person in shape if not color, complete with arms and legs and miniature breasts. Her eyes were a deep purple that looked almost black against her bright yellow body. Only her mouth completely failed to mimic something human. Instead of lips, there were a pair of chelicerae, gory with my blood.

I threw her on the ground and watched her blink out of existence the moment her body touched the fake wooden floor, the same way the bits and pieces that Sherwood was leaving behind did.

I took the container of salt I'd tucked under my arm and pried open the spout. I poured a pinch onto my hand and dribbled it on my wrist. The nasty bugger chewing there made a popping sound, turned gray, and fell to the ground, a dead husk. It did not disappear in a flash of light. Hah.

I took a spare handful and scattered it on the fae bugs attacking Sherwood, and it sounded like popcorn cooking.

I took the container and ran a gauntlet of biting fae bugs, one arm crooked above my eyes. The fae that Zee fought scored a hit. It wasn't a hard hit, but Zee responded by increasing the speed and fury of his attacks. I poured salt in my hand as I jumped on top of an upended pew and scattered the handful of salt on the last of our enemies.

The salt landed with a crack of noise, and wherever it hit turned gray. He turned on me. Gray powder fell on the ground, and the sparkly bugs all returned and landed on him, reabsorbed into his odd body.

He raised his hands before I threw another handful, and in a voice like smoke he said, "I surrender."

Zee snarled but sheathed his sword at my look. Sherwood negotiated his way through the mess of the sanctuary with a little more trouble than a man with two good legs might have, but there was nothing wrong with the speed with which he killed the woman with the crushing injury. He managed to do it before she shot the crossbow I hadn't noticed when I'd first seen her.

He cleaned the ax on his pant leg, then continued to pick his way to Zee and me. He looked at our prisoner.

"What are we going to do with that?" he asked.

11

We let him go. It was pretty obvious to anyone who thought about it for two seconds that we weren't going to be able to keep him prisoner unless Zee wanted to babysit him. Ropes and duct tape don't work on someone who can dissolve into nasty insectoid thingies whenever he wants to. I especially didn't want to be around him in a car—I almost died once when my college room-mate was driving a bunch of us to the movies and a hornet flew in through an open window.

Once Zee was sure that all of Mr. I-Am-Really-a-Hive-of-Female-Fae-Bugs was gone, and there were no more fae of any size or shape hanging around downstairs, we went upstairs. All the way, Zee muttered about stupid sprite lords who were weak and stupid— but not bothered as much by cold iron as most other fae.

"Cockroaches of the fae," he pronounced. "Can't hurt much, but they won't *die*."

Sherwood tossed his ax up in the air and caught it. I thought, by his attitude, that he was surprised at how comfortable he was with the ax.

Zee was still complaining about the sprite lord when we walked into the room with the hostages.

"I thought he'd get your dander up," said Uncle Mike happily.

"What do you have yourself mixed up in?" Zee asked him in an exasperated tone. "Sprite lords. You've sunk to a new low dealing with such as those."

Uncle Mike grinned. "Someone has to, Zee. If they'd managed to kill these humans, they would ruin any chance of an alliance with the werewolves. They don't understand the connection between this pack and the Marrok's—and I'm not inclined to enlighten them because they are too stupid, as this situation makes quite clear. They are too likely to think about it as an opportunity instead of a danger. Alas, this brave new world that has such idiots in't."

"There is no connection between our pack and the Marrok's," I said. "Not anymore."

Uncle Mike looked at me like I was an idiot, too. "As you say," he said blandly.

"Will you be in trouble for helping us?" I asked. "Are you going to be safe?" I didn't quite offer him sanctuary—I could see the billboard now: COLUMBIA BASIN PACK WELCOMES DISENFRANCHISED OR ALIENATED FAE.

Uncle Mike laughed, a warm belly laugh. "If fate favors me, I hope not. There's no fun in safety, is there?" He waved a hand at the salt circle, and a tickle in my throat I hadn't been paying much attention to made itself felt by going away. Then he put his foot on the ring and broke the circle. When that was done to his satisfaction, he pulled open the single large window and, after peering left and right, jumped out.

I ran to the window to make sure he was okay because there was nothing to break his fall, but he was nowhere to be seen.

Salt circle broken, Sherwood had wasted no time in freeing the prisoners, starting with the hands of both men. The pastor reached up as soon as his fingers were free and ripped the duct tape off his face.

"How dare you?" he said to me, his voice rough. "This is a house of God. How dare you bring your supernatural evil into God's house?"

His first instinct, as evidenced by what he'd said on the phone, had been to protect me. Apparently, he'd gotten over that. The other man took his time peeling the tape away from his mouth.

"Other way around," I said in as mild a tone as I could manage. Another day, I'd feel bad about this, but right now, I needed to make sure Pastor White and the man he'd been counseling were safe, then go find out what was happening at home. "That supernatural evil brought *me* here." I couldn't help a bit of temper, and added, "I suppose I could have stayed away, and they'd probably have killed you."

"Pastor," said the other man.

"Married to a werewolf," Pastor White said, spittle leaving his mouth with his words he was so upset. "I should have asked you to leave as soon as I found out."

"Pastor," said the other man again, his voice very quiet. Sherwood had freed both men's hands first and was working on the stranger's feet. "Pastor White, I think some reflection might be called for." There was just a hint of something in his voice that made me think that he'd been called to reflect on things by the pastor once too often.

"This lady just saved both of our lives," the man continued.

"And I think the fae who jumped out the window cured my need for alcohol because I swear to God that this is the first time in twenty years I haven't had the thirst. Not since that witch cursed me down in Bogotá." He looked at me. "Josh Harper, ma'am. You must be Mercy Hauptman. Thank you for coming."

Bemused, I shook his hand while Pastor White continued to be very unhappy with me, the werewolves, and most everything about this church in a rant that no one listened to, except for Zee.

That might not be healthy for Pastor White.

"Fear is a hard thing," said Sherwood as he finished the last cut to free Pastor White's feet. He patted the pastor on his knee. "You should give yourself some time to think about that."

Impelled by Sherwood's touch, the pastor surged to his feet. He opened his mouth again, looked at us, closed his mouth tightly, and made haste out of the room and down the stairs. I followed him, and I guess everyone else followed me down because we were all there when the pastor saw the chapel.

"Who is going to pay for this?" Pastor White whispered. "We'd been saving up for a new roof. It's taken us two years to raise half the money we need."

"You should wait until the morning and call someone to board up the windows," said Zee.

"What happened to the bodies?" Sherwood asked. Because neither the woman Sherwood had killed nor the one Zee had beheaded were in the sanctuary.

"Bodies?" asked Pastor White.

"We fade when we die," Zee told Sherwood. "At least, most of us do. There aren't any bodies."

"Look what you've done," said Pastor White. There were tears in his eyes. "This stained glass cannot be replaced. Look at the pews."

While he took inventory of the destruction, I tried to call Adam and got a "this customer is not available" message. I tried to contact him through our mating bond, but it was being obstreperous again. I could *feel* him, but I couldn't contact him.

"We need to go," I said. And I let my actions follow my words.

As we drove up to the house, the first thing that I noticed was that there were no lights. No house lights, no yard lights, nothing. It wasn't just our home. The nearest house was a twenty-acre field away, and it was vacant, with a FOR SALE sign out front. I guess living next to a werewolf pack was too exciting for some people. But that didn't explain the darkness that had swallowed the rest of the homes along our road.

Or Mary Jo's car pulled mostly out of the road and empty. About a hundred yards beyond that, a black SUV that was a near match to Adam's down to the elegant HAUPTMAN SECURITY hand-lettered on the driver's side was parked—Adam was here.

I pulled into the crowded driveway and stopped the car. No one was dead, I reassured myself. I'd felt it when Peter died. If someone else in the pack died, I'd know it.

The three of us got out of the SUV and shut the doors quietly.

There was a howl and a crunching noise from the back of the house—at the same time the big glass window in the front room shattered, a dark shape hurtling through it. It smelled of rotting bog and salt and looked a little like a horse—it had four feet and hooves—but its head was more reptilian than equine. Its body was shaggy with fronds that made a slithery sound, like a wet hula skirt. The Fideal screamed when it saw me—long yellow-white teeth flashing for a moment in the still-lit SUV headlights.

I pulled out my Sig and shot the Fideal in the body twice as it galloped toward us. It reared and screamed again—but not because of the bullets. Sherwood threw the ax and hit it in the head. The ax dislodged from the Fideal's head and slid down to his shoulder before it bounced off to the grass. The touch of iron left a brown gap in the plantlike hair from the top of the Fideal's neck and down his chest.

Zee hopped onto the hood of the nearest car, ran to the top, and launched himself into the air, his sword raised. He seemed to linger in the air—but that couldn't have been true because his sword flashed down on the Fideal before Sherwood could pick up the ax.

The Fideal shifted to human shape, a sword in his left hand that met Zee's black blade with a noise fit to wake the dead. Sparks flew like fireflies and disappeared into the darkness. It wasn't magic, I don't think, just a bit of physics.

I heard Jesse scream, and the distinctive crack of my .444 Marlin rifle as it fired four times in succession. A moment later, there was a flash of fire I could see clearly through the broken window. I left the Fideal for Zee and Sherwood and bolted up the porch stairs. The front door was unlocked, and I opened it with a bang.

Jesse was on the second floor, at the top of the stairway, the rifle ready to fire. Cookie was pressed against her leg, growling ferociously. Their attention was focused toward the living room.

"Stay down there," she said. "I won't let you have him."

Something the size of a car boiled out of the living room. My eyes didn't want to focus on it because it was so ugly or beautiful. It had a lot of insectoid legs and some sort of flowing, luminous, blue-green carapace that moved like silk blown in the wind. But when Jesse shot the fae again, the bullet ricocheted off the carapace, hitting the wall two feet from my head.

"Stop firing," I shouted, and raised my Sig.

I dropped to one knee on the ground, aiming under the carapace at an angle that wouldn't allow me to bounce a bullet up to the top of the stairs. I emptied the gun into the fae, and blue-green blood sprayed onto the white carpet. That was good, because some of the fae can't be hurt with lead bullets.

The fae creature whirled on me in a snakelike motion. I got a confusing glimpse of a beautiful woman's face with skin of amber and eyes of ruby. I surged to my feet, running toward her even though I was weaponless. Running away would only have caused her to charge me. As it was, she hesitated, doubtless reasoning that, if I was running toward her, I must have some sort of an attack in mind.

I tripped on the walking stick and rolled with the fall. I used the momentum to power my thrust, and the walking stick's sharp spearhead slid into the amber fae's mouth. It wasn't exactly unexpected that the walking stick would show up—but I hadn't counted on it. I'd been planning on running past the fae creature and luring it away from the kids to the backyard, where I could hear a battle raging.

The fae creature dropped to the ground, the light fading from its carapace. I held the walking stick at the ready, but the fae stayed where she was, not breathing.

Aiden, appearing beside Jesse at the top of the stairs, made a motion with his hand, and the amber fae's body began to burn with a smoldering, angry blue flame. There was a cracking boom from the kitchen that sounded like a door being ripped from its hinges. Then the tibicena, a great gash opened on his hip from which molten rock dripped, bolted into the foyer and closed his great jaws on the amber fae's face. This time the tibicena was built like a wolf rather than the foo dog of his last appearance. Upright ears topped a muzzle that was long and narrow. His body was finer-boned than a werewolf of his size would have been, more like a wolf's gracile and narrow form. His tail was covered with molten hair, and it curled a little.

He jerked his head, and there was a snapping sound before the fae's amber face melted like wax in his teeth. Between Aiden's sullen blue fire and the tibicena's red flame and black teeth, the fae was definitely dead. Aiden closed his fist and spoke a word of power that emitted a sharp magical smell that made me sneeze. His fire died to nothing as the last of the fae's body turned to ash.

Aiden slipped past Jesse and trotted down the stairs. Joel snarled at him, then at me when I moved. I froze, but Aiden kept coming.

"It's done, it is," Aiden told Joel. "That was the last of them. Can you hear the silence? It's the good kind of silence, not the silence that listens back. Hear the silence and feel the air. There is only death that visited our enemies and the blood of our wounded. No more battle, no more enemies to kill. Time to sleep, fire dog," he said, and touched his hand to Joel's forehead.

Joel took a deep breath and turned his head to lick Aiden's hand twice before settling on the floor in the ashes of the amber fae. A few breaths later, Joel's naked human form lay in the tibicena's place. He sat up, and Cookie bounded down the stairs and licked his face anxiously.

Joel began laughing. He looked up at Aiden, and said, "Thanks, *mijo*. That was the first time I've ever let the tibicena free, because I knew you'd be there. That was fun." His voice slurred a little, as if he were drunk.

Rapid footsteps from the direction of the kitchen had me gripping the walking stick, which was once more a stick. But it was only Mary Jo, armed with a pickax that was covered with various substances that might be fae blood; she skidded to a stop, her hand half-raised.

"Which one was that?" she asked, gesturing at the ashes.

"Glowed blue," I told her. "With a face that looked like it'd been carved in amber."

"Caterpillar Girl," said Mary Jo. "That only leaves Water Horse."

The front door opened, and Zee and Sherwood ran in, weapons in hand. "Water Horse was the Fideal," I told her. I looked at Zee. "Did you kill him?"

Zee relaxed and made a quick movement that my eyes didn't quite follow, but after which his sword was gone. "I warned him not to come back," said Zee, and he glanced at Sherwood. "I've seen you fight before. What did you say your name was?"

Sherwood gave him a half smile. "Sherwood Post."

Zee blinked at him. "That sounds like a fence built by Robin Hood."

"Don't ever forget your name when Bran is around," I told Zee. "I figure Sherwood got away lightly. Just think if Bran had been reading *Moby-Dick* and *The Old Man and the Sea* instead. Sherwood could have been Herman Hemingway."

"Or what if he had been reading Louis L'Amour?" asked Mary Jo. "Sherwood L'Amour would have doomed you to stripper jokes for the rest of your life."

Zee frowned. "If I've seen you fight—and I have, long ago. Somewhere . . . it may take some time to come to me. But if I've seen you fight, it's a fair and sure thing that Bran knows who you are. There aren't that many old wolves running around, and none that old bastard doesn't know."

I opened my mouth to say something—and shut it because it would have been bitter. Bran had made the decision to cut us loose based on what he thought would be the best for the werewolves. It was no use being bitter at Bran for acting like himself.

"Mercy," Adam said.

I hadn't heard him approach. I turned just in time to be enveloped in warm arms that closed just a little too hard. He smelled of blood—his own and others'—but I was reassured by the strength of his embrace. I just stood there for a moment and breathed him in.

"So I see you made it here alive," he said after a moment.

"You, too," I said. "Congratulations." I might have been shaking a little. Now that it was all over, that we'd all survived—even poor Pastor White—and we'd kept them from taking Aiden, now I could shake.

When I felt the weight of eyes on my back, I took a deep breath and stepped back. "How did we do?" I asked.

"Paul's hurt the worst," Adam told me. "Mary Jo brought Carlos with her, and he's doing wound care out in the backyard. Paul will feel it for a few days, but he'll be fine. Ben got messed up pretty badly, too—he and Paul were on the front lines on their own for about five minutes before Mary Jo and her band of merry wolves got here."

"I'm sorry," said Aiden, his voice solemn.

"Yes, you are," said Jesse stoutly. She'd come down the stairs while I wasn't looking. "But that doesn't mean that they can come here and feed you to a monster on our watch." She patted him on the head. "And while I'm at it, thanks, squirt, for saving my life." She looked at her dad. "They came out of the river. Ben was the first one to notice them—we were stargazing in the backyard. He yelled at us to get in the house, to get to the safe room." She frowned. "We should have, but there were a bunch of those things, and only Paul and Ben to fight them. So we ran up to your bedroom and I grabbed the .444 and ran to the sitting room and started shooting. You're going to have to get that window replaced."

"There are a lot of windows that need replaced," I said.

"The back wall of the house needs to be replaced," said Mary Jo. "One of them had some sort of earth magic. She took the huge rocks that Christy had placed around the backyard as décor and hurled them. A couple of them hit the house."

"I think I killed her," said Jesse, suddenly sounding younger. "I tried to anyway. She threw that granite boulder and hit Paul with it."

"That's about when I arrived," Mary Jo said. "Ben's pretty proud of you, kid, you hit her right between the eyes. You are the reason that Paul and Ben aren't dead—and if the fae had taken those two out that early, I'd have shown up too late."

Adam started to put a hand on Jesse, and I caught his eye and shook my head. She was holding on, just barely. If he hugged her, she'd lose it—and she deserved better than that.

Jesse caught his hand and gripped it tightly, giving me a smile. "Anyway, one of them climbed up the side of the house—and bullets didn't do anything to him. He got through the window in the sitting room, and Aiden touched him." She swallowed. "I'm not actually sure he's dead. We got out of there and shut the door. There was a lot of noise by that time, and the blue-silky caterpillar lady was downstairs, so Aiden and I crouched in the hallway and waited."

Mary Jo said something under her breath, dodged into the kitchen, and grabbed the fire extinguisher from the counter—we now had a lot of fire extinguishers stashed around the house—and ran up the stairs.

"If the house were going to have caught fire," Jesse said, "I think it would have done so by now."

"Reflexes," I told her. "Remember, Mary Jo fights fires for a living—and Aiden has been doing his best to refine her response time."

"It's okay," Mary Jo called down after a moment. "But you're going to have to replace some furniture and the carpets in the sitting room."

Mary Jo had been right: the back of the house was going to need major repairs. The yard was a real mess. Christy's careful landscaping had been ruined. Four of the five giant boulders were scattered at random, to the detriment of lawn furniture and trees and garden spots. The fifth boulder was in the middle of the kitchen floor. There was now no question that we'd have to retile the kitchen. The big window in the living room was shattered, as were, as far as I could tell, all but one of the windows in the back.

Werewolves trickled in as word spread to those not actively involved in the actual battle, and they came over to help with cleanup. Someone rustled up tuna-fish sandwiches, and the night took on the oddly festive air of a work party. When they were done, the yard didn't look pristine, but it was neat. Paving stones were stacked in piles. Things broken beyond repair, like the cement benches, and a lot of garbage bags from the house were set aside for the next garbage run. We did the best we could with the inside of the house, mostly sweeping or vacuuming up glass and throwing away broken things.

Ben and Mary Jo brought out plywood sheets from the garage, and I helped put them in place over the windows. Windows are fragile, and werewolves are not. Putting up plywood wasn't a skill I would have actively sought out on my own, but I was pretty good at it. We were four sheets short of getting the job done, so we left the front window open until someone could get to a hardware store in the morning.

Adam came over when we were getting the last one up.

"Ben," he said, "Auriele and Darryl are headed home; you can ride in with them."

Ben's truck had gotten smashed in the battle between Zee, Sherwood, and the Fideal. I'd told him that he'd be better off taking a settlement from his insurance and buying a new truck rather than repairing the old one. Once the frame was bent, it wasn't usually worth the trouble of fixing it.

Ben stepped back from the job and stretched. He had a long cut the length of his face from the tip of his eye, down his jaw, and onto his collarbone. It had mostly healed up, and he looked as though he'd been in a car wreck several days earlier. "My croaking fat frog will shag my fucking Aunt Fanny before I'll go now," he said. "Until we get matters straightened out with the fae, I'm living right the fucking hell here."

And, as if in answer, the lights all over the world—or at least our part of the world—turned on as the power company figured out how to fix whatever the fae had done.

Ben took a bow and accepted the applause of the pack.

We spent the next couple of days repairing what we could and carting away what we couldn't. Adam's contractor friend was optimistic that the stucco on the front of the house could be saved.

Adam and I were repairing a planting bed crushed by the granite boulder when it landed on Paul, who was mostly back on his feet now. We were discussing the merits of a rosebush in place of the dogwood, which was not as tough as Paul and had suffered unrecoverable damage, when the house phone rang.

"I've got it," called Jesse. I heard her voice as she answered the phone but didn't catch what she said. Then she called brightly, "Hey, Dad. Baba Yaga is on the phone for you."

I followed him into the kitchen, where Jesse stood with the handset. She gave it to him. Then she looked at me and raised her eyebrows in an exaggerated fashion that made her eyes bulge, and mouthed, "Baba Yaga. Really?"

I nodded and mouthed, "Really."

She hugged herself and, as she passed by me on her way out of the room, she whispered, "Now, how many people have gotten to say that? 'Hey, Dad. Baba Yaga is on the phone for you'?"

Aiden was coming in as she was going out. Fighting together seemed to have broken the cold war and initiated a detente between Jesse and Aiden.

Her tone was relaxed as she said, "Hey, short stuff. Offended anyone bigger than you lately?"

"Everyone is bigger than me, Daisy Duke," he said.

His attempt at teasing was lame, but he was making an effort. Last night, the werewolves had run a *Dukes of Hazzard* marathon in Aiden's honor. The whole pack were trying their best to help him climb into the modern era with the help of TV shows and movies. It might have been more effective if they'd chosen something filmed in this decade, but their hearts were in the right place. I hoped that Aiden didn't think that cars really could jump rivers and barns and whatever.

He seemed to know that he'd gotten it wrong with the Daisy, but he cleared his throat and tried again. "Bigger is easy. Finding someone smaller to offend is a real challenge."

"I'm sure you're up for that, too," Jesse said, teasing him back. "You show some real aptitude in that area."

He grinned at her, but then he turned his attention to me. "The witch is calling for a meeting with the fae, right?"

Jesse paused, and they both looked at me.

"That's what it sounds like," I agreed.

"You need to take me to this meeting," he said. "Zee says that Underhill won't leave them alone. They can't afford for me to escape."

"We're not giving you to them," I told him.

"Excuse me," said Adam. He covered the mouthpiece, looked Aiden in the eyes, and said, "You stay here. No question."

Aiden opened his mouth to argue, but Adam stared him down. Only when Aiden dropped his eyes did Adam go back to his call.

We agreed to meet at Uncle Mike's. It was as close as we could come to neutral territory. The once bar was in east Pasco near the river, on the edge of the industrial district. The bar had been shut down for more than half a year. I expected it to smell musty or unused. But when Uncle Mike opened the door, his face somber, it smelled exactly the way it always did: alcohol, sawdust, peanuts, and the scents of hundreds of individuals. The last were faded and mixed into a musk from which it would have been impossible to coax a single thread free. And it smelled of magic.

When it had been open, the light had been kept low. But all the lights were on, and it was nearly as bright as it would have been had there been windows. Most of the tables were stacked in a pyramid in one corner of the room, large tables on the bottom, smaller on top. The chairs were mostly stacked, too, awaiting the day when the bar reopened.

One of the big tables had been set in the middle of the mostly empty room, and chairs were set around it.

"The others are here," said Uncle Mike, "in the back. I'll get them."

He left us, Adam and me, alone in the room. The rest of the pack, all of them, were at our house protecting Aiden and Jesse. Darryl hadn't been happy that we weren't taking any extra wolves with us. But the fae had no reason to kill us, and the pack could protect Aiden and keep him safe. Or else, I'd been happy to point out to Darryl, nothing we could do would keep anyone safe at all.

Uncle Mike returned, escorting Beauclaire and the bald man whom Margaret had forced to her will. Goreu. The discrepancy between what I would have expected from a knight of the round table, fictional though it was, and Goreu left me bitterly and irrationally disappointed. They'd brought the good fairy and the bad fairy. I looked at Beauclaire and frowned at him. He looked cool and composed, as he had every time I'd seen him. Maybe we were meeting the bad fairy and the worse fairy. I had expected to be facing more. We apparently weren't, Adam and I, as important as Margaret. I might have been offended, except the fewer Gray Lords we sat down with, the more likely we would be to walk away alive.

We all went to the scarred table and sat down, virtually at the same time. Adam was slower because he held my chair out.

"Are there any other fae in the building or adjacent lot?" asked Adam as he settled.

"No," said Uncle Mike. "Just the three of us—and I don't count."

"What do you want?" asked Adam.

"There are nine fae dead," said Beauclaire, very softly. Yep, I thought, my stomach clenched, bad fairy and worse fairy.

"They attacked us," Adam told them. "That makes their deaths their own fault."

"Point," agreed Beauclaire, and he glanced at Goreu. "They were on their own," he told us, "as, I understand, Uncle Mike informed you."

"How often," said Adam dangerously, "are we going to be discussing how many of your people have been killed by their own stupidity before you stop them instead of making me do it?"

"We have discussed this very thing," said Beauclaire grimly.

Goreu pushed back his chair and sighed. "As well as a whole rotting cesspool of other things."

He sat in silence a moment, examining Adam without meeting his eyes—and avoiding any kind of dominance game. Finally, he leaned forward, and it was as if he peeled off a glamour without changing his form at all. When he spoke, his voice was still tenor, but it had softened and lost the squeak. Instead of a parody, he became . . . someone who might once have ridden beside Arthur. "Some old king," Goreu said, "some old time or other proclaimed that if the Welsh had all started fighting one enemy instead of each other, they would have conquered the world—that goes double for the fae. Still, we did passably well for the past couple of hundred years, protecting the weak and reining in the strong and vicious." He flashed a humorless smile. "Coexisting, you could call it. Then Underhill opened unexpectedly—on one of the reservations, then on all of the reservations, thousands if not tens of thousands of miles from the nearest old door."

"Unexpected by some," murmured Beauclaire.

Goreu nodded gravely at Beauclaire. "You were behind the drive to create the reservations. I followed your lead because it made sense to have a place of safety to keep those who were too frightening or too frightened. I don't know five fae who thought that you'd be right about Underhill, that she would follow us."

He looked at Adam again. "While we were still debating what should change, what could change—this one killed a human for the sake of Justice." There was a capital letter starting that word; I could hear it in his voice. "And then he issued a recall, and all of us were penned up in the reservations." He pinched his nose and gave Beauclaire a pained look. "There were probably less . . . eventful ways to handle it."

Beauclaire pursed his lips. "Are you sure that we should spill our secrets here?"

Goreu smiled, a smile as sweet and innocent as sunshine. "And what do you think they will do with our secrets, this warrior and his softhearted coyote mate? If our side in this battle prevails, it won't matter—if not, well then, we'll probably be fighting on their side anyway."

Beauclaire gave a reluctant nod. "Point."

Goreu's smile widened a little, then died. When he spoke again, it was to us. "Afterward, we thought for a while that we could stay on our reservations. No humans could get in, not with their fighter jets or tanks. A bard might have managed, but your bards are not given to wandering in the wilderness in this era. We had, after all, Underhill to live in. Underhill exists in a different space and time. Infinite space."

He and Beauclaire exchanged a glance. Beauclaire snorted abruptly and threw up his hands.

"Why not?" he said, and it was Beauclaire who continued. "But Underhill is different. I will spare you the dozens of explanations we've thrown at her and had thrown back. No one knows why.

She's volatile. Unpredictable. We lost four selkies on one of the other reservations. They apparently had found a doorway—" Here he paused, and said, "A doorway is not, strictly speaking, a doorway as you would think of it, though it can be. Some of the doors to Underhill are invisible and impossible to detect unless you happen to stumble through one."

He sighed, which didn't bode well for the four selkies, I thought. "They found a place where there was a big salt lake, cold and clear, a fifth selkie told me, that they could see to the bottom of, though it was a hundred feet down. They disappeared for a couple of weeks— which would not normally have been a concern because time can pass differently in Underhill. But the fifth selkie had gone to the salt lake and couldn't find them. We searched and asked Underhill, who quit talking to us for a couple of days. Then the fifth selkie found the skeletons of the four selkies laid out on the sands of their lake."

"A predator?" I asked.

"Selkies are tough," said Goreu. "And there were no teeth marks on the bones."

"There are some of us who are very old," Beauclaire said. "Baba Yaga is one of those. She remembers a time when Underhill killed as many fae as traveled through her, a time when Underhill was very young. She told us that Underhill mellowed with time. Five or six hundred years."

"So you couldn't stay on the reservations," said Adam. "There are too many of you for the land you have if you can't trust Underhill to be a home."

Goreu nodded. "So we were going to have to resume living in the humans' world. But we would do it on our own terms."

"We had quite a lively discussion on the matter," said Uncle

Mike with an unrepentant grin. "Not that I was a participant, mind you. But some things should be witnessed."

Both of the other fae gave him an unamused look that bothered Uncle Mike not at all. "I have some very nice hard cider in the back room," he said. "Would anyone care for some?"

Goreu gave him a sharp look.

"I like humans," Uncle Mike said seriously. "I might be the only fae alive today who can say that and not mean as a meal. I want them to survive. I want to survive. I'm on your side."

"Cider would be good," said Adam. "This sounds like it will take a while. And, though we are intrigued with the story—I'm not sure why you are telling it to us."

"I want you to understand that our options are limited," said Goreu. "I want you to really, really understand why we find ourselves here in this place at this time. If we—and by 'we,' I mean the fae, the werewolves, the humans, and anyone else who wants to live a full life—are to find our way out of it, then we—Beauclaire and I—need your help."

Uncle Mike excused himself, and we waited quietly while he made glass-clinky and cider-getting noises behind the closed doors marked EMPLOYEES ONLY in bright green letters. He brought back a tray with five clear, frosty mugs, and a glass pitcher filled with a golden liquid that bubbled and sparkled like champagne.

I generally don't drink alcohol. I have too many people's secrets in my head—and alcohol affects me oddly. But to refuse it in this place and time was more of a statement than I wanted to make. I took the glass that Uncle Mike poured and brought it to my lips—and stopped.

I set it down on the table with a shaky hand, gave Uncle Mike a tight smile. "I had a bad experience with drink and the fae."

His eyes grew sad. "I'd forgotten that." He touched the glass, and the liquid cleared. "It's water now, cool and sweet. I give my word that water is all it is, safe for you to drink. But if you'd rather not, I will not take offense."

I took a sip, and it tasted like water. Goreu glanced at Beauclaire, who shook his head. Neither of them had heard that story— they could get the whole tale from Uncle Mike when we were gone. I mostly trusted Uncle Mike. But as soon as no one was paying attention to me, I set the water down on the table and left it there.

"So," I said, as the others drank their cider. "When we left off, the fae were stuck between a rock and a hard place. Let me guess— the result of the discussion that Uncle Mike is so gleeful about was the release of a few of the nasties that the Gray Lords have been keeping a choke hold on. We had a little excitement, and some werewolf friends of mine had trouble in Arizona." I let them see what I thought about their solution. The two that I knew about both preyed upon children.

"I was unhappy with the decision," Beauclaire said. "I was unhappier with the way it was carried out. The fae who were released were all under a death sentence. After they had caused a stir, one of us was supposed to go out and kill them. Making us heroes of sorts."

I gave him a sour look. The years I had spent working with Zee had given me more than the know-how to rebuild an engine: I had Zee's patented sour look down cold. "That's not what happened."

"No," agreed Beauclaire. Maybe he'd hung out with Zee at some point, too, because his sour look was pretty good. "I thought it was overly optimistic. I was outvoted." He gave Goreu a cool look.

Goreu grimaced. "I had no choice. We need someone in with

the genocidal bunch. Since I'm the one with the harmless look and no reputation for stuff, it's got to be me. We vote as a block."

"The genocidal bunch?" I asked cautiously.

He nodded. "The majority of the Gray Lords want to deal with the humans from a point of strength: appease us, and we won't kill you. But there is a cadre of us who look at Underhill, look at our numbers—and at the fact that our population has dropped by half since we left Europe and traveled here—and they don't believe we can survive. They want a war, a war with the humans or a war with the werewolves that will devolve into a war with the humans. They think that if all of Faery fight, we can kill humankind and die in glory."

I felt like someone had knocked the wind out of me.

"Are they right?" asked Adam. "Could you destroy humanity?"

Goreu shrugged. "I don't know. Maybe."

Uncle Mike took a deep drink of his cider, and said, "The only thing that has saved us so far is that they are aware that most of the fae, the ones who are not Gray Lords, would like to live. We don't care so much about the fae as a race, we care about ourselves and our families. And there are still enough of us that we'd have a fair chance of stopping the Gray Lords who want war. Which is why they have to make the humans or, failing that, the werewolves make war first."

Did Bran know this? I took a deep breath. Of course he did. He'd abandoned our pack so that if we failed to negotiate with the fae, they couldn't use that as the flash point for a war with all of the werewolves. Was it better that Bran abandoned us not just for the safety of the werewolves, but of the humans, and, probably, the fae, too? Yes.

"The Widow Queen is one of the suicidal, genocidal group?" I hazarded.

Goreu shook his head. "No. She's part of her own small group of delusional idiots. She thinks that if the werewolves don't come in on the humans' side, we can actually kill all the humans who live on this continent and survive. Happily, you've just killed most of her followers. She thought she could use Aiden to gain control of Underhill as part of some further and complicated plot to destroy the other Gray Lords and take control. She likes to rule."

"To be fair," Uncle Mike said, "we watched the Europeans do a fair job of killing off the people who were originally on this continent." He gave me a sly look. "You could ask your father's people about that. But she doesn't have smallpox or the black measles, so she's trying out a few other things. The last one was a troll who was nearly mindless—there are a few of them who are quite brilliant by troll standards at least, Mercy—but who had the delightful talent of growing in strength every time he ate a human and, in the water, was impossible to kill."

I stared at him, trying to imagine that troll being stronger.

Uncle Mike gave me a cheery smile. "Happily for our side, he was too dumb to jump in the water before your pack killed him. Had he made it to the city and started killing hundreds of people, none of *us* could have stopped him." He paused. "Well, maybe Nemane or Beauclaire. But the Widow Queen forgets how much power she's lost."

"Our storytelling this night is at an end," Beauclaire said softly. He got up from the table. "If you would excuse me for a few moments. Goreu will continue our conversation."

Goreu leaned forward. "The situation with your pack has presented us with a unique opportunity. We need to negotiate with the human government—and have scared them to the point that there is no path for communication. But you killed a troll."

He let that statement sit in the air.

"And you did it on national TV. In the past few months, several fairy monsters have been publicly taken down by werewolves." He tapped on the table. "If we can manage to sign a nonaggression pact that would make the Tri-Cities a neutral territory, somewhere that we have agreed that no aggressive act can take place—enforced by someone the humans can trust in, trust in their honor and in their ability—then it is just possible that we might avoid a war with the humans and go back to how we have been. Coexisting."

"Are we negotiating with Beauclaire and Goreu?" asked Adam softly. "Or the Council of the Gray Lords?"

"The Council," Goreu said. "Beauclaire to represent the majority and I the minority opinion. It took some doing for that to happen. If they'd been able to locate Órlaith, this would have been much more difficult."

"Goreu," I said, "did you hurt Zee?"

He met my eyes. "No."

"So why did you cringe from him?"

He smiled. "Because it was the action that the male who I pretend to be would have done once the wristlets had proven him weaker than the half-dead daughter of one of the Old Kings. Such a fae would know that Zee was a threat he could not face."

"They believed that?" asked Adam. "That a Gray Lord would be so weak?"

"They remember the Old Kings," Uncle Mike answered. "They remember what Zee can do—they fear him themselves. And Goreu is powerful enough that the battles he fought to become a Gray Lord looked . . . like a political animal wiggling his way into power." He smiled. "And most of them would have been afraid to share those wristlets with the daughter of the Dragon Under the Hill."

"All right," I said, and looked to Adam.

"You know that we would sign a nonaggression pact," he said. "So why the story hour?"

"Because nothing is that simple," agreed Goreu. "The humans might believe that your killing of the troll was enough to make us sign such an agreement. But those of Faery know better. It would be a loss of face—and might spell the downfall of the Gray Lords. The individuals are strong—but there are those, like your Zee and Uncle Mike"—he nodded to Uncle Mike, who grinned and drank his cider—"who hide what they are. If we appear too weak, we shall be brought down—and chaos will rule. That would not be good for anyone. So." He stood up. "Two things. First, a show of force, something to demonstrate that it is no weakness of the fae that makes us sign a treaty. Beauclaire should be ready for his demonstration."

I felt a slow, rolling anxiety. Beauclaire had once, not long ago, told me that he could create hurricanes and tidal waves. That he could drown cities. The Columbia was a mile wide and sixty feet deep.

12

We followed Uncle Mike and Goreu through the double doors marked EMPLOYEES ONLY. I'd expected a kitchen, but there was only a stairway that led up or down. We took the up. Uncle Mike's shouldn't have had an up. From the outside, it was clearly a single-story building. Apparently, that was an illusion or this was a different kind of stairway. We climbed more than one floor. I started counting on the third-floor landing, and I counted seven more. I don't know that there is a ten-story building in the Tri-Cities—maybe the new hospital building in Richland.

Goreu said, opening the door at the top of the stairs, "We wanted you to have a good view."

It was windy, but warm enough, as we stepped out onto a flat roof, the kind of roof I'd have expected Uncle Mike's to have, with battered machines happily humming away, keeping the tavern a steady temperature, and a knee-high barricade to keep people from walking off the edge. Just the right height for a tripping hazard, I thought. Someone stood on the edge of the roof, looking out over the river.

I'd once caught a glimpse of Beauclaire without the glamour that made him appear human. It hadn't prepared me for the whole deal. He was, unlike a lot of fae, almost entirely human-shaped, and his height was somewhere between tall and average, an inch or so taller than Adam and of a similar build.

He turned to greet us, and I could see the hints of the Beauclaire I knew, parts that he'd pulled into his glamour—but he didn't look like a human. His cheekbones were high and flat beneath eyes like expensive emeralds, clear and deep. Other than his eyes, his coloring came from the sun: his skin would have been the envy of a California bikini enthusiast; his hair, which reached past his shoulders in a thick, straight fall, held all the colors of gold with hints of red. Was he beautiful? I couldn't tell. He was extraordinary.

"You are just in time," he said. "I have pushed the last of the humans off the bridge—so I am ready for our little demonstration."

Goreu huffed a laugh, then turned to us. "He didn't mean that like it sounded. He *encouraged* the people who have been working on the bridge to find something else to do. We don't need to kill people for this demonstration."

"One of our Council members was convinced we should flood one of the towns—Burbank or Richland," Uncle Mike said. "It took a while to persuade her that killing that many people would ensure that we'd never get a treaty of any kind with you, and it would play right into the hands of our foes on the Council."

I shivered, though it wasn't cold, and walked as close to the edge as I dared. We had a spectacular view, not as scary as the one from on top of the crane the other day, but spectacular. The Lampson crane was to our left, but it was the view of the Columbia and the Cable Bridge that was breathtaking in a different way than it had been from on top of the crane. From the crane, it had looked distant and small. From our current vantage point, it felt like we were standing right on top of it—and it was huge.

Beauclaire raised his hand and said something. It might have been a word, but it sounded bigger than that. It resonated in my chest and in my throat. Below us, under the center of the bridge, the water of the Columbia started to swirl.

Magic, thick and rich and warm as the noonday sun in August, pressed down on me, and I went to my knees. Adam put his hand under my elbow, but he had to wrap his arms around me before I could stand. I breathed like a racehorse, and my face grew hot, then very cold, and still the power moved.

The swirling water started small, but grew until the whole river circled beneath the bridge like traffic negotiating the stupid round-abouts that had been showing up where the four-way stop signs used to be. Gradually, the water moved faster, climbing the banks on the outside edge as the center dropped.

The pressure of the water made the bridge groan, I could hear it from where we stood. Overhead, a helicopter flew in and hovered.

Adam said something that I, consumed by the force of Beau-claire's magic, missed, his voice just another rumble in my ears and chest.

I heard Goreu's reply, though it didn't make much sense to me at the time. "Our helicopter. We called the news agencies about ten minutes ago, but we wanted to make sure this was recorded for the media. We'll give the footage to the local stations and let them dis-seminate it. That worked well enough for your killing of the troll." He looked at me. "She is sensitive to magic."

Adam grunted rather than answering, and Goreu smiled at him.

For a moment, he looked less human to me, too, and I had the feeling that the real Goreu was a lot bigger than his glamour would suggest. But the bridge groaned again, and all my attention returned to the sight before us.

The water on the outside of the whirlpool was level with the bridge deck, much higher than the banks of the river, though Beauclaire's magic kept all the water where he wanted it. Beyond the whirlpool, the Columbia's waves grew choppy and white-edged, but the level of the river didn't appear to be affected.

The whirlpool quit growing, but it continued to speed up and drain the middle to feed the edge until I could see bare ground beneath the bridge. The circle grew until the entire section between the two towers was empty of water. The bridge was shaking under the force of the water that now hit the railed edge before rushing over or under the bridge with twisting force.

Beauclaire spoke another word—and for a moment my eyes wouldn't focus. When I could see again, there was no more dirt beneath the bridge. There was just . . . nothing, a hole, so deep that, from our perspective, I could not see the bottom.

The fae cannot lie. Beauclaire had told me he could drown cities, but until this moment, I hadn't really understood what that meant. And this was nowhere near the limits of his power. He might have been able to fake his relaxed stance, but I could feel the magic he channeled to the river and the earth, and there was no end to it.

It took maybe three more minutes, and the bridge gave in to the twisting water, breaking free of its supports and foundations. The noise was tremendous, Uncle Mike's shook, and I could hear someone's car alarm go off. For a moment, just after it was ripped from the bank, the bridge held its structure. Then it collapsed, torn apart by the water and by gravity. Some of the bridge dropped into the hole immediately, some of it was carried by the water to bang back into the supports that had held it up. Battered by water and by debris, the supports for the towers slid into the black hole beneath. The water swirled and spat bits of cement, metal, blacktop, and long, snapping cables into the hole until the water ran clean and nothing more fell out.

Beauclaire said another word, a release of some sort, because it was easier for me to breathe again. The hole in the earth closed up, and this time I could watch it happen, the soil building up from the outside and working in until there was nothing but disturbed dirt and rocks where the hole had been.

Beauclaire said another word, and the water slowed, the whirlpool edge leveled, and the center filled with water. Eventually, the Columbia quit swirling altogether and flowed with deceptive mildness in the same path it had taken an hour ago—except that now it didn't flow past a bridge. It looked beautiful and peaceful. I could see people, some of them in uniform, on both sides of the river, and they were all staring, just like me.

Adam turned me around so he could see my face. He wiped my cheeks with his thumbs—that's when I realized there were tears running down my face. I didn't know why I'd been crying, I wasn't sad—just overwhelmed by Beauclaire's magic.

He bent down to me. *Are you all right?*

His voice slid through the mating bond, caressed me, and cleared my head. I felt like I could take a clean breath for the first time since Beauclaire had called his magic.

"I'm fine," I told him out loud, because if I spoke through our bond, he would hear too much, and I was afraid that the echoes of magic still rattling my bones might cross and hurt him. I didn't know why it was a worry, just that it was, and I had learned to trust my instincts.

He looked at Goreu, standing patiently beside Beauclaire. Sometime while Adam and I were talking, he had regained his usual, unremarkable, glamoured appearance.

"You said two things," Adam said. "This was the first—a demonstration of what the fae can do. So that no one thinks that you were driven to treat with us because we killed your troll, and you're scared. I found your demonstration very convincing."

"The mortals and their government will be very grateful to you for achieving a neutral territory where they can be safe," Goreu said. "The second thing is that you need to find a reason for us to treat with you."

"The Fire Touched would work," Beauclaire said. "I would guarantee his safety and his well-being."

"Since he left our care, Underhill has been more difficult," said Goreu. "She didn't seem to mind while he was on the reservation grounds, but when he left, she was unhappy."

Beauclaire shook his head. "She didn't care that Neuth and Órlaith tortured him," he clarified. "She only cared when he left her influence. Had I realized that, I would have taken him under my protection in the first place. But it would have cost me political power I needed at the moment, to step in to rescue a human—no matter how altered. So—" He stopped speaking.

"Don't worry," said Goreu. "I knew you helped the Dark Smith and his son escape with the Fire Touched. No one had to tell me—who else would have done it? Don't worry, most of them are blinded by the fact that the Dark Smith killed your father. They wouldn't forgive someone's sneezing on them, and couldn't comprehend you in a million years, my friend."

"We won't send the boy back," I said.

"Do you doubt me?" asked Beauclaire. He didn't sound offended, but it scared me all the same. It didn't change my opinion, but it did scare me.

"No," I said firmly. "But he wakes up screaming in terror on the nights he can sleep. He's afraid of you—all of you. If you'd stopped the Widow Queen and her ilk when he first escaped Underhill, if someone, if anyone had cared for him, he wouldn't have come to us. I don't think that he'll go back willingly. And I think he has suffered enough. I won't encourage him to go back. I trust you and your word, Beauclaire. But I don't think that he will survive if he's forced back to you. I won't force him, and I won't allow anyone else to, either."

Beauclaire turned to Adam. "Does she speak for you?"

"She speaks for herself," said Adam. "But I agree. He cannot go back."

"You will risk the survival of the pack for the happiness of a boy who will not be harmed," said Goreu. There was no judgment in his voice. "A boy who is not a child at all."

I looked at Adam.

He smiled. "My wolves would not thank me for sending a scared kid to the people in his nightmares just to keep them safe. Safety is not always the key. He belongs to the pack now, and we take care of our own."

And that right there was one of the differences between Adam and Bran. Bran kept his eye on the end game. Adam understood the end game all right, but to him, the people mattered more than the game.

The werewolves needed Bran, who could make the tough choices to make sure they survived. I needed Adam because he would never abandon someone who loved him, the way that Bran had abandoned us. Abandoned me. Twice. I swallowed and reminded myself I was a grown-up. But I was so grateful that I had Adam. "Name something else," said Adam.

Goreu turned to Beauclaire, and said, "I told you that would not happen." He looked at Adam. "I'm afraid, then, it is up to you."

"You can't give us a better clue about what we could offer you?" Adam said.

"Ask Zee," said Goreu. "Our people are hungry for magic, and Zee has been collecting the weapons he has made."

I raised my eyebrows. "Now, *that* makes sense. We find ourselves on opposite sides in a conflict—and to stop it, we give you a powerful magical artifact, a weapon?"

Goreu grinned at my logic. "It might work."

Uncle Mike, who'd been a silent witness to it all, shook his head. "That old man has been destroying his toys ever since his wife died. I'm not sure he has anything big enough to matter."

I looked at him, and Uncle Mike shrugged. "He was forced to marry her, and he thought it would be easy so he allowed it. Then he fell in love for the first time in . . . for the first time, I think. When she died—he was very angry. Angry at the Gray Lords who made him make himself vulnerable. So he started to destroy any of his own work that came back to him—and most of it does, eventually. He also destroys other things when he can, too. The Gray Lords would stop him if they could." He gave the two Gray Lords present a merry look. "But they can't. So they pretend not to notice."

"This is weird," said Jesse at dinner two days later. "Last week, I was a social pariah at school. Hell—"

Her father cleared his throat.

"Heck," she said. "Heck. Since the troll died? I could run for class president and win."

"Don't fret," Aiden said, eating the spaghetti I'd made as if he was afraid it would run off his plate, "I'm sure you'll be a pariah again soon enough."

"That was pretty good," Jesse said, dumping another helping of spaghetti on his plate without his asking. "It would have been better, though, if you'd swallowed before you started to talk. We eat with our mouths closed around here."

"How do you get the food in?" asked Aiden.

She stopped eating. Opened her mouth, then shut it again.

"Gotcha," he said happily, still talking with his mouth full.

Adam, I noticed, was looking pretty worn. He hadn't said much since we'd sat down to eat. Tonight, it was just Jesse, Aiden, Adam, and me.

Joel, who was still experiencing better control of his shapeshifting, had taken his wife out to dinner. No one knew he was a pack member, so they didn't have to worry about reporters following them around.

Adam was taking the brunt of the attention. The local newspeople knew him, the Feds knew him, and a fair number of the national press knew him from previous stories—and he was handsome and articulate. So he was the one they aimed their questions at.

How had we known what the fae were going to do? Why had they done it? Were they planning on doing it again somewhere else? After the first wave of reporters, Adam drafted a statement, which he read for the local TV stations.

"It was the fae," Adam told them. "They came to us and told us that they wanted people to understand what we were dealing with. They are not just the boogie monsters hiding in fairy tales. Some of them are more powerful than that, some of them were worshipped as gods by our ancestors for very good reasons. The bridge was chosen because it was highly visible, and because it was easy to clear of people—because the Gray Lords don't think that killing people will accomplish what they want. And because it was where we killed the troll. Could they do it to a bridge full of rush-hour traffic in the middle of Seattle, Portland, or Washington, DC? Yes. But they could have done that last year or ten years ago, too. They don't want to. They and we are trying to negotiate a nonviolent end to our situation here in the Tri-Cities, in hopes that it might allow them, and us, and our government to negotiate a nonviolent end to the situation that occurred when our justice system made it clear that justice was for humans only. Thank you."

And when the Feds came, Adam told them the same thing, mostly word for word except where pronouns needed to be clarified.

The newspeople took their photos of my handsome, sincere mate and wrote up what he could give them. But the Feds . . . they were pushier. We had the whole alphabet soup on our doorstep (figuratively speaking) because terrorist attacks belong to the FBI, and paranormal anything belongs to Cantrip. But the NSA was here, too. Adam told me that two of the people claiming to be Cantrip, and one who was supposed to be FEMA, were actually CIA. He told me he could tell by the way they made the back of his neck itch—he recognized it from Vietnam, where he'd first encountered their kind.

The Feds threatened, cajoled, and stopped just short of arresting Adam. We kept a patrol of werewolves who watched out for the fae. As a side benefit, the wolves kept the Feds off, too.

When the director of Cantrip called to complain about our lack of cooperation, Adam told him exactly where he could shove it and how far. Adam used some of Ben's favorite phrases to remind them that a rogue Cantrip agent and his rogue-agent pals had killed one of our own not six months ago. That we'd found illegal tracking equipment on our personal vehicle that Cantrip had admitted to placing (when they'd summoned Adam to a closed-door meeting while I was talking Sherwood down from the crane). Cantrip would rot before we ever cooperated with them. And he hung up while the director was still talking.

Five minutes later, the FBI called and asked us to cooperate with Cantrip's investigation. Adam said, "No." When the man kept talking at him, Adam threw the phone through the wall.

My husband has a temper. Especially he has a temper when dealing with stupid people. It was why Bran had tried very hard not to use him as a spokesperson. There were no cameras on him when the phone landed in the entryway, so it didn't matter as far as Adam's public face.

Our favorite contractor was still working on the damage the fight with the fae had done to the house. One more wall wasn't going to add that much to the overall bill, so the hole in the wall that the phone made wasn't important, either. Two more walls, because Aiden had burned down the wall between the safe room and the adjoining bathroom.

The phone survived. That protective case proved that it had been worth the money.

The real reason for Adam's short temper was frustration. We still hadn't been able to come up with anything the fae would want or need.

Other than Aiden.

Despite Uncle Mike's words, I'd have asked Zee, but he and Tad had left the house the morning after the fae attack, and I hadn't seen them since. Zee's house was empty—there was no sign that he'd been back there since he'd escaped the reservation.

In the meantime, life went on. Adam got his work done mostly from home to avoid the rush of reporters (and the Feds of whatever alphabet variety). Ben and Warren took turns escorting Jesse to and from school. And we ate breakfast and dinner together. Tonight, it had been spaghetti that I'd made from scratch. The noodles were packaged, though. If Christy had made dinner, the noodles would have been freshly made from scratch, too. I hoped she had met the nice young billionaire of her dreams and decided to stay in the Bahamas. Heck, I even hoped she lived happily for the rest of her life, as long as she did it in the Bahamas.

The phone rang while Adam and I were cleaning up the dishes. He started the dishwasher while I answered the phone. He had gotten less and less polite since the Sinking of the Cable Bridge, so I had started answering the phones first when I could.

"Hauptmans'," I said. "What can I do for you?"

"Mercy," said Baba Yaga's voice. "That is not a question you should ask until you know who you're talking to."

Adam spun to look at me, and his response stopped Jesse and Aiden in their tracks. I raised an eyebrow, and he made a rolling motion with his hand. I was, it seemed, to carry on with the conversation.

"Just because I asked what I could do, doesn't imply I would do it," I said peaceably. "Hello, Baba Yaga. What can I do for you?"

"Well, you could have called me," she said. "Here I all but gave you an engraved invitation . . . no, no. I did give you an engraved invitation, didn't I? I gave you my card and told you to call me when you needed information. And yet here I sit uncalled."

The kids couldn't hear what she was saying, but Adam could. He nodded at me.

"Okay, then," I said, and asked her the question we hadn't been able to find an answer to: "What can we do for the fae that will allow the Gray Lords to sign a treaty with our pack that sets up the Tri-Cities as neutral territory?"

"You could give them the fire-touched boy," said Baba Yaga brightly. "I am sure that Beauclaire gave you his word that the boy would be safe. Beauclaire would die before breaking that word."

She placed a slight emphasis on her last sentence. She thought that if we sent Aiden into Beauclaire's hands, he would die keeping Aiden safe. Not that he would die before letting anything happen to him—but that he would die. Or she wanted me to think that. I pinched the bridge of my nose.

"I think we can agree that we don't want Beauclaire dead," I said.

"Oh, I think we can indeed agree to that," she replied.

"So we won't give Aiden back to the fae," I said. "Since we didn't intend to do so, we're doubly convinced that would be the wrong thing to do. What do you suggest?"

"You could steal the sword of Siebold Adelbertsmiter," she said. "The blade that cuts through anything and takes any shape it desires. The one he used a few days ago to kill his fellow fae. I assure you that the fae would consider that a gift worth signing a treaty that benefits them far more than it benefits you."

"No," I said. "No. I couldn't steal the sword or any other artifact from Zee. It would not be possible. Besides, he's off somewhere. I will ask him if he has something the fae would consider worth signing the treaty for, but, as Uncle Mike said, I do know he's been destroying anything he thought too dangerous. Anything he doesn't think too dangerous, the fae probably wouldn't want."

"True," said Baba Yaga. "True." She made a humming sound. Then in an apparently complete change of subject, she said, "Órlaith is missing."

I started to ask her what that had to do with anything. But then I remembered that Órlaith was the Gray Lord who had tortured Zee. Maybe it wasn't a change of subject. So I held my tongue. Aiden was staring at me, his expression frozen. I looked at Adam and tilted my head. He saw Aiden's face and went over to him, putting a hand on his shoulder.

"We won't send you back," he told Aiden.

"I thought we'd already agreed upon that," said Baba Yaga, though she couldn't have seen who Adam had been talking to. Probably, it was only a good guess.

"What is it that the fae need?" she asked. "I always look at that first when I'm bringing someone a present. What *do* they need?"

I blinked at the phone, then I looked at Adam. Who shrugged.

"They need Underhill to play nice," I ventured.

"Yes," Baba Yaga agreed. "We're not going to give them . . . uhm, let me rephrase that. *You* aren't going to give *us* Aiden. That's right. But you might listen to what he's going to tell you. I'll give you a call back in five minutes or so, and you can let me know if he says anything interesting. Ta."

She hung up before I could respond.

Aiden and Jesse had been clearing the table; Aiden still had the plastic-wrapped salad in his hands. He seemed to become aware of it after I put the handset back in its stand. He moved away from Adam and put the salad in the fridge.

"I will go back," he said, turning to face us. He looked at Jesse for a moment. "She should be safe—and while I am here, she will never be safe."

And moments like that were why, even though sometimes he was very difficult, I still liked him.

"You're not going back," said Adam. "And are you implying I can't keep my daughter safe?"

"Or she can't keep herself safe?" Jesse said. She looked at me. "I forgot to thank you for teaching me how to shoot your rifle."

"No trouble," I said. "I enjoyed the company."

Aiden tilted his head, then shook it. "You can't stop me."

"Maybe I could," said Adam. "But I won't. I misspoke earlier. You can't go back and be our tribute for the fae so that they will sign a pact with us. You can go back. But we will tell them that you did it without our knowledge or consent, and so they owe us nothing."

I fought it for a second—but then I kissed Adam, the kind of kiss that made Jesse say, "Really, Mercy? Dad? Get a room."

I stepped back and met Adam's eyes. "You know I love you, right?" I looked at Aiden. "So your sacrifice is refused. Baba Yaga seems to think you are the key, though she made it clear that returning you to the fae would be a bad idea. You are outvoted and outnumbered. Help us think outside of the box."

Jesse said, "She told you not to return Aiden to the fae? Good. Artifacts might work, but Zee isn't here, and he's the only one who would have an artifact that would be powerful enough to make them accept." She held up a hand to me. "The walking stick won't work because it won't stay with them. Giving them something that will only take itself away again will force them to abandon any pact they make."

"Right," I said.

"Back to Baba Yaga," she said. Her father watched her with a smile on his face. "She said something about Underhill."

"Not quite," I told her. "She asked me what the fae needed—and I told her that they needed Underhill to behave."

Aiden sat down on a chair. "Underhill contains a lot of arti-facts," he said. "I know where some of them are."

"You can't go back there," Adam said.

Aiden nodded. "Yes, yes, I can. I can get out, too. The same way I got in, I know how to open the doors to Underhill whether she wants me to do so or not. Water figured it out—and she taught all of us."

"One of the other elemental changelings?" asked Jesse.

I was still stuck on the "I know where some of them are" part of what Aiden had said.

Aiden answered Jesse's question. "There were only four of us who survived. Sort of survived anyway. I guess I'm the only one who got out and survived the fae afterward."

Jesse said, "Good for you. So if Dad can get the fae to guar-antee you safe passage to and from Underhill, you can go in and get an artifact that is powerful enough to please the fae? Some-thing that will let them interact with Underhill better?"

He stood up and took Jesse's hand and kissed it. "Yes, my lady, that is exactly what I have to say."

The phone rang.

"Hauptmans' mortuary," I answered. "You stab 'em, we slab 'em." Baba Yaga was wearing off on me.

"Hard-boiled is the best way to eat eggs," said Baba Yaga. "But I've quit eating eggs—it upset my household. What did the boy-who-isn't-a-boy have to say?"

I decided I didn't want to know what inspired the information about eggs. "He said that if the fae will guarantee safe-from-them passage, he knows of an artifact that will help the fae deal with Underhill."

"Very good," she said in a chipper voice that was more usual in bad children's programming on TV. "So you and yours have safe passage to Underhill and back from Underhill. We will sign the treaty before you go in—just in case you don't come out again. That way no one's sacrifice is in vain. No, I'm not listening in, Mercy— that would be rude." She rolled her "r" on rude. "People are just so predictable. You should bring your walking stick, Mercy. Oh, and that oh-so-handsome Russian-blooded wolf. Just you four should be enough."

"Four?" asked Adam.

"You, Mercy, Aiden, and the walking stick," she said. "That should be enough. The right ingredients make the stew, you know." She hung up.

I'd just replaced the handset when it rang again.

"Yes?" I said.

"I'm waiting for more cleverness," Baba Yaga said. "Hauptman House of Horrors, don't mind the screaming—we don't. Something of the sort."

"Okay," I said. "Hauptman House of Horrors—"

"Sssss," she said. "You and that Coyote are always ruining my fun. Anyway. I forgot to tell you—we accept your bargain. You should come tomorrow early."

"Come where?" I asked.

She laughed. "To the reservation. Guides will meet you along the way so you won't get caught up in the protections. I don't think I'll see you there, but I'll see you sometime. Ta', darling. Give that wolf of yours a nudge for me—I do love Russian men."

She hung up, and I set the phone back on the counter and watched it. While I waited for her to call again, Adam told Jesse and Aiden what Baba Yaga had said.

Jesse frowned at him when he was done. "Okay. You, I understand. You can keep everyone safe. Aiden has to go in, but why

Mercy? Why not Zee, who is fae, or Tad, who is nearly fae? Or another werewolf?"

"The walking stick," said Adam after a moment. "It only follows Mercy."

I nodded thoughtfully. "One of the things it can do is show us the way home. That might be useful in Underhill."

"Every boarding party needs its guide to light the way, its wizard to defeat the magic, and a tank to kill everything that tries to stop the party," Jesse said. She had been playing too much ISTDPBF with the pack lately, and it was affecting her thinking. She looked at her father. "The tank is *not* sacrificial."

"Aye, aye, Captain," said Adam with only a little irony in his voice.

"You come home, Daddy," she told him. "I love my mother, but if I have to live with her for very long, one of us will commit a homicide. And you bring Mercy and the pip-squeak back."

"Am I the wizard or the guide?" I asked our captain.

"Aiden is fire touched," she told me after considering the matter. "You can only turn into a coyote. So he's the wizard, even though he has to guide the party in. You guide the party out. And Dad makes sure you all get out alive."

"Next time," said Aiden, who'd been learning the fine art of playing pirate on computers, too, "I want to be the tank."

Jesse came with us.

"No one will touch her," Zee told Adam, breaking into the middle of the heated after-breakfast discussion. "I will be there. Tad will be there. Nothing will happen to her."

Zee and Tad had shown up in the middle of the night, neither of them willing to talk about what they'd been doing. Since Baba Yaga had sort of told me already, I didn't ask. I didn't want to know.

"What do you mean, you'll be there?" asked Adam.

"Underhill doesn't like our kind," Zee said. "So we won't follow you in. But Tad and I will come with you, we will watch over Jesse and see that nothing befalls her. I agree that Underhill is no place for someone who is wholly human." He glanced at Aiden, who grimaced and nodded emphatically. "But Jesse is no longer a child. It is her right to witness what her father does."

The Alpha wolf and the Dark Smith held each other's eyes.

"Daddy?" asked Jesse.

The Alpha stare-down broke up with neither participant a winner or loser.

"Please?" she said.

"Fine," Adam huffed, because Jesse's awesome, seldom-used secret power was that she had her father wrapped around her little finger.

"Now that that's settled," I said, "we should go."

I took my dishes to the sink and stopped to kiss Adam's cheek as I passed him. I would have moved on, but he held me against him for a moment. He smelled of me, of our early-morning lovemaking, and of the pack. But mostly he smelled like himself: mint and musk and Adam.

We loaded ourselves in Adam's SUV. I took the middle of the front while Jesse took shotgun, leaving Aiden, Zee, and Tad to sort themselves out in the backseat. As Adam backed the SUV out of its parking space, I saw Joel, in human form, leaning against the frame of the front door. He wasn't happy at being left behind, but that was an argument Adam had won.

Ben, who had listened in, had quipped lightly, "You know you've got a good Alpha when everyone beats each other up trying to throw themselves in the tar pit after he jumps in." But he'd patted Joel on the shoulder, and said, "Enough. We all know you're willing—and if you weren't, there are a dozen of us who would have his back if he needed it. He appreciates it, but you're distracting him from what he needs to do."

And so Joel had given in. He watched us drive off with an unhappy expression on his face, but he would wait. He was pack; he knew he was valued, that he had purpose. That didn't mean he had to be happy about obeying orders, just that he obeyed. Which is why he mostly fit in the pack a lot better than I did. Suggestions I might follow: I had trouble with orders.

It was still dark out as we pulled into the road. Adam's shoulder against mine was warm. For an accidental moment, I caught his thoughts.

It was just a visual of my face, lit by the blue light of the dash. It wasn't the face I saw in the mirror every day. He thought I was beautiful. He was worried for me.

I saw his hands tighten on the wheel and put my hand on his thigh. I don't think he knew I'd caught what he was thinking. I was lucky he wasn't thinking I should lose a few pounds or clean under my nails better. Or how gorgeous that early-morning jogger we just passed was (and she was).

"Adam?" I asked.

He didn't answer, still lost in his thoughts.

"Hey, Adam," I said again.

"Woolgathering," he told me with a faint smile.

I grinned at him. "An appropriate activity for a wolf."

"Did you need something?" he asked.

For this trip to be done. For all of us to be home and safe.

"No," I said lightly. "Or if I did, I've forgotten what it was."

Silence fell in the SUV again. It was early. I wiggled to get comfortable—the center seat was more suited to a child than an adult. From the backseat, the scent of fear was getting stronger.

To distract him—because it wasn't Zee or Tad who was worried— I asked, "So, Aiden, what do you think we'll find in Underhill?"

"Underhill," said Aiden stoically. He was afraid, but he also smelled resigned, like the rabbit who knew it was dead and quit struggling. The confidence he'd shown us last night was gone. He cleared his throat, and said, "Sometimes the terrain is forest or desert, sometimes it's a snowy mountaintop or an ocean so deep, you can't find the bottom. If you blink, it can change—but it doesn't matter where you are, Underhill is always there." His voice tightened. "Watching."

"What do you *think* will happen?" asked Jesse.

After a moment, Aiden said, "She'll pretend to ignore us at first, I think. She'll be mad at me, and she'll want to take her time to decide what to do."

"Why mad?" asked Jesse. Since Aiden was telling her more than he'd told Adam or me, I thought I'd just keep quiet and see what Jesse could pull out of him.

"Because I left," he said. "None of us was supposed to leave her. And I was the last one. Water. Earth. Air. Fire. Her creations, she called us. Her children. The others died or were killed when they left her. She told me about it." He hesitated. "I think she caused their deaths. Or did something that made the fae cause their deaths. I left last because I was afraid to leave."

"So why are you going back?" Jesse's voice was cool. "If she caused their deaths, don't you think she'll kill you?"

"No," he said, when, I could tell, he hadn't intended to say anything at all on the subject. "Not while I'm in Underhill itself—because that would be cheating. If we get attacked, and I can't defend myself, that's a fair death, but she can't turn her hand specifically toward that end, or she'll ruin her own game."

When Adam turned off the highway and took the road that used to lead to the reservation, dawn was lightening the sky, though the sun herself wouldn't be up for fifteen or twenty minutes. He drove steadily past vineyards and cornfields into the hill country. I was pretty sure that he'd driven farther than it had taken to get to the reservation, but it didn't seem to bother him.

The road took a sharp turn I didn't remember, then Adam had to hit the brakes hard so he didn't run into the horsemen lined up across the road. There were three of them, each riding a white horse and dressed in gray. As soon as the SUV stopped completely, they turned their horses and began trotting down the road.

"Our guides?" Adam asked the backseat denizens.

"*Ja,*" said Zee. "Good to know that drama is still alive and well among the fae. *Schimmelreiter.* Bah. Theatrics."

Adam was smiling his hunting smile as we followed the three galloping horses who moved as fast as the SUV could safely negotiate the narrow mountain road that bore no resemblance to the road that used to go to the Ronald Wilson Reagan Fae Reservation.

The road might go different paths, but the walls around the reservation had been left, block cement topped by stainless-steel razor wire. The guard towers were apparently empty, and the gates hung wide open. It looked abandoned, but it didn't smell that way. It smelled green and alive, even through the filter of the SUV.

The horses slowed to a walk to cross through the threshold of Fairyland, and Adam slowed the SUV to follow them.

Zee made no sound as they crossed into the reservation, but I could smell Tad's sweat. Aiden's heart beat double time. Jesse and Adam were the only ones in the car who weren't affected. I include myself as the affected. The one time before that I'd been in Underhill had been a scary, scary thing.

We followed the walking horses through streets that could have been in any unimaginatively-laid-out suburb in America as the sun rose and lit the world. The streets were set in a numbered grid—as if the original architect feared that people might get lost here. I knew how they felt, but I also thought that the hope that a sign could lead someone out of Faery was the belief of an innocent.

Magic was stronger here than it had been the last time I'd come. I gripped Adam's thigh and practiced a swimmer's breathing, in through my mouth and out through my nose, in an effort to block the overwhelming rush. It wasn't as bad as when Beauclaire sank Cable Bridge, but it was bad enough.

"Are we feeling Underhill?" asked Adam in a low voice.

I looked at him. Adam wasn't very sensitive to magic, but his wolf looked out through his eyes, so he was feeling something.

"Yes," said Aiden. His voice was faint. "This is what happens in places where there are too many doors in too small an area. Her magic leaks out."

"Even though the doors have long been closed in the Old Country," Zee added, "there are places that people avoid because the spill of magic lingers. And others that they visit in hopes of miracles."

There were still fae in Europe, I knew, but most of them had come to the New World fleeing the spread of cold iron. Iron had followed them here, too, but they seemed to have come to some sort of terms with it. Tolkien's elves had traveled to the West, and there were scholars who argued that Tolkien had known some of the fae left behind who spoke with longing of their kinsfolk who had traveled to the New World.

The horses stopped in front of what had once been a municipal building of some sort—the sign in front of it was hacked into indecipherable splinters, the bits of wood left where they lay, though the lawns were mowed and tidy.

As soon as the riders began to dismount, Adam turned the SUV off and got out. I scooted out behind Jesse because I wanted to make sure she wasn't standing alone in the reservation for long. Of the six of us, she was the most vulnerable—which was why Adam had tried to leave her at home. Standing here, among our enemies—or at least our unpredictable and dangerous acquaintances—I wished he'd succeeded.

Two of the riders led the horses away, but the other one waited to escort us into the building. Adam went first, Zee and Tad took the rear guard, and the rest of us spread out between them.

The building wasn't much to look at. Built to the military specs of the eighties, cement steps took them to a plain painted door set into uninspired vinyl siding. But inside . . .

Jesse sucked in her breath, and said, "It's a TARDIS."

"A what?" asked Aiden.

"Bigger on the inside than it is on the outside," Jesse said.

She was right, because we'd entered not a small antechamber that probably had originally been the first thing visitors saw, but a spacious room with marble floors and pillars. The marble was pink, flecked with patches of black and gray. The room was empty, and our escort didn't slow down as he crossed the room and out through one of many doorways. This one led to a large office, easily large enough it didn't feel crowded despite floor-to-ceiling bookcases and the seven of us. In contrast to the size of the room, Beauclaire's desk was of normal size. The fae lord himself sat behind it.

"Sir," said our escort, "I bring you the guests you were expecting." He didn't wait for acknowledgment, just turned and left the room.

Beauclaire cleared away the papers he was working on and set them in a folder without hurrying. His desk was as hyperorganized as Adam's. Adam had learned to organize in the army; I wondered where Beauclaire had picked up the habit. Only when the papers had been properly stowed did he turn his attention to us.

"Gentlemen," said Beauclaire, his gaze drifting past Adam's face and lighting on mine briefly before stopping to dwell on Jesse's. "Ladies."

"My daughter," said Adam, answering the question the fae wouldn't ask. "She needed to see us off on our journey."

Beauclaire knew about daughters. His face lit with appreciation of our predicament.

"I told him no harm would come to her here," said Zee.

Beauclaire met Zee's eyes in a way he hadn't Adam's. "I am pleased to help you keep that vow."

Zee inclined his head regally.

"You wouldn't happen to know why Órlaith and several other fae of her cadre are missing, would you?" Beauclaire asked Zee.

Zee smiled and said nothing.

Beauclaire smiled back. Evidently, none of the missing would be missed by him.

Beauclaire reached into a desk drawer and brought out a roll of vellum. He stretched it out across his desk, so the lettering faced us, putting a paperweight at the top and the bottom to keep it rolled out. "The others have signed," he told Adam. "When you have read it and signed, I'll make my mark, and the bargain will be made."

Adam nodded, pulled up a seat, and began to read. I read over his shoulder.

> We, the Gray Lords of Faery, representing themselves and all of Faery, do make this bargain with Adam Alexander Hauptman and his mate Mercedes Athena Thompson Hauptman, who represent themselves and the Columbia Basin Pack . . .

When Adam was finished, he stood up and looked at Zee. "Would you mind going through it as well?"

Zee nodded. It didn't take him as long as it had us. "It says what we think it does," he said, his smile brief but real. "It helps that the fae want this more than you do."

After Tad nodded, too, I wrote my name in the space left for me, then handed Adam the quill pen to sign. Beauclaire rounded the desk to sign rather than turn the sheet around.

When he was finished, he set the pen aside and put his hand on the vellum. He took three deep breaths, and magic swelled. I sneezed twice and still couldn't get the tickle out of my nose.

Beauclaire bent his head then, and spoke a *word*. Adam put his hand on my shoulder, but Beauclaire didn't use the kind of power he'd called when destroying the bridge. When he took his hand off the document, there were two copies.

He rolled them both and wrapped some kind of keeper around the rolls. One of those he left on his desk, and the other he gave to Zee.

"I'll take you to a door," he said, and started out of his office, only to pause in the doorway. "You should take off any iron or steel you have on your persons."

But Adam had spent the night going through the go-bags he kept ready and waiting in our closet. He'd substituted plastic and nylon for most of the metal.

I had a thought. "Adam. Your dog tags. What are they made from?"

"Stainless steel," Adam told me, and started to take his off.

I had one of his tags on the necklace I always wore. I undid the clasp and looked at it. It was an untidy mess—a gold lamb charm, my wedding ring, and the tag. I put out my hand and took Adam's steel necklace with his remaining tag—and then I put both necklaces around Jesse's neck.

"These are our promise to you," I told Jesse, "that we'll do our best to get back to you if we can. That we will do our best and expect the same from you."

"That's my Mercy," Adam said. "Not too good with words until it counts. And then she'll pull the rug right out from under you."

Jesse blinked hard and gave Adam a "help me" look out of her watery eyes.

He grinned at her. "Just remember whose daughter you are," he said. "And whose daughter she is." He tipped his chin at me.

I felt my jaw set hard. But I didn't protest. "Joe Old Coyote," said Jesse.

Who had been Coyote wearing a human suit. Joe Old Coyote had died, not abandoned my mother. Coyote had abandoned my mother—and me.

"Joe Old Coyote was tough," Adam told Jesse, putting an arm around my shoulders. "He hunted vampires, and he took on Mercy's mom. Of the two, I know what I'm more scared of."

That made me laugh. "My mom isn't that bad."

Adam gave me a look.

I bit my lip, then gave up and laughed again. "Okay, okay. She is. Worse. I'd rather face vampires any day than my mother."

"I found her charming," said Zee.

Laughter, I thought with satisfaction, is a terrific way to start an adventure.

13

I stepped in front of Adam when he started to pull his clothes off. Not that Jesse hadn't seen him naked before. Like me, werewolves have to strip to change. Modesty is for humans. But it wasn't only modesty that had made me step between Adam and the rest of the room. Werewolves in the middle of shifting could and did protect themselves, but they couldn't do it well until they were fully in either form. I wasn't worried, really, that anyone would attack him—we had Baba Yaga's word on it. It was more the way Adam always walked on the traffic side of me when we walked around town. He didn't expect anything to happen, but he wanted to be there if it did.

I could feel Adam pulling on the pack bonds for speed. If it hadn't been for the necessity of signing the bargain, he could have changed at home, could have taken his time. But he couldn't afford to be weakened in any way for very long on the reservation, so he pulled on the bonds and asked for help.

Beauclaire said, "I've never seen a werewolf change."

"New experiences are hard to come by," Zee agreed. "Unless you work with Mercy. I've been having all sorts of new experiences since I met her."

Beauclaire smiled appreciatively.

I said, "We decided it would work best to go in with Adam as wolf. Guns don't work in Underhill." And wasn't that too bad. "And we can't take steel or iron. So our best weapon is going to come in ready to defend us."

"You will stay human?" he asked.

I shrugged. "At least I can talk to Aiden this way." The only other time I'd been in Underhill, I'd been in coyote form. The very scary fae I'd met there—a fae that Zee had treated with more caution than he did any of the Gray Lords—had known exactly what I was anyway.

If my coyote skin wouldn't serve as camouflage, there was no reason not to stay human. I could carry more that way. I wasn't entirely sure that I could change shape in Underhill. I hadn't tried before, and Zee worried that only fae magic would work there. But Aiden needed a cheering section and, if the walking stick cooperated, I probably needed to be in human shape to use it.

I also probably should have grabbed the walking stick off the chest of drawers when we left. But it had seemed wrong. When the walking stick chose to come to my aid—it just came. Taking it with me . . . I worried that it wouldn't work.

Adam's change took a little less than five minutes. Not as fast as Charles's—the Marrok's son, who had been born a werewolf, could sometimes change as fast as I could, between one blink and the next. But it was faster than most werewolves. He shook himself and stretched like a cat, his claws making clicking sounds on the marble floors. Then he walked up to me as Tad gathered his fallen clothing.

I grabbed Aiden's pack and helped him to settle it comfortably. My pack was a lot heavier. Adam, we decided, needed to be free to move, so I carried most of our supplies. Food for a week, water for a day, and a very light boatload of technology-lightened-and-miniaturized backpacking supplies. Also six hard-boiled eggs from the dozen I'd made at breakfast. Baba Yaga might not have meant anything when she'd told me that hard-boiled was best, but I wasn't taking any chances. Aiden had a pack, too, but however old he really was, his body was that of a ten-year-old. His pack was mostly his bedroll and freeze-dried food.

We hadn't brought a tent. Even if it rained, we couldn't afford to blind ourselves like that when we slept.

"We're ready now," I told Beauclaire.

He took us back out to the main room, through two more doors, and into a room that was so utilitarian, it must have belonged to the original building. There was a closet door on one wall, and it was to this he led us.

Zee took a deep breath. "This one wasn't here last month. There are too many doors to Underhill in too small a space."

"We know," said Beauclaire.

"It's not safe," said Zee.

"We know that, too."

Zee snorted. "Well, somebody doesn't, because she can't make doorways where she isn't invited."

"Is this doorway acceptable?" Beauclaire asked me, ignoring Zee's taunt.

I looked at Aiden, who shrugged. We both looked at Zee.

"It doesn't matter where you go in," he said. "These doorways are all too new to have found an anchor in Underhill. That means they'll drop you someplace random. Just make sure you are holding on to each other when you go—or you'll all end up in different parts of Underhill." Beauclaire opened the door and stepped back. Jesse hugged her father, hugged me, then hugged Aiden.

"Don't get them killed," she told Aiden.

"I'll try not to," he said earnestly.

"Don't get stuck," she said.

"I'll try not to," he told her.

"Good enough," she said. "If you try, Dad will do the rest."

"Safe journey," said Zee.

"Don't do anything I wouldn't do," said Tad.

"I love you, too," I said, and, holding on to Adam with one hand and Aiden with the other, crossed over into Underhill.

We had to go down three cement steps to get to the ground. When Aiden went back and shut the door behind us, I turned to see that the door was set in the back of a building that looked like the back of the building we'd gone into.

But my bones hummed with the magic—it was like standing on a washing machine permanently caught in the spin cycle.

"It's a good idea to shut doors behind you in Underhill," Aiden told me. "People who are chasing you usually go somewhere else."

He looked around, his breathing a little fast, and his weight shifted from foot to foot like a deer waiting to see where the danger emerged, so he could flee in the opposite direction as fast as he could.

We had emerged into an anticlimactic, bland landscape that looked very much like the area around the reservation. We were on the top of a small hill at the base of larger hills. Below us was a grassy valley with a river running through it. If it hadn't been for the lack of civilization—roads, wires, squashed beer cans—it could have been anywhere near Walla Walla.

Okay, it could have been anywhere near Walla Walla if there had been beer cans on the ground and a sun in the bright blue sky. There was no sun in the sky. There were shadows, and, from how the shadows lay, we were approximately the same time as it was back on the reservation. I just couldn't see any reason for the shadows.

From what Zee told me, time in Underhill could be capricious— but not as badly as in the Elphame of the fairy queen I'd encountered. We might lose or gain a few days or possibly a week. But we were unlikely to lose years or decades.

I turned slowly. We had a clear field of vision, but I couldn't see anything that looked out of place. At the thought, I turned to look for the small building we'd exited from—but there was no sign of any building anywhere.

"Do you know which way to go?" I asked. "Have you been here before?"

"I don't think that I've been here, precisely," he said. "But I know which way to go. Mostly I find my way around by the way it feels here." He thumped himself on the chest.

I tried, but I couldn't feel any kind of pull or push in the magic.

"It took me a while," he said. "This way."

And he set off, straight up the hill. We walked for hours. Aiden's terror subsided, though it never quite left him. Adam ranged a little, his nose to the ground and his ears alert, but he never traveled out of sight. He didn't chase the white bunny that first appeared in glimpses, then ran across our path. Twice.

"He's not a dog," I commented loudly, spinning in a slow

circle to look for something, I don't know what it was. "He's not going to chase a rabbit and leave us behind."

I could feel the urge to chase that rabbit, and I seldom felt the need to hunt when I was on two feet. Adam didn't even lunge at the rabbit when it emerged from a hollow just beyond his nose.

He did growl, though.

"It's not a real rabbit," said Aiden unnecesssarily. "After a while, even before I had magic, I learned to tell the difference. I survived a long time without magic—but I had friends then."

"What happened?" I asked.

He laughed without humor, but his voice was relaxed. "No need to sound so careful," he told me, his gaze on the strange sky. "It was a very long time ago, even by my reckoning. There were five or six of us humans left behind when the fae were banished. At first, we were overjoyed. We played all day long and ate the food in the larder—and there was always food in the larder. Last time I went back there, a very long time later, there was still food there—but there are other things living in the Emerald Court now, things that feed on those weaker than they. Like me and like you.

"Evander died first," Aiden said. He was walking faster as he talked, and he kept looking behind us. "He was the youngest of us—you learned caution very quickly in that court, or you died. I don't think Evander would have survived long even if we hadn't been abandoned in Underhill. Evander first, then Lily and Rose—I don't remember what their human names had been. Lily just disappeared from her bed one day, and Rose quit eating. Then it was just Willy and me. For a long time, it was Willy and me. Then we found this pretty little girl crying next to a stream. We took care of her and told her stories."

There was nothing behind us that I could see or smell. I touched

Adam lightly on his head and looked at Aiden. Adam watched him a moment, then broke free to run down the hill half a dozen yards before circling back.

There was nothing following us. Aiden didn't seem to take note of Adam's useless search. He looked up at the sky again, and as he did so, I realized that warm feeling on the back of my shoulders was gone. Above us, dark gray clouds roiled, and as soon as I saw them, a chill wind picked up.

"Willy figured it out first," Aiden said, picking up the pace again. We weren't running, but it was a swinging walk that would take us places fast. "He said it was because she always knew where to find berries and which path we should take. But Willy always had a bit of the gift—he could see things that others didn't."

He paused, this time looking down at the path we were on. He turned a little to the left, a steeper climb. "Never follow a path while you're in Underhill," he told me. "The only things here that make a path are things you don't want to meet."

The hill was steeper than it had been, steeper than it looked.

"He talked to me about it first," Aiden said. "But I didn't believe him. Underhill was just where we were—like Caledonia or Ulster, right? Willy could make up things, too—he was the best storyteller. I thought he was making up a story right up until he died and proved himself right."

For all that he'd said it was a long time ago, Aiden's breath was shaky. "Underhill can't kill, not directly. But if she wants you dead, you die. Sometimes quickly but usually slower. She can't feel pain, so it fascinates her."

A cold wind blew down my neck just then. "Aiden," I said, "we're on a path again."

We walked—and now Aiden wasn't the only one who could

feel something following us. I felt as though if I turned around, I would see someone. When I did, there was no one there—except the ghosts.

Underhill was a haunted land. Most ghosts I've been around—and I've been around a lot of them—haunt places where people might be found. Churches, homes, stores—places like that. The ghosts that I'd been seeing were tucked into hollows under trees and hiding under branches. All of them were children. One of them had been following us since Aiden had started talking about the children he used to run around with. I wish I could believe that it was the ghost who was watching us—but his regard felt desperate, as if he thought we might be able to save him.

The watcher who made my shoulders itch, that one was not desperate, just . . . predatory.

But the ghost was worrisome, too.

"I think it might be smarter not to talk about dead friends while we are here," I told Aiden. "Can you tell how much farther?"

"Not far," he said. "But I thought that was Underhill watching us, and it wasn't. I think we should move faster."

He broke into a jog that I kept up with easily—one thing I do very well is run. I could have maintained that pace for hours. Knowing that Adam was behind us was the only thing that kept me from looking.

Normally, running is the last thing I would do when I thought we were being pursued. But Aiden had survived this place for a very long time, and he was, as Jesse said, our guide.

We topped the rise and found ourselves on a flat, broad plain with waist-high grass. The wind whipped through the grass and sent the few stray hairs that had escaped my braiding this morning straight into my eyes. A huge old tree stood in the middle of the plain, and about thirty feet up the thick trunk, there was a tree house perched where the trunk split into three.

"Run," shouted Aiden, heading for the tree at full speed.

Adam hesitated, looking behind us—but there was only the endless plain. If there was something hidden in the grass, the wind disguised its passage.

"Don't ignore your experts," I told Adam. "Run."

I bolted, catching up to Aiden in ten strides. The kid could run—but I could run, too, and my legs were longer. Beside me, Adam followed at an easy lope.

Aiden ran like a sprinter, head back, arms and legs pumping as fast as he could. Ahead of us, I could see that, though there were hand- and footholds carved into the side of the tree, the first ten feet were smooth.

"I'm going to go ahead," I told Aiden. "When I get to the tree, I'm going to make a foot pocket of my hands. I want you to step into it, and I'll toss you up."

He nodded, and I threw myself forward, imitating Aiden's very good technique. Adam stayed with Aiden. I spun when I reached the tree, letting the trunk on my back eat up the excess momentum. I laced my fingers, and Aiden, not slowing a bit, stuck his boot in my hands and I tossed him up. He landed on the tree like a spider monkey and scrambled up.

Adam braced on his hind legs, and I put one foot on his chest and used that as a step stool to get my hands up high enough, and I climbed as quickly as I could, because Adam wasn't going to start up until I was all the way.

Aiden waited on the crude little porch in front of the tree house, his back against the wall, breathing hard through his mouth, sweat dampening his shirt. He smelled like fear.

"Come on, come on, come up," he chanted. "What's taking him so long?"

"I'm up," I shouted, scuttling over the edge of the porch on all fours.

With the howl of the hunt in his throat, Adam sank his claws into the trunk and climbed the tree with the grace of a jaguar. Werewolf shoulders are built more like those of a bear or a cat. It meant that they were excellent climbers.

Aiden opened the door of the house and waved his hand at me. There wasn't room on the porch for all three of us, so I wasted no time getting inside. Adam came in after me and Aiden after him, shutting the door firmly and locking it.

Something hit the tree and rocked it.

"You lost," Aiden yelled. "Go about your business."

Something roared, and I had the feeling that my ears weren't picking up the whole thing—as if some of that roar wasn't just sound. Skittering sounds came from the walls and the ceiling. There were no windows in the tree house and part of me was grateful. Whatever was making that noise sounded like a thousand rats or something with a thousand legs. Most of me hated hearing a threat I could not see.

Adam snarled.

"You lost," said Aiden again. "This is doing you no good. If you don't leave, I'll light my wards."

That horrible aching roar traveled through the walls and into my skull, sending hot pain through my nervous system.

"I warned him," said Aiden. "He should know better."

He pressed his hand on the door and . . . his magic wasn't as big as what Beauclaire had used on the bridge, but it was plenty big enough to make me sit down on the floor harder than I'd meant to. There was a whoomph sound, like when a gas burner is turned on—only an order of magnitude bigger than that.

Silence fell.

Aiden took his hand from the door and shook it. "It won't have killed him—not the flames nor the fall from the tree—but he won't come up here again for a while."

"What was that?" I asked.

Aiden shrugged. "I call him the Unseen. I don't actually know what he is supposed to be. He's one of the things that escaped from the prisons the fae left behind, and a lot of them started out as fae. He's difficult to see except in strong sunlight. He's slow, or he'd have killed me a long time ago."

He looked around the room and blew out a huff of air. "Welcome to my home. It's safe here—as safe as anywhere in Underhill. We can spend the night and look for a way back out tomorrow. The artifact is here."

Now that we didn't have unknown monsters trying to get in and eat us, I looked around. Without windows, the interior was dark except for a little light that snuck in between the hand-hewn boards— that looked more like they'd been scavenged than cut to build this tree house. The widths would be consistent for a section, then change. Right next to the door, there was a panel that was six or seven feet wide. Another plank looked more like a tabletop than a board.

Aiden lit some beeswax candles. Maybe if I'd been human, it would still have been too dim, but I see pretty well in the dark.

The room was big enough, maybe fifteen feet square. Rough

shelves lined three of the walls and held a collection of treasures—literally in some cases. A bird's feather was displayed next to an elaborate silver crown studded with cabochon gems set in silver flowers and vines. In a world where you were mostly alone, the feather was as valuable as the crown. There were books, too, but not very many—none that I could have read.

On the fourth wall there were a pair of wardrobes. The first was itself a work of art. Every bit of the wardrobe was elaborately carved in abstract designs. The second, like the walls of the tree house, was cobbled together out of bits and pieces of other things.

"I've never had anyone in here," Aiden told me. "I built this after most of the others were already dead."

"It's charming," I told him, seriously.

"Aboveground gives you a lot of protection," he told me. "The first one I built here had windows—that was a mistake."

He opened the elaborate wardrobe and pulled out some thick rag rugs and threw them at random on the floor. "I sleep . . . slept on piles of these," he said. "We can use the bedrolls, but the rugs will soften the floor."

"Sounds good to me," I told him. In lieu of speech, Adam stretched out on one of the rugs and rested his muzzle on his front legs. "Adam approves, too."

"I might as well get the artifact," he said, and opened the second wardrobe. As soon as the doors separated, I could feel a wave of power.

The wardrobe was split into two halves. The right half had shelves filled with bright-colored fabric bags of all sorts of sizes and colors, with small boxes of bone, wood, or lacquer, and larger, jewelry-box-sized boxes. The bottom shelf was full of folded cloth. The left side held staves and swords and pole arms of all kinds.

"Are these all artifacts?" I asked.

He nodded. "I keep them in this wardrobe because it doesn't let the power leak. Around here, power attracts attention."

"When the fae come back," I said slowly, "could someone find your house and your treasures?"

He shook his head. "Once a place belongs to you, it *belongs* to you. No one will ever be able to find this place unless I'm with them. No one can come inside unless I invite them in. It's how Underhill was set up—and even she can't change the rules. That's why, even though she's mad at me, she couldn't actually make us wander for long before I found my home. If I die, Underhill will reclaim what is here. She has her own treasure rooms—I've seen them. Some of this stuff comes from there."

I looked at the contents of the wardrobe. "Don't ever tell anyone this is here," I told him. "The fae would never have let you go if they knew what you have."

He nodded, reached in to the shelves, and brought out a small box and opened it. The box he put back on the shelf. In his hand was a crude bronze key. He gave it to me, then closed the doors of the wardrobe.

The key was warm in my hands.

"What does it do?" I asked.

"Pressed against a door, it makes any door a gateway to Underhill," he said. "If you keep in mind where in Underhill you want to appear, that doorway will take you there."

"How do you know that?" I asked.

"Underhill isn't opposed to sharing knowledge," he told me. "Not if she's in a good mood."

He looked unhappily at the key in my hand, and thinking he was worried I wanted it, I handed it back to him. But, though he closed his hands on it and stuffed it in a pocket of his jeans, the scent of his unhappiness didn't change.

"It's a good pick," I told him. "Not a weapon, but valuable all the same."

"She never abandoned me," he told me. "She gets very lonely." He looked up at me. "Am I doing the right thing?"

"You aren't doing anything wrong," I told him. "There might be other right things you could do, but that's not the same as doing something wrong. She isn't alone anymore."

He snorted. "The fae. They don't appreciate her—they use her like a slave, with no more thought to her than they give their shoes—less."

And that didn't sound like someone repeating a rant they'd heard once too often, I thought.

"We'll tell Beauclaire that's how she feels about the fae. Maybe they can do something about it," I told him. "If you want to stay here, that's something different. But thinking that you are the only one who can possibly keep her company—that's a trap."

We ate lunch from our packs and drank from our canteens.

"Is there a reason that we need to sleep here instead of heading out?" I asked, gathering our garbage and, after putting it into a plastic bag, stuffing it into the pack.

"It might take us a while to find a door to leave," he said. "I can hurry it along a bit—that's the real trick. Underhill can't seal the doors from the inside, but she can make it hard to find them. That's why she locked the fae out, and not in." He got to his feet and paced a bit. "Night's dangerous, more dangerous, here. It's safer if we leave at first light in the morning."

320

And this was lunchtime. I looked at Aiden pacing and exchanged a glance with Adam.

"Okay," I said brightly. "While we wait for nighttime, why don't we tell each other stories?"

So I told him about Bran, the Marrok, and what growing up a coyote in the woods of northwestern Montana had been like. He told me stories about living in Underhill, the creatures terrible and wonderful who made their homes here. Once he warmed up, he was a pretty good storyteller—and I developed a new perspective on Underhill, who had first appeared to him as a small girl, though she sometimes was a great lady or an animal.

She was not evil, just . . . thoughtless. She was like a toddler who breaks her toys because she doesn't know any better. Doesn't realize that once they are broken, they will never play with her again. After she had killed Aiden's friend Willy, she had mourned him for a very long time. But she didn't learn from her errors—it sounded as though she'd been hardwired to be who she was.

She had damaged Aiden more than she would have been able to if she had truly been evil, I thought. Because sometimes she was funny and good company, and at other times she was vicious. She couldn't, herself, hurt someone. But she could taint food, turn the weather foul, or attract one of the dangerous ones (Aiden's term) wherever she wanted. Aiden was alive because Underhill loved him.

Eventually, the storytelling wound down, and we ate dinner. Aiden fell asleep. Adam got up from the rug he'd claimed and sat next to me, his muzzle on my thigh.

She's not going to let him go easily, he told me.

"I caught that." I threaded my fingers through his fur. "It's a good thing that we have the walking stick." Sometime during the storytelling, the stick had appeared in my lap. "It should show us the way home."

There was, I noticed, a faint green light that danced in the runes etched on the silver of the head of the walking stick. Aiden turned and, when I followed, the glow faded. I stopped and moved the walking stick in the direction we'd been headed. The green glow returned.

It wasn't the way the walking stick had shown me how to get home last time, but it was clearly unhappy about following Aiden.

"Wrong way," I said. "Home is this way."

"Right," said Aiden. "But we have to go around until we can find a way down."

Down?

I leaned the walking stick against Adam's shoulder, unwilling to merely set it on the ground—or hand it to Aiden, though I wasn't sure why. When I did, I saw that the others had been climbing up a steep mountain—though the whole time I'd been walking on a flat cave floor. The direction the walking stick wanted us to go appeared to be an impassable cliff face.

"I see," I said. "Come here and give me your t-shirt."

Aiden's expression was a little wary, but he pulled his t-shirt off and handed it to me. I blindfolded him and, taking up the staff again, walked him through a tree root I'd seen when I wasn't holding the staff.

"Okay," I said. "That worked."

I turned him around and had him walk the same path. He stumbled over the root—I caught him before he fell. He reached up to take off his blindfold, and I tapped his hand. "Leave it for a minute. Trust me."

"You just made me trip," he said.

"You didn't get hurt," I told him.

Adam posed a different problem. I wasn't going to blindfold him. Not when something had been following us. We needed Adam free to act.

"Close your eyes and lean on me?" I asked. He did. And I took him over the same root—and he picked his feet up and stepped over the root because he paid attention to his environment.

But he followed me right off the cliff. Or where he thought the cliff would be, anyway.

With Adam leaning against me, I took Aiden by the arm, held the staff in my free hand, and took them in the direction the staff dictated.

"The ground feels hard," Aiden said after a few minutes.

"Yes," I said. "Don't think too hard about it. Just walk."

It wasn't that the cavern floor was flat. Finding a path where the three of us could walk abreast wasn't always practical. Once, traveling on a worn wooden bridge over a river, I had to leave one of them behind and escort them across one at a time. But mostly I could push Aiden ahead of me and keep Adam against my side as the green light in the walking stick got brighter and brighter.

We stopped to eat . . . lunch? Dinner? I couldn't tell. We just needed food. Before I took off Aiden's blindfold, I cautiously released my hold on the walking stick, leaving it balanced for a moment on its own. In the time it took for the stick to fall back into my hand, the light dimmed, and we appeared to be in a rocky ravine. But no one was standing in midair or anything.

"Okay," I said. "You can take your blindfold off."

Adam stepped away from me and shook himself.

Aiden and I had meal preparation down pat. I'd open the bag of freeze-dried food and fill it with water, and he'd heat it up—no fire needed. The first three bags went to Adam, who needed a lot of calories. When I'd eaten as much of my food as I could, I opened up the packet and held it down for Adam to finish off. But Adam was standing alert, taking in deep breaths of air.

I stood up and gripped my walking stick and sucked in air to see if I could catch the scent that had alerted Adam.

"What is it?" asked Aiden.

"Fae," I said, only that moment certain.

He frowned at me. "Which fae?"

"I think she means us," said the Widow Queen, appearing out of thin air. She was accompanied by three others, two men and a woman. None of them were familiar to me except for the Widow Queen. All of them wore armor, though not the kind of armor I'd have expected. Theirs was the sort that soldiers or police might wear, except for the colors. Most police SWAT teams wore black or blue, not silver, gold, green, or, in the Widow Queen's case, lavender. Kevlar, I thought, didn't have any cold-iron components. These fae were traditional enough that they carried swords strapped to their hips or over their shoulders. I didn't see any guns.

"Good afternoon, Aiden," the Widow Queen said. "Have you retrieved it yet?"

He stared at her mutely. I could scent his fear.

"Retrieved what?" I asked, stepping closer to him.

"The artifact, child," she said to me. "The artifact."

I put a hand on Aiden's shoulder. "Are you here as a representative of the Gray Lords, to receive the artifact in fulfillment of our bargain?" I was pretty sure I knew the answer to that, but it was best to get everyone's cards on the table to avoid a misunderstanding.

"They want to make peace with the humans," she sneered. "That is a fool's game. A game of attrition that we can only lose as we watch them reproduce like rabbits while we ever so slowly die off. Making peace with cockroaches makes more sense. The trick is to kill them off or, better yet, get them to kill themselves off for us." She smiled. "I'm very good at that last one."

"I take that as a no," I said. "So why do you want the artifact when you don't even know what it is?"

"I'm not the only fae or even the only Gray Lord who despises humans," she said. "But I need a bigger power base to gain the support of the fae for my plans. They need to see me as a Power, someone who can back up her ideas with action. An artifact retrieved from Underhill, stolen from under the noses of the Council of the Gray Lords, would do nicely. As long as I do it before you hand it over, the other Gray Lords can do nothing but wring their hands. Retrieving artifacts that have fallen into human hands is an acceptable venture and not a crime at all."

"I see," I said.

"If you hand it over to me," she said, "I'll let you live."

"It will void the bargain," Aiden told me in a low voice.

I nodded. We had promised to do everything in our power to bring back an artifact. Handing it over just because we were outgunned wouldn't qualify. I couldn't remember all of the exact words, but I was pretty sure "even unto death" was in there.

"Why bring them?" I asked, nodding at her three minions. "You are a Gray Lord. It sounds like you're going to take a stab at ruling the fae all by yourself—and you can't take on the three of us without help?"

"She cannot use magic to attack us," said Aiden suddenly. "Before Underhill let them come back, she made them swear not to use their magic here."

"It matters not," the Widow Queen said. "You are both unarmed, and the werewolf is no match for the four of us by himself."

Aiden nodded. "Maybe that would be so," he said, "if you were right about that unarmed part." Aiden sucked in a breath and gestured with his hand. Flame spilled out of his fingers and— I didn't see what he did with it; I was too busy dodging a bronze broadsword wielded by the man in green.

In martial art terms, a broadsword is by definition an outer-circle weapon. There has to be a certain amount of space between the combatants in order to properly swing a sword of that size. The Widow Queen had a rapier, which would have been harder to deal with, because a rapier is quicker and more flexible. Not that the broadsword was easy. Still, the first strike the fae aimed at me I dodged. I managed it not so much because he couldn't have hit me, but because he'd assumed I'd be a lot slower than I was—and because he'd expected me to try to get away. I stepped into him.

He was a better fighter than I was, but he wasn't faster than me. Nor was he as motivated, and I think he underestimated me. He thought he was fighting a girl with a stick when he was fighting Adam's mate, Coyote's daughter, armed with Lugh's staff.

As I closed with him, I hit him hard in the abdomen with the end of the stick. I think he let me make the hit because he started to do . . . something. I expected the stick to bounce back off his armor, and was ready to roll to the side, but the walking stick stayed where it was—and so did the male. In my hands, the walking stick came to life. I felt its outrage that someone would have attacked us without provocation. It had never spoken so clearly to me before. I couldn't tell if it was the blood or Underhill, though both sang through the old wood.

The male fae froze where he was, and the stick finally pulled free, the spearpoint black with blood. The point was longer and thinner than I'd ever seen it. The fae man fell to the ground and didn't move. He was dead by the spear and by the magic in the walking stick, and his death greatly satisfied the old artifact.

Kevlar was no match for a spear made by Lugh.

But there was no time to wonder about the stick. Adam was fighting the Widow Queen. He'd bloodied her leg, but had taken a slice in return along his side that was bleeding badly. The female in silver was lying on the ground, her head and shoulder burned away. Aiden lay on the ground not far from her, unconscious or dead—I couldn't tell which.

The final fae, the male in gold, struck at me with his sword. This one had some magic in it; I could feel its hunger. It was a short sword and more agile than the broadsword had been.

The walking stick had, once before, used me to fight. This time it was more of an inspiration, using things I already knew. I wasn't the walking stick's puppet this time; I was its dance partner. It was like the hunt song, like a dance in which my partner was the more skilled of us, and I followed his lead. *Step and duck and thrust and parry* blended together as called for by our dance, in a syncopated rhythm that followed a random beat to keep our opponent from catching our dance step. It would have been fun—I could feel the walking stick's joy—but I remembered Aiden's crumpled form.

And then magic flashed. I stumbled but recovered in time to counter the sword and put my foot behind my opponent's weight-bearing leg. When he tried to step back to regroup, he stumbled over my foot. I could have struck before he recovered, as the walking stick urged. But Adam's agony, a direct result of the surge of magic that caused my misstep, flashed through our mating bond and made me take two steps away so I could center myself again for battle. It couldn't matter, right now, how badly he was hurt. Or if he was worse than hurt.

Adam's agony faded from our bond as the male attacked again, his mouth twisted in concentration. I fought with everything I had, focus possible only because of years of training with Sensei first, and later Adam. I set aside my fears and fought as coolly as I could manage, my attention on the here and now, and not on anything else. I couldn't afford to make another misstep.

When the blade of the walking stick slid into the gold-clad male's throat, it was just a part of our dance.

I could feel it when the walking stick called death to our enemy, felt the moment the male died of a wound he might have recovered from.

Adam lay still on the ground. I couldn't see if he was breathing, and I couldn't take the time to look. The Widow Queen, who, to defeat Adam, had broken her word to Underhill about using magic, crouched over Aiden, searching him, muttering to herself, "Where is it? What is it? It's got to be somewhere."

I tried to stab her with the spear, but she sensed us at the last moment. We danced, the walking stick and I, and between us we kept her busy, but she was slowly winning. Her armor was better than the armor of the man who'd died beneath our shining blade. I hit her hard with it, and she shrugged it off without the spear blade leaving even a surface scratch.

Magic, the stick told me. Magic armor.

She gathered magic as we danced, and there was nothing I could do about it. When she chose, because she was in control of the fight, she broke free of our dance by knocking me onto my side. I scrambled up, but it was awkward and too slow. It gave her the moment she needed to throw her spell at me.

The walking stick knew what it was, therefore so did I: a spell that would make it impossible to move, not even enough to breathe or for my heart to pump.

I felt the artifact make a decision as the magic came toward us, because Coyote had seen that it was becoming aware and coaxed it to free will. The stick twisted in my hands and intercepted the magic directed at me by a Gray Lord of the fae. Lugh's walking stick ate the Gray Lord's spell, and in doing so, it died.

To save me.

The Widow Queen had dropped her guard when she cast the spell. Confident, I think, that there was nothing someone like me could have done to save myself. And she was right. The walking stick bought me that moment of grace—and I launched into a spinning back kick, and felt it land with the precision of a move I must have done ten thousand times in practice. I heard the snapping of her neck, watched her body fall as quickly as mine. I rolled to my feet; she stayed in the awkward position she had fallen in, her breath rasping in and out.

I reached down and grabbed the spearhead of Lugh's walking stick and thrust it under her chest and into her heart. She stopped breathing then.

The fight was over, and I was the only one standing. For a moment I hesitated, bewildered by the unexpectedness of my survival. But only for a moment because Adam was still down.

I ran to my mate but there was already someone there. Three someone elses.

The first was Aiden. He looked as though he'd crawled through the ashes of the female he'd killed. The expression on his face was very old.

The second was a child, about Aiden's age. Her hair was bright red, short, and very curly, her face rounded with blue eyes and pretty but unremarkable features. Her bottom lip was stuck out in a pout. I had no trouble recognizing her from Aiden's descriptions.

The third was Baba Yaga, wearing the guise she'd worn the last time I'd seen her.

I fell to my knees next to Aiden, who turned to me. "He's dead," he said starkly. "He died to keep me safe."

"No," I said because I could feel our mating bond. There was nothing useful coming through it, but it was still there, so he couldn't be dead. Even though there was no breath in his body and his great heart was still under my shaking fingers.

"The Widow Queen always was good with death curses," said Baba Yaga. "Fortunately, I'm better."

"He was taking Aiden away again," said the little girl belligerently. "He should die."

"If he hadn't helped me," said Aiden in a very calm tone, "I would have died."

"She promised not to kill you," Underhill said. "I wouldn't lead her to you until she promised."

Aiden looked at her, his face grim and sad. "Tilly, the Widow Queen didn't have to kill me herself. The fae woman over there would have done it." He lifted his shirt to display a red mark. "Adam knocked her away, and I scorched her with my fire. But in doing so, he left himself vulnerable. He saved me, and that gave the Widow Queen time to hit him with her spell."

"She lied to me," hissed Underhill—and like the thing that had attacked the tree house, her voice carried more than mere sound. "And she used magic. She broke her word."

"So she did," said Baba Yaga briskly. "She was always like that. She was after the artifact, I'm afraid. I told her that she had no business trying to keep something that powerful for herself."

I looked up at Baba Yaga. I'd seen her raise someone from the dead once. "Can you bring him back?"

Baba Yaga shook her head. "Can't do, dearie. At least, not right now. He's not dead yet. Not like that other one. I could wait if you want, but what you want to ask me is whether I can break the Widow Queen's spell."

"Can you break the Widow Queen's spell?" I repeated her instructions, my bloody hand clenched deep in my husband's silver fur and my heart in my throat.

"Only with Underhill's permission," Baba Yaga said. "I keep my promises."

"No," said Underhill.

"Tilly," Aiden snapped. "You aren't being nice."

"It isn't nice to run away," she snarled at him, and her voice made my chest hurt.

"I wouldn't have run away if you hadn't set the fae on me as soon as I got Outside," he said. "On all of us. They all died, Tilly. They can't come back because you taunted the fae, and they thought they could get something from us if they just took us far enough apart. No more Ice, no more Cloud, no more Terra. They died as mortals do. They cannot come back. But I can. I will. But you have to let Baba Yaga break the Widow Queen's curse."

I held my breath. He'd lived with her for centuries—he loved her, and she loved him back in her own way. His word would sway her more than anything I could say.

"If he dies, I will hate you forever," he told her. "I will leave and never come back. And I'll tell everyone I meet how mean you are."

Underhill's face flushed angrily, but I could see that the threat meant something to her.

"I'll allow a bargain," she said finally, folding her arms on her chest and obviously unhappy. "A bargain for the Witch's service. A bargain I approve of." She looked at me and smiled, a slow, cruel smile. "A life-for-a-life kind of bargain."

Baba Yaga said, "Give me an unborn life, then, Mercy, so I may restore his."

I put my hand over my belly—but I wasn't pregnant. We'd talked about it but had decided to wait before we tried.

"An unborn life is acceptable," said Underhill slyly, taking in my gesture and my expression.

"You can't do that," said Aiden in a low voice. "He'd never want to buy his life with another's. Especially not his own child's."

I got up and went to the backpack and took out one of the hard-boiled eggs, chills sliding down my spine. What if I had just dismissed her remark over the phone? What if I hadn't decided to bring them along? What if we had eaten them for lunch yesterday, as I'd almost suggested?

I handed Baba Yaga the egg. "One unborn life," I told her, my voice shaky.

"Hard-boiled are my favorite," she said, popping the whole thing, shell and all, into her mouth. "I can't eat them much anymore at home. I keep telling her that just because she stands on a chicken leg doesn't mean she is a chicken."

Underhill looked back and forth between me and Baba Yaga. "You tricked me," she said, looking at me like I was interesting. She looked at Baba Yaga and suddenly smiled—a smile that didn't belong on a young face, so wise and joyous. She laughed and clapped her hands. "That was fun," she said. She looked at me. "You should come visit me. We could play a lot of jokes on each other. It would be fun."

"It could be fun," I managed. That was the truth, right? The possibility existed that it would be fun—but I'd have put my money on terrifying.

Baba Yaga waved her hands at Adam—and he sucked in a breath of air so hard he choked, and the wolf convulsed, trying to breathe.

It hurt. I could feel it along our bond, but if he hurt, he was alive, so I didn't mind. Much. I fell to my knees beside him and put my head against his heart so I could hear it beat. He coughed as the pain faded, and tried to get up. It took him two tries, but once he was on his feet, he shook himself briskly. I held him for a moment more.

He was alive. I breathed in, breathed him in, and believed. I wiped my tears—of fright and grief—and then loosened my hold.

"He's okay?" asked Aiden, sounding, for once, the same age that he looked.

"Of course," said Baba Yaga. "Everything was done right and proper."

Adam turned to Baba Yaga and bowed his head. And then he did the same to Underhill. If his gaze was wary, I don't think anyone else there knew him well enough to notice.

Underhill sighed. "I suppose you want to leave again," she told Aiden. "I won't make you work for it. There's a door about a half mile that way—" She pointed. "Baba Yaga knows where it is."

"I will visit," Aiden said. "But you have to promise not to make me stay here."

Underhill bounced on her toes, and her voice was shy as she said, "Visiting would be better than lost forever. But you will die out there."

"Death is part of life," he told her. "Without the one, it is hard to have the other. That's what my mother used to say. But I could visit until then."

"You used to not remember your mother," she said.

"I'm remembering more Outside. I could come and tell you stories about it."

She gave him a tentative smile. "I like your stories. All right. I promise not to make you stay here."

Baba Yaga took us to a different door than the one we'd used to come in. This one was set in one of two walls belonging to the remnants of a hut that had seen better days. When she opened the door, I could see only the empty, overgrown patch that had once (presumably) been the hut's interior, but stepping through it, with Adam beside me, landed us in the same little, nondescript room that we'd entered Underhill from.

It had been light in Underhill, but it was evening here.

"How much time has passed?" I asked urgently.

Baba Yaga shrugged. "As much as needed to." She paused, then smiled at me. "Oh, yes. I forgot that you had some adventures in an Elphame court. Underhill is far more stable, and her ties to this world are stronger. Time passes differently, yes, but not all that differently. If you had stayed in Underhill for a year, you might find that you'd spent a year and a half. But with a short visit, generally you might lose or gain an hour or six, but mostly it's not enough to matter." She smiled again. "Generally."

I caught my polite "thank you" before it left my tongue. "Good to know," I said instead.

She looked at Aiden, who was frantically patting his clothing. "Here, boy," she said, digging into a pocket. She pulled out the key and gave it to him. "It's probably better if you have this now. Otherwise someone might say that I brought the artifact back and not you, hmm?" She looked at me. "Remember to dot your tees and cross your eyes"—which she did—"when dealing with the fae." She smiled broadly. "Now then, we should go to Beauclaire's office, I think. You can be sure that someone from the Council will be awaiting our arrival—and Beauclaire's office is as good a target as any."

Two someones were waiting for us—or at least, they were in Beauclaire's office talking quietly. Goreu and Beauclaire seemed awfully startled by our entrance to have been actually waiting for us.

"That was quick," said Goreu. "We didn't expect you for another day at least."

"How quick?" I asked.

"Twelve, maybe thirteen hours," said Goreu.

"Huh," I said. "We were there a day and a night and most of another day." I'd gained back about twelve hours of the month that the Elphame court had stolen from me.

Adam's clothes were folded and awaited him on a chair near the fireplace, which held a merry little fire. He walked over to the chair. I don't think that anyone except me knew how sore and tired he was.

"What are you carrying?" Beauclaire asked me.

I'd used one of the dead fae's shirts to collect what I could find of the walking stick. I laid it on the desk in front of Beauclaire and opened the shroud to reveal shards and splinters of gray wood, some silver bits, and the spearpoint, still stained with the Widow Queen's blood.

Beauclaire touched the silver spearhead lightly and raised an eyebrow.

"The Widow Queen thought that she'd like an artifact all to herself," I said.

Goreu growled. "I told you she acquiesced too easily. That she took the defeat of her people at the werewolves' hands with too much grace."

"You took care of her?" Beauclaire asked me, ignoring Goreu. He didn't raise his eyebrows in disbelief, but it lurked in his tone.

"Aiden, Adam, and I," I said. "But we had help. She couldn't do great magic without Underhill's consent, which she didn't get. The walking stick . . . helped me, too. In the end, that's what killed her. Without Baba Yaga's help, Adam would have died."

"Baba Yaga," said Beauclaire with a frown. "What was . . ." He quit talking, but his frown didn't go away. "Coyote's daughter," he said quietly. "He and Baba Yaga are akin, tricksters and unreliable champions of the underdog. I can see why she might be inclined to help you."

He was talking about her like she wasn't in the room.

"She didn't have much use for the Widow Queen," said Goreu.

I glanced discreetly around, but she wasn't in the room. I started to say something, I don't know what, when Adam drew on the pack bonds to do another quicker-than-usual change. The power flowed to him, I felt the edge of it. But more than power, I felt the joyous welcome that sang through the pack as they celebrated Adam's return.

When I paid attention to the others again, Beauclaire was once more examining the remains of his father's work. Aiden was fumbling in his pocket, and Goreu was watching me.

"Interesting," he said. "I hadn't realized how much magic resides within the werewolves. That magic produces their condition, yes, that I understood. That they themselves could produce and use magic . . . that I didn't know."

I gave him a faint smile. "Every day brings something new," I said.

His smile was a fraction wider than mine had been, and his eyes were warm. "Not if you have seen as many every days as I have," he murmured. Then he cleared his throat, and said, "You went to Underhill to retrieve a gift for my people."

Aiden held out the key, which looked like nothing so much as a nail that someone had gotten creative with. Its consequence was not added to by the dirt on Aiden's hand. I glanced down at my hands—they were dirty, too, and bloodstained.

Unprepossessing sight as the key made, Goreu and Beauclaire both focused on it intently.

"Oh yes," said Beauclaire. "This, *this* is very good."

Goreu smiled at Aiden. "Good choice," he said. "But let's not tell anyone it was a choice, shall we?"

"It was the only one I could find," Aiden said, his voice ringing with truth. He didn't say what exactly the "one" referred to. That's the secret of dealing with people who can tell if you lie.

"Excellent," said Goreu. He looked at me, then glanced over my shoulder, where Adam was just finishing dressing. "Our bargain is made, and you have fulfilled all that you promised to try. None shall gainsay."

"It is done," said Beauclaire, and magic surged, spread, and flowed outward.

"It was done before," I pointed out. "When we signed the agreement."

Beauclaire nodded. "Yes. But that you were successful in your endeavor gave additional power to the bargain. Not only have we promised to maintain neutrality in the Tri-Cities but the bargain will itself enforce the neutrality on any fae in your territory." He smiled. "As defined in our contract."

"I have a further bargain to propose," said Adam. He came up behind me and rested his hand on my shoulder.

"Oh?" Goreu examined my husband's face warily.

"I think you'll be happy with it," Adam said, a smile in his voice. I glanced over my shoulder and saw his dimple.

"Underhill," Adam said, "has requested that Aiden visit her now and then. She misses him. For him to do that, you have to guarantee him safe passage from my territory, through yours, and through a door to Underhill."

I watched the understanding spread across both Gray Lords' faces, but it was Goreu who said, "A very interesting bargain you propose. We shall have to discuss it."

"Underhill would be obliged if you agree." Aiden said aloud what everyone was thinking. "If you'd like, I could put in a good word for those who have dealt true with me and my friends."

"Aiden has had a very long time to learn how best to deal with Underhill," I told them.

14

It was Pirate night at our house, and I had, once again, died an ignominious death. So I'd left the vicious cutthroats to their play and gone upstairs to make brownies with the orange oil I'd bought from Izzy's mom. She was right, they tasted better with the oil than with the extract I'd used before.

I'd buried the walking stick in one of the garden beds near the back door, with Aiden, Jesse, and Adam as witnesses. It seemed like a good resting place for an old object of power, a safe place where pretty things grew. I planted lavender on top of it because I like lavender. Once we replaced the plywood with windows again, I'd be able to see the lavender from the kitchen window when I was doing dishes.

The Tri-Cities was a neutral territory—and none of us really knew what that meant yet. I knew what the fae wanted it to mean, I knew what the pack needed it to mean—but no one knew exactly how it was going to work. Uncle Mike's was open for business again—but this time it was open to humans and others alike. The local police stations had asked to meet with Adam to discuss what being under the protection of the pack really meant—and what they could expect from the fae. So had the Feds. Adam had made appointments to meet with the police. He was letting the Feds stew. He was still mad about the tracking device on the SUV.

I couldn't control the Feds, the fae, or the future, but I could bake brownies. I dipped a spoon into the last of the dough and took a bite.

Yes, still good.

"What are you cooking?" asked Aiden, coming up from the basement where he'd been playing computer games. He had only set the house on fire once since we'd returned from Underhill. He'd told me that Underhill promised she could help him stop lighting fires in his sleep. He planned on going for a visit next week to see what she could do.

"Brownies," I said.

He flinched.

Jesse, who'd come up behind him, laughed. "Not that kind of brownie, dummy. It's a cross between a cookie and a cake. You'll like it." She sniffed. "Smells good."

"Here," I said, handing them two plates filled with frosted brownies. When I make brownies on Pirate night, I bake four pans to ensure that there is some left for me. "Take these downstairs."

Brownies in hand, they disappeared downstairs without another word. I frosted the batch I'd just pulled out. Technically speaking, I should have let them cool all the way. But if I frosted them while they were still warm, the frosting soaked deliciously into the brownies. It didn't look as pretty, but it tasted marvelous.

I was smoothing out the frosting when I heard Adam's footsteps behind me.

"Just a minute," I said, turning toward him. "Let me get these cut . . ." My voice trailed off at the expression on his face. He'd left the game and gone into his office to take a call from Bran. "Something wrong?" I asked.

"Not exactly," he said. "As we thought, Bran would like us to stay independent for a while longer, until we see how the treaty is going to work out for everyone."

"No surprise there."

"No," he agreed. He looked at me steadily, and said, "Bran is the reason Baba Yaga left Russia to come here."

I put down the knife I'd been using very carefully.

"He told me that it was a calculated risk. She owed him a favor, but she is unpredictable." Adam put his hand on my cheek. "But he said he couldn't just sit and hope things worked out for us. He knew that she liked you, so he took a chance." He wiped my eyes and hugged me. "He didn't abandon you."

"No," I said, my throat tight.

"So do I get a brownie?" Adam asked. I sniffed, pushed back, and cut him a brownie.

He bit into it, paused, and swallowed. "This is amazing."

I gave him a smug smile. "I know, right?"

"Hey, Mercy?"

I looked to see that Aiden and Jesse were back. Aiden had two empty plates, and Jesse had her cell phone—which she handed to me. I glanced at it, started to look back at her, and returned my gaze to the phone.

"Darryl wanted to know where you got the essential oil, so I looked it up online," Jesse said. "And Aiden came over to see."

Jesse had found the Intrasity Web site and the front page had the founder of Intrasity. She wore a bright green silk suit and a great big smile.

Jesse continued, "Aiden says that Tracy LaBella is Baba Yaga."

Adam leaned over to take a look. He laughed and handed Jesse's phone back to her.

"I guess you don't have to worry about talking to Elizaveta," he said.

I gave the kids another plate of brownies to take down with them.

"Baba Yaga is a multilevel marketing guru," Adam said, still smiling.

"I need another brownie," I told him.

He followed me to the counter. When I cut into the last batch, he put a hand on either side of me and leaned against me. His breath was hot on the skin of my neck.

"Nudge," he said.

ACKNOWLEDGMENTS

First, I'd like to thank Evelyn Walkley, who won the dedication of this book in an auction held to benefit Safe Harbor, which provides support for families in crisis. I'm very pleased with this because Safe Harbor is an awesome charity and because both Evelyn and Nanette are awesome people.

Second, I'd like to thank Lampson International, Bruce Stemp and Lana Laughlin in particular, who put up with us roaming (escorted by Bruce) all over their yards and showed us Big Blue in person.

Very special thanks to the Ed Hendler Memorial Bridge, better known as the Cable Bridge. This book would not be the same without you.

And, of course, I'd like to thank everyone who helped with this one: Collin Briggs, Mike Briggs, Dave Carson, Michelle Kasper, Ann Peters, Kaye Roberson, Bob and Sara Schwager, and Anne Sowards. Last but never least, thank you to Michael Enzweiler for another fine map.

As always, the mistakes are mine.

ABOUT THE AUTHOR

Patricia Briggs lived a fairly normal life until she learned to read. After that she spent lazy afternoons flying dragon-back and looking for magic swords when she wasn't horseback riding in the Rocky Mountains. Once she graduated from Montana State University with degrees in history and German, she spent her time substitute teaching and writing. She and her family live in the Pacific Northwest, and you can visit her website at www.patriciabriggs.com.

Find out more about Patricia Briggs and other Orbit authors by registering for the free monthly newsletter at www.orbitbooks.net.